THE PRINCE OF PROHIBITION

MARILYN MARKS

Book Cover by Rin Mitchell

Interior Artwork by Rin Mitchell

Editing by Noah Sky

ASIN: B0BRHQQ55V

ISBN: 9798987571606

For sweet Melissa,
who was undoubtedly an ethereal flapper in a past life.

Love you eternally.

PART ONE

THE HIEROPHANT

ONE

THE COLTON FAMILY WAS strange. It was something I never thought of when I was small, skipping beside my papa to the river every night. I carried the salt and Tommy sat on the porch, scanning the darkened tree line with a rifle in his lap. But that all changed when I turned six and told Papa about the lights.

"Aren't they beautiful?" I had asked, waving to one across the river. Round and blue, it tumbled over itself like silk in a breeze. Tommy and Papa shared a look. A look that said my brother was nine years older and knew far more than I did. After that, Tommy followed close behind on our nightly walks, iron-loaded gun pointed across the water.

But these things were normal. No different than attending church on Sunday or coffee in the morning. We were a family that loved each other—three peas in a happy pod—hardworking farmers who took to our fields, and devout Christians just like everyone else in Fairville, Georgia. Only we didn't pray in a church or worship the Lord, but performed our traditions. Our rituals. Once, I asked Papa why we didn't sing to God like the others did. "Because God isn't coming for us," he'd said. "The Devil is."

I never questioned it. When your papa told you a truth, you didn't wonder if he was wrong—you listened. So I followed him to the river every night. When the moon shone in the sky and cicadas sang in the

1

grass, I hummed the opening line to Papa's song. *Down to the river we go, down to the river and the lake and the bog* . . .

I poured the salt circle. Papa continued the rest. *To the ashwood tree and the midnight fog* . . .

And like that we'd continue. Dancing, praying, forming the ward of salt around the property along the rivers that enclosed our land. Tommy had iron bullets and I had an iron cross necklace. On our land, protected by our liturgy and the knowledge Papa gave us, nothing could ever find us. It was right there in the song we sang, the one Papa wrote himself.

The summer I was eight, I tried asking him why we always sang it. The three of us sat on the porch. The men sipped whiskey and I played at their feet, trotting the wooden horse Tommy carved across the weathered boards. Papa and Tommy shared their sacred look. The one I didn't understand. I ignored them, staring down the hill to our river. Across it, a woman with skin like birch bark waved at me.

My father grabbed my hand in his, smoothing back my hair. My attention left the strange creature. "Because one day you'll listen, Adeline. You'll understand. When the Devil kills saints, he kills slowly."

It was Papa's favorite line, sung at the end of every verse of his special song. Something he said often whenever I asked why I couldn't attend school. Why we never crossed the bridge that took us over the iron-laden rivers circling our property. Why Tommy and Papa were the only two people I was allowed to speak to, even when visitors came to buy our crops. Why my mama was dead and I wasn't, taking my first breath when she took her last. It was the answer to everything, which made no sense, but it was Papa's truth, so it was mine.

"Is Papa a saint?" I whispered in Tommy's ear. I was ten when I asked that question, a little too skinny and shy as a mouse. Tommy had his arm around me, pointing at words for me to read from our faded copy of Alfred Lord Tennyson's completed works. Since I didn't attend school and we never went to a real church, they educated me themselves. Tommy liked war books, but I liked poetry, so we compromised. Down the hall, in the darkness of his bedroom, the quiet notes of Papa's guitar drifted through the door.

"No, you are." He said it as plain as mentioning the weather, ending my questions by pointing to *The Charge of the Light Brigade.*

"I think Papa is," I had said. "That's why he's afraid of dying slowly."

My brother's arm froze around me, stiff as the leather cover between his fingers. His next words came so low, so deadly, I still wondered if I imagined them.

"Saints don't sell their souls, baby."

It never bothered me until I turned eleven.

That year was 1917. While war never touched our borders, the papers spoke of it every day. Living in nowhere Georgia, I'd never heard of the places spoken of in the press. We had our books, yes, but I knew little of Wales, Belgium, Germany, or the forests in France where so many lost their lives. Papa let me venture into town for the first time, then. Something I hated, because each time we did, he made me turn my clothes inside out and wear bells around my ankles. Worse, the townsfolk stared. Spoke in whispers. Between recounting how strange we were, that my visions made me Satan's daughter, that Papa sang to a dark lord, they'd whisper their fears about the war. That the Americans would soon join, because if we didn't, the Germans would come and kill us all.

Back then, that was my worst fear. The Germans. It could have been a synonym for the Devil. The children playing in town center no longer recited folklore of the Appalachia, or worried if they didn't brush their teeth they'd be sent to hell. In 1917, everyone feared the Germans. Everyone but my brother.

The day Tommy's draft card came in, I cried until darkness touched the sky. I didn't stop until dawn broke the next morning.

But Tommy wasn't afraid. He kept telling me it would be fine. That there was no way in—excuse his language—goddamn hell he wouldn't come home. The day the war ended, the first thing he'd do was give me the biggest hug, take me to town to buy those white shoes I wanted with his soldier pay, and then we'd finish reading our book. We only had six poems left. Some goddamn Krauts weren't getting in the way of that.

In April, the three of us stood in town center, watching the horses kick up dust around the community well. A group of boys straggled back from the mines, their tired faces dusted with soot and coal. They washed their hands in buckets before entering the schoolhouse for afternoon class. All the shops had American flags in their windows, even the bawdy tavern the church ladies always tried to shut down. Four other families stood with us, saying goodbye to their boys. Tommy and them clasped hands, talking and laughing like they never thought of us as devil-folk, the new enemy far worse than our family's heathen ways. Then a covered truck stopped with more boys in green uniforms sitting in the back, guns fashioned across their laps. And just like that, Tommy was gone. One half of all I'd ever known.

We received letters from him. Plenty, in the beginning. I even convinced Papa to get a family portrait of us, and even though the photographer said we shouldn't smile, that we'd be sitting there so long our faces would ache, I fought my quivering lips the entire time. Then, I helped Papa gather calendula and willow bark for the pharmacist. The extra money was enough to ship our faded copy of *Tennyson's Completed Works* to Tommy's battalion in France. I'd taped the family portrait on the back cover, adding a note that when Tommy came home, we needed a new one with all three of us.

But the letters got fewer, then for six long months, they stopped altogether. I sensed the omen in the air, in the whooshing current of the river surrounding our land. First, I stopped eating. I saw Papa sob for the first time in my life, shoving candied peaches down my throat after I fainted in the field. Then, sleeping. Speaking. The weight of death pressed closely, a dark foreboding so deep, it lay on my chest like a weight and stole the air from my lungs. One day I woke up, and it was as if I were never alive at all.

Maybe the townsfolk were right. Maybe the Devil walked our farm, and it was Satan's dark shadow that haunted me. I'd written a note to Papa, asking if we could go to a real church for once. He put me in ballet lessons instead.

"If you won't speak, then you can dance. Just like we do at the river." He ran a hand through my silky, wheat-colored hair. Looked deep into my brown eyes that matched my Mama's. "I promise you, he's coming home, baby. And God has nothing to do with it."

He was right. God had nothing to do with it.

I did.

We arrived home from ballet one evening. The only studio in our county was three towns over, so Papa popped me on his saddle and we trotted to Calverston every Tuesday evening. The stars flickered to life as we crossed the bridge to our land, illuminating the twig men and tree women dancing in the wood. I'd grown used to seeing devil creatures in the forest, even more after Tommy left. When I stopped speaking, Papa bought me a sketchbook and charcoal to draw what roamed the trees, so he always knew what lurked around. It was mostly the same things—little winged people flitting through the trees, hairy men no taller than cats and the tree women with floral hair, but what rested on our shore that night was something I'd never seen.

"I'm putting Scout in the barn. Go clean up for supper," Papa said. I nodded, but drifted toward the river bank instead.

White, everything from her satin slippers to her stunning veil was a crisp and clean white. White hair spilled over her shoulders around

5

pupilless, eggshell eyes. The only spot of color was a uniform she washed in the shallow bank, a green military one soaked in blood. A ribbon of red curled from the soaked jacket and slithered down the stream.

I stopped on the slippery rocks, watching her across the water.

"You have sensed me for some time now, haven't you?"

For the first time in eight months, I spoke. I had little desire to, but something about this woman demanded words, a command I couldn't disobey. My voice came scratchier with each word, autumn leaves scraping over the rocks. "I'm not allowed to talk to devil-folk."

A smile curled her lips. Razor teeth glimmered in the starlight. "It's fair folk, wee one."

Swallowing, I scanned the forest. The usual monsters were gone. Even the bugs had stopped humming, the birds silent in the shadowed wood. "How can you sit in the river? Papa says iron makes the devil-folk sick."

"Most of them." Her voice crackled like fire in a hearth, cold like freshly turned earth.

"Are you a devil-folk, then?"

Her milky eyes lifted to mine. I stepped back.

"You know my name." I did know it, but refused to say. I had felt her presence for months.

My heart sank beneath the river. "Did you take my brother away?"

"We shall see." She ran her thumb over a hole in the uniform's breast pocket. Blood poured forth like an open wound. "After all, it is you I truly want."

The flesh rose on my arms. "Why?"

She leaned her head to the side, empty eyes scouring me. "Because you cheated."

"I haven't cheated at anything, ma'am."

"But you have, sweet girl." She released the uniform. It became a plume of scarlet, bubbling noxious red before drifting away on the

6

current. "*He* thought he could play me for you, but he forgot the most important rule. I always get what I want, in the end."

Behind me, the porch light flickered on. Papa's slow whistle cut through the yard, his footsteps smacking the mud as he entered the house. I sank lower into the grass. "My father?"

She shook her head.

"The devil?" I tried again.

She smiled, all teeth. "Is that what you call him?"

My palms grew cold and clammy. I shrugged.

Her throaty laugh echoed into the night. "When he finally finds you, when he finally gets his claws in you . . ." Laughter faded into sighs, and she beckoned to me.

"Would you like to make a bargain, Adeline?" The bottom of her beautiful dress pooled around her shins, floating and pulsing in the current. "Thomas may still come home, but you must give me something in return. Not today, not tomorrow, not for many years— but in the end, you must give it to me."

Anything, anything for Tommy. "What do I have to give you?"

"Your life." The two words were so simple, spoken like they meant nothing at all. "In childbirth. So you may end this life the way you were supposed to."

Fear seeped from my skin. Childbirth seemed so far away, any thoughts of marriage and children far removed from my immature mind. Besides, I could simply not have children. I had Papa and Tommy to take care of me, anyway.

But I still had to know. "What if I refuse?"

She raised her hands above her head, a grotesque imitation of my beloved ballet. "*Theirs not to make reply. Theirs not to reason why. Theirs but to do and die.*"

I knew the poem, could have recognized it anywhere.

I'd lost the urge to eat, to sleep, to speak . . . to live. Papa and Tommy were all I had, all my isolated, eleven-year-old mind could recognize. I'd never experienced life without them, therefore one didn't exist at all.

I nodded. An icy breeze billowed over the water and the Woman in White disappeared. Just like that, my fate was sealed.

Life went on as it had. I still didn't speak, throwing myself into dance and drawing to express myself instead. But I ate. I slept at the foot of Papa's bed, curled up like a puppy dog with Tommy's shirt tucked beneath my arm, sleeping soundly with the knowledge I'd saved him.

Then came November of 1918. The World War was over. The evil Germans were beaten. Thomas Colton was coming home.

I waited in the yard, skipping circles around Papa in my nicest dress. My only clean ribbon tied back my hair. The dress was blue, my stockings yellow. Tommy promised he'd buy me the white shoes with his soldier pay, and I wanted my outfit to match. But first, I'd give him the biggest hug in the world, and make sure he didn't finish our book without me. Even if I barely remembered the poems anymore.

A truck hummed down the dirt road to our property, slowing as it approached the bridge. I vibrated in my old slippers, clasping my hands behind my back when Papa cast me a warning look. I didn't understand it, less when he said, "When they bring him in, don't stare."

I nodded too soon. The truck stopped. Three soldiers hopped out the front and circled back to the bed. There were some scattered words, then they heaved a gurney out the back. Something curled up on top of it, covered in faded, white blankets. A thing. A creature. It couldn't possibly be Tommy.

But as the soldiers carried the gurney up the porch, I recognized a tuft of blonde hair the same shade as my own. A single, brown eye, rich as chocolate, vacant and pointed at me. Bandages coated the rest of him.

I opened my mouth to speak, but no words came out. The soldiers stopped, looking to me and Papa, to the shriveled man on the cot. None of us said a word. They carried him inside.

I never got the white shoes. We never finished our book.

Most days, it was like the war never ended. Tommy never left his room, and Papa never let me inside. We did everything we could for spare cash. For a few harsh weeks, I even dressed as a boy, joining the others in the mines until I developed a cough so bad Papa forbade me from going back. All the money went toward medicine, bandages, doctors and special earrings that were supposed to help Tommy hear again.

I still didn't speak. Nor did I eat. Even on the nights I found sleep, I woke to Tommy screaming from his shadowed bedroom. It was always the same word, over and over again. *Argonne.*

But one cold December night, he screamed from the living room.

I cracked my bedroom door open. Yellow light washed the wooden floors, pouring in from the hall.

"Tommy, *calm down.*"

Something shattered. Guttural moans filtered down the hall, whispered words on an endless loop. *Grenade, where's my fucking grenade. Argonne. The captain's dead. Argonne. Kill me. Kill me. Kill me.*

I drifted into the hall.

A dull thud against the floor. Labored breathing echoed in and out and Tommy hollered. More thumping, then Papa pinned Tommy to the floor, right beneath the portrait of my mama in her Sunday best. Below it, Papa had hung up Tommy's citation star, the ribbon the army gave him for being a hero. For taking down the bad guys.

Tommy released another guttural scream.

"Calm down, boy. You'll scare your sister."

"I can't hear you." An ear-splitting cry left my brother's throat, a wailing keen that coated my bones. "I can't fucking hear you, Dad. I can't hear you, I can't hear you, I can't—"

Papa reached for Tommy's ear, fiddling with his special metal earring. *"Get off of me."*

He slammed into Papa, so hard he knocked him into one of the wooden dining chairs, sending splintered shards across the floor. He kept repeating those words. *Grenade. Captain. Argonne. Kill me.* His thunderous pacing echoed down the hall, the smack of his hands repeatedly hitting his head—the mottled skin covering the left side of his face like wax someone had swirled up.

I whimpered.

His eyes snapped to mine. So red, so swollen, I could barely make out the chocolate brown. "Adeline."

I took a step back.

His voice broke with a hushed crack. "Addie." Papa groaned beneath him, pushing off the floor. I stepped back again. "I'm sorry. Please don't look at me like that, baby. I'm sorry. I'm fucking sorry." The strange skin on his face scrunched, red and raw.

Hot tears dribbled down my cheeks.

Tommy screamed again, then stormed outside. Papa got to his feet as the wooden door smacked the frame.

A shuddering breath left his throat, and he ambled toward me. "Come on, baby, you're supposed to be in bed."

He tugged on my nightgown sleeve, but I remained still as stone.

A withered sigh. "Tommy's fine, he's just going through a rough patch. Let's go to sleep, you can come into my room if you want."

I shook my head, shuffling back to my bed. Waited until Papa shut his door and the sound of his guitar wafted through the wood, then grabbed my drawing book and Tommy's medal. I made sure the wooden door didn't smack behind me.

The night was cool. The leaves fell off all the trees but the evergreens, sparkling frost painting the ashen grass. It was too cold for the lightning bugs and the moon was new, the only light provided by flickering stars and the burnt, orange bulb on our porch. Lifting one of Papa's new propane lanterns, I scanned the property. A hunched shadow shook beside the river bank, stilted breaths echoing up the hill.

Tommy said nothing as I settled beside him. Frost seeped between my slippers and coated my dress in frigid mud. A little patch of ice floated down the river, getting caught on a low-hanging branch before shattering.

"I guess we both see shit that ain't real now."

I folded my arms around my knees, drawing them to my chest. Then, for the first time in over a year, I spoke to another human. "Papa says only bad men swear."

He didn't answer, but maybe he couldn't hear. I didn't know how his special earrings worked, but Papa had played with them when Tommy couldn't hear anything. I reached for one, but he smacked my hand away. I flinched.

More tears. Men didn't cry, at least they weren't supposed to, as far as I knew. But Papa cried when I wouldn't eat, and Tommy cried every day since he came home from the war. I wanted to cry too, but that would hurt us all worse, so I blinked my tears away.

With a long, drawn-out breath, Tommy reached up and fiddled with his earring. "You have to talk loud."

I swallowed, ignoring the scratching pain from an unused throat. "Papa says only bad men swear."

He blinked, long and slow at something across the river, but for once, there was nothing there.

"I am a bad man, baby."

Shaking my head, I muttered, "No, you ain't." Producing his ribbon from my pocket, I dangled it in front of his face. "Papa said you got this because you were a hero. Like the soldiers in *The Charge of the Light Brigade*. Bad men don't get ribbons and metals, Tommy." I grinned, confident that would get through to him. Instead, his harsh face twisted in the yellow lantern light.

"I don't want to look at that right now."

Frowning, I dangled the colorful ribbon closer. "But look, you were one of the good guys. There's nothing to be sad about, Tommy. You're a hero."

"Addie—"

"You promised you'd come home to me and you did. You fought the bad Germans and won and good men don't swear and cry, Tommy, so—"

A vicious growl left his throat. He ripped the medal from my shaking hands, yanking me to the ground as he threw it into the river. He overshot. The dull sound of it hitting a tree across the water echoed through the night.

Tears brimmed my eyes. Cold mud squelched around my fingers and seeped through my knees. I tried not to cry, but it wasn't working anymore. Dull sobs echoed from my throat, mingling with my brother's.

"I'm sorry, baby. I'm sorry." His cold arms encircled me, tugging me to his chest. I sniffed and pushed at him, but he crushed me against his jacket, shivering. *I'm sorry, I'm sorry, I'm sorry . . .*

An owl hooted in the distance. Another patch of ice broke in the river. Tommy's muffled tears sounded against my cheek.

He smoothed back my hair, rocking me back and forth in his lap. Stars dotted my vision, but I evened my breaths, wrapping my arms around his neck and hugging him back.

"Why aren't you acting like yourself anymore?"

He shook his head. More owls filled the silence. But silence, I'd grown used to that. Without Tommy and without my voice, Papa had no one left to speak to. Empty words filled our house like weeds in the field.

I stood, holding my hands high above my head. A little twirl. Then I did that thing Mrs. June taught us in ballet, to make your arms float, to make your body look sad. I streaked my fingers down my cheeks, mimicking tears, and wilted back to the ground.

Tommy watched, lips a flat line and red eyes following each movement. Papa never told him I took ballet, never mentioned I stopped talking, but big brothers worked that way. We were siblings, and that was stronger than anything. He nodded. "That's right, baby. Because I'm sad."

Curling up next to him, I laid my head on his thigh while his fingers stroked my hair. We stared at the water.

"It's okay if you see things."

His fingers left my hair. "No, it's never a good thing to see things that aren't there."

"But they are there." I pushed to my knees, pulling my journal from my coat. "Papa got me this, so I could draw all the things around our house. Maybe it'll help you too. You can draw . . . Argonne," I finished, recalling the name.

His pale lips flattened into a line again, so I continued, "Don't worry, Argonne can't hurt you. That's why we pour salt around the house, and devil-folk can't cross the river."

He swallowed, the word catching in his throat. "Argonne is a place, Addie. Not a thing."

"Oh." I frowned. That was strange, how could Tommy see *places*? I only saw bad folk.

"You can still draw it," I said. I opened my notebook in his lap, showing him my pictures. The first one was a little winged creature made of flowers. Below it, I scribbled *flower pixie*. "A few months ago, a troll man said he'd tell me all their names if I gave him the dress I was baptized in. Papa was angry because I ain't supposed to bargain with devil-folk, but then he was happy when he saw all the names I got. Maybe we could get your baptism outfit and the troll man can help you too." I smiled.

A tight frown slashed his lips. He flipped the page. The next was of the birchwood woman, naked as sin, but that was how she always looked. My face turned hot and red, but Tommy only flipped the page again. The knobby-faced trolls. Then, the nasty water horse called a kelpie. The furry little brown men called brownies, then the nuckelavee. His fingers froze on that one, drifting over the monster scratched on the page. It was a horse and rider, both skinless and connected by flesh and sinew. I only saw that one once. I had nightmares for weeks.

His voice took an odd tone. "You see these things?"

I nodded. "Not all the time, but sometimes. They never cross the river though, don't worry. And I never see them off the property as long as my clothes are inside out. Especially when I have my bells and iron necklace on."

His eyes flicked up to mine.

"It's really not that bad once you get used to it." I tried to pull my book away, but he held it in his lap. He looked scared, but that made no sense. "You always knew I saw the devil-folk, Tommy."

"I know, but—" His voice drifted on the frigid breeze, the icy current roaring behind me. "I just . . . I just thought you were imaginative and Papa was superstitious . . ." He shook his head. "You really see things? Like this, in this much detail?"

I smiled. "Well, I ain't that good of an artist. They're a bit different in real life."

"And Dad . . . encourages this?"

I nodded. "He said it was good for me, keeping an eye on them and learning more about the devil-folk. So I'd stay safe."

He twisted, staring at the fogged windows like he could see Papa in his bedroom, strumming his guitar.

"These things ain't real, baby."

I frowned. "Of course they're real. Just like Argonne—"

"*They ain't real*, Addie." Swallowing deep, he placed his hands on my shoulders. "The entire time I've been gone, you've been doing what? Seeing things, drawing them, and Papa keeps telling you to? He keeps saying this is okay?"

I didn't think it was a good time to mention I didn't eat, sleep or speak much either. "It's okay. The devil-folk can't hurt us here."

Tears brimmed his eyes, his lower lip coming between his teeth. "Baby, I want you to listen to me, okay?"

I nodded.

"They ain't real," he repeated. I opened my mouth but he rushed in, "I didn't understand before, but I get it now. I do. Papa talks a lot and you've barely ever left this farm. I hadn't either, but when I left for the war I met people, Addie. Many people, from all over the world, and no one sees things, not like this. It's not normal."

Vibrating beneath him, I tried to shake from his grip but he held tight. "Addie, you got to listen to me. I haven't been good, I know I haven't been good since I came back, but you need help, baby, real help. Like, a doctor or medicine or maybe . . . maybe we should go to church, I don't know, but these things Papa is telling you ain't good for your brain. If we keep letting this go on it might last forever."

"The devil-folk are real, Tommy, I—"

"Look." He released me, pulling something from his coat pocket. *The Completed Works of Alfred Lord Tennyson*. I smiled, thinking maybe he would change his mind when he flipped it over. My picture was still taped to the back, Papa and I smiling in black and white. At least, I was smiling. Where Papa stood beside me, a bullet embedded in the thick cover.

I shrank into the mud.

"I won't ever tell you everything. I won't ever tell you most. But I've been to hell, Addie. The real hell, the only one that exists. I didn't see a single one of your devil-folk there. No one did."

Casting my eyes to the ground, I ignored the book he held out by wringing my dirty skirt through my fingers.

"You know what's real, though? What's true?"

I shook my head.

"You saved my life." He dropped the book between us. "This book was in my chest pocket, you know that? Right over my heart. You saved me, and I'm going to save you now, baby. I'm going to make you better. I'm going to fix this."

"They're real," I whispered one more time. I saw them. They were real. Papa's song was real, my drawings were real, the deal I made to save him, the devil coming for our daddy's soul because he made a bargain, was all *real*.

"Sh, it's okay. It's okay." I hadn't realized I was crying again. Hot tears slipped down my cheeks, mixing with the mud and frost staining my dress. Tommy wrapped me in his arms, stroking my hair. Even though he didn't believe me, even though he was *wrong*, even though his face didn't look the same and he cried and swore now and he'd no longer dance with Papa and me at the river, I let him. I let him hug me. I let him pick me up, even though Papa said I was too old for that. My arms came around his neck, my legs around his waist and I buried my face against his skin. He was wrong, but Tommy loved me and Papa too, so I'd just have to show him.

"I love you, Addie. We're . . . we're going to fix this." He kissed my tear-matted hair, pushing to his feet. I didn't let go. "Come on, let's get you to bed. It's late."

Tears pooled and kept coming, pouring down my cheeks even as Tommy held me tight against him, stroking my hair as he carried me up the hill. I could tell the difference now from all the other times he carried me. He marched with determination, pushing his injured legs harder and harder up the slope. I was bigger and my feet dangled past his waist. His eyes focused behind me, on the soft lighting of the house and all the demons he trudged back to. But I faced the river, the creatures that inhabited our woods, the things Tommy forgot to protect me from while he fought enemies across the sea.

Stars flickered, the river babbled and critters roamed the underbrush.

All at once, the world went silent.

The lantern light faded, retreating from where it splashed across the grass. The noise from the river became a hush, the hooting owls and the fracturing ice. Even Tommy's whispered words faded into nothing, empty smoke on a frozen breeze. The stars flickered to black and the mighty evergreens froze in the wind. The entire night dipped into a silence so heavy, nothing remained but the blood rushing in my ears. I lifted my face from Tommy's shoulder. I froze.

A pair of golden eyes blinked across the river.

A man stood in the trees' shadows, drawing darkness to him like he absorbed the night. The dusk caressed him, coating like a second skin so only a flicker here and there could be discerned. The sharp curve of a jaw, flexed fingers brushing his throat. Nothing apparent, nothing my eyes could grasp onto for more than a second. Except for the eyes. They glowed like beacons in the dark, slitted and narrow like a snake's. My pulse grew thick and hot in my throat. My heart thudded against my chest.

When the Devil kills saints, he kills slowly.

Tommy's arms tightened on my ribs, but I didn't feel them. The eyes scoured me and my brother's back as he marched us farther away from them. They tilted to the side. I couldn't decide if they were friendly. If those eyes sought answers, or prey.

Ice froze my veins, but something else trembled against my bones, a feeling I couldn't ignore. I raised a tentative hand, unfurling my fingers one by one. Tommy still mumbled assurances, smoothing his fingers over my spine. In the shadow-kissed darkness, those golden eyes smiled.

My brother's words found me, garbled and muted like he spoke underwater. *These things aren't real. There're no evil creatures walking our farm.*

I melted into those inhuman eyes. A deep understanding, a foreboding, unfurled beneath my skin. I knew we were strange. I knew the townsfolk said things about us. But it wasn't until then, trembling in the crisp darkness against my brother's chest, that I truly understood. Tommy was wrong, and Papa too.

"The devil ain't coming for Papa's soul."

I nodded against his shoulder. For the first time and only time in my life, I was grateful he could no longer hear.

"I know," I whispered. "He's coming for mine."

TWO

There was a pixie in the drug store, and it wouldn't quit staring at me.

It was always best to avoid looking at them, but as it gnawed on a tiny, porous bone, hopping from shelf to shelf behind Mr. Laney's head, I made that grave mistake. Sage-green skin stood colorful and strange against the background of glass jars. It sat on a bed of cotton bandages, rabbit-like ears twitching and sharp while shiny, black eyes followed me. Its tiny head cocked to the side, sharp teeth ripening into a smile when Mr. Laney coughed. "Is everything alright, Miss Colton?"

Tearing my focus back to the pharmacist, I lifted a hand to the iron crucifix dangling from my neck. Once my fingers brushed the cool metal, the pixie disappeared from view. "Sorry?"

"I asked if you were alright. Looked like you were seeing something." He frowned, but instead of waiting for an answer, pushed the vial of codeine I'd bought across the counter with my change.

Grabbing my things, I adjusted my hat on my head, smoothing my dress while the eyes of Mrs. Joyland and Mrs. Farley followed me out the store. The bell chimed above my head, matching the tune of the ones around my ankle. One of them whispered, "That girl is *disturbed*."

19

I paused only a second before leaving.

The sun winked in and out of roiling, gray clouds. A hot breeze took the air, scattering dust and dirt across the main road. The weather vane on top of Tully's General Store twirled round and round like a ballerina. Children held their hats, running past me in their dirty clothes to the end of the street. In front of the tavern that shut down six years ago—a casualty of prohibition—the pastor's wife and her three sisters fanned their faces, clutching purses in crisp gloves.

"Miss Adeline!"

Two little boys ran up to me, so streaked with dirt I hardly recognized them. But as they came closer, the faces of Gregory and Robert Baker became clear. The brothers looked so much alike, I could only tell them apart based on their missing teeth and personalities.

I halted beside the community well, clutching the codeine and my purse. Robert stopped in front of me, pushing his brother out of the way. "Miss Adeline, we think we found a dryad in the woods!"

My eyes snapped to the four women on the old tavern's porch. The pastor's wife, Belinda, stared with pinched eyes and lips.

I bent down to Robert's level, dropping my voice. "You know folks don't like when you talk like that."

"I don't care what any of them think." He beamed, revealing a black space where a front tooth should have been. Gregory stood behind his brother, toeing the ground. The two boys grew fond of me last year when I warned them away from a copse of trees teeming with sprites. It wasn't often I revealed what I could see to other people, but sprites were particularly nasty and the boys were only eight. Their little sister, Florence, usually followed close behind—no one else watched her since their papa passed and mama fell ill—but she was nowhere to be seen today.

20

"What do I tell you boys about staying out of the woods?" I sat on the faded stones of the well, crossing my legs. "Not to mention, shouldn't you two be in school right now?"

"No school this week. The teacher quit," Gregory said.

I frowned. "I thought a new one came last month?"

Robert bounced on his heels. "No one stays here long. Mama says it's because Fairville is a shithole."

I closed my eyes, sighing. Belinda stood from her chair, clutching the wooden arm with white knuckles. I prepared to lecture him on the language, but one look at their soot-streaked faces told me otherwise. The man of their house was dead, their mama could hardly get out of bed, and their little sister just learned to walk. With no school they'd spent the whole week in the mines. If the coal on their cheeks didn't give it away, the gaunt hollows of their cheeks did.

"You should be the new teacher," Gregory said.

I'd love to. I'd tried to, many times in fact. I loved children. They were so much simpler than adults, their little minds not warped by the world just yet—and since I could never have any of my own, teaching seemed fitting. But each time I applied, there were too many protests to count. No one wanted the devil girl educating their kids.

I smiled. "I ain't old enough yet. Don't you have to be gray-haired and sour-faced to run a schoolhouse?"

Robert made a face. "You are old, Miss Addie."

I narrowed my eyes, but laughed anyway.

They both went silent, waiting.

Tommy and I barely made ends meet anymore. The mortgage was overdue and the crops failed this summer, the third year in a row. Everyone in Fairville was half-starving from the continued droughts. But the boys looked worse than I did, and they kept looking at my bag. I sighed, retrieving the loaf of bread I'd just bought with the last

21

two dollars I had. I broke it in half. "Save some for your mama and Florence, alright?"

Robert dived for the bread, but I held it back. "Just because you were raised like wolves doesn't mean you can act like them." He folded his hands behind his back and smiled, releasing a quiet wolf howl. Gregory whispered, "Thank you, Miss Addie," behind him.

They were already halfway down the road before the bread left my fingertips. "And stay out of the woods!" I called, to which they each gave a thumbs-up. Fanning my face, I stole a deep breath and scurried past the old tavern.

Belinda's face quivered. "Shame on you, Miss Colton. Shame on you filling those boys' heads with such evil."

"I didn't fill their heads," I mumbled under my breath. "I filled their stomachs."

Focused on the ground, I followed the lonely dirt road home, rubbing my cross between my fingers.

A storm would begin soon, and while I never minded a little summer rain, it was best to get home before the thunder set in. Tommy never did well with all the noise. I'd been planning on stopping by the cemetery, but it would have to wait until tomorrow.

The dryads were out in droves today, released from their trees and skipping at the edge of the forest. They giggled when they noticed me, caressing their tree bark skin and flowery hair.

"Look! The glamour-touched girl has arrived."

"Come play with us, sister."

"Please, sister, come dance with us in our woods."

I knew exactly what happened when living things wandered too close to their trees. The bloody remains of an animal who did just that rested at the base of a towering oak. Their silken voices followed me down the road, more arriving and skirting the tree line to woo me closer. Touching my iron necklace did no good, so I popped the crucifix in my mouth and sucked until metal tinged my throat. After a moment, their voices dimmed and their willowy bodies faded away.

I reached the end of the road. Across the bridge, parked with the top down beside our porch, was a sleek, black Rolls Royce. I frowned, surveying the tall grasses, the river, and the farmland beyond the house. All empty. Mid-afternoon in June, Tommy should have been out in the field.

Low chatter filled the hall when I stepped inside and hung up my hat. I rounded the corner, eyeing the stranger sitting at my kitchen table, sipping coffee with Tommy.

Noise hushed in their throats. The stranger grinned, gray hair slicked back on his head and sharp suit free of any wrinkles or stains. Across from him, Tommy wore his Sunday best, which included Papa's faded, striped shirt, worn leather suspenders and the black dress shoes the army gave him for his medal ceremony.

Tommy's lips pulled into a pained smile. "Addie . . . I wasn't expecting you back until later."

"There's a storm coming in. I came home early." I folded my arms, not bothering to greet the guest. Silence swirled around the three of us as he waited for introductions. Tommy sharpened his eyes on me, a battle of wits brewing until he realized I wouldn't leave.

"Agent Morris, this is my sister, Miss Adeline Colton. Addie, this is Mr. Morris."

My eyebrow hit my hairline. "Agent?"

To his credit, Mr. Morris smiled. "With the Federal Bureau of Investigation, ma'am. Why don't you take a seat, I was just discussing some things with your brother."

The look on Tommy's face warned me to find somewhere else to be, but I wasn't twelve anymore, and if this man was in our home it was probably important. I settled into the seat beside my brother, digging deep enough into my shallow pool of etiquette to offer Mr.

Morris something to eat. He declined, so I followed up with, "Is there a problem?"

"Oh, no, not at all." Mr. Morris folded his hands on the table. "Your brother and I were just discussing his future. You should be very proud, Miss Colton. The FBI has offered him a job."

My eyes flicked to Tommy, who looked everywhere but me. I was on his right side, his good side, with smooth skin, a sharp brown eye and golden stubble dusting his jaw. A jaw that clenched as I said, "He doesn't hear too well, you know that, right?"

Mr. Morris nodded. "Which is why he's the perfect candidate for this job. We've been looking for someone who's particularly skilled at lip reading."

Well, Tommy certainly had that down. He busted enough hearing aids over the years; it was the only way to communicate in between earning cash for new ones. He refused to learn sign language. "Tommy never mentioned he applied for this job."

Mr. Morris looked between us. Tommy swiveled his head toward me. "We can discuss it further in private."

"We're farmers. Always have been, always will be," I said, ignoring him completely. The smile wilted off Mr. Morris's face. "But thank you for stopping by."

Tommy closed his eyes, releasing a drawn sigh. "Agent Morris, may I stop by your hotel tomorrow to discuss the rest of the paperwork?"

"Of course." After thanking us for our time, nodding his head at me and retrieving his hat, Tommy walked him to the door and said hushed goodbyes. The wooden door smacked against the frame and he stormed back into the living room.

I didn't get up from my seat.

"Really?"

Turning my slow gaze on him, I hissed, "*Really*? You want to tell me what in the hell that was all about?"

24

"You're a lady, Addie. Watch your mouth." He went into the kitchen, rolling up his shirtsleeves to wash the sweat from his clammy palms. "I didn't want to tell you anything until I knew it was a done deal."

My hands balled into fists. "What's a done deal?"

"This job." Flicking water at the counter, he grabbed another mug from the cabinet and slammed it down in front of me. "How was town today?"

I didn't pour myself any coffee. "Don't change the topic."

"I'm not." He settled into the seat across from me, rubbing at his temples. "I didn't have a choice. We need the money."

"I've been making plenty with the pharmacist." Mr. Laney and I had a deal going, as long as I kept it quiet. No one in Fairville wanted others to know they worked with the devil girl. Each Sunday while everyone gathered in church, I brought him willow bark, hawthorne, primrose and whatever else he requested for the season. Half the town took medicine grown on the devil farm without realizing it.

"It's not enough." He produced a letter from his pocket, flicking it across the table. "We lost it, baby."

My lungs squeezed in my chest, sweaty fingers clutching the letter as I scanned it once, twice, three times just to be sure. *Dear Mr. Thomas Colton, this is a formal notice from The Bank of Georgia . . .*

I shook my head. "We paid the mortgage on time last month."

"And we're still five hundred behind." He took the letter back. "I tried, alright? I'm sorry I couldn't make it work, I'm sorry the rain didn't come last season, I'm sorry we couldn't hold onto this place but he's been gone six months now and we can't—"

"It's only been *six months*. The bank can't work with us for a few more? We can find the money—"

"We can't." There was a death knell in his words, the frown slashing his lips. "I loved Papa just as much as you did and I'll never speak badly of him, but he was always behind. His eyes were too big for his stomach when he purchased this land and we always struggled to maintain it even when there were three of us. We haven't been able to keep it afloat just the two of us, Addie, and we're not going to. Not like this."

Tears pricked the back of my eyes. I turned away, gritting my teeth and blinking them away.

"They're offering me three hundred dollars a month to start. That's a good salary, Addie, and I know how you feel about this place, but maybe after we've lived in New York for a while—"

I cut off whatever he was about to say. "What do you mean New York?"

"The job is in Manhattan."

I shook my head. "Then you ain't going."

"I am going. And so are you." He played with the handle of his cup, ignoring my face turning redder and hotter. "We have no house to live in anymore. Papa's with Mama and the lord now. You're twenty years old, a young woman, and it's about time we both moved on from this place. It's never been good for you."

I slammed my palms flat on the table, rattling the glass lantern in the center. "I need this place. You know I can't leave, Tommy. It's not safe for me."

He stared at me. I'd never admit it, but sometimes, when I looked at him head-on like this, it was like I spoke to two different people. There was right-sided Tommy, with smooth skin and a warm brown eye. A crooked half-smile that used to charm the socks off every lady in Fairville. He was my big brother, my other half, the gangly teenager who whittled me wooden horses and taught me to read. Then there was left-sided Tommy, the empty shell that came home from the war. Burned and scarred, unrecognizable, cold and distant and so vastly different from me, we may as well have been strangers.

Especially as he said, "Addie, Papa was insane. He loved you, but all he ever did was hurt you."

I jumped to my feet, ignoring his grimace as the dining chair smacked the floor behind me. The grandfather clock struck three times from the living room, the wooden door slammed the frame behind me, and thunder rolled in the distance. I didn't go back inside to make sure Tommy turned his hearing aids off.

THREE

Down to the river we go. Down to the river we go . . .

Bells chimed on my ankles and the inseam of my dress rubbed against my neck. Scattered lightning flickered the sky, thunder drumming in the distance, but I ignored the impending storm as I carried my salt pouch to the river. Six months ago, Papa drew his last breath beside the water, a final request when a cough took him so bad, even I knew he'd never recover. But it didn't matter that he was gone, that his old guitar sat dusty and unused beside his bed since last spring. I still heard the notes humming inside my brain, his husky baritone singing the opening lines of his song.

> *Down to the river we go.*
> *Down to the river we go.*
> *Down to the river and the lake and the bog,*
> *To the ash wood tree and the midnight fog.*
> *In the summer, in the rain, in the wind's harsh blow,*
> *Speaks a message from your god and his friend down low.*
> *For the sinner, for the father, for the girl he borrowed,*
> *When the devil kills saints he kills slowly.*
> *When the devil kills saints he kills slow.*

Closing my eyes, I took a moment to breathe, to let myself get swallowed by the memory. Tommy always said my visions weren't real, but if that were true, then I would have conjured Papa months ago. All I had were my memories, the rituals he gave me, and the song I knew so well I could sing it in my sleep.

I took off my shoes, laying them in a dry patch of grass so my feet could dig into the earth. A quiet hum filled my bones, the sense of connection, of life, as I unclipped my salt pouch from my waist and began my circle around the house.

"So down to the river we go . . ." I murmured, but my voice didn't want to come today, just like it didn't so many other days. I imagined Papa's low drawl instead, his golden throat and graying beard bobbing with each syllable.

So down to the river we go.
Down to the river we go.
With the son and the daughter and a stolen night,
With his salt on the earth and her bones in the light.
With Adam and Eve and their whisper through the trees,
When a serpent strikes a deal you obey his creed.
For the daughter that you seek you will pay his toll,
But when the devil kills saints he kills slowly.
When the devil kills saints he kills slow.

Lightning crackled against the sky, striking far too close. It was dangerous being out here much longer, especially with all the tall trees and water, but I needed to finish. Needed to practice Papa's liturgy lest one day without him, I forgot it. I never sang. That was all him—he was the voice I abandoned and Tommy lost with his hearing, but I could still dance, just like I always did, face to the sky and feet in the dirt and wind tugging my hair at the nape of my neck.

Across the river, the mighty evergreens groaned in the lifting wind, leaves rustling toward the sky and casting shadows along the water. I followed the path of scorched grass around our house, burned brown from years and years of salting it. Wind barreled across the water and drew goosebumps to my skin, but I didn't stop salting, humming, falling into the rhythm until my eyes closed and I walked by memory alone. My shoulders swayed with the breeze, dress whipping my ankles. When I sank deep enough into the melody, Papa's haunting guitar joined his voice in my head.

Down to the river we go.
Down to the river we go.
For the liars, for the beggars, for a dead man's fears,
For a mother's last breath and a widower's tears.
Where the father lays his head on the dark river bed,
And the stones eat his bones, not the daughter's instead.
And when Satan comes taking it's my daddy's soul,
For when the devil kills saints he kills slowly.
If the devil takes me he'll kill slowly.
Cuz' when the devil kills saints he kills slow.

The last line left my lips and the last of the salt fell to the dirt. On instinct, I lifted my eyes to the forest, scanning the darkened, swaying tree line for any life. Mostly, for a pair of golden eyes. But it had been years since I saw him that way, the mirage of his presence just beyond our land no longer a concern. People said the devil walked our farm, and they were right. He visited my dreams every month.

Rain shattered from the heavens like God flipped a switch. My dress clung to my legs and my hair smacked against my face, but I didn't move. Sometimes, I wished a cold breeze would come and take my lungs too. That there would be an end to all this waiting, this anxiety, the ridicule, the grief.

I went inside. The rain washed away my freshly poured salt. All I'd accomplished was getting wet.

RAIN RATTLED THE HOUSE, beating like war drums on the tin roof. The windchimes on the porch screamed a melody and the candles dotting our living room flickered with the draft. Tommy's untouched dinner sat cold on the table with our dirty coffee mugs.

I wrapped my mama's pearl necklace around my throat, laying it over my iron crucifix. Then I put on my nicest heels, my favorite lipstick, and cranked the gramophone in the living room. Mrs. June gifted it to me when I was fifteen and could no longer afford ballet lessons. "You have a gift, Miss Colton," she'd said. "Don't ever stop using it."

That simply wasn't true. I had a curse, but it didn't matter because I needed something to fill the silence without Papa taking to the task. Neither me nor Tommy were good at it.

I did several pirouettes—a struggle in kitten heels but my old slippers were long destroyed. First position. An arabesque, then I gave up anything technical and swayed along with the music. Mikhail Fokine's *Carnival of the Animals* drifted across the rug, slow and haunting.

Dancing was how I spoke most days, so I was half-tempted to stop when Tommy shuffled from his room, shirt untucked and hair disheveled. He sank onto the sofa, dark eyes following each of my movements, hearing aids noticeably absent.

The song ended. I went to flip the record when he said, "I know. I'm sorry."

My fingers twitched around the crank handle. He wouldn't know what I was saying unless I turned around, letting him read my lips. He did it on purpose. He always did when he wanted me to look at him. No one else would. Averted eyes became Thomas Colton's new normal in 1918. I was the only one who wasn't afraid to stare.

31

Turning, I leaned against the table and crossed my arms. "No, you're not."

"I'm sorry you're hurting," he said, which was a nice way to say he wasn't sorry at all.

I cranked the gramophone, dropped the needle on the record and swept across the faded carpet. It was how things usually went these days. Words were thrown into the void between us and left there to perish. He used to hear me out, even when words were nothing but twirls on the carpet and jerking limbs, but that was before. It was never that he lost the ability to hear. He lost the ability to listen.

"What will I do in New York?" I asked, pausing just long enough for him to read my lips.

He didn't answer at first. I thought I may have spoken too fast, but he finally said, "Whatever you want. They're setting me up with a nice apartment, a two bedroom so you have somewhere to stay too. I made sure of that." He played with a frayed string on his shirt. "And after we're settled then I don't know. They say ladies in New York do lots of things all day. Maybe you could get a job, or use your unwitting charm to dine with all the rich city folk. Meet a nice man or something."

"I'm never getting married." I pushed to my toes, completing a turn. "I have the conversation skills of a boar and last I checked, there ain't much farming in Manhattan."

"You know, you're twenty now, Addie. Maybe you should try and meet—"

"I ain't ever getting married," I snapped. My hands came down from their position over my head, my skirt rustling around my knees. "Why don't you go meet a nice lady if the thought is so important to you?"

I regretted it the moment I said it. There was a reason I didn't speak much, because when I did, I either said the wrong things or bad things. Tommy would have loved to have a wife, and eight years ago, he was so handsome half the girls in Fairville didn't care their mamas said he was a devil worshiper.

I sank to my knees, pressing my thumbs into my temples.

"I need this, Addie."

Eyes flickering to his, I pressed my lips into a tight line.

"I really need this," he repeated. "It's been so hard since . . ." His voice departed like a cool breeze, eyes far away, drifting across the ocean to settle in the blood-stained scars of Argonne.

"I'm useful for once," he finished.

"You're always useful."

"No, I'm not. I couldn't save the farm. Couldn't run things like Papa did, not with all my injuries. I've been looking for work for years, long before Papa got sick, so I could make my own way and get you the hell away from this place. But there ain't much opportunity out there for a mostly deaf veteran, so . . ." He shrugged, refusing to look at me. "Nothing good has ever come out of this, baby. All those things that happened to me, they never came with opportunities, just shut doors. The FBI needs someone like me, no one else does."

"I need you."

He nodded. "Yeah."

The record finished on the gramophone. Pattering rain filled the vast, empty space between us. It stretched wider with every second.

I didn't say what we were both thinking. It wasn't enough. Nothing would ever be enough to fill the hole in Tommy the war left behind, only deepened further by Papa passing, whether he liked to admit it or not. For the past eight years, they hadn't seen eye to eye on pretty much anything, but Papa was still there every time Tommy woke screaming in the night. Papa was the only one who could calm him down when the war visions got bad.

Now, it was just the two of us. Two lonely peas in a very unhappy pod. The broken soldier son and the crazy devil-worshiping daughter. The deaf man and the woman who refused to speak.

"I wish we could have left sooner." My eyes found Tommy, but he wasn't looking at me, or anything on this side of the Atlantic. "Maybe you would have been better then, but this is the best I can do now. At least try. Give it a chance. I'll put some money away and, in a few months, if the house is still up for auction I'll see if I can get it back, if you're really not doing well in New York. But try first, please, for me."

There it was. I could scream, I could sob, I could pitch myself on the carpet and fall prostrate before him on the floor. In the end, Tommy was the man of the house with Papa gone. I was the unhinged little sister left behind. He made the decisions, and the best I could hope for was he considered what I had to say, but he wouldn't. Papa was the only thing that kept our two worlds separate—what was good for Tommy and what was good for me. Tommy already had opinions on what was best for me, inflamed by many, many years of arguing with Papa. So, he would not listen. He would do what he thought was best, and because I was a woman and his burden to bear, I would listen.

I nodded, already resigned to another curse revolving around my brother. "I'll try."

FOUR

CLUTCHING ONE OVERSTUFFED SUITCASE, I fanned myself beside Tommy on the crumbling platform. Across the tracks and baking in the sun sat the community well where Tommy left for the war, the old schoolhouse, Tully's General Store and the pharmacist. Beyond that, the cemetery where my parents laid in eternal rest, and a little farther past that, the farm I spent my entire life on. The only things I'd ever known. It wasn't much, and I had no lost love for Fairville, but I couldn't help a sense of loss knowing my entire life was about to roll away.

The train blew past. Thick smoke clogged the air, sour and staunch against my nose. Wind whipped my hat clear from my head and Tommy ran after it, telling me to stay put. His suitcase rested on the ground next to mine. Our whole lives, stuffed into these little bags. Everything else, sold back to the bank.

The aforementioned bank flickered through the train's windows, dark and light and dark and light as the locomotive roared between us. It rolled to a stop, steam hissing on the tracks as a gangly conductor hung off the side. Down the platform, Tommy still chased after my hat.

Our tickets grew damp and soft in my palm.

Maybe—

"Got it." Tommy appeared beside me, placing the dirty felt back on my head. Swiping the tickets from my palm, he handed them to the conductor. "First class."

We were too poor for first class, but I didn't say it. Just like I hadn't said anything the entire day, choosing silence as I circled my home for the last time, picking and choosing the most important things. If I had it my way, I'd bring nothing but a suitcase full of memories, but Tommy told me over and over, clothes and valuables only. We couldn't afford to bring much else.

Everything was valuable. Papa's soul sang in that house, settled in the wooden floors and draped across the furniture. But a whole lifetime couldn't fit in a suitcase, and Tommy didn't see things the way I did. That house was full of bad memories for him, not good ones. The most he allowed was Papa's guitar and Mama's portrait before stating we'd purchase new things up north.

In the city.

New York City.

We settled into velvet seats directly across from one another. A boy with dirty suspenders took our luggage and stored it above our heads. Then a server came over, dressed to the nines, asking Tommy if he'd like a cigar. Steam roiled out the window and the train lurched forward. Colors swirled past us, so fast you could barely make them out. Then Fairville was gone, just like a young man wearing a green uniform and holding a gun, promising he'd come home.

Tommy folded his ankle over his knee and flicked open today's paper. Not the local one, but the Times. A grainy shot of a sharp-dressed man filled the front cover. Above his hat the headline read, STOCK PRICES SOAR FOR J.W. OIL COMPANY. Beneath the photograph in smaller print, THE BLOODY BOWLERS STRIKE AGAIN! VIOLENCE SOARS WITH ILLEGAL SALE OF ALCOHOL.

I leaned forward.

Murder and mayhem have become commonplace in New York, rivaling Chicago in incidence of violent crime. Mayor Hylan states the sale of alcohol is to blame, pointing the finger at prohibition laws for the rise of criminally run—

"Did you have any of your visions today?" Tommy folded the paper down, eyes roaming over me like he could figure out what went wrong with my brain.

Tilting my head to the side, I continued reading the crumpled article beside his thigh. *While the New York Police investigate claims—*

"Adeline, I asked you something."

Sighing, I leaned back with a scowl. "No."

"You keep rubbing your necklace."

I dropped the cross. "Nervous habit."

"What are you nervous about?"

There was no point in telling him. He either wouldn't believe me, or he'd think I was more insane than he already did.

"It's a new moon tonight," I said.

Tommy frowned. "We're not taking a boat or anything, no need to worry about tides."

"I know." I left it at that, not adding on what I really wanted to say. Tonight was a new moon. So, tonight, I'd see the devil.

DARKNESS TOUCHED THE SKY when the conductor showed us to our sleeping cars. My bed was private, a room off to the side with a heavy door between me and the hall. I'd never been on a train before, but it was easy to see the arrangement didn't come cheap. Most slept in tiny open bunks attached to the wall, fighting for space in a smelly car I accidentally found instead of the powder room. The place we should have been.

The lights went off but I lay awake, staring out the window. Tonight, the moon was new, showcasing nothing but shadow and the blink of faded stars.

He always came on the new moon. The first time had been shortly after I turned eighteen. I went to sleep, warm in my bed and woke up beneath the river.

I had known it was a dream, but with the frigid wetness of the water, the visceral murky darkness, I panicked anyway. My lungs screamed, skin burning where the current ripped at my arms. I thrashed against the water, white dress tangling between my legs, but only fell deeper . . . and deeper and deeper, then *he* was there.

At first, I saw nothing but his golden eyes.

Then, hovering in the silty water above me, was the strangest creature I'd ever seen.

He looked like a man, but I knew he wasn't. Thick, black hair swirled around warm skin. In the little light, I could just make out the tapered points of his ears, the sharp edges of his teeth. Tattoos of violet and black encased his arms and chest, traveling up his neck to the curve of his jaw. Even his hands hadn't been spared, the inky whorls on his fingers writhing as he reached out for me.

He ran a lock of my pale hair through his fingers, letting it drift away on the current. The strands fanned out in a curtain of ivory, and I woke up.

I had that dream three times, once a night during the new moon's cycle. When a sliver of it appeared back in the sky, my sleep went quiet and empty again. Until four weeks later. Each month since, the dreams became stronger, the noises louder, the feelings more . . . real.

Tonight's dream played on the train. Though the sky was black and empty when I went to sleep, a bright full moon shined through the window now. Thick fog blanketed the ground, knee-high and smooth as glass. Tendrils of it swirled around my legs as my bare feet hit the floor, further disturbed when I pushed open the hallway door. From the carpet of white grew vines, dark green and thick as my arms. They clambered up the metal siding, snaking around the windows in a web of veins across the walls. Wisteria grew above my head, so dense it made a swaying ceiling of violet. There were no other signs of life.

I stood in the empty car and waited.

A warm breeze caressed my feet, dragging the fog around my ankles with the heady scent of oleander. Rain dripped in the distance, mixed with the steady pounding of drums. Between the beats came a whisper, threaded with a dare. *"Annwyl."*

The oleander grew stronger. Rain ran down my hair and face as I exited our train car, feet digging into the grating as I pushed into the next one. Rows of bunks stared back at me, stacked three high along the walls. Each bed lay empty except one. In the last row on the very top, a leg dangled off the side, swinging to a whistled tune.

I leaned against the door.

The whistling stopped, the swinging, and the leg vanished into thin air. Only the vines hissing across the walls made a sound.

"Well, if it isn't the object of all my adoration."

I turned, not at all surprised to find him on the top bunk closest to me. He lounged on his side with a lazy smile, cheek propped in his hand. Long fingers drifted over the blanket with slow circles, echoing the tattoos on his bare torso. Along his side, a vicious battle looped a warrior's final moments. Over his ribcage, a woman performed an inviting dance on a tabletop. A snake slithered like a living armband around his bicep, and over his heart, two children held each other in a violent wind. Even the spaces in between writhed with movement, thick waves of gray and black swirling between the larger pictures.

Somehow, I still found his eyes the most inhuman.

Leaning my head against the door, I gave him half a smile. "Hello, Devil."

"You know I loathe when you call me that." A vicious grin pulled at his lips, sharp incisors on display.

"If you told me your real name, I wouldn't have to."

"I'll tell you mine if you tell me yours."

"Would you prefer Satan?" Another rule of Papa's I never questioned—never give out your name. Whenever asked, I said I was *called* Addie instead of Adeline, and never Colton. I could have done the same with my dark prince, but a shiver in my bones warned me otherwise. That even giving him my nickname—even in a dream— came with great risk, one I was yet to understand the consequences of. Threat pulsed in the power around him, the aura of black and gold coating him like a second skin.

"Such a cruel, little thing." He clicked his tongue, stretching his arm above his head like I bored him. "Tell me, my beloved, where are we going?"

"Home." Not quite a truth, not quite a lie. He could always see right through my dishonesty.

"Hm." In the space of a blink he was gone again.

He reappeared in front of me, dressed in a suit. A snap of his fingers and my robe left my shoulders, replaced with a heavy gown more befitting my mama's generation than mine. The corset hugged my waist and ribs, pushing up my breasts beneath a square hemline. Silk sleeves ended at my elbows, dripping with pearls and lace. Even my hair had been fixed by magic, curled and framed around my face with golden pins. Diamonds choked my neck and dangled from my ears, catching the full moon's light as he tugged me forward, an arm around my waist and his hand in mine. Phantom strings struck a haunting tune on the oleander breeze.

"I've missed you." He pulled me close, so close the heat of his body licked through the layers of silk. Heat bloomed on my skin, setting fire to an incessant pull deep in my blood. The closer I inched to him the more it was satisfied, only giving me space to breathe when my chest went flush with his.

"Every four weeks." I had no reason to assure him. These were dreams, apparitions of a dark lord I should have never indulged. It was surely all his master plan to lure me in. Especially as his warm lips glided up my neck, sending shivers across my skin.

"Tell me where you are, *annwyl*." His hand tightened on my waist. Those strange eyes grew dark and heavy, melting around the nickname I didn't understand.

I tilted my head to the side. "Then you would never miss me."

"True." His thumb ran beneath the lace at my back. "You could find other ways to punish me."

Chills raced down my arms, meeting a heat low in my stomach I was desperately ashamed of. Thankfully, he moved on from the offer quicker than he blinked from sight.

"How are your flowers?"

"Good. You were right, the pharmacist paid well for the bark." A copse of willows dotted our land, separate from the forest and therefore safe to wander into. When my calendula didn't sell too well last month, my dark prince suggested the bark instead.

He didn't know why I needed the money, only that I was desperate for it. Most months we spent the dreams outside Papa's farmhouse, just outside my circle of salt. It made sense for me to dream of my last known surroundings, though it never explained how he spotted things I didn't. Like the circle of willow trees on the edge of the land or the cluster of primroses beside the river. When I woke up, those things were always there, exactly as he said.

His voice dropped low against my ear, seductive and quiet beneath the haunting strings. "Try foxgloves next."

"Those are poisonous."

"Medicine is nothing but a well-dosed poison."

He dipped me, low enough to grant a perfect view of the ceiling. Just like the last car, wisteria dangled in amethyst droves, but here, small indigo flowers mixed in with the vines, their bright, yellow centers marking them clearly. Atropa belladonna . . . better known as deadly nightshade.

"Your druggist will know what to do with it." He pulled me back to his chest with a mysterious grin. "Besides, how beautiful will you look laying among them?"

Another omen dripping with charm, a threat so tantalizing you escorted yourself straight to peril. His presence had always been that way—a hypnotic beckoning into the dark.

I'd spent the last two years deciphering these moments, going as far as buying books on how to interpret dreams. Through all my readings, contemplation and forced sit-downs with the pastor, a solid conclusion couldn't be reached. Dreams weren't supposed to feel more tangible than life. Dreams weren't supposed to teach you things—give information—you didn't know existed before. The books told me next to nothing and the pastor said I let the devil into my heart. Unfortunately, the latter was right.

"Foxglove," he breathed along my neck, tugging me from my thoughts. His hand left my waist to reveal a handful of seeds. "Just like these, grown in the shade. Tell them your darkest secret and they'll be full grown in two weeks."

A wry smile pulled my lips. "Does it truly work like that?"

"Do you prefer something different?"

I lifted a shoulder. Lightning shot up my side when his hand resumed its position on my waist. "It's not as simple as that. I can whisper and wish all I want. It doesn't change how fast flowers grow."

"It's not a wish, it's a command." He placed a lingering kiss to my jaw, filled with something so dark I feared I'd lose the light. "The flowers, the earth, the darkness, the woods. They're all yours if you want them. One day, you may even command me."

Phantom strings turned to the frenzy of beating drums. The silk gown disappeared, replaced with my slippers and robe and the dark prince vanished, leaving only a handful of seeds pressed to my sticky palm. My breath came uneven, fast and frantic with the pulsing drums. I—

Woke up.

I blinked, frowning at the sunlight streaming through my window. People hurried up and down the corridor, casting shadows beneath the door.

Just a dream, just like always, but maybe something more. The Devil always found things I never noticed, things I withheld from even myself. Commanding the flowers, the earth, my own imagination, *him* . . . control over anything in my life was my only true wish.

Most days, I was terrified of what would happen if he actually found me. Others, I secretly prayed he would.

FIVE

NEW YORK CITY WAS . . . large.

Our train pulled in earlier that morning, depositing us into the gaping cavern of Grand Central Station. Gold brocade coated the walls and marble took the floor. Everywhere I looked there were people, women in fine dresses, men in their day suits and children hawking newspapers and spewing, "Get your shoes shined, only two cents!" The chaos didn't stop there, pouring us first into the streets and then a packed subway terminal where I fought to keep hold of my suitcase. We traveled downtown, against the crowds to a nondescript city block and Tommy pulled forth the keys to our new apartment.

It wasn't home, that was for sure, but as far as my expectations went it could have been far worse. The front door led to a spacious living room connected to a narrow hall and narrower kitchen. There were two bedrooms, shined wooden floors and freshly painted walls, though I missed the floral paper that covered the farmhouse. Furniture was sparse but had been provided for free. The curtains were dusty and the beds unmade, but everything else was clean.

"Needs a woman's touch," Tommy had said. He handed me a fat stack of paper bills and declared he had to check in with the office, but would be home later. "Knock yourself out."

Now, I fiddled with my purse on the stoop of our massive, stone building. According to Tommy, our block was *quiet*. I had yet to see what *loud* was, but if this was quiet, then I feared I'd never sleep again.

Everywhere I looked, there were people. Short people, tall people, rich people, poor people, young and old, white and brown, just . . . *people.* Back in Fairville, the entire town could fit inside the old church. I hadn't met too many folks outside of that few hundred either. On occasion, I'd stop to talk to people coming through town, but Papa was distrustful of strangers and Tommy worse. Distrust rubbed off on me by the time men from the outside looked a little too long whenever I walked the street. I always thought myself fairly pretty, but at home there wasn't much to choose from. The women passing in their expensive clothes had me fixing my hair and dabbing my lipstick.

Most roads were paved, something else I wasn't used to. Instead of dirt kicking up into the air, a thick smog bellowed down the alleys from the factories across town. Mixed with the exhaust of car fumes, the very air felt like it was choking the life from me. All around was talking, chatter, endless energy. Children in tattered clothes played feet away from men meeting in sharp suits. A group of ladies strutted past, dressed to the nines in short skirts and felt hats. I eyed their ankles and bare shins, wondering if their fathers and husbands allowed them out like that. Tommy always told me to look like the lady I was.

Taking a deep breath, I made it a single step before a pair of blue eyes hovered before me.

"You seem lost, chicky," the woman said. She had ivory skin and hair the color of fire, cut so short it barely brushed her chin. Perfect, tight curls lined her round face and stuck to her pearlescent skin. She wore a dress and summer jacket of deep burgundy, stylish shoes without a single scuff and a string of pearls around her neck. A warm and inviting smile greeted me, but I was weary of those most.

"I'm fine, thank you. About to do some shopping."

"My god, what an *adorable* accent." An ironic statement since she boasted one of her own, the posh lilt of something I guessed was European. She shifted her velvet purse to her other arm, offering me a hand. Then, thinking better of it, leaned in and kissed both my cheeks. "Though I'm sure you're tired of hearing it. God knows I am, you Americans are *obsessed*. Anyway, the name's Lillian Carter. I live across the hall. You and your daddy just moved in, yes?"

Mouth gaping like a fish, I struggled for something to say as she reached into her purse and pulled out a cigarette. With a pinch of horror, I watched her light it and take a long drag.

She noticed my stare. "Women smoke here and no one bats an eye. They don't call it the Big Apple for nothing."

There was so much to take in, my only reply was, "My daddy's dead."

A barking laugh echoed out of her, so loud the nearby men turned their heads. "No, darling, not your daddy. Your *daddy*." She chuckled at my blank stare. "Don't worry, you'll pick up the slang. A New Yorker in no time," she declared. Looping her arm through mine, I tried not to flinch as she yanked us down the sidewalk. For a woman so waifish, she was shockingly strong. Her fingers brushed mine and she paused, giving me just enough time to slip some words in.

"I think you mean my brother," I told her, horrified at what I was fairly sure she meant by, *daddy*.

She shook her head, wide smile reappearing. "Oh! A brother, how delightful. Is he seeing anyone?"

My mouth gaped again, but she filled the empty space.

"Mr. Warren said to expect new tenants and to show you around. Furniture's nice, but it needs a woman's touch, doesn't it? I know all the best places. Fifth Avenue is gorgeous, but goddamn expensive. Head into the village and you have affordability and fashion." Pulling us hard to the left, she prattled on, "Us women have to stick together, you know? Can't have your place absolutely drab, especially when you start taking visitors."

My legs went double speed to keep up with her long, slim ones. "Who's Mr. Warren?"

Another enormous laugh. "Who's Mr. Warren? You're funny."

"I wasn't joking." Casting my eyes to the sidewalk, I avoided the leering stares of a group of men across the street. Tall, lithe, and more stunning than I'd ever seen, Lillian garnered more attention than if I danced down the road naked. But if she was uncomfortable, she didn't show it.

She jerked me to a halt. "Truly? You don't know who Mr. Warren is?"

I shook my head.

"Oh no . . . that simply won't do."

She tugged me along faster than before, "Mr. Warren owns the building, along with half of the city, if we're honest. Nearly every man who lives there works for him." She beamed. "Or woman."

My eyebrows furrowed. Before I could ask, she continued, "I'm his secretary. The best one, if I do say so myself." She tossed me another award-winning smile. "Commitment repulses me and I never had a domestic touch."

Before she could get another word in, I blurted, "Does Mr. Warren need any more secretaries? I ain't ever typed, but I'm a quick learner."

A little frown took her lips. "Not that I know of, but it couldn't hurt to ask. Not looking to get shacked up anytime soon, huh?"

I thought my blank stare said it all, but she leaned in close. "I think we'll be great friends."

Not trusting myself to speak, I nodded, pressing closer to her as a pair of women passed on the sidewalk. Their clothes, hair and posture were familiar, but their faces were . . . they were dryads. They gave me strange looks as I openly gaped. Their bark skin melted into ordinary flesh and I shook my head, wondering if I was losing it.

Then, something stranger. A heady dizziness stole my thoughts, the sweet taste of blackberries popping on my tongue. A warm heat licked across my skin, gone quicker than it came when Lillian stepped away. My cloudy thoughts sharpened and a massive storefront loomed ahead. Lillian ushered me inside.

After picking new china, gossamer curtains and better linens for the bed, Lillian pulled out a business card and handed it to the cashier. "All on Mr. Warren's tab, please."

I rushed forward but the teller was too quick, taking the card and my information into the back for delivery.

Horror swelled in my gut. I'd never even met this man, and his secretary pinned all my purchases on him. The indecency of it made me sway. Tommy would flip his lid when he found out.

"It's no problem at all." Lillian blew me a kiss, oblivious to my plight. "Mr. Warren lets me use his tab whenever I please. Believe me, he won't mind. Consider it a welcome gift."

Palms sweaty and head faint, I tried not to panic as the teller reappeared with instructions to be home tomorrow at ten. What kind of secretary received an endless tab, and what kind of man could afford such a thing? I eyed Lilian from the counter, taking in her gentle curves and plump, round lips. The thought couldn't take full form before she looped her arm back through mine, already set on the next shop.

Resisting the urge to dab at my forehead, I whispered, "So, what is it exactly Mr. Warren does for a living?"

"All sorts of things—he's a businessman. Made his money a few years ago when he found oil on some land he owned in the states, then immigrated from Wales. Since then it's a little of this, little of that. Automobiles, trains, infrastructure and a few other more *nefarious* things." The word came with a waggle of her eyebrows. "Though you have nothing to worry about with that."

Except, I did. We lived in his building, after all, and my brother was signing his name on an FBI contract that very moment. We passed a newsstand, fresh with today's paper. The one from yesterday flashed in my mind, the words read sideways beside Tommy's thigh. *J.W. Oil Company.*

"Does Mr. Warren have a first name?"

"Jack." She clicked her tongue. "Though few call him that."

Heavens knew why, but either way, I had no doubt yesterday's paper held news of my current landlord.

More shopping, more decor. I picked up a pack of Lucky Strikes for Tommy before Lillian escorted us home. The entire way she babbled about the city, the current elite, the parties and how she sometimes missed Wales, where she emigrated from shortly after Jack Warren did. By the time I unlocked my door, my head was so filled up I could hardly think.

Lillian kissed me on each cheek. "What a fabulously eventful day. I'll be seeing you tonight, then?"

My fingers clutched the doorway until they turned white. "Tonight?"

"The party?" For reasons I couldn't explain, her coquettish smile chilled my skin. "You really are such a sweet, little chicky, aren't you?" Tugging at the shoulder of my summer jacket, she frowned. "I'll bring something for you to wear at eight. Make sure you and that brother of yours eat a good dinner, you'll need it." A protest bubbled on my lips, but she was already across the hall, shutting her door with a wink.

Dammit.

TOMMY TELEPHONED TO LET me know he would be late, so I shouldn't worry about setting a dinner plate for him. I damn near jumped out of my skin when the thing trilled on its hook. I'd never used a telephone before. It screamed out its last ring before I figured out which end was the speaker.

As promised, Lillian knocked on my door at eight, already dressed like the Queen of Sheba—a very scandalous version. My jaw dropped at her bare knees and rolled stockings, taking in the ensemble of feathers and sparkles like she was a creature of another world. With glitter across her cheeks and jewels dusting every inch of skin, she could have been. When she displayed the dress I was to wear, I turned three shades of red.

"I can't wear that."

"Of course you can." She laid the dress on my bed, eyes roaming my figure like I was her own porcelain doll. If the ensemble she had in mind was anything close to hers, Tommy would have a stroke.

"I don't think my brother would approve of that."

"Why does he get to be the boss?" Offering nothing else, she shoved me down before a paint-flecked vanity. "Now, would you be terribly opposed to cutting your hair?"

I eyed her stunted cut in the mirror. My hair had been long my entire life, but all the ladies here wore it short. I shrugged, covering my fears with nonchalance. I didn't like change. I didn't ask to uproot my life or adapt to new customs, but I'd promised Tommy I would try. Back in Fairville, fitting in was my biggest weakness, but maybe I could be something different here. At least until we earned the money to pay back the bank.

I nodded, giving Lillian free reign. This delighted her so much it made my head spin, but in a strange way, her exuberance melted some of the ice around my heart. Besides the little Baker boys, I couldn't recall a time someone outside my family showed so much joy around me. I'd never had a friend before.

When she was finally finished, navy blue dusted my eyes, shimmering with gold flakes. Red touched my cheeks above burgundy lipstick, applied so my lips looked round and plump just like hers. The dark makeup would have me run out of Georgia, but made something ethereal in the low light of my bedroom. Something mysterious and enchanting—something not at all like me.

Lillian helped me into new undergarments—*corselettes are* all *the rage now, darling*—then pulled the slip dress over my head. As I feared, it barely touched my knees. The empire waist hung low and shapeless, but my stylist appeared pleased. Fabric of dark emerald clung to my shoulders, capped with lace sleeves sewed in with glittering jewels. More adorned the entire garment—a small fortune's worth—giving way to gold fringe that tickled my calves. I protested when Lillian rolled down my stockings, but she insisted it was *in*.

"Chanel couldn't have done better herself." She kissed her lips, removing clips from my hair and fixing my "finger waves." Another fashion I had no knowledge of, but apparently my newest cut was *just divine for it.*

She stood me up in front of the mirror, admiring her handiwork. "And a final touch." A band of gold found its way around my forehead, just above my freshly plucked brows. Diamonds, pearls, and bits of gold hung from it, framing my face like a seductress's crown.

For a moment, I forgot all about my worries. My dead father, my brother, Fairville and all their strict social etiquettes, even the devil haunting my dreams. I'd never felt comfortable in my own body, in the brain Tommy said was broken, Fairville said was evil and my father said was cursed. The vessel keeping me tethered to this earth was just that—a hollow, timid thing that could never be shared, or the Woman in White would keep it forever. A farmer with dirty hands and wind-burnt cheeks, not a thing of beauty. Perhaps it made me vain, but I liked this hidden side of me.

"Do you like it?" The pleased lilt to her voice told me she already knew.

I tilted my head to the side, not convinced it was my own reflection staring back at me. "Forget being a secretary. Open your own boutique."

She laughed, loud and boisterous and full of life. "Off we go, then."

The new moon didn't show its face in an empty black sky, a realization that sent shivers down my arms. Thick, August heat wrapped around us like smog, drawing perspiration beneath all my heavy makeup. Even still, it didn't deter Lillian's erratic energy. Only a day with her revealed a vital flaw: she loved to talk about everything and everyone. While useful for navigating a new social sphere, weariness prickled the back of my mind. It had been a hard lesson to learn through the church women—if someone gossiped about others, they were more than happy to gossip about you.

Therefore, I chose all my words very carefully, adding nothing more than noncommittal noises with an occasional *yes* or *no,* even though I decided I liked Lillian. Walking through the city, I learned that most of the men who lived in our building were young and unmarried. This made me uncomfortable, but Lillian was delighted at the prospect. When I asked if she planned to marry, she laughed so hard I tripped on my heels

Even so, she was wonderfully pleased to finally have another woman around, as there generally weren't as many in *these crowds*— an odd comment she wouldn't elaborate on. Social circles were small, elite, and exclusive, something else that bothered me but I didn't dare comment on. For a circle so small, elite and exclusive, two farmers from Georgia found it awfully easy to wiggle in.

After reiterating everyone knew everyone and listing several names to memorize, she explained more about Mr. Warren. He often threw large, elaborate parties but only those invited could attend. He owned a large hotel in the business district where these parties were usually held. According to Lillian, the top three floors became a sinner's playden five nights a week.

"I swear, the man never sleeps," she said, a note of dreaminess touching the words. "Really, he doesn't." With a coy wink, she looped her arm through mine, a position I'd become used to. Like before, that heady dizziness overtook me, the taste of ripe fruit on my tongue, but in a blink it was gone again. "Anyway, stay far away from Margaret Freeman. Dreadful, that one. She'll spend the entire night discussing politics if you let her snag you."

A smile touched my lips, dying a quick death as she stopped us in front of a hotel. I wasn't sure what I expected, but it wasn't the looming stone monstrosity swallowing half a city block. Intricate, gothic architecture carved its way through the stones, ending in a massive archway that housed a stained glass entrance. *The Glamour Hotel* stretched above it in dazzling, golden letters. Men and women dressed to the nines revolved through the doors, their glittering diamonds catching the streetlights and sweet smoke clogging the air. Chatter filled the sidewalk, loud and drumming, as a thick pulse started in my head. Light flickered through the lobby like daytime, but something arcane lingered beyond the doors.

Hesitating on the sidewalk, temptation snapped at my heels with my growing anxiety. Words bubbled on my lips, a request for Lillian to smoke another cigarette just to buy some time, but still, something about that darkness drew me in. Called to me. A feeling so deep and primitive it couldn't be of this mortal plane. I'd felt it before, but only ever in my dreams.

Telling myself that was absurd, I followed my new friend inside.

At first, everything appeared normal. Busy along with some more scandalous dresses, but normal. For such a late hour, I found it hard to believe so many people loitered in the lobby, but the seductive energy changed my mind. A dangerous hum echoed in my chest, crackling like lightning in the air, standing the hair on the back of my neck.

A long line waited for a peculiar door, but Lillian sauntered to the front of it. A handsome bellhop whistled and winked at her, but she only rolled her eyes, demanding he open the entryway. When we stepped inside it, he asked us which floor.

"The top of one, of course."

He gave her a ceremonious bow. "As you wish, my sweet Lillian."

She rolled her eyes again, but it was accompanied by a little smile. The box of a room had no other doors and there was no staircase to speak of. A metal grate slid in front of us and the floor jolted. My stomach bottomed out, hands snatching the railing as a yelp escaped my throat.

"Never been in a lift before?" One chiming laugh and a puff of smoke later, she shook her head. "Such a little chicky."

She dabbed her cigarette in an ashtray while I held on for dear life. "Before we get to the top, a little warning. No matter what anyone offers you, no matter how simple it seems, do not drink or eat *anything* in this hotel. Am I understood?"

I stared at her.

"And keep your mouth shut. You look like a carp." Placing two fingers beneath my chin, she snapped my jaw closed. "I hope you're ready, darling, because you've never seen a party like this."

SIX

I'D SEEN PARTIES. PLENTY, in fact. Church get-togethers, weddings, the yearly banquet at town hall after harvest season. Once, I'd even glimpsed a belle's debutante where Tommy was hired for catering. This was not a party. This was a madhouse.

If I had thought the lobby was packed, the top floor of Mr. Warren's hotel put it to shame. It suddenly made sense how two Georgian farmers became *elite* and *exclusive*, because if those were the requirements, then half the damn city were aristocrats. Hundreds of people packed shoulder to shoulder. Tables littered the outer edge of the open floor, teeming with men smoking cigars and playing cards. A few boasted women in glittering outfits, spinning in heels on the tabletops. A well-lit dais took the back of the room, raising up a five-man band playing music I'd never heard before. The partiers responded, dancing to the sensual drums like I did when I salted the earth. Colored fabrics laid over lamps, casting the walls in rainbow colors. Jewels and glitter and glass hung from the ceiling, fracturing all the light around the room. Hardly able to hear, hardly able to *think*, I grabbed Lillian's arm like she was a raft in a stormy sea.

"Marvelous, isn't it?" Her gleaming smile turned blue in the shadow of a nearby lamp. "And to think, the night's still young. Just wait until the rabble arrives."

If the rabble hadn't arrived yet, I wasn't sure I wanted to wait for it. My teeth set on edge with the licentious melody from the stage.

Sweat and smoke clogged the air, suffocating each breath I took. Everywhere I looked, there were people. Dancing people, kissing people, angry people, *drinking* people.

My mouth fell open at the sight of a fizzy drink, green as grass bubbling in a woman's glass. "Is that . . ."

"Oh, you'll see a lot of alcohol here, chicky." Lillian tugged me closer, biting her lip to contain her grin. "I told you, Mr. Warren dabbles in a few nefarious things."

Revulsion swelled deep in my chest. Beside us, the woman swallowed her fizzy drink. "He's a gangster?"

Lillian clicked her tongue. "Such a nasty word."

For a reason. Gangsters were the reason the city descended into crime. Gangsters were the reason a gin mill blew sky high in Calverston, killing three boys working the illegal plant. The reason Tommy, my only sibling, my last relative, was recruited by the FBI for a job so dangerous it made my skin crawl.

Lillian swam in my vision, wearing a little frown. "Are you worried about the fuzz? No one breaks up these parties, darling."

I shook my head, not trusting myself to speak.

For all her gossip and blabbering, she had great intuition. She took my elbow and pulled us to the edge of the room. One brilliant smile later and a group of men scattered from their table, allowing us to sit.

I frowned, watching the men walk away. What kind of woman —

"I'm sorry, I assumed you knew." Leaning her head in her hand, she watched with an intensity that rattled my bones. "I'm guessing your brother just started working for us and you're a tad nervous?"

I nodded, letting her run with the lie. I couldn't very well tell her what Tommy actually did.

"Well, I think he should have told you. Men are all bastards, aren't they?"

A short breath puffed from my throat. "Most are."

"Don't worry, we'll take good care of both of you." She winked for the thousandth time that night. "Anyway, you look like a society woman, so let's play the part . . ." Her voice faded off as she scanned the room. I sat there, frozen to the overstuffed booth, wondering if that was a promise or a threat.

"Let's see, let's see," she mumbled, searching. "Over there. Gray hair, ridiculous waistcoat, smoking cigars far more expensive than he can afford, see him?"

I nodded, though I hadn't bothered to look. My mind still raced from the newest revelation. Tommy's new job found the apartment for us, so did they know, intentionally putting us in harm's way? Worse, did my brother know and not tell me?

"—so the quick and dirty, avoid his little mistress and there's very little drama." Lillian glanced at me with a frown. "Are you listening? This is important."

I nodded, but all my focus was on my fingernails digging into my thigh. Lillian shook her head. "Look at me, darling."

I did.

"This is *important*." She reiterated. My blank stare must have spoken volumes, because she sighed. "Everyone underestimates us girls, yes?"

I nodded.

"That's because they forget." She tapped the corners of her eyes, then her ears. "We're the background noise. The little flies on the wall. I've developed a soft spot for you, so I'll tell you my secret. Men deal in violence, we deal in talk." She gestured around the room. "You're in it now, darling, so here's how you play the game. Listen. Get smart. You can't shoot a gun or throw a fist, but you have something far more valuable at your expense." She leaned in close, a vicious grin glinting around sharp teeth, "Secrets. Gossip. The sway of society. And even better? You're very, *very* beautiful."

57

My face turned so hot the air around us went to boil. "I ain't like that."

"Don't need to be," she said airly. "Truthfully, it's better if you don't give in. Dogs like the chase more than the meal. More power that way." She winked again. "I can tell you're upset, so I'll tell you this. Tonight, you are a goddess. A queen. No man can tell you no right now. Watch and learn a little, forget bastard men and their bastard ways, and let's have a little fun." Reaching across the table, she took my hand in hers. "Now, remember what I told you about Margaret Freeman?"

I nodded, listened, learned. Margaret Freeman was the senator's youngest daughter, an outspoken feminist and aspiring politician, but she had a penchant for gossip and couldn't stay away from scandals. No one took her very seriously, but she was a go-to source for information. Or dope.

Her sister, Gladys, was far more liked, once had an affair with a Rockefeller, and appeared beside her father more often than not in newspaper clippings. Her husband, Richard, was a drunk dimwit and many suspected they'd divorce soon.

Among others were Theodore Greenley, a famous pianist who attended parties three nights a week. Howard Daniels, an old money philanthropist who moonlit as a loan shark. I was warned to stay far away from Agnes, Nellie and Lucille Morrigan—three sisters who married far above their station and crucified anyone who stood in their way. I'd learned half the room's names, careers and social standing before the clock even struck eleven. It all felt so trivial, but if Lillian was right these things could serve me. The right connections, the right names, and I could work my situation to an advantage. Find a way to pay back our mortgage before it was too late to return home.

Between a lengthy explanation about Helen McKinley and her marital woes, a woman caught my eye. She caught everyone's eye, drawing attention to her presence like moths to the light. Rivaling even Lillian in beauty, she possessed the same tall and lithe figure, but with ivory skin and hair darker than pitch. She wore all black — dress, stockings, headpiece, even her gloves. The drummer missed his note as she sauntered across the stage, ignoring the singer's lustful eyes as she looked down on the crowd with boredom. A wrathful goddess, sneering down on her disciples. As if that weren't strange enough, she had —

"Is that . . ."

Lillian rolled her eyes. "Yes. And yes, it's real."

Despite being dressed for a funeral — in color only, I suspected she had the shortest dress of any woman here — she wore one terrifying and peculiar accessory. A massive snake, golden as the sun, slithered around the back of her neck. The tail of it stretched her slim shoulders, hanging between her breasts like a necklace. The rest curled around her arm from shoulder to wrist, resting its massive head on the back of her hand where she clutched a flute of that fizzing, green drink.

"And disastrously venomous," Lillian added. "Rumor has it she allows the viper to bite anyone who vexes her, and you shouldn't take that as hearsay."

That should have been enough to ease my curiosity. After all, the kind of woman who wore poisonous snakes like a scarf was best to be avoided. But something about the woman captured my attention. Her cold expression, hardened eyes, the way she carried herself off the stage into a throng of onlookers like a queen, waiting for everyone to kneel. Her dark energy filled our corner of the room and stifled it. Like giving her your attention drained your soul, but looking away would be far worse.

The clambering noise swallowed my whispered words. "Who is she?"

Lillian sniffed, unimpressed. "Violet Warren."

"Mr. Warren is married?"

"He's not," she answered, more bite to her voice than necessary. She shot me a glowing smile. "Violet is his twin sister. You almost never see the two apart, even with business. Attached at the hip, they say. It's quite untraditional for a woman, but don't believe the gossip. They're nothing but *very* nasty rumors. Dirty, dirty politics."

Whatever assumptions people made, I didn't want to know. Scanning the room like I knew who to look for, I wondered if I would find Mr. Warren in the crowd. If he looked anything like his gorgeous sister, he'd be impossible to miss.

"Stay away from her for now," Lillian murmured, but it was too late. I'd been so distracted by the ethereal woman, her venomous snake and crowd of worshippers, I hadn't noticed she'd been staring at *me*.

Something flickered in her bored expression. Dull disinterest no longer flattened her eyes, but a moment of shock, so misplaced I barely registered when it shifted to panic, then pure wrath. Each emotion smoothed over quicker than the last before she sauntered over with cold indifference again.

Lillian stood. "Maybe we should—"

"I don't think I've seen you before." Violet stood before me, even more stunning up close. Her smooth skin could have been porcelain, black hair ink pouring off a page. But it was her eyes that were so unique they were almost uncanny in an otherwise sculptured face. Some may have called them brown, honey even, but that wasn't true. Golden as the snake wrapped around her shoulders, the goddess analogy resurfaced in my head.

"Enchanted." Standing, I leaned in to kiss her cheek but she stepped away. The snake hissed from her hand.

"How old are you?"

"You never ask a lady her age," Lillian said, drumming her fingers on the table. Violet gave her a sharp look, but the former held her gaze, chin lifted high. Lillian worked for Miss Warren's brother, but something lingered that went beyond business. Something personal.

"Twenty." I answered to ease the tension, but there was something else as well. A tickling in a cobwebbed corner of my brain, enticing me to obey. I didn't understand it, less the strange draw she had on me and everyone within ten feet.

"When did you turn twenty?"

"About six months ago."

Violet's eyebrows pinched together, just a fraction of an inch. If we weren't standing so close, I wouldn't have noticed.

"I just moved into one of Mr. Warren's apartment buildings." I didn't want to say it, but the words rushed forth against my better judgment. I never offered information about myself, but the enchantment of this woman lured me in like flies to honey.

"Interesting." She drew out the word as if to taste every letter, then turned to Lillian as though I didn't exist. "Has my brother seen her yet?"

Lillian gave her head a small shake, crisp eyes turning sharp when they landed on me.

"Good." Violet changed her expression, no longer bored but . . . I couldn't be sure. A serpentine smile stretched her lips. The cold chip of her golden eyes burned with malice. "I'd like you to have a drink with me."

Hair rose on the back of my neck. Music and chatter surrounded us at a deafening volume, but it all faded into a numbing background. I shook my head. "Apologies, m'am, but I don't drink alcohol." Once, I did. Not anymore. Not since prohibition made it illegal, gangsters made it common, and the FBI took my brother to fight against it. Violet Warren had a brother. Maybe she'd empathize.

"I wasn't asking." She held out her own glass, untouched by her lips. The green liquid fizzed like champagne, but held the viscosity of a liqueur. I'd never seen anything like it.

Besides that, Lillian's cryptic warning haunted my thoughts. The one about not eating or drinking anything in the hotel, no matter what. It made little sense to me, but nothing about these city folk did.

Her snake released a drawn hiss, as if impatient with my refusal. Its tongue flicked at the glass still clutched between Violet's fingers.

Behind Violet, Lillian shook her head.

"I really don't—"

"Addie?"

I whirled around. Tommy turned to stone two paces away, dressed in the nicest suit he owned. Someone had slicked his blonde hair back so all of his facial scars were on display, a look I hadn't seen on him in years. Even stranger, he clutched a flute of champagne.

My eyebrows drew together. "What are you doing here?"

"What are *you* doing here?" He clutched my arm, leaving his drink on a table to yank me closer. If he noticed the women watching with unconcealed interest, he paid them no mind.

Shaking my arm from his grip, I gestured at Lillian. "Tommy, this is Miss Lillian Carter, she lives across the hall from us and invited me out tonight. Lillian, this is my brother, Mr. Thomas Colton."

Her eyes went alight. "Your brother?" As if the recent tension never occurred, she sauntered toward us like a feline stalking its prey. An electric hum crackled the air. Behind her, Miss Warren's mouth became a deep frown. "You never mentioned he was so handsome." In a move that made my skin crawl, she ran light fingers down Tommy's coat sleeve.

Tommy turned beet red, running a fumbling hand through his hair. I cast my eyes to the ceiling. "I don't exactly talk about my brother that way."

He ignored my clear discomfort, grinning at the lithe redhead pursing her lips. "Across the hall, you say? I can hardly believe that, Miss Carter. I think I'd remember seeing a face like yours around."

She fanned her lashes. "A face like what?"

"Excuse us a moment." Violet appeared ready to protest, but I snatched Tommy by his coat and dragged him toward the door. He practically dug his heels into the floor calling after Lillian, inviting her over for coffee tomorrow.

I didn't stop until we passed the doors to the ballroom, made our way down two halls and settled into an alcove where a handful of drunkards slumped against the wall. A sheen coated Tommy's eyes, a blush still etched into his cheeks, but like a fog lifted from his brain, he blinked, staring at me with rising annoyance. "Addie, you can't be here."

I threw my hands up, gesturing around. "*I* can't be here? I thought you were in the FBI, what are you—"

"*Sh.*" He threw a hand over my mouth, glancing around to make sure no one paid attention. One of the drunkards hiccuped and slumped to the floor. Tommy leaned in with a smile, removing his hand from my mouth. "I'm undercover, alright? They wanted me to hit the ground running today."

"Well, I'm glad you look so pleased. Since when do you do undercover work?"

"Since always. It's in my contract. No point in having me read lips if I can't get close enough to anyone." He stuffed his hands in his pocket, doing another look down the hall. "You didn't drink anything, right?"

"I don't drink alcohol since it's illegal and all, but it looked like you did."

"It's all for show, I've been dumping it in the plants. But you shouldn't be here, alright? Not a good place for a young woman like you. Come on, let's get you home."

A bitter laugh chimed in my throat. "Home? You mean the building where Jack Warren sets up all his employees?"

Tommy frowned. "How do you know about that?"

"Lillian told me. She works for him too."

Tommy turned pale. "Did you mention what I do for a living?"

I shook my head. "No, I'm smarter than that, but apparently you ain't. Why wouldn't you tell me what you're doing, where we're *living*? Do you understand how dangerous this is?"

"That's exactly why I didn't tell you."

"What if I unknowingly compromised your position? You ever think of that, Tommy, huh?" I pointed a finger at his chest. "You said this was a fresh start for both of us, a chance to move on. Instead, we're living in a building owned by a criminal, you fail to tell me I need to keep up a facade for our safety and now I have to worry about you coming home in a box every day working undercover? Have you read the papers recently? These men don't mess around, Tommy, they shoot and kill and torture. After everything, you're willing to risk that? You're willing to do that to me?" My voice trembled on the last word, an involuntary motion I attempted to cover with anger.

If this entire move up north with its opportunities and clean slate was a farce, I would survive. But whether Tommy liked to admit it or not, I couldn't live without him. I knew life without me would be easier, that he'd be free to live on his own, worry only about himself and all the war-shaped wounds he carried, but not like this. Not putting his life on the line, risking death or worse while I sat at home, wondering if he would come back. I already did that once and it nearly killed me. In fact, it did kill me.

His voice lowered, revoltingly soft, and suddenly I was a child again, a little girl sniffling beside the river with a faded book of poems. "Addie . . ."

His head snapped to the side. A sharp-dressed black man breezed past us and continued down the hall. Tommy's eyebrows came together, mumbling half to himself and half to the man, "Will?"

The man stopped, but didn't turn. Tommy called out again, "Will Porter, is that you?"

Slowly, warily, he faced us. He was handsome, unnervingly so, the fine clothes fitted to his lean body like rags beneath such a spectacular face. He held a stack of papers beneath one arm and a cigar bobbed between his lips. When he spoke, he possessed the same lyrical accent as Lillian and Miss Warren. "That would be me."

Tommy drifted across the marble. "William Porter, from the Welsh Regiment?"

Mr. Porter nodded, glancing around for a quick escape. "Yes, but I'm sorry, I don't believe I know who you are."

"Thomas Colton." This garnered no response, so he added. "Corporal Colton, from the 77th battalion. Argonne."

Something shifted in Mr. Porter's expression, eyes scanning my brother's ruined face before recognition lit them. "Tommy! Yes, of course, how are you, lad?" He rushed forward, patting Tommy on the back while the two volleyed standard greetings, exclamations of disbelief, questions of what the other has been up to, and so on and so forth. Meanwhile, I melted against the wall, gathering my bearings for another social interaction I didn't have the energy for.

"And you have to meet—Addie, Ad, come here." Tommy jerked me forward and threw his arm around my shoulders. "This is my baby sister, Miss Adeline Colton. Addie, this is—"

"Mr. William Porter, from the Welsh Regiment," I finished. I nodded, holding out a hand. "A pleasure."

"The pleasure's all mine." Mr. Porter took my hand, bending his head down to kiss the top instead of a standard shake, but something stopped him. A frown cut through his flirtatious smile. Icy prickles traveled up my arm. "You can call me Will," he said and dropped my hand, the peculiar expression never leaving his face.

Tommy was too high on life to notice the fresh tension. "I can't believe you're alive," he said, removing his arm from my shoulder to gesture to Will. "Really, I can't believe it. We all saw you go down and thought you were a goner. I mean, you were shot no less than six times. In the chest and all." His joy melted into sad confusion. I took his hand.

Will seemed uncomfortable. "Just got lucky, I suppose."

"I know, but—" Tommy shook his head. "That's some incredible luck."

If only Tommy had a little more of it. Why did William Porter get shot six times in the chest and walk away unscathed while Thomas Colton lost his hearing and half his face?

Mr. Porter swallowed, then faced me with the strangest question imaginable. "Have we met before?"

Attempting to remain cordial, I shook my head. "I highly doubt that, sir. Tommy and I just moved up from Georgia a few days ago."

"You seem really, *really* familiar," he said, leaning in far too close for my comfort.

I took a step back. "Maybe Miss Carter spoke of me. Do you two know one another?" I couldn't imagine there was a huge population of young welsh immigrants who just so happened to party at Jack Warren's hotel. Nevermind I'd only met Lillian that morning, there was no other explanation.

He frowned. "You know Lillian?"

"She lives across the hall."

"And she brought you—" He cut himself short, looking between us. Confusion gave way to a curt smile that set my teeth on edge. "Would you two like to meet someone?"

I glanced at Tommy, who only asked, "Who?"

"The man of the hour, of course."

I shook my head, knowing immediately who he spoke of. "We really ought to—"

"We'd love to," Tommy cut in, shooting me a look. "I've been meaning to thank our host anyway. Please, lead the way."

SEVEN

MR. PORTER LED US down several hallways, each more ornate than the last. Persian rugs ran over the white marble floors and gilded paintings lined the wall every three feet. The pieces themselves were unusual, growing more scandalous the farther we walked. Near the alcove, there had been nothing but solemn-faced, black-and-white portraits of men who worked for the company. As we stopped before a set of gold french doors, I stood face to face with a pair of dancing women in the nude, bare feet pressed into a grassy knoll and a bright moon shining on their slender forms.

Will pushed through them like he owned the place. I took the opportunity to lean to whisper, "This is a bad idea."

Tommy wouldn't look at me. "It's fine."

"What if he knows who you are?"

"Nothing will happen with a lady present. Just smile, nod and we'll leave as soon as we can."

An elegant antechamber spread out, more befitting of a palace than a hotel in New York. Here, the stonework of the outside bled into the room, making up the floors and walls like a gothic castle. Still, the room boasted a warm glow from modern red and green lamps. Another lush, intricate rug covered the floor and mahogany furniture scattered the room. In the corner, a brass bar cart lifted cigars, a decanter of brown liquor and a bottle of that green champagne. Will poured himself a drink before offering some to us. I was about to refuse when Tommy bumped my arm. I smiled and accepted a flute of the viridescent bubbly.

Clutching the stem glass between white knuckles, I followed behind as we approached a second set of doors, even more detailed than the previous ones. A vast array of wildlife was carved into the wood, but largest of all were two vipers facing one another, fangs bared and tongues flickering.

This family had a strange proclivity for snakes.

Heat hit me like a stormfront. Despite the stifling August air, a vast fireplace crackled along the back wall. Adjacent to it, floor-to-ceiling shelves held gold-embroidered books and baubles of every oddity. Potted trees and swishing flowers filled every floor corner and open wall space. In the center of the room a hodge-podge of velvet settees and armchairs circled a coffee table. Behind those, silhouetted by the fireplace, stretched a desk as wide as I was tall, teeming with paper, books, and to my horror, two pistols. Three men reclined on the settees before it. I ignored them all, because waiting behind the desk, reposed in an armchair more like a throne, hands folded on his waistcoat with a vicious smile blooming beneath dark eyes, was a man I'd recognize anywhere.

The Devil sat on the top floor of The Glamour Hotel.

The glass slipped from my hand and shattered.

"*Addie.*" Tommy gave me wide eyes, then a placating smile to the demon in a three-piece suit. "Apologies, Mr. Warren. We can clean up the mess."

Mr. Warren—a man who could be a doppelganger to the Devil himself—waved a dismissive hand and jerked his chin. A man rose from the settee and cleaned up the glass at my feet. Mr. Porter nodded at him and took a seat, not bothering to introduce us.

"How very fortunate I am then, that she chose to make an appearance tonight." Jack Warren grinned, slow and serpent-like. His voice wrapped around me like a sinful song, honey-like with a faint Welsh accent. Heat flushed across my skin. My pulse thrummed in my throat.

I shifted, clearing my thoughts. "My sincerest apology for the mess, Mr. Warren. I'm known for being clumsy."

Golden eyes narrowed on me, sensing the lie. I shuffled, trying to decipher his stare, and wondered if I was well and truly losing my mind. He looked like the Devil, but that couldn't be. The Devil had sharp, inhuman features that were certainly not present on this man. Jack Warren had no tattoos, and the rounded curve of his ears was obvious beneath neat, black hair. More than anything, his pupils were normal—perfectly round and human within bright, golden eyes.

Mr. Warren was a public figure. His face landed in the papers more often than not since his oil company made him rich. There was an explanation here. A reasonable one that maybe had nothing to do with heaven or hell. Perhaps Tommy was right and I possessed an overactive imagination at times. I could have seen Mr. Warren's face before and implanted it in my dreams, altered it to accommodate my visions.

Still, dangerous energy curled the air. Shivers broke across my flesh.

"Take a seat," he said, waving to an empty settee. I sat as far from him as possible. "I'd offer you another drink, but I don't think it would agree with you."

Tommy tensed beside me. Mr. Warren gave him a pointed look and continued, "I'm not accusing you of being a lush. I only mean our drinks can be rather . . . unpalatable for certain people."

Unsure what to say, I crossed my legs and tried to emulate Tommy's placating smile. I failed. Terribly.

Mr. Warren stood. The simple motion rooted me to the cushions, frozen with an unfamiliar, primitive fear. Wood clicked along the stones as he rounded the desk with an elegant cane. He could be no older than thirty, and it seemed out of place clutched in his leather glove. The pommel was monstrous, literally—steel carved into the head of a dragon, scales flared around open jaws dripping with two lethal fangs.

He stood in front of me.

"Jack Warren." He held out his hand. For a moment, I only stared at the black leather covering each of his fingers. My eyes roamed higher, over his storm-gray waistcoat and silver pocket chain, to his black tie, pressed collar, and finally to the face that haunted my dreams every month. A cool sensation coated my skin, sharp as the wind and just as deadly. Warm skin stretched over his sharp jaw beneath a pink, sensual smile. High cheekbones and angled brows gave him a severe look, but he was undeniably handsome. Devastatingly so. In fact, I couldn't think of any man more gorgeous than him.

I stood, murmuring, "It's a pleasure to meet you." His hand encased mine and even through the leather, a warm ecstasy tingled along my skin. The hair rose on the back of my neck as he raised an eyebrow, waiting.

Tommy stood beside me. "Mr. Warren, I'm Thomas Colton and this is my little sister, Miss Adeline Colton. I believe we just moved into your apartment building downtown."

That fear struck again, firing like a bullet between my lungs. Mr. Warren's smile curled wider. "Did you?"

I wrenched my hand back. "We did."

"It's a pleasure to have you." Completely ignoring Tommy, he said, "How are you liking your new accommodations, Miss Colton?"

My tongue turned to lead, the blood in my veins to iron. Dark energy ebbed between us and *snapped,* stopping my pulse. I scanned the room, wondering if anyone else felt a demanding tug in their chest, dragging them to the man in front of me. Perhaps it was his demeanor, his manner of dress, or the extravagantly wealthy room we now stood in, but he exuded power. Life and death. So suffocating, I fought for the air he seemed to claim as his own.

Only then did I take note of the other men in the room. The first, a lumbering beast of a man that took up an entire couch to himself. The second, a weasel-faced fellow counting bills. In a chair to his right, a slight, fidgeting blond of mid-thirty, sharp eyes trained on me with unsettling interest. Lastly, Mr. Porter, who lounged in his chair with the confidence of a prince. He caught my look and offered a warm smile, barely concealing the tense edge behind it.

"The apartment is lovely. Thank you."

We stared at one another. I tried not to, but something about those eyes dragged me under. I was no longer in the present but twelve years old again, clutched in my brother's arms as I waved to a monster across the river. Then I was eighteen, lost in golden eyes and the tattooed fingers sifting through my hair. Twenty, the mouth of the devil caressing my neck as he whispered everything I could become.

My breath hitched. The tug grew stronger, inching my feet closer to his leather shoes. Heat scored my skin and settled low in the pit of my stomach. I wanted to be closer to him. I wanted to touch him. I wanted to *taste* him.

He leaned his head to the side, evaluating my face like I was something he'd long been searching for. I leaned with him, forgetting my own breaths the longer I melted into honey and gold.

My lips moved of their own accord. "How does one get eyes like that?"

Tommy coughed beside me. "Apologies, Mr. Warren, but we ought to be heading home. I don't think my sister is feeling too well."

Mr. Warren's expression turned nothing short of lethal. Golden eyes narrowed to slits, hands pushing his cane into the floor until the wood groaned. Behind him, the brutish man leaned forward with

71

savage interest, the blond excused himself for the bar and Will shook his head, smiling nervously.

In a flash it was gone. Sensing the quick turn of the room, Tommy looped his arm through mine and stepped away. It did nothing to ease the tension, even as Mr. Warren gave me an apologetic smile.

It was over. Too late. I had no room in my life for a violent man.

"Are you feeling unwell, Adeline?" The sound enveloped me, but it was tainted, ruined. His beautiful smile did nothing but mask a silver tongue. Those lurid eyes were a weapon of another kind.

"Very unwell." I faintly recognized I said goodnight to each man, thanked Mr. Warren for the invitation and hovered outside myself as we exited.

I held my iron necklace the entire way home.

ANNWYL.

A full moon shone through the window where darkness should have plagued the sky. Silver light washed the blurry room and the dark figure beside me. I blinked, pressing my hand to a soft, warm shirt. How could I forget? My dark prince visited each night of the new moon.

"I don't want to see you tonight." Useless words. He never missed a visit. With my forehead to his chest, the Devil held me flush against him, tight and safe within an unfamiliar bed. An apartment I hadn't yet called home, and likely never would.

Maybe Tommy was right. Everything was only my imagination, cultivated over years and years of affirmation. The Devil wasn't real, my visions, the comforting hand sliding up my back, even less so. It made sense. I'd been alone for so many years, sheltered and isolated on our land with no one but Papa and Tommy to keep me company. Then Tommy left and my sanity barely survived. He came home a changed man, our family unit splintered, and I had no one else in

Fairville to provide what I'd lost. Now my father was dead, my brother practically a stranger, and I had no one to turn to but the apparition my mind created.

But what did it say about me if all that were true? If my mind was truly fractured . . . and found solace with the worst sinner of all.

Small sobs choked the back of my throat. The arm around my waist tightened. The scent of rain circled me, stronger with each kiss he pressed to my face, streaking pathetic tears away with his lips.

Rough fingers smoothed back my hair and I melted into the feeling. The endless night only he could provide. He was darkness, beauty, so unnatural I didn't question when a warm ecstasy filled my bones and replaced all the pain.

"Is that better, darling?"

I nodded, hushed cries withering to faded smoke. I reached beneath his jacket and tugged him closer, clenching his waistcoat until our lungs matched inch for inch.

Warm breath danced over my eyelids. "I know where you are now, *annwyl*. Anything you want, anything at all, all you need to do is ask for it."

I needed more of this feeling. His hypnotic beckoning into the dark. The way I seemed to forget all my pain, all my loss, all my endless misery inside these dreams. If I was nothing but insane, that was the purpose he served, after all.

God wasn't here, but the Devil was.

I wrapped my leg over his hip, pulling entirely different parts of us closer together. I never kissed him back in my dreams, some foreign sense of morality forbidding me. I didn't care anymore. If this wasn't real it didn't matter anyway. Digging my hands into his dark, satin hair, I brushed my lips against his and breathed.

Desire rushed through my veins, hotter than the blood pounding in my chest. I'd never done this, never indulged, but once I did there was no turning back. I wanted—*needed*—him so badly I knew I would die without it.

A low sound went off in his throat, hands tightening on the fabric of my dress. Heavy pants fell from my lips, body taking over as he ran his nose up my throat. It wasn't enough. I'd never been good with words, so I'd show him. I turned, granting myself one look into those serpentine eyes before I grabbed his face in both hands and *bit*.

I tugged his bottom lip between my teeth and a darker, needier sound rumbled through his chest. His tongue slipped into my mouth and pure ecstasy swallowed me whole, threatening to drown as his hand roamed up my side, as I kissed him with every desperate memory he would make me forget. Heat flushed my skin and pressure pooled low in my stomach. Wetness coated my inner thighs and I tugged his bottom lip again, asking for more, demanding more. Heavy breaths mingled between us, my bare leg tightened around his waist, then I allowed just enough space to reach between us and show him what I wanted most.

My hand flattened over the hard length of him, a ragged moan breathing past my lips. God, what would that feel like inside me? I hiked my dress higher, kissed him harder, seized the collar of his shirt and—

The Devil flipped me onto my back.

No, not the Devil.

Jack Warren hovered over me, hard breaths echoing between us as he locked my wrists above my head. A strangled noise blew past his lips, then a guttural, "Not yet."

I blinked and the Devil was back. Again, and it was Jack. Back and forth, the image of the man above me flickered between reality and my dreams, an apparition and a man I met a few hours ago. When he finally settled back on inhuman features, I closed my eyes and released a breath.

"You're not real." But the hands around my wrists tightened, locking me to the mattress with a tangibility that couldn't be conjured. Labored breaths warmed my cheeks and the hard length of his body pressed in, igniting little sparks between his skin and mine. I opened my eyes and Jack Warren was back, his silver pocket chain dangling over my breasts.

"Not yet," he repeated, pained restraint edging each syllable. His next words came low and heated, a promise and a threat rolled into one. "Ask for me, Adeline. I'll give you anything you want."

I shook my head. "Are you the Devil?"

He leaned in. Close, so close oak and rain and gunmetal washed over me, slathered across my lips. "For you, I'll be so much fucking worse."

"Addie, is everything okay in there?"

I squeezed my eyes together, opening them to a room with no full moon in the window and no Devil caressing me. Tommy hovered in the doorway, backlit by the golden lamp in the living room.

I ran a hand over my face. "What?"

"Nothing, I just heard you mumbling. Thought maybe you were having a bad dream or something."

Because Tommy had bad dreams. Because sleep eluded him more than it found him. Because deep down, maybe he wanted me to be just as screwed up as he was. That way neither one of us was ever alone.

"I'm fine," I said. I wasn't fine. I was beginning to wonder if I'd lost my mind.

His head dipped to the side, fingers clenching on the doorframe. "I'm sorry for waking you up. Goodnight."

Papa was insane.

That girl is disturbed.

How does one get eyes like that?

I needed a distraction. Something, anything, to get my mind away from all the evidence saying my father was wrong, that I didn't want to leave Georgia because I'd have to face the truth about myself, that I was too far gone for anyone to ever fix. So I sent my thoughts somewhere those things didn't exist. Train cars filled with wisteria. Forbidden forests teeming with golden eyes. Haunting music floating down a dark hall and a crackling fireplace in a luxurious room. So far away, so disconnected, so lost from everything and everywhere I was, I didn't notice what was clutched in my hand until morning. A thin chain, the kind that hung from men's waistcoats, flashing silver between my sweaty fingers.

EIGHT

WHEN I WAS SIX, Tommy found a rabbit den on the edge of our north field. Papa caught the mama eating our grain and shot her dead, unknowingly leaving the babies to starve. By the time Tommy found them only one still lived; a tiny, sick thing I begged Papa to take home.

The first day, it seemed fine. Weak and hungry, but it took to feedings well. When dusk reddened the sky, it even hopped around the milk crate I'd stuffed with hay. But the next day it refused to eat. It sat in a corner until noon, then spent the next few hours doing nothing but banging its fuzzy head against the wood. It would sniff, scratch, then ram against the weathered boards until it squeaked in pain and started the cycle again. Three more hours went by before Papa put the kit out of its misery.

The following days felt just like that. Not the blinding anger when I realized what Papa did, or the anguished grief when he let me bury it next to my mama. The redundancy. The endless cycle of slamming my head against a wall, only to hurt myself. Scratch and sniff for the umpteenth time and begin the wheel of insanity all over again.

Tommy worked. I cleaned in the morning, made dinner, and waited for him to get home. At first, I had Lillian over for coffee almost every day. Having a real honest-to-god friend was one of my few reprieves. But when her face suddenly sharpened and shimmered, I barred the door from any of her visits. I practiced our traditions, but something about this place didn't agree with me, or anything Papa taught me. The bells on my ankle no longer warded away strange creatures. When I walked the streets, rubbing my iron necklace did nothing to stave off the visions of monsters roaming the sidewalk. I salted the apartment every evening, prayed to a God I was taught not to trust in, but the harder I worked the worse the visions became. I kept banging my head against the wall, marching myself toward the end of my own misery.

Two weeks passed and I stopped leaving the apartment.

Three, and I covered all the windows, screaming with Tommy when he came home and said I needed to see a doctor. I spent the rest of the night curled up beside him sobbing, only to resume our argument first thing in the morning.

Four, and Tommy got sent off to Chicago for training with a new unit, instructing me to send letters every day and promising an intervention when he got back.

Five, and there was a knock on my door.

A look through the peephole revealed Lillian, red hair perfectly curled and a delightful smile on her face. I only opened the door a crack, but she barged through before I could send her away.

"I have some news—oh, dear god, what happened here?"

I glanced around. The few belongings I had were strewn around the living room. Dishes stacked in the sink and dust settled in all the corners. Papa's guitar lay on the kitchen table like an altar and two of my three dresses were tacked over the windows. Salt was scattered the floor, a noticeable break in the circle where I'd kicked it attempting to shut the door. Unease curled through me.

A full minute ticked down on the clock in silence. She sighed, gesturing toward her apartment. "How about you come over for something to drink?"

"TEA, COFFEE, OR SOMETHING stronger?"

"I'm fine without, thank you."

Lillian bustled around her kitchen while I sank into her overstuffed, shrimp-pink couch. I observed her apartment, which appeared to belong to the illegitimate child of a chronic hoarder and eccentric curator. Between the mismatched furniture, baubles covering every flat surface, and unconventional paintings covering mismatched walls, a headache formed.

"I suppose there's enough energy to go around." She settled across from me with an empty teacup, which she discarded to a littered coffee table. "Now, what's happening with you? You're clearly unwell."

I didn't think she was one to talk. I shrugged, ignoring her pointed stare.

"Are you getting on well with your brother?"

I refused to meet her eyes. "We're fine."

She nodded, the low dip of her chin all I could see with my head down. "Family is complicated sometimes. Especially so soon after losing a parent."

More unease flickered through me, until I remembered I had told her my father passed. Another side effect of my insanity, perhaps. Memory loss. "It's a part of life."

"And I'm terribly sorry for it." The little frown never left her face, but she said nothing else. For that, I was grateful, and I didn't protest when she stood and retrieved us tea. "I do have some good news."

"Oh?"

"I spoke with Mr. Warren, and it appears a position has opened at his office. He was insistent it go to you, no interview necessary." She paused. "But there is one, sort of peculiar condition."

Of course there was. "What is it?"

"He wants to take you to dinner." She observed me, my sunken eyes and sallow skin. The clothes that hung too loose off my shoulders, since I refused to visit the grocer and Tommy was no longer home. Her frown became so deep I feared it was permanent. "I think getting out could do you some good."

Except, out there, there was nothing more but those things. Real or not, I wasn't even sure anymore, but how could I go to work, how could I sit in an office, how could I hold my sanity if I was constantly surrounded by monsters only I could hear or touch or see?

Shaking my head, I murmured, "I appreciate the offer, Lillian, I do, but I think right now it would be best if I didn't work."

Again, silence swallowed us whole. Birds chirped outside the window and children laughed on the street. Three separate clocks ticked in the background, scattered across Lillian's walls like keepers of this tense moment. She folded her hands in her lap, tucking an unruly curl behind her ear.

"Do you need help, Adeline?"

I stared at her.

"Us girls, we have to stick together, remember?" She gave her tell-tale wink, but it was so half-hearted I may have imagined it. "But sometimes there are even better solutions."

I said nothing. Her expression turned serious, something I didn't quite understand. "Mr. Warren is a very powerful man. And whatever you said to him at the party, it left . . . an impression. I promise if you ask him, he would be very, *very* inclined to help you. In any way you need."

I frowned. I'd barely said anything at all. In fact, I stuttered and dropped a glass on his carpet.

He probably wanted to sleep with me. Undoubtedly, he slept with Lillian. I noticed a pair of his cufflinks—gold and engraved with his initials—on the coffee table the moment I arrived.

The silver chain I'd carried all month burned my skin, buried between the folds of my dress where I tucked it against my waist. But Mr. Warren hadn't been there. The Devil hadn't been there. Only

Tommy was, checking in on my fitful sleep, and I was so close to losing my mind I couldn't remember how I acquired the damn thing. Maybe I'd done something with Mr. Warren I'd forgotten about. Maybe the pastor was right and I had evil in my heart. Maybe I'd already succumbed to the madness I knew deep down clawed its way to me.

I needed a safer mind.

I needed to go home.

I needed my papa.

There was nothing Mr. Warren could give me.

I WAS THE RABBIT. Slamming my head against the wall, waiting, falling, doing the same thing over and over again. It never seemed to end. I forgot my rituals, the liturgy Papa once taught me, my brother's smile and an old farmhouse fading into the distance. The more numb I became the worse it got. Late at night I heard the sounds of devil-folk skittering across my floorboards, laughing and shrieking as they terrorized me.

I broke.

It made sense then, why desperate people did terrible things. The consequences didn't matter when you had nothing to lose. So after only five weeks in New York, I penned a letter to Tommy assuring him I was fine and made a quiet phone call. I had nothing but a common name, but he was so well known the operator knew exactly who to call. I left a message with some nameless secretary, then I went to the newspaper stand. I'd been listening to the paperboys hawk headlines from my windows for weeks.

Devil-folk crowded the street. I ignored them. Pretended they didn't exist. Soon enough, this would all be over. I'd be safe again. I stopped by Lillian's and smiled through an hour of small talk to get what I needed. Then, I went home and waited for a return call. I prepared.

That Friday, someone knocked on my door at six o'clock sharp.

I knew Tommy was still in Chicago, but silently hoped it was him as I opened the door. It wasn't. It was Jack Warren, eyes their strange shade of honey-gold, dressed as impeccably as last time and holding a bouquet of roses.

"I'm flattered, but I don't date."

He leaned his head to the side. Everything about him was relaxed, confident, but there was a sharpness behind those eyes that cut like glass.

"These are for a friend," he said, tone implicating quite the opposite.

I swallowed, taking a large gulp of his potent scent into me. Fresh rain and oleander, with a hint of gunmetal underneath. Sharp as the factories down the road and warm as the barrels he stored his liquor in. The scents themselves weren't unfamiliar, only the quality. So intense the aroma wrapped me like a funeral shroud.

"I don't know you," I said, trying and failing to maintain composure. Dangerous heat curled beneath my skin.

The corner of his lips tilted upward. "Would you like to?"

NINE

"I SHOULDN'T BE OUT too late."

"You don't need to worry, Miss Colton."

Two things warred in my brain: the unwelcome guilt at this plan, and the lies I told to both my brother and the man beside me. His cane clicked on the sidewalk as I made my way to a gangster's car. I'd only been in the Tully Brother's rusted Ford, and it was nothing like Mr. Warren's. Sleek and black, the fresh chrome lining caught the pink light of dusk and scattered it across the road.

Blissfully, we spent the ride in silence. Any attempts he made at pleasant conversation were quickly squashed by my lack of responses, and it only took several attempts for him to get the hint. I clutched my purse tighter against my chest, running over my speech for the thousandth time. I'd done nothing this week but prepare, or as Lillian so elegantly put it, research. Quite the term for eavesdropping and social sabotage.

Twenty minutes later we stopped in front of a restaurant. One look at the gilded front door told me this wasn't an establishment meant for dirty farmers. Despite wearing the nicest clothes I owned, embarrassment flooded me.

If Mr. Warren noticed the light dimming in my eyes, he didn't say. After shooing away a valet, he came around the side and opened my door for me, offering one leather-gloved hand.

No less than ten people nodded at him as we entered, a troupe of waiters and doormen and hosts greeting him like old friends. Offering to take his hat, my purse, asking if he'd like the usual, who I was, if we wanted the normal seating arrangement or something quieter? I'd never seen one person garner so much attention, but he regarded this all with cool composure while men buzzed like bees around him. I was practically pushed toward a seat in the back, a wave of disquiet washing over the restaurant as we sauntered between tables. By the time he pulled out my chair and asked me to sit, low chatter filled the nervous silence again.

Surveying the crowded room, I wondered just how deep Mr. Warren's reputation ran—and more importantly, what he did to get it. Men didn't walk into a room and set the place on fire unless they had a history of watching the world burn.

Sensing my unease, he leaned back in his seat, offering me that millionaire smile. If he didn't rule the world with fear, that would certainly be enough. "You seem nervous."

"I'm not." The lie sounded poor, even to me, but it wouldn't matter because he'd understand exactly why as soon as I had the courage to speak.

I'd gotten this far.

I had plans, legitimate plans.

I only had to survive a little longer.

A stiff waiter in black filled our water glasses and asked if we'd like something to drink. I only had a moment to be surprised at Mr. Warren's request—whiskey on the rocks—before the stoic man faced me. I hadn't drank in years, and made it an explicit point not to after prohibition. But tonight was special, and I was going to hell anyway. I ordered myself a glass of red wine, whatever they recommended, not knowing the name of anything acceptable since all I'd ever had was homemade hooch.

Then I leveled my eyes on the man I avoided until now.

He wore no expression. Slouched in his chair like a king, surveying the room with cool indifference, I wondered if we would spend the night in silence unless I was the first to break it. Unbidden, the dream I had of him came full force. The flush of his skin, hands wrapped around my wrists, weight sinking me into the mattress . . .

Red stole my cheeks. I looked down. That wasn't at all what I was here for. I would pay the price for all my sins later, but in order to do what I must, I had to cast all those thoughts from my mind.

Even still, that . . . tug had me watching him again. Like our souls were magnets and the energy pulsed between us, heavy and dark and a few other things I couldn't begin to name. His gaze flicked to mine and a sharp breath fell from my lips.

"Thank you for dinner, Mr. Warren."

A smile curled his lips, filled with far too much dangerous intent. "Call me Jack."

"I'll stick with Mr. Warren."

His expression sharpened, eyes narrowed and jaw clenched. All his actions held an uncanny intensity. That indescribable *tug* grew stronger, becoming an aching in my chest, thick heat between my legs, a depthless fog through my brain that could only be satiated by his attention.

"Friends can call each other by their first names." He rested his cane between his knees, clutching the top in an iron grip so unlike the rest of his relaxed demeanor.

"We're not friends yet."

"That's why you're here."

I took a long sip of my wine, ignoring the urge to gag. "Actually, I'm here for another reason."

"Which would be?"

It was now or never. I stole another sip of wine, no longer flinching at the fire rearing down my throat. "I've heard some things."

A single eyebrow arched skyward. "Things?"

"Things," I repeated, pulling out my purse. "In the papers on Monday. They say you plan to buy a very large portion of Mr. Roger Letterman's shipping company."

"Is that what you like to discuss at dinner? Business?"

"If it concerns me." I laid the infamous news article on the table, beginning my pile of mounting evidence. "It was an interesting choice for you, I believe, because it takes very little chatter and gossip to know Mr. Letterman is an excessively devout Catholic. One who is known to only work with other men who share in his devotions."

If he had any indication where this conversation was heading, he didn't show it. His eyebrow resumed its normal position, his warm skin smooth and unimpressionable. Even those damning eyes flattened into stoic indifference.

"I am Catholic."

"Yes, I've heard that. You claim to be quite the believer." I gestured toward his low glass of whiskey. "But I'll be honest with you, Mr. Warren, I've spent my entire life around obnoxiously faithful men. You're not one of them."

A smile flicked his lips and frigid energy cooled the air. That tug grew undeniable, sharpening like steel knives between us.

"A reputation is very important, and from what I've gathered, you've worked very hard to secure a certain influence about you, one that would satisfy the proprietor of this deal you're striking."

That was a hunch, but the next part wasn't. I laid down a receipt, stolen from a casefile Tommy brought home from work. "This states a buyer in Wales purchased ten thousand pounds worth of pipes from you."

He shrugged. "Europeans love their cars."

"You know, I've wondered how you manage to keep your second, more *lucrative* business so quiet." We stared at one another. His hand clenched tighter on the pommel of his cane. "But it makes sense, doesn't it? Why sell alcohol here when you can export it to your home country, where you undoubtedly have more influence, connections and means to keep your *nefarious* ongoings quiet. All you need is a shipping company."

He neither confirmed nor denied it, but that part I knew for sure. All it took was a little snooping at my very chatty neighbor's apartment.

Guilt pierced my ribs. I ignored it.

"So, wouldn't it be quite the scandal if you were sleeping with your female employees?"

At that, he broke into a grin. A breathy laugh passed his lips, and he shook his head, running his tongue over his teeth. "You lost me there, darling."

I reached into my purse one last time, pulling forth two golden cufflinks. Custom engraved ones. I dropped them one at a time onto the table, letting them fall through my fingers like sand. "These were in Lillian's apartment. Along with several other things I believe are yours, and have now been acquired by *Society Talk*. Additionally, there are several eyewitness testimonies that you and I left my apartment and came here for dinner tonight."

He cupped his chin in his hand. Something sparked in his eyes, a deadly mix of intrigue and challenge. "The gossip paper?"

"That's the one." I snapped my purse shut. "I think Mr. Letterman will have a few understandable doubts about your pious, unsoiled nature if that story breaks."

He said nothing. Low chatter filled the empty space between us. I took another sip of wine, clutching the glass until my knuckles whitened. As I lowered the cup, Mr. Warren appeared nothing short of amused.

"There's one problem with your blackmail, darling."

"And it is?"

His stare burrowed into mine. "I haven't fucked you yet."

My thoughts scattered like marbles, colliding and bouncing around *fucked* and *yet.*

A victorious smile took his face. One I had no doubt led to many instances of said fucking. But I wasn't like that, and I came here for a reason that wasn't Mr. Warren's salacious nature.

The dream flashed back to my consciousness. Heavy eyes, the hand sliding up my thigh, the low groan of a man—the Devil—in my ear.

"The truth doesn't matter, only the public's view of it." Only because those two words wouldn't stop invading my every heartbeat, I added. "I'm a respectable woman, Mr. Warren, and I'd like for you to speak to me as such."

"While you're in the midst of blackmailing me, you mean?" He drummed his fingers on the table, any touch of playfulness in his voice erased. "What is it you did all this marvelous research for anyway?"

"Five hundred dollars."

He raised an eyebrow. "That's it? Not even a thousand?"

Blinding red swept my vision. *That's it?* As if five hundred dollars wasn't the difference between losing my home forever and being stuck here. As if five hundred dollars wasn't the difference between a full night's sleep and waking up screaming. My safety and sanity versus an asylum.

"That's it," I seethed.

His eyes narrowed on my face. I hated it. Hated everything about how that stare dug beneath my skin, rooting and burrowing into places I hadn't known existed. Darkness curled around him, soaking the air with his presence, with the look I had no name for and prayed I never would.

He dug through his pocket, producing a checkbook and a pen. Scribbled something. Then slid the banknote across the table. He wrote it out for a thousand.

"For tonight's company," he said.

I had been sheltered my entire life, but even I knew what *company* meant. "I am not a whore."

"By entertainment, I simply meant dinner and conversation." He tilted his head to the side. "Very interesting conversation if I might add. I would have paid a thousand just to know I left cufflinks at Lillian's. Next time, bargain for more. Extortion becomes you." He fanned a menu open with a snap. "Now that that nasty business is over, would you like another drink?"

I stared at him. "You're joking."

"No, not at all, but I do believe you can find it in yourself to call me Jack now that we've become financially intimate." He reached across the table and snatched my *evidence*. "You have to tell me where you found this. Very clever ruse by the way, I'm impressed."

A full hour could have passed before I muttered, "You're a terrible criminal."

"Tell that to the FBI. They've been up my ass for weeks." The rough language rolled off his tongue without effort, without remorse. I expected any man who willingly broke the law to be improper at worst, immoral at best, but there was absolutely nothing traditional about him.

I should have run. Taken my check and fractured morality home, packed my things and prepared for a train home. Instead, I found myself saying, "You're not what I expected."

"Much more handsome in person, I agree."

The corner of my lip twitched in an almost smile. Meanwhile, Jack mumbled something about the lobster here tasting like fresh shit.

"I should go now."

I hadn't risen from my seat when he said, "Sit down and eat with me, please. I just paid five hundred dollars for the pleasure."

"You paid a thousand."

"No, I paid a thousand in total. Five hundred for the extortion and five hundred for the pleasure."

"Why am I here?" I snapped. Not that I didn't know. He made that abundantly clear with *fucked* and *yet*, but I needed to know if he felt it too. The tug. The only reason I hadn't grabbed my money and my wits and fled the moment he handed me the check.

"I enjoy dinner and good conversation."

I was hardly a conversationalist and we both knew it. Besides my very rehearsed speech just now, I could barely utter a sentence in his presence. "While I'm flattered, you'll have to excuse me if I find your sudden interest in a stranger unusual. But I will be candid in admitting I don't have much experience with your kind."

"And what is my kind, Adeline?"

"Gangsters." That word set a little twitch to his lips. "Apologies for my frankness, but I'm not easily impressed by wealth and booze."

"So it's safe to assume this bothers you about me?"

"It does."

"Why?"

It was none of his business why. My brother was none of his business, yet he was dragged here because of it anyway. "The way I see it, you cause more harm than good. And there isn't room for that ugliness in an already ugly world."

His wry smile broke free. "That is a very assertive argument."

"I value honesty. So when you say we'll be friends, Mr. Warren, that's why we won't be. It's a matter of character and choices."

"Character and choices," he repeated, using the same lazy cadence as before. "Yet, you just blackmailed me. Live in the apartment building I own. And you seemed *very* impressed with the check I just handed you."

"I don't have a choice, unlike you."

Unsure if I spoke for my situation or a subconscious defense of all my recent decisions, I clutched my napkin with ferocious intent. But all my jagged edges smoothed to dull lines when he tilted his head to the side, eyes lifting to mine with sincere intensity. "I'm sorry you don't have that choice."

I swallowed. The waiter arrived beside our table again, but Jack waved him away. Refusing to meet his eyes, I took in the decor of the room instead. All the lush flora, hand-carved moldings, railings gilded in gold and the rich, mahogany carpentry. Wealth of another kind, something people like Mr. Warren could never have attained all that long ago. New money was just that for a reason—up until recently, old fortunes were the only kind to exist. My family knew damn well just how deep the scars of poverty ran.

"Lillian was right."

My focus snapped to him. Those eyes . . . god, those eyes. I melted into them faster than I could conceal, slipping through my own fingers as desperate need unfurled beneath my skin. "About?"

"I asked her what you were like. She said you were very kind, but very sad."

I wondered if she would have the same assessment if she knew I deceived her. "I'm not sad."

He tapped his fingers on the table, the sound muted by the leather still encasing them. Strange, that he hadn't taken them off. Straining for a change in conversation, I asked, "Is there something wrong with your hands?"

He released a short breath, glancing around the room like we were co-conspirators. "For this crowd, yes, but you can see if you would like to."

I would like to. Not only to satiate my curiosity, but I now realized we'd never actually touched. I wondered what his hands would feel like—plagued by the rough edges of a working man, or as smooth and soft as a thoughtless life. But when he slipped the gloves from his hands, splaying his fingers on the crisp tablecloth, I saw neither.

Tattoos. Intricate, realistic, disturbing tattoos. Not an inch of skin was left uncovered, shadowed ink forming gloves of another kind.

Patterns, symbols and complex knots filled the empty space, but two large pieces dominated the top of each hand. On the left, a copse of trees so detailed I felt them sway in the wind. On the right, a pyre brandished with rope, engorged with flames reaching for a starless sky.

Heat crackled along my spine, searing and oppressive.

Letters scattered his knuckles, three rows to each finger in a language I didn't recognize. "What does that say?"

"*Yn y bywyd hwn neu o hyn ymlaen.* In this life and hereafter."

"In Welsh?"

He nodded.

It made . . . well, no sense at all, but the feeling in my chest became a wildfire, battling his inky flames for who could burn hotter. I'd never met a man with tattoos. Tommy always said only sailors and rabble acquired those, but something so beautiful, so *evocative* couldn't be wrong. I ached to touch him, to run my fingers along those trees and caress those elegant words. My hands twitched at my sides, a kernel of rationality telling me otherwise. But a moment later I caved, laying my hands over his.

A small breath left my lips. A delicious honey coated my veins, pulling me under. That simple touch was ecstasy, a symphony, a feeling so lurid that pleasant shivers broke down my spine. I craved more—more touches, more nakedness as images flitted behind my eyes faster than I could catch them: my dark prince in the forest, waiting beyond the trees as the moon waned down to darkness. Swollen lips kissing me, touching me, following a hand up my bare thigh. A ceiling of swaying wisteria and deadly nightshade. Then Jack's eyes—my dark prince's eyes—blinking in the darkness, the current of a river roaring around us. A swath of my white dress unfurling between us and a whisper. A promise. A question . . .

Annwyl.

He pulled away.

I blinked. The low hum of the restaurant swelled into rowdy laughter and conversation. The golden lights came back into focus, the greenery dotting the room, the waiters in their stiff outfits and Mr. Warren's piercing stare.

I pressed the back of my hand to my head, feeling ill.

"Are you all right, Adeline?" I heard the question as if underwater. I nodded, accepting the handkerchief he offered not to wipe my head, but in the hope his fingers would brush mine again. My lips went numb, a fierce heat clambering across my limbs that could only stop with his touch, but he pulled the gloves back on his hands. Nothing but cool leather caressed me as he leaned over, dabbing at my head.

"This was a mistake."

For a moment, I didn't realize I was the one to speak. Once the words were out there, they couldn't be taken back. This was a mistake, all of it. I should have stayed in Georgia. I shouldn't have promised Tommy my compliance. I shouldn't have indulged Mr. Warren with good conversation, dinner, anything. A panicked fever hit me I couldn't explain. All I knew was a deeper, primitive piece of me screamed it was time to *run.*

I leapt to my feet, causing the table nearest to us to tense in alarm. Dozens of eyes landed on me, but I only saw two. Rich gold darkened with each passing second, haunting my thoughts as I ran away from them.

TEN

I DIDN'T STOP UNTIL I reached my apartment.

It took me two hours to find my way back, a midnight sky stretching above my head by the time I scrambled through the door. I grabbed my salt pouch and scattered crystals in front of the door. *Down to the river we go, down to the river we go . . .*

A harsh sob left my throat and the bag slipped from my fingers. Salt exploded on the floor and I sobbed harder.

What was I doing, what was I—

Something hard slammed into my head. My vision went dark.

"DON'T WAKE UP YET."

I tried to focus, but only muted moonlight swirled around my vision. Cold hardwood ran beneath me and a shadowed face hovered above.

Pain arced behind my eyes, face throbbing as I choked for air. A strangled noise I couldn't possibly make cut through the silence. A slender finger pressed against my lips. "*Sh, sh, sh, sh,* no, none of that, darling. You have to go back to sleep."

The silhouette sharpened into details. Violet Warren straddled my stomach, hair dangling around her face and arms pinning my own. At least, I thought it was Violet Warren. The monster above me looked like her, sounded like her, but wasn't the woman I met at The Glamour Hotel. She wasn't a woman at all.

"Quiet, now." The sound brushed me like scattered leaves. Her eyes honed in on me, but they were so gold they glowed in the dark. Vertical pupils slimmed and widened as she swayed above me. A cloying scent infiltrated my nose and vomit roared up my throat.

"None of that." Pointed ears twitched through her hair, so dark the night bled from each silky strand. All her features were sharper, stronger, an already beautiful face now devastating in its intensity.

"None of that," she repeated. Her thumb brushed my cheekbone, streaking a pus-filled tear across my skin. "You just have to fuck everything up, don't you?"

A ragged breath passed my lips. She smothered it with her hand. "If you don't calm down, he'll sense you. You can still run away, but you have to be quiet."

She leaned in until we were nose to nose. Hot breath danced across my ear, the hushed sound of, "Georgia, the farmhouse," seeping beneath my skin. "Isn't that what you want, Adeline, to go home? All you have to do is sleep. I promise I'll come back for you soon."

This wasn't real. My heart slammed against my ribs, a serrated breath hissing past my teeth. This wasn't real. *This couldn't be real.*

"Go back to sleep," she whispered. Then Violet Warren cupped my face and pressed her lips to mine. A breath of a kiss, barely a touch, but I couldn't think before darkness jerked me under, a cruel current wrenching me beneath murky waters.

IT WAS STILL NIGHT when I woke again.

The busted clock across the room said it was three in the morning. A breeze blew through the open window, sending glittering shards of glass and dust across the floor. Moonlight seeped between the floorboards and chatter wafted up from the street, but in the apartment, I was alone. Violet was gone.

I shook my head, pressing the backs of my hands to my swollen eyes. That was a dream. Another ridiculous, psychotic dream feeding me information from my own conscience. It was time to go.

My dress was destroyed, torn and coated in blood from a wound weeping on my forehead. As my other two were still tacked to the windows, I threw on my nightgown and robe. Glass crunched beneath my feet, stinging with little wounds as I pulled on stockings and tights, grabbed Jack Warren's check, and ran out the door.

I was halfway to the bank before it occurred to me what time it was. The world spun and my bleeding feet ached. Drunkards and night owls swarmed around me, but I paid them no mind as I sank to my knees on the sidewalk, pressing my forehead to my tights and taking a deep breath.

I couldn't wait until morning. My strange dream told me that, Violet's warning of return an omen I didn't wish to fulfill. If I hurried, I could still make the six a.m. train.

There was no time to form another solution. Pulling off my shoes and discarding them in an alley, I clutched Jack's check and walked to his hotel. It was three in the morning, but Lillian said it herself. The place was a sinner's playden five nights a week, and sinners didn't go to bed until sunrise.

As luck would have it, tonight was one of the quiet two. No one stood on the sidewalk or loitered in the lobby. A tired doorman slumped against the entrance, eyes closed and breath whistling on each exhale. I shimmied past him.

Not only was the rabble absent, but anyone else. The front desk lay empty and cold, not a bellhop could be seen and the elevator boy was missing from his station.

Shivers broke across my skin. Stagnant air pushed through my teeth, sharp and coated with my blood. Something about this place felt dead, empty . . . wrong.

You hit your head and you're losing your mind, Addie. Of course it feels wrong. That seemed reasonable enough to me. I set the lever myself in the elevator, praying I remembered how to navigate the top floor. If I retraced my steps from the ballroom, I could find his study, which in hindsight, I believed to be an apartment. I'd explain I needed the money now, and would like to switch the check for cash he undoubtedly kept in a safe, with assurances he'd never have to speak to me again if he did. If that didn't work, I'd sob and beg. If that didn't work, I'd threaten him again. And if *that* didn't work, I'd fuck him for it.

A chime cut off my maniacal laughter, caught somewhere between a sob and a scream. I lifted my forehead from the wall I leaned against. The doors slid open.

This . . . wasn't the right floor.

Fog coated the ground, obscuring the marble under a layer of swirling white. Vines meandered along the walls, pouring out of cracks in the plaster and stone, curling around pictures frames and suspending them midair. Wisteria hung from the ceiling in droves. A swaying sea of violet.

Right, I was dreaming.

I sighed in relief, then more crazed laughter. Of course, this was nothing but a dream. And to think I had been so worried . . . .

Cupping my hands around my mouth, I shouted, "Devil!" Air blew from my lungs into the roiling fog, sending alabaster waves against the walls. The vines slithered and the ceiling creaked, but no one answered.

"It's *annwyl*." Still, nothing. I frowned, turning inside the elevator. He always summoned me, never made me go find him. But tonight was only a half moon, not a new one, so perhaps the rules changed. I dipped one foot into the layer of fog, watching it scatter around my ankle.

"Can you at least give me a hint?" I shouted down the corridor.

"What would be the fun in that?"

I whirled. The voice belonged to a woman, high-pitched and lyrical, but no one stood behind me. No one stood in the hall, the elevator, any of it.

"*Annwyl,*" a second voice mocked, male, but still not the devil. The nasally sound echoed off the walls. "On the fucking fates, who's been calling her that?"

"A blind man, obviously." The female voice tittered. The male voice broke into raucous laughter.

"I think she's fine enough to play with," a third voice added, another man. I turned in a circle, but the hall was still empty.

I threw my hands to my ears and crouched to the floor. *You're losing it, you're losing it, you're losing it—*

"Do you want to play with us tonight, little *annwyl?* I don't think your devil's here."

"There's no one here," I sobbed through clenched teeth. "There's no one here."

The third man sighed. "It's always such a gamble with the glamour-touched."

Someone snapped and three people stood around me. Creatures. Devil-folk.

The woman with the lyrical voice was not a woman, but a waifish dryad, tall and slim with skin of bark and hair of apple blossoms. Beside her stood a bare-chested man with hooves for feet and horns curling from his long black hair, and beside him, a demonic, humanoid version of swine.

I screamed.

The dryad sighed, throwing her hand over my mouth. "She's not going to be any fun." Another scream bubbled up my throat, but my lips remained together, stuck like they were coated in glue. I screamed and grunted against the closed wall of my mouth, but they ignored me to squabble with one another.

"We just need to give her an elixir. She'll loosen up."

"I don't know if I wish her to. Look at that face, it's like she got mauled by a wyvern."

"But she's blonde. You know how much I love the fair ones."

Back and forth, back and forth, until finally, the hooved man's eyes widened. "Who did she say she was looking for, again?"

The swine and the tree woman halted their bickering, the latter huffing, "The Devil?"

"What does the human devil look like?"

"How would I know that?" The dryad threw her arms in the air. I screamed against my sealed lips.

"No, no, no, he's always compared to a serpent, yes?"

"I think he's right," the swine said, huffing and snorting as he wagged his finger. "Something about a garden, right? And a snake?"

"Yes, and if that's who she's referring to, then who do we think the human belongs to?"

For a moment neither replied. Three sets of eyes widened.

"On the fucking fates," the dryad hissed. "What do we now?"

"We could deliver her."

"Are you mad? We should send her back."

The squabbling continued until the hooved man screamed, "*Enough.*"

The other two went silent.

"We don't want him thinking we did that," he said, gesturing toward me, and presumably, my wyvern-mauled face. "Nix, heal her face a little, make her look pretty and we'll deliver her ourselves. Perhaps even gain a favor for the task."

The swine groaned. "I thought we were avoiding the Calamity tonight?"

"Would you rather be the subject of it?" The hooved man kneeled before me, clutching my chin between his fingers. A soft moan met my lips, tears springing to my eyes.

But my lips finally parted. Before I could emit another scream, the dryad, Nix, kneeled beside him.

"Yes, I'll make her very pleasant. Would you like that, little *annwyl*? Then we'll take you to your devil and you can tell him just how wonderful we treated you."

"How gracious we were," the hooved man added.

The swine. "You'll ask for our favor, won't you, sweet human?"

A heavy breath fell past my lips. "Oh my god, I'm fucking insane."

"Splendid," Nix squeaked, clapping her hands together. She clenched my face. Lightening-hot pain ricocheted through my skull and I collapsed against the floor.

"Wake up, little *annwyl*." I blinked . . . and blinked and blinked. Three creatures of hell swam back into view.

"She looks much better."

"Indeed."

"She's much more tolerable this way. Perhaps I see the appeal now."

"Right then, up we go, girl." The hooved man grabbed my arm and jerked me to a stand. Swaying on my feet, dizziness tilted the world while he pulled me down the hall. Any attempts to stop his march made me stumble over my feet.

The hall grew warmer, the lights brighter and the swirling fog less dense. We passed a familiar portrait when sound met my ears, beautiful and horrible. Discordant music clenched my soul, cawing laughter and savage shouts like war cries mixed with grunts of pleasure. The ballroom stood with open doors ahead, throwing flickering firelight and shadows against the walls.

Above the cacophony, a shrewd voice bellowed into the night. "And will we stand for this? Will we sit idly by while House Valdivia allows the annihilation of our kind?"

Nix brushed my sweat-soaked hair back and pushed me inside.

Devil-folk crowded every inch of the marble floors. Some that could be human if not for the animalistic features adorning them, tails and horns and other monstrous things. Some that weren't quite like anything at all, boasting flowing hair of rocks, water, sunshine as if it streamed from the heavens down a woman's back. Then more of the beasts that resembled Violet Warren when she appeared in my dream—tall and lithe, more beautiful than words could describe, with shimmering eyes and pointed ears. And ones I recognized— dryads and brownies and sprites arcing through the air. Twig-limbed spriggans, knobby-faced trolls and sage green pixies. A man who could be human if not for the aura of pulsing darkness around him stood on a chair, speaking to the crowd.

"My faction has a better answer," he declared, eyes swollen and mad with fury. "We were created by the Bogorans to rule worlds, and that is what we shall do. Stand by your current master if you wish, but if you seek the future, you will follow me."

Raucous jeers erupted, clicking claws, pounding hooves and howls that paled my flesh.

"If only you were created by a Bogoran," a dull voice called. A voice I'd recognize anywhere. I swiveled my head, but could see nothing through the riotous crowd. Nix shoved me forward, and all at once the devil-folk noticed my presence.

"What is it we have here?"

"Hello, little human, do you find yourself in need of company?"

"Look at that poor, pathetic thing."

"Does it sing? Let's see if it will sing for us."

Music rose above the swell of noise and a twitch started in my feet. My body ached to move with it, languish in it, even as the jarring notes scratched my ears. Oppressive heat licked my skin, roaring from a massive fire in the center of the room. Vines slithered across the floor, moving between the devil-folk's feet.

"What is it now?" The speaker called, honing his stare where the crowd thickened, creatures swarming me to get a closer look. They laughed and taunted, poking my exposed skin and clawing at my nightgown. My shoulder left its socket as Nix and the hooved man trudged me forward, releasing me before a stage on the far side of the room. A stage that once occupied a five-man band, but now held a throne with a smaller one beside it.

The Devil sneered down at me with Violet Warren beside him.

Air fled my lungs. Gasping, I stared into the cruel and vacant eyes of the man who haunted my monthly dreams, who I was fairly sure I saw earlier tonight. He reclined across the ornate throne with boredom, fingers clutching a glass of fizzy green. His eyes widened a fraction as the creatures stepped away, smoothing over into indifference in the space of a blink.

He gestured to Nix. "What is this?"

She bowed, and not just any bow, but a full prostration upon the floor. "This *lovely* little creature requested an audience with you."

A round of sharp, gleeful laughter. The Devil held up his hand and silence descended. "And you thought I desired to grant it?"

The hooved man sank into his own worship before addressing him. "She spoke of you with familiarity. Were we wrong to assume you had . . . relations?"

More tittering laughter, now quieter and behind cupped hands. Violet cast her golden snake eyes over the room and the sound grew riotous.

The devil beheld me. "Perhaps. They all look the same to me." Taking a tentative sip of his drink, he eyed me with malicious resolve. "Though she may do for some entertainment tonight. Do you hear that, Delsaran? The humans *are* good for some things."

At the far end of the room, the speaker, Delsaran, turned a mottled red. "You called this Calamity, not I. If you wish to hear me speak, I will not do so in the presence of swine."

"I do not wish to hear you speak, actually. I simply allowed this little display for my own entertainment, which you regretfully have not fulfilled." The devil raised his glass into the air. "But go on, hawk your preachings if you must. You have not swayed my mind, nor the minds of any of my followers. Why dispose of humans when they have so many *wonderful* uses." Thunderous agreement roared throughout the crowd, stomping and war cries.

"You usher in the ruin of the fair folk."

"And you usher in the ruin of my fucking patience." He downed his drink and smashed the glass upon the ground. Cackling laughter filled the room, the swine man heaving and snorting beside me.

The speaker, Delsaran, balled his fists. "Inform me, what use does that one have?"

My breath came in heavy pants, blood pounding in my ears. The devil-folk swarmed me, fighting, demanding to see the human. Malignant energy charged the air. It was all too much, drowning me in panic and chaos, but in the midst of the commotion was a simple tug. A lifeline wrapped around my ribs, twisting along the floor and stopping at the serpent king before me. Nothing was there, but I could *feel* it, along with an emotion so unlike the ones around me. A potent drop of fear.

I must have imagined it, because his face twisted into a savage smirk. "Does she not bow before her king?"

Someone shoved me to my knees. They hit the floor with a crack, shockwaves reverberating up my limbs. This had to be a dream, it had to be. This couldn't be real.

Papa's voice fluttered in my ears, smooth and strong. *Because one day you will listen.*

But it wasn't his song I decided to sing. I pressed my hands together, forehead to the stones.. *Our Father in heaven. Hallowed be Your name. Your kingdom come, Your will be done, on earth as it is in heaven—*

"Oh, how sweet, she's praying to God."

"Will He save you now, little human?"

The room burst into a symphony of hysterics. Nix dragged me across the floor, over the steps of the dais until I kneeled before the devil's feet. His fingers came beneath my chin, lifting my eyes to his. He smiled.

"Your god's not here, sweetheart. You can pray to me."

Tears burned the back of my eyes.

"Retrieve me another drink." He dropped my chin and gestured to a willowy steward beside him. The monster bowed, blinked from existence, and reappeared with green champagne.

The Devil seized me by my dress and pulled me into his lap. I squirmed and screamed but his arm locked around my waist, anchoring me to his leather-clad thighs.

"Relax, darling. We're only having fun. This is what you wanted, is it not?" To Delsaran, he shouted, "Would you like me to demonstrate her use here or in private?"

The tug snapped, fear and anger and of all things *concern* fizzling between us. I gripped the arms of the golden throne, grounding myself against the cool metal and heat seeping along my backside. Perverse desire hit me, swift as the fear pouring through my veins, but none of it made sense. None of it felt like it was *mine*.

"Darling, look at me." I didn't. His fingers encased my jaw, jerking my face toward his. I had no choice but to lean fully against him. The room held patrons of hell, but something told me to keep my eyes on him. That the real threat shivered against my body, smoothing his hand down my exposed thigh.

Warm breath, the tainted scent of honey and poison, brushed against my ear. "The things you think I will do to you, I promise they will do much worse." He raised his glass toward the room. Music rose into the air and the laughter and cawing resumed. "Just because we don't wish for your death, does not mean we are your friends."

The steward appeared before us, sinking to his knees and offering me a second glass. The Devil nodded and my trembling fingers ensconced it. A whimper erupted in my throat, and he gripped me harder, lowering his voice still. "Don't give them any reasons, *annwyl.*"

Heat plummeted to my stomach. I stared into those alluring, inhuman eyes. My hypnotic beckoning into the dark. If only I knew how right I'd been.

"Drink," he hissed.

I did.

"I declare this Calamity over. You may retreat back to your hovel now, Delsaran. And do bring your lecherous fucking court with you."

There was more, several exchanges of words but a fog like no other shrouded me, warmth and fear and light and darkness, warring for territory in my skull. Sickness hit in a swift wave and I sank deeper against him, desperately grasping for the awareness sieving away from me. Somewhere, some place outside myself, I recognized the hands gliding over my stomach. My thighs. The heated words dancing along the shell of my ears and the pounding of feet blending with grotesque songs. Only god knew how much time passed before the Devil straightened his legs and sent me colliding with the floor.

Cold marble burned against my flushed skin. Sweat and tears dribbled off my face to the stone.

"I'm bored," the Devil declared. He threw a withering stare at Violet. All this time she eyed me with quiet resignation, but her own devilish smile now curled her face.

"Take her." Dismissive words, empty words, nothing like the playful flirtations I received in my dreams. Violet stood from her throne, muscles roiling like a predator beneath her skin. In one smooth motion she pulled me to my feet, pressing my back against her chest and holding my head against her shoulder.

Her sharp nail ran down the side of my face. "What would you like me to do with her, brother?"

"Throw her in the Abstruse. I'll make use of her later."

She bowed her head. "As you wish."

Cheering followed us, poking and prodding, licentious shouts. Fog nipped at our ankles as she dragged me down one hall, then another, until the sounds from the ballroom faded to silence and familiar double doors loomed ahead.

She marched through the foyer, then the study, pushing aside a colossal fern to reveal a hidden hall with a door at the end. She kicked it open with a swift crack and threw me to the floor.

I stared at her from the carpet, finding no words to speak.

She shook her head. "I warned you to stay asleep." The door slammed shut and darkness pulled me under.

ELEVEN

SOMETIME IN THE NIGHT, I'd crawled across the floor and into a sprawling, decadent bed. A fluffed, ivory comforter twisted between my legs and sparkling gossamer hung from four gold-capped posts. The curtains hung from the ceiling at random, turning the room into a labyrinth of swaying gauze. Embers burned in a stone fireplace, light leaked through floor-to-ceiling windows, and thick, green vines crept across the walls.

Despite my hammering head, I jerked upright.

"Take it easy."

I froze. I knew that voice. I knew it like the sky was blue and the grass was green and the reverence of silky river water flowing through my outstretched hands. Heart thudding against my chest, I willed my breath to slow and turned. Breezy gossamer swayed on a warm breeze, and serpentine eyes blinked behind them.

But when I pulled the curtain aside, Jack Warren stared at me.

Dark circles ringed his eyes. A crumpled suit hung off his shoulders and he clenched his cane like it personally offended him.

I waited for him to speak. He didn't. I fingered the edge of my nightdress, willing my heartbeat to slow. One sharp canine tugged his lower lip into his mouth. He closed his eyes. The flowers and sparkling curtains flowed around us, picking up as if in a momentous breeze, but all the windows were closed.

"I will spend the rest of my life rectifying last night." His eyes sprung open, normal eyes, human eyes, so I couldn't understand why my muscles ached to run. "Someone was here that would have killed you if he knew what you are. I did not want him to suspect anything, which I know is not entirely convincing, but I hope you know I mean you no harm."

"What am I?" I gripped the comforter between sweaty fingers. "Better yet, what are you?"

"Well, to start, I'm not the Devil." He ran his thumb over his lips. "Though if I ever run into him, I'll be sure to take notes."

I wasn't sure if that was meant to be a joke. My breath shuddered past my teeth, fingers still clenched tight around the blanket. The room was unfamiliar, the *bed* unfamiliar, and I suddenly wondered if he had made good on his promises last night. Memories returned in flashes—arriving at the hotel, a lithe dryad gripping me by the hair, my dark prince's cruel smile and the feeling of a hand roaming my thigh.

I'll make use of her later.

"And I?"

His head tilted to the side, golden eyes scouring me. "You are mine."

"I think I would remember agreeing to that."

"You didn't," he whispered. "But that does not change fate, *annwyl*. So, here I am—" He lifted his cane, snagging a monstrous fang against my shoulder strap, tugging it until it slipped down my shoulder "—and here *you* are."

I shivered, pushing the pommel aside and sweeping the lace back onto my shoulder. "This is inappropriate."

"Is it?" His eyebrow lifted. "You begged me in your own bed just last month."

My blood heated to a boil, then solidified back to ice. Two truths lay before me, equally terrifying with disastrous results: I was not insane. But since I was not insane, since everything was real, that meant . . . that meant that . . .

"What *are* you?" I asked again.

"Fair folk, nothing you have not seen before."

"I've seen devil-folk, and last time I checked they don't look so . . ." The word I was about to use died in my throat. Human. I was about to say human.

His eyes narrowed, evaluating. I had an awful feeling I just revealed something important. "Then I would say you have only seen low fae."

"And that makes you . . ."

"High fae, the sidhe, people of the hills; rotten bastards, take your pick."

That was certainly a joke, but I didn't laugh. Neither did he. In fact, he stared at me with an intensity that made me shudder. *Just because we don't wish for your death, does not mean we are your friends.* He said he meant me no harm, but I'd be a fool to believe him.

I scanned the room. Besides the gossamer curtains, vines, and hellish creature seated beside me, there was an empty armoire and dresser, a mirrored vanity throwing back my reflection, and a door leading to a marble powder room. The door to exit was shut. Even worse, I would have to pass Mr. Warren to reach it. Or whatever his name really was.

"Do you require something?" He asked.

More memories, this time Lillian's lyrical sing-song. *Whatever you do, don't eat or drink* anything *in this hotel.*

My head pounded ferociously, my mouth parched. I shook my head. "I think I would like to leave now."

Ignoring that, he murmured, "We call this room the Abstruse. It can be warded against anything, but what makes it especially important is that no one has the ability to lie in here." He leaned forward and I back, keeping equal distance between us. "So I will ask

110

you this, and I would like you to choose your next words very carefully. What brought you here last night?"

"Money." I could have mentioned Violet's visit to my apartment, but decided to omit it. The less he knew the better.

My answer dissatisfied him. Survival instincts told me to placate him, but when I opened my mouth no words came out. I spoke them in my mind, *And I wanted to see you,* but there was no sound.

"Did anyone bring you here?"

"No."

"Did you speak to anyone inside the hotel?"

"The dryad and two others who brought me to the ballroom, but that was all." The words rushed out before I could stop them, the dam of my teeth failing to halt the flow of confessions.

"Did you recognize that man, Delsaran?"

The foggy image of a man with an aura of darkness surfaced. I shook my head.

"Where did you come from?"

I pressed my lips together, nose scrunching as I gritted out, "Georgia."

"Where in Georgia?"

Sweat broke on my hairline. I shook my head.

"Where in Georgia?" Each word came slower than the last, my face twitching as my mouth scrambled to answer.

"Shouldn't you already know that?" I asked instead. He followed that question with, "Where is your father?"

My heart squeezed in my chest. "Dead."

His teeth clenched. "Thought so."

Breaths froze in my lungs, my fingers rigid where I splayed them in my lap. Clearly, he didn't kill Papa, but had he planned to?

I needed to leave, now. But who knew what this man was capable of, or what else roamed this cursed hotel. If I spent the remainder of my days with no answers about what Jack Warren was or why he

111

could enter my dreams, it was a minor sacrifice. The only problem: I didn't think he was about to let me go. I had no weapons, no help, not even an idea of how to escape this.

"What do you want?" I asked.

His answer took a long moment to form, as if he had to choose carefully. "You."

Not the answer I desired to hear. A tepid breeze fluttered through the room, billowing the sparkling cloth drifting from the ceiling. The edge of one lifted beside the bed, obscuring Mr. Warren's face. Through the film, pointed ears stuck from his hair and black tattoos scattered his neck. It drifted back to the floor and he appeared human again. My eyes drifted to his hip. The breeze took the edge of his jacket, revealing a pistol strapped against his hip.

"You want . . . me?" Both a familiar and foreign sensation swirled in my chest. The tug. Oppressive energy pushed against my ribs, a dark warmth that soothed my breaths. My skin heated, hair raising along my arms. Jack leaned forward.

"Yes."

The tug swelled, growing to the point of suffocation, taking every inch of space that air should have occupied. Warmth deepened, becoming need. Dark thoughts formed, clashing with remnants of clarity. "Why?"

He ran his tongue over his teeth, hand clutching the armchair. "Reasons."

"How do you want me?" I pushed the covers back. My pale legs shimmered in the watery sunlight, the simple swath of satin gathered at my hips. His eyes traced the lace hemline, skimming every dip and rise of my legs and back up again. Power rolled off him in landslides, drawing me deeper and deeper into his orbit.

Another breeze curled the room, warm as red wine and colder than ice. The tug no longer pulled. It *snapped*. My focus shot to Mr. Warren's face, his golden eyes, his dark hair, the heated breaths he tried to quell under a facade of calm. Rain and oleander overtook my senses, rich and heady. Suddenly, I was cold. Cold and desperate and *empty.* But if I could touch his skin, if I could taste his lips, if I could feel him inside me . . .

"How. Do you. Want me?" A cobwebbed corner of my mind screamed to stop. To grab the gun off his hip and run and run and run. But it wasn't strong enough, not compared to the beckoning of his presence. Images flitted behind my eyes, of color-streaked hills, poison flowers blooming and shrinking beneath a tattooed palm, ragged whispers and warm skin. If I followed him, if I let him, that was where I would go.

He didn't answer. I fell to my hands and knees, sinking into the mattress. It put us at eye level, and that felt right. To be on equal grounds. To edge closer to him. To feel the air leave my lungs and enter his.

His golden eyes darkened, pupils swallowing the sunlit color. The arm of the chair creaked beneath his grip, but he slid closer and closer to the edge of his seat. "Just like that," he whispered.

I moved forward.

He growled low. "Just like that, darling. Crawl to me."

Heat shot down my spine and pooled low at the base. I was panting my needs now, my desires. The thin nightgown fell forward revealing my breasts, stealing all of Jack's attention. My hands slid to the end of the bed and I leaned forward, nose-to-nose with him. The musky scent of him rolled off in waves, the heat from his body licking at my skin. My eyes flicked to his lips, waiting, asking . . . *This isn't me.*

His fingers came beneath my chin. "I've missed you."

My eyes fluttered close, a ragged breath passing my teeth. He clenched my face, smoothing his thumb over my lips. I tasted leather. He still had those goddamn gloves on, and I needed them gone. I needed to feel him. A pathetic whimper trembled in my throat. When I opened my eyes, he sucked the last remaining light from me.

"Anything you want, *annwyl*." He leaned closer, breath skirting my cheek, lips only a hair's breadth from mine. "Anything at all."

His head jerked to the side, preternatural stillness seizing him. Not a single hair on his head moved. His eyes didn't blink, and I felt his pulse all but leave the fingers around my jaw. I'd never seen a human simply . . . stop, like that, only animals frozen beneath an impending threat.

But there was no threat. This man was not twitching game hidden in the grass. He was the predator.

His nostrils flared, teeth clenched. He turned back to me and he was no longer a man at all. Eyes like a serpent shimmered in the morning light, his vertical pupils narrowed on my lips.

"Don't leave this room." He didn't so much as glance at me, rising with unnatural grace. My eyes snagged on his fluid movements, the muscles roiling beneath his clothes. The door clicked shut behind him.

What the hell.

I pressed a fluttering hand to my heart, breathing heavy through the racing beats. My mind cleared into a cloudless sky, but it left more questions than answers. What were we just doing? Why did I think like that, why did I *act* like that? The tug returned to my chest, but grew fainter with each second. Now was not the time to think. Now was the time to leave.

I jumped to my feet and ran to the door. Nothing but silence filtered through the thick wood. Counting to ten, I steeled myself and turned the knob, not daring to breathe.

The study was empty at the end of a dark hall, but voices carried down from the foyer.

"Why the fuck do you smell like that?" Jack.

"I had some fun myself last night, and since you have kept me so busy with all your drama, there wasn't exactly time to wash." Violent Warren, I had no doubt about it. Two thumps hit the stone, presumably her shoes.

I released the doorknob as softly as I could, shimmying through the crack in the doorway.

"Tell me, how is our human guest faring?"

I inched across the stones, clutching the shadowy jungle of greenery encasing the walls.

"What do you want, Violet?"

"Nothing, truly. I simply enjoy watching my brother sink deeper into his biggest mistake. It's quite entertaining."

I reached the end of the hall, not daring to breathe as I peeked around the corner through a lush, potted tree. Jack and Violet—or whatever their real names were—stood in the open doorway between the foyer and study. She leaned against the doorjamb, sipping a drink.

"An excellent show you put on, by the way. Though I wonder how much our little mortal enjoyed it." She pouted, hands pressed together in a bastardized prayer. "You put the pretty little thing on her knees and she prayed to the Christian lord. That must have been *so* disappointing for you."

His jaw set, casting a look to where I stood. I flattened myself against the wall, squeezing my eyes shut.

After a moment, he sighed. "Go home."

"I would, but clearly you don't understand the consequences of your fucking actions anymore."

"I understand them fine."

"She is not the answer to our problems. She will create them, and whatever lies between you shouldn't have obscured that. You've had your time."

"So the better answer was to hide her from me again?"

"You don't have the fucking balls to send her away. I was doing you a favor."

Their argument turned low and hushed, but I'd already heard all I needed. I looked around, thinking of any way out. I had no way to know of more secret halls or doors, and the siblings stood between myself and the only exit I knew.

The Abstruse's door creaked open on a phantom breeze. Sunlight poured through the massive window. A window with no screens. A window with no lock, as far as I could see.

My heart jumped to my throat.

The bickering ceased. Violet asked something, but Jack told her to hush. I stood, shaking, willing my pulse to slow. Finally, he said, "I don't have time for this."

"We are *not* done here."

The hushed moment felt too sudden, too timed. He sensed something, through hearing or scent or some other sense, I couldn't be sure. After all, it seemed he had scented Violet coming through the door.

Like an animal.

My heart kicked up as another thought came to me.

If you don't be quiet, he'll sense you. Violet had said that in my living room. And the tug, it had to mean something. It wasn't all in my head.

I surveyed the shadowed hall. Flowers and vines ensconced the walls, wisteria, deadly nightshade and many others, all poisonous. To my right, a cluster of foxglove grew from crevices in the stone.

In my dreams, Jack always instructed me to harvest certain flowers and plants, most deadly in large doses, but he said it himself. Medicine was nothing but a well-dosed poison, and I'd been taught what ingesting these plants could do. Deadly nightshade caused hallucinations, wisteria induced vomiting, azaleas made one foam at the mouth and hemlock caused one to seize, but foxglove slowed down the heart . . . in small doses. In large ones, it killed you.

Before I could think better of it, I tore off a single petal and chewed. Slowly.

The effect was immediate. I spit out the rest, breathing easier, my heartbeat turning dull and slow in my chest. As if sensing that too, Jack's voice grew more demanding, insisting they discuss this another time.

The hall tilted sideways. Ignoring it, I padded back into the bedroom and shut the door with a soft click. I flung the window open and peered out, praying my dropping stomach wouldn't give me away.

High up was an understatement. The street loomed several hundred feet below, already busy with rushing people and cars blowing exhaust into the warm, breezy morning. But a stone balcony jutted into the air only two stories below. The building was old, styled with endless nooks, crannies and ledges. If I was careful, if I was slow, I could make it.

I debated turning the sheets into a rope, but there was little time. I'd have to scramble the walls, praying that a drop would put me on the balcony and not the street. Then, pray hitting the balcony wouldn't snap my legs.

I took several deep breaths, fighting against a wave of nausea. My heart echoed in my chest with a dull thump. It was only fifteen feet, possibly less. I stood at five feet and seven inches, so really, it wasn't that far of a drop. Nothing I couldn't handle.

My vision went black the entire way down. Somewhere, faintly, I recognized the tear of my stockings on gravelly stone, my bleeding fingers digging into crumbling crevices and my glass-torn feet braced against wind-blasted ledges. I fell to the balcony and took a deep breath, willing myself to stand. Glass doors swung open to an empty hotel room, save for an open suitcase and messy sheets. Mind slipping back into darkness, I only came to when I stood on the street, braced against a lamppost while a doorman asked if I needed assistance.

Great, I had escaped, but what now?

Bleeding feet moved beneath me and my head lolled on my shoulders. The check was gone, probably eaten by the swine man or ceremoniously burned in the fire last night. I had no money, and just because Jack wasn't there didn't mean my apartment was safe. But I still had one resource left.

"Good morning, chicky! What a pleasant surprise." Lillian's face dropped as I swayed in her doorway. "What the hell happened to you?"

"Can I borrow two dollars?"

"Um, well, I suppose." She didn't move. "You don't look so good, Addie. And why are you in your nightgown? Heavens, where are your shoe—"

"I really need it," I breathed, conveying silently there would be no more questions. Guilt ate at me knowing I'd already stolen from her, and used her in a plot against Jack Warren; but none of that mattered now. I had a high fae to run from, and for all I knew she was one of—

I stopped. Thinking, breathing, all of it. Taking in her tall, lithe form, her ethereal beauty, I wondered just how large Jack's network was. How many of these *things* roamed the streets, wearing human disguises and living among us?

Crossing her arms, she frowned, leaning against the doorway. "Can I be honest, Addie?"

My fingers bunched in my dress. "Of course."

"You really don't look good," she said, scouring my face. "I heard some noise last night and made a call. I know someone came to help you."

Yes, someone did. Violet Warren, demon incarnate. "It's been handled, thank you."

Chewing on her bottom lip, she continued, "Saying this as plainly as possible, you look terrible. May I at least ask what the money is for? Perhaps I can help."

"It's personal. Please, Lillian, it's only two dollars. I can pay you back in a few days."

"I know it seems strange, but if you need help you should ask Mr. Warren. He'll—"

"No."

She blinked.

"I don't feel comfortable with that, we're strangers."

"Okay." She retrieved the money, holding onto the bills longer than necessary. I crumbled them in my fist.

"Don't tell Jack."

Neither of us moved. A heated second passed before a pained smile stretched her lips. She nodded. "Of course not."

We said rushed goodbyes, neither admitting we knew it was a lie.

TWELVE

I RAN FOR GRAND Central Station like my life depended on it. Which, funnily enough, it did. I had two dollars to my name. I wore nothing but torn stockings and a dirty, satin nightgown. Men leered at me and women covered their children's eyes. A police officer cornered me on 46th street, but I ducked into an alley and outran him.

A tired teller eyed me from behind a window in the glittering, extravagant ticket booth. "Where are you going?"

"The soonest train I can depart on for two dollars. Chicago, if you can." My first mission was to get as far from here as possible. I'd have no more money, but I'd worry about that at the next stop. Once I had a few more dollars I would contact Tommy and rendezvous with him in the midwest. Then, we were getting the hell out of dodge. Forever.

I shoved the crumpled bills beneath the glass, bouncing on my heels.

He stared at me.

"*Now.*"

He muttered something under his breath, stamping a ticket and tearing it off the roll. "Chicago. Track eleven. Departs in three minutes."

I made it just in time, collapsing on a faded, wooden bench. Another sprouted from muddy carpets directly across from me, running beneath the windows. Anyone sitting near me scattered. A woman with two young children gawked from the opposite side of the car, urging them to move along and find somewhere else to sit.

My feet were torn to ribbons, coated in a nice layer of dirt and blood. My nightdress hung dangerously low and the hem fell just below my knees. I hadn't looked in a mirror in days and doubted my face fared much better. Purple bruises swelled up and down my arms.

That was only what you could physically see. After the train ticket, I had exactly twenty-five cents left. I rubbed the green-tinged quarter between sweaty fingers. It was enough for food, salt and a phone call. Tommy would have anything else we needed.

No longer caring about decency, I pulled my knees to my chest and wrapped my arms around them. An older woman turned three shades of red across from me. Her companion made a strange noise and turned away. A door slid open and men's rowdy laughter filled the car, smoke billowing out the window as the train rolled forward.

The older couple exited for a different car. I pulled my arms tighter around my knees.

Four men fell into rows of seats where the wooden benches ended and became an aisle. All wore impeccable, gray, double-breasted suits, but that wasn't of concern. They each donned a bowler hat, dyed a peculiar shade of maroon.

One of them caught my stare, sporting a wolfish grin. "Nice gams, sweetheart."

I pulled what remained of my nightgown over my legs.

He folded his arms on the seat in front him, resting his chin on his wrists. "Come on, we were enjoying the view."

The other three burst into laughter. I stood, wincing when my aching feet hit the hardwood, breezing past them for the next car. Before I could pass the row of seats, one reached out and latched a hand around my wrist. I froze. He pressed his nose to my skin and took a deep, guttural breath.

121

Then he *licked* me. Right over the pulsing artery he clasped.

I wrenched my hand back as a memory swelled. The last time I was on a train, reading Tommy's folded newspaper beside his thigh. *THE BLOODY BOWLERS STRIKE AGAIN.*

Their red hats glinted in the morning sun. I stepped back.

"What does she smell like?" One asked, his nasally voice a companion to his weasel-like face.

"I can't be sure, but she's glamour-touched," said the man who licked my wrist.

Nerves fired behind my skull, discomfort to unease to startling awareness. Chills erupted in rapid succession, fight or flight hitting in full force.

I'd only taken one step when another caught my ankle, sending me face-first into the floor. My forehead smacked the hardwood and iron exploded behind my teeth. Screaming and clawing the ground, I fought sharp nails digging into my shins while two men dragged me to the back of the car. The rows of seats ended, leaving the floor wide open between the empty benches lining the wall. I sobbed, kicking and shrieking with a sound that split my own ears.

"Lock the doors," my captor called. A doughy man with ruddy cheeks set off to complete the task. The remaining three fell to their knees, pinned my limbs to the floor and observed.

"She seems familiar."

"Her face *and* her scent, don't you think?"

"Shit, that's what it is."

"What?"

"The scent. It's Jack Warren."

Oh no. God, please no. No, no, no.

I thrashed harder, screaming through their serrated nails tearing my skin. It did nothing to dissuade their conversation, now echoing with scratchy laughter. The man who licked me covered my mouth.

He shrieked and jerked his hand back when my teeth sank into his thumb.

"Bitch," he spat, sucking on the wound. "I recognize the stupid cunt, but she didn't look glamour-touched last night. You think he was hiding it?"

"Does it matter?" Weasel-face said, hat tipped low on his brow. He yanked my wrists above my head. "Kill her and soak her blood. We can give whatever's left to Delsaran."

My foot connected with the doughy one's jaw, eliciting a howl. I sobbed, throwing myself side to side, pitching my limbs from their greedy claws, but it was no use. When one hand left another replaced it, when one creature hissed in pain another held me down. I would die. All of this, my survival in New York, my blackmail, my escape from Jack, just to die on the train that was supposed to lead me to freedom.

"Oh, Danny boy, the pipes, the pipes are calling . . ."

The fae men froze, glancing at one another in snarled confusion. The melodic voice rose above the train's horn, soft as a summer breeze, *" . . . from glen to glen and down the mountainside. The summer's gone and all the roses dying, tis you, tis you must go and I must bide . . ."*

Weasel-face dropped my wrists. "What in fucking hell?"

The car door slid open at my feet, revealing Violet Warren. Golden eyes shimmered, a massive snake wrapped around her shoulders, and a sword dangled from each hand.

"What in fucking hell?" I echoed.

A savage smile lifted her lips. The metal grating clanked and sparked beneath her kitten heels. *"Oh Danny boy, I love you so."* Dragging the last note long and slow, she sighed with theatrical flair. "I simply adore a depressing ballad. How about you, boys?"

The doughy man growled. "It's neutral territory, Violet."

"Yes, but that's not," she said, pointing a taloned nail at me. Her snake hissed beside her head. "Anyway, I will be taking the girl now.

You may want to scatter before my brother arrives. I do believe he plans to kill you all."

The man who licked me hissed, rivaling the snake.

"Oh, come on, don't make me dirty my dress." She swung a sword over the floor like a pendulum, loose between her fingers. "I just had this cleaned."

"You have no right," Weasel-face snapped.

"I have every right."

"Under what laws?"

She frowned, tossing a hand in the air. "Under the law of 'I am Violet Warren and may do whatever the fuck I wish?'"

"Then you will answer to Delsaran."

She clicked her tongue. "Wrong thing to say." One second she hummed Danny Boy in the doorway, the next she stood before weasel-face, plunging a sword through his neck.

Hot blood of the darkest black sprayed the car. I screamed, scrambling back until I lay beneath one of the faded benches. A large thump hit the ground and Violet's snake slithered past, flickering its forked tongue in my direction.

I slapped a hand to my mouth, holding back a sob.

A crack split the air. The man who licked me fell, limbs bent at odd angles, but Violet was nowhere near him. A second sharp crack. A third. His arms snapped at the elbows, knees fracturing backward. The impeccable suit writhed over his skin, limp where it used to be fitted. The velvet hat melted around his face, transforming into a cloak. The decrepit beast dropped to all fours.

Eyes of pitch black fell over me.

I screamed, clawing from my place beneath the bench, but there was nowhere to go. The monster scuttled across the floor, screeching and spitting blood. I covered my face, waiting to be torn apart. Instead, heavy, suffocating silence descended.

My fingers spread, slowly, just enough to see dark fog roll through the car.

A hushed thump hit the floor, a man's shoe. Another. Darkness crept across the ground, leaching from the black leather—circles of death with each step he took. A cloying scent infiltrated the air and vomit roared up my throat. Deadly nightshade sprouted from the burn marks scorched in the wood, bright violet petals writhing in the fog.

A sword struck down from the heavens and buried itself in the floor. The creature screeched and dark fluid sprayed my hands and face. I rubbed acrid blood from my eyes, sputtering and seething. Black, leather shoes filled my vision.

I stopped breathing. Stopped thinking. My gaze slowly lifted up. Golden, serpentine eyes met mine, but this time, they didn't belong to Violet.

At the other end of the car, her laughter danced with the clang of steel.

Jack sheathed his sword—one with a pommel identical to his cane—into a black metal holster. Only when he rapped it on the ground did I realize they were one and the same. I remained frozen. A derisive smirk took his lips.

He held out a hand. "Please, get up."

I stared, entranced by the face I saw every month for the past two years. The face my pastor thought a hellish apparition, my brother thought a fantasy and my father thought the Devil himself. But he was none of those things—he was alive, and in front of me. He reached down and yanked me to my feet.

"Well, that's just wonderful. The last bastard ran." Violet sheathed her swords, staring out the back of the train car. "Take your girlfriend home. I'm going after him."

"I'm not—"

"I don't give a fuck," she snapped. I stepped back and she lowered her voice. "He will tell Delsaran what she is."

Jack jerked his chin at the open door. "Go. I will see you back at the hotel."

Without a moment of hesitation, she leapt from the train car. In a flickering, sunlit moment, I watched her duck and roll onto the grassy plain we roared past.

I stumbled backward. "I'm not going anywhere with you."

"*Annwyl*, let me—"

"Don't call me that." I shivered, wrapping my arms around my torso. I'd never seen those things before, whatever they were. How many fae existed, how did they appear human and roam the streets . . .

I'd been so lost in shock, I didn't notice the moment he reached for me. His bare hand met mine, black leather glove tossed to the blood-soaked floor. A moment of euphoria. Sun-kissed bliss, peonies perfuming the air, the crackling warmth of flames—

We were in Times Square.

A barrage of horns went off and a car swerved around me. People yelped, ducking out of the way. Lights flashed and taxi drivers cursed, a man from the press cornered the sidewalk, flashing pictures as people passed. Officers on horses trotted down the street and children chased each other through the crowd. I turned in a circle, panting, losing feeling in my fingers and toes.

Jack cursed under his breath. "Addie, I need you to work with me. We can't be here."

I shook my head and plunged into the crowd.

His cane clicked the asphalt behind me, echoing through the cacophony of sound. "*Adeline.*"

Running to the nearest cop, I clutched his horse's mane in my fists and screamed, "You have to help me. There's a man, and he's following me, and—"

Eyes wide, the police officer nodded along as I rambled complete nonsense. His frown melted into a smile and he tipped his hat at someone behind me. "Good morning, Mr. Warren."

Jack seized my waist, pulling me against his chest. "Sorry lad, you might have to excuse this one. She had a bit too much fun at the hotel last night."

"I wouldn't expect anything less," he said, tipping his hat once more and trotting to another street corner. I screamed, turned in Jack's arms and rammed my hands against his chest.

"Get off of me."

"If you would just let me—"

"No!"

He released me and I fell into the road. Before he could grab me again, I clambered to my feet and dove for an empty side street.

Again, that goddamned cane clicked close behind, a heated voice calling, "What do you want to know?"

I whirled. *"Everything.* Tell me *everything,* Jack!"

Still as stone, both hands clutching his cane, he watched me through the streaming crowd. Horns blared, people chattered, birds chirped, buskers sang, foot traffic filtered around and between us, a never ending current of noise and light and sound. He raised his hand and snapped.

Everything stopped.

The people. The birds. The very air set to stone. All around us, people froze halfway into their stride, lifting cigarettes to their mouths, mid-chatter, as if god himself came down and declared time no longer existed.

Maybe he did.

I dropped to my knees.

"What . . . what did you do?"

"It only lasts a few minutes." He fell beside me, grunting as he folded his bad leg beneath him. As if my body had had too much, I melted into the ground, not stopping until I lay flat against the pavement, facing a bright summer sky.

Jack lay next to me, folding one arm beneath his head.

"You're not human." Laughter bubbled up my throat, high-pitched and ridiculous because truly, the notion was absurd. Tamping it down, I folded my shaking hands over my stomach and focused on a drifting cloud.

"Never have been."

"And you have god-sent magical powers?"

"Not your god." A moment of hesitation, then he added, "What gods mean to humans and what they mean to us are very different."

Clutching the fabric of my blood-stained dress, I whispered, "Those things on the train, what were they?"

"Redcaps, nasty species. They soak their hats in the blood of their kills. I prefer not to allow them under my jurisdiction, but my rival doesn't share the sentiment."

Delsaran, I assumed. "Everyone keeps saying I'm glamour-touched, what does that mean?"

Wind whistled down the silent alley and the sun beamed down. A full minute passed before he said, "Somewhere, very far back in your ancestry, someone had a child with a fae. Power doesn't follow standard inheritance patterns. Sometimes it skips entire generations, sometimes it doesn't appear at all. But a piece of it got into you, making you for all intents and purposes, a small percentage fae."

"What does that do?"

"It varies." On a telephone wire above, a bird shook out its feathers, releasing a croaking chirp. "For most, it allows you to see through glamour if the fae using it is unsuspecting, or it isn't a particularly strong illusion."

"So glamour is an illusion? That's how you can look human, or why no one but me sees the other fae?"

He nodded, hair crunching against the road.

"Is there anything else?"

"With you, I don't know yet. As I said, it varies."

With you. He had an unsettling interest in me, but I didn't understand it yet.

"Was I truly seeing you in my dreams?"

A second pigeon broke free of the spell, shaking its fat, slate-gray body. "Yes. The iron necklace you always wore, the salt and the river, these things hid you from me. But during the new moon, the veil—the curtain between this world and another—is at its thinnest, so our powers are stronger, both yours and mine." He spared a glance at me. "I couldn't see where you were, or find you, but I could see and talk to you in those dreams."

Shivers ran down my spine. Tommy always told me to follow my instincts, that my gut was smarter than my brain. Right now, every fiber of me screamed once I asked my next question, there would be no coming back from it.

"Are we connected somehow?"

Out loud, it sounded so ridiculous I almost wished I could take it back. Even with the dreams, the feeling in my chest, the strange thoughts and feelings whenever he was near, it had to be something else. A connection between us was completely implausible, something that shouldn't be possible.

Any notion of my brain creating false realities faded as he whispered, "Yes."

My voice cracked. "Did my father know?"

It took so long for his answer to come, I feared he would leave me in the dark. "Yes."

Horns blew, voices erupted and a bicycle rider careened around us, spitting curses. Jack pushed to his feet faster than any man with a cane should have been able to, reaching for me. "It's not safe here, but we can talk more at the hotel."

His outstretched hand hovered before my face, tattoos reflecting the morning light.

A choice. Take his hand and discover the truth or take my chances and attempt another escape. The latter tempted me, the ignorance in bliss a draw I could no longer deny. Yesterday, my biggest problem was paranoia, a brother in Chicago, and the uphill battle of finding my way home. Today, it was everything I never could have imagined.

Closing my eyes, I placed my hand in his.

THIRTEEN

ONE MOMENT THE SOUNDS of Times Square flooded my ears, the next, crushing silence. A sense of free-falling dropped my stomach, a darkness so thick I wondered if this was hell. Air whooshed past, condensed and suffocating like liquid but cold and dry as bone. My limbs pushed forward, fighting a current dragging me deeper. I blinked and we were in the study.

Stumbling, the world tilted and warped as I smacked a hand against one of the wooden bookshelves. A fire roared in the back of the room, vines rasped along the wall, and a bright voice exclaimed, "Thank goodness, you are both alright."

The room came into focus. Lillian stood from one of the velvet settees with a hand over her heart. Beside her sat William Porter and the reed-thin blond I saw the night I met Jack. The former played with a dagger while the latter became suspiciously interested in his book.

"Where's Violet?" Mr. Porter asked.

"She will return soon." I jumped, forgetting all sense of time and space as Jack appeared next to me. It was a testament to how poorly I felt after . . . whatever he did, because I didn't protest as his arm came around my waist and he dragged me to one of the couches.

"The first few times are the worst, I promise," Lillian said, falling beside me and dabbing at my forehead with a silk cloth. "If you need to vomit, just let me—"

I doubled over, retching onto the expensive carpet.

"It's only seven hundred years old," the blond murmured.

"Be polite, Arthur. You must remember what it was like." Lillian rolled her eyes around a grin, shrugging as if to say, *Men, what will we do with them?*

Men, women . . . were any of these people actually—

"I have to say, I am so delighted you know everything now. It was getting quite tedious always having to hide and lie, and gods, glamour can be so *itchy* on your face all day and . . ." I tuned out her nonsensical stream, only focusing again when she added, " . . . but now that you are aware of the parallel and all that, we can start planning your ceremony. I have to tell you, I've never seen one of these and I am just bursting at the seams. I've heard some humans like to use traditional wedding gowns, but if that's not your style I know a veil-crosser who can get—"

I held up my hand. "What did you just say?"

But at that moment, Violet kicked open the study doors. Blood doused her head to toe, scowling and hissing like a cat thrown in water.

"He got to the boundary before I could catch up. I hope you're happy we are all fucked now." The last line came directed at me. Throwing her swords onto the floor, she collapsed upon the futon closest to the blond man, Arthur.

Mr. Porter grinned. "Violet, you look absolutely radiant today."

"Oh, piss off, Will," she spat, then turned to Jack, who had done nothing but stand quietly against the desk this entire time. "He will report this to Delsaran, you know that, right?"

"I'm aware."

"Well, I'm glad everyone's just so fucking nonchalant about this." Her hands rocketed into the air before smacking back to the cushion.

"We always expected him to find out, it was just a matter of when," Lillian added.

"Yes, but it could have been later rather than sooner," Arthur murmured, still focused on his book.

"It could have been never," Violet snapped. "Was it worth it, Jack, really—"

"I would like five minutes alone with Adeline." The bickering stopped. When we all did nothing but stare at Jack, he quietly added, "Please."

A cruel smile curled Violet's face. "Shouldn't there be a chaperone? You know, just in case you can't control yourself?"

No one rebuked it, whatever was intended. The two stared at one another. His voice dropped to a deathly chill, the low note of, "Get out."

She snickered, pushing to her feet. "Remember, don't touch him," she called back to me. A moment later, the rest shuffled out. Will, avoiding eye contact, Lillian, smiling sheepishly and Arthur, still reading his book.

That left the two of us.

Jack settled directly across from me, knees apart and cane resting between them. We didn't speak. He looked human again, but something about those too-bright golden eyes settled beneath my skin, coiling like snakes under my flesh. His mouth formed a tight line when I asked, "What was Violet talking about?"

A dismissive wave of his hand. "She's just being Violet."

I highly doubted that was the whole truth, especially considering what happened earlier. Resisting the urge to bounce my knee against the faded, seven-hundred-year-old carpet, I said, "What did you need to speak about?"

Closing his eyes, he leaned his head back and sighed. "Nothing, I just needed five minutes of silence before dealing with all of this."

Unsure if that was a polite way of telling me to keep my mouth shut, I wrung my hands in my lap and pretended this was all perfectly, pleasantly normal. That the man sitting across from me wasn't some inhuman creature wearing human skin, we hadn't just . . . *popped* into the middle of a room on top of a skyscraper, and four other people weren't undoubtedly standing outside the door, listening to heavy silence.

He stared at me.

That visceral energy coated my skin, heavy and warm. The sensation of skin drifting over mine, softened breath, something deep and primitive. No other words existed to explain the pulsing presence between us, so thick and tangible I almost swiped the air to see if an invisible string tugged me toward him. In a foggy corner of my mind I remembered Violet's harsh retorts about control, not touching him.

I really, really wanted to.

I couldn't explain why. We didn't know one another outside of dreams, we weren't even the same *species*, yet his presence in the room was more familiar than my own flesh. Like where my soul ended his began, where he existed I did too, and that was the most terrifying part of all of this. *If you don't calm down, he'll sense you.* Because there was something between us, some connection, that went beyond my understanding.

Dark eyes raked up my body, starting at the tips of my feet and hovering at the curve of my waist. Suppressing a shiver, I pulled my arms around myself and casually said, "What is it you need to deal with?"

I both prayed for and dreaded the answer having something to do with me. But arcane sensations and feelings aside, I had to approach this with a level head. I was in danger, that much was obvious. He knew how to find me, knew how to *sense* me, and I had a feeling taking his hand in Times Square was something I would sorely regret.

My pulse stopped and pooled low in my stomach when he answered, "What I plan to do with you."

134

I had ideas—several, in fact—about what he could do with me. That dream I didn't think was a dream fluttered to the forefront of my memory. Lips devouring mine, hands roaming up my thighs, an insatiable need only one thing could satisfy.

I shook my head. "You promised me answers."

"And I will give them to you," he said, slowly, restrained. I wondered if I should have requested that chaperone after all.

But he only stood, leaning a little too heavily on his cane and gesturing for me to follow. Legs wobbling, I pushed to my feet and followed him around his desk, where he sifted through a pile of news clippings, shoving one my way. It was a story about some gangster in Chicago, a black and white mugshot I vaguely recognized.

"Have you heard of him?"

I shook my head.

"Daniel Harrow," Jack murmured. "As this world currently knows him, at least. Everyone else calls him Delsaran."

Right, the person who kept murderous fae close to him. The one who those same creatures said they would send my carcass to. The man standing on his soapbox in the hotel last night, an aura of darkness pulsing around his skin, telling a crowd how he wanted to . . .

I swallowed. "Is he like you?"

"No. He is a druid." Realizing I hadn't the faintest clue what that meant, he continued, "Once, he was human. Glamour-touched. They all start that way, but once they become this, they're just as powerful as any high fae. Some even moreso."

"And you didn't want him to know I existed?"

"No," he said, the word a little too heated to be casual. "But that was inevitable, since I need you to help me kill him."

If I had anything left in me to laugh, I would have. About a million reasons why that was the most ridiculous thing I'd ever heard crowded my brain, but I wasn't given time to utter a single one of them. "Before you give me your vehement refusal, allow me to explain the rest of it."

"Absolutely not." A nervous chuckle escaped my throat, and I stepped back. "Let me guess, this is mob related. Is he also a bootlegger? I don't want any part of that, Mr. Warren, so I think it'd be best if I—"

"That feeling you are having right now—you know the one I'm talking about." It wasn't a question, and my mouth snapped closed. "The first time I felt that . . . tug, or however else you want to put it, was the day you were born."

I froze. "And?"

Golden eyes settled on me, heavy with inhumanity despite his current form. "I followed it to a hospital only a few blocks from here. To a room where a woman had just died giving birth to her second child, and the baby wasn't doing much better. They told the father she had the umbilical cord around her throat, lost too much oxygen and would likely only live for a few hours." He cocked his head to the side. "So I made a deal with him. I would save his daughter's life and she could remain with him until she was twenty years and twenty days old exactly, and then she would return to me."

"Instead," he continued, leaning closer. I backed away. "He ran off to Georgia with her and his older son, taught her to make salt circles around the house and mold iron bullets, all the time forgetting that a fae bargain is something you can never go back on. So when that girl turned twenty years and twenty days . . ." His voice faded off, and I lost the will to breathe.

"I don't know how he knew those things would hide you. That touching iron—" He jerked his chin at the empty space where my crucifix usually laid "—would effectively poison you, dampening your glamour-breaking abilities so you wouldn't see or hear fae. And I wish he knew those actions would eventually take his life, because that was never my intention, Adeline. Our powers just work that way."

"What do you want from me?" My papa. The man who always tried to protect me, who walked me to the river every night and taught me traditions that would keep me safe, keep me with *him*. The person who kissed every scraped knee and sang me to sleep every night. Who loved me so much he was convinced he made a deal with the Devil himself so I could keep my life.

"Right now, I want nothing more than for you to listen to me."

He lied. He had to be lying, because he just told me the reason I had no father anymore, the reason my papa left this world was all because of a bargain they struck twenty years ago.

"No," I said, backing away. I knew I should be careful, but I no longer cared that he wasn't human, that he had powers I couldn't begin to understand. I had no doubt he could kill me without lifting a finger, but none of it mattered. My papa. Gone because of a gangster, these fae creatures, a twisted game I somehow found myself in without ever agreeing.

Papa warned me the fae would come for him my entire life, and he was right.

"Humans are in danger." For all the emotion he gave those four words, he may as well have said the sky was blue. "This man, Daniel Harrow, he isn't a man anymore. He has no allegiance to humans and he has plans that will change everything. What he wants and what I want are two very different things, Adeline, and I assure you once you hear the rest you may be more inclined to help us."

"I know what you are. I will never work with your kind."

Silence swirled around us, heavy and thick. The fireplace popped and crackled, the vines slithered along the walls, but I said nothing. Felt nothing. Because if I let all that rage and fear consume me now, there was no way I could survive.

"I am going to let the others back in now," he said. His stoic mask cracked, his deep swallow filling the room. "Hear what they have to say before you make up your mind."

FOURTEEN

I'D BEEN CORRECT IN my earlier assumption. They all waited directly on the other side of the door.

One by one they shuffled in, silent as death, settling among the hodge-podge of seats and plants forming the middle of the room. Only Violet seemed unbothered, wearing a self-satisfied smirk as she sauntered in and reclined across a chaise all to herself.

"Everything alright, darling?" Lillian asked, sitting next to me. I inched away from her, scanning the room for any signs of pointed ears or strange eyes, but that magic—glamour—either hid their true nature, or they were as human as I was.

Though, supposedly I wasn't as human as I thought. Their blood mixed with mine, making me something else. Not quite what they were, but not what my parents were either.

"Adeline has some reservations," Jack said, sinking into an ornate red and gold chair at the head of our disorganized circle. Between the monstrous cane clutched in his leather fingers and the fire crackling at his back, he looked every bit the hellish king I originally thought he was.

"Of course she does," Violet murmured, petting her snake with disinterest.

"I thought if we all discussed our current plans, she may be more inclined to aid us in them."

"No pressure though," Will said, grinning despite the somber energy. "I'm sure this is a lot for you, so we can shut up whenever you'd like." That last part was spoken with a sharp look at Lillian, who crossed her arms and pouted.

"Okay." My desire to hear them out closely resembled my desire to stick ice picks in my ears, but I doubted I had any choice in the matter. They all glanced at one another with flickering unease. Arthur, the reedy blond with wire glasses, spoke first.

"Well to start, does she know how your magic works?"

Your magic, not ours. Likely, there was at least one person in the room who was less like Jack and more like me. It was a strange comfort I held onto, shaking my head as he offered a weak smile.

"Oh, well, that's fine. It *is* my job to explain these things." He took a deep breath, folding his hands in his lap like he had prepared a great speech. "Fae magic has always been nature-based. They gain their power from the natural world around them, and it's always reflected in their abilities. Even glamour is nothing more than bending light, scent and matter to one's will. It's an illusion, but one strong enough to transform."

He paused. I nodded, urging him to continue. "But, in this world, the preservation of nature isn't emphasized. Humans don't have magic, so they rely on ingenuity and technology to advance. Unfortunately for the fae, this has a neutralizing effect on their abilities. The more technology, the more inorganic structures and objects around them, the less power they have.

"For someone like Jack, this is not really a problem. But for those less powerful, even so much as contact with an object of human making can render them completely useless. For example." He pointed to a radio sitting on a side table beside Lillian. Reaching out one slender hand, she turned the dial and static crackled through the air. At first, nothing changed, but for flickers of seconds, so quick one may blink and miss it, her rounded ears turned sharp and pointed,

140

her skin held an unnatural glow, and the bones in her face appeared sharper and disastrously more beautiful.

She turned it off, returning to her normal, human look with a little smile and shrug.

"Well . . . that doesn't make much sense." Arthur blinked, gesturing for me to elaborate. "You all run around looking human and using magic all the time."

"There are two reasons for that," Lillian said. "One, Jack is very powerful. A lot more than most of our kind have ever been, so for anyone in his court, he's able to cast a sort of net of magic. It holds up the glamour when we interact with the human world so we don't give ourselves away. And it's very powerful, so even the glamour-touched can't see through it."

Anyone in his *court*. Like . . . like a noble, or a king. That didn't have time to settle before Lillian continued, "The second reason is where we are. For a bunch of nature-based creatures, it seems a little silly to set up home in a city, right?"

I nodded.

"That's because this hotel was built on an undercroft. That's what we call the place of burial for . . . well, it's a bit hard to explain. But they give off extremely large amounts of power, sort of like a battery that never runs out, so it's far more advantageous to stay here."

"They are not burial grounds," Violet said, much less bored all of a sudden. "They are sites of genocide."

Lillian sighed. "You know what I meant."

"Genocide of what?" I asked.

"The Bogorans," Will said. Then quickly added, "We will get to that in a moment. Like Lillian said, it's a bit hard to explain."

"Yes, so, anyway . . ." Arthur looked around the room, waiting to see if anyone else would interrupt. "This makes day-to-day life for us much more difficult, as I am sure you could imagine. And while many have been happy to find solutions to our dwindling abilities—"

"Others would rather just kill you all and take your world," Violet finished. Arthur shot her a look. She blinked innocently. "What? There's no polite way to put it."

Our world, their world. "I thought you were all from Wales?"

Lillian fluttered her hands in the air. "Well, not really. We are sort of from . . . *behind* Wales."

I stared at her.

"I am actually from Wales, since I'm a druid," Arthur chirped, grinning around the crooked glasses sliding off his nose. "The rest of them are from behind the veil, in Ildathach. The fae world."

Ildathach, the other world. Wonderful. "Then why come here at all? If it's such a struggle to be in this world, then go back to your own."

They all shuffled in their seats, silent. All except for Jack. "We're banished."

"Banished?"

Lillian gripped my hand and squeezed. I bit down the urge to recoil. "It's a lot more common than you think, and since we're all immortal, our numbers tend to add up over time."

My face paled. "Did you say immortal?"

She smacked her forehead with the palm of her hand. "Yes, of course you wouldn't know, silly me. Magical creatures don't age, isn't that fun?"

I was going to be ill.

Looking around the room, I stuttered, "So . . . you're all . . ."

"A young, spry three hundred and one," Will said.

Then, Arthur, "Seven hundred and forty-nine." He frowned. "I think. The Middle Ages were sort of a blur."

"Two hundred and twenty-eight," Lillian chirped, placing her hands on her knees and winking. "I'm the baby of the group."

142

Violet glared at me. "A lady never reveals her age." Jack sighed and cast a withering look at his twin. "We are three-hundred and something toward the end, we only started keeping track a few centuries ago."

Centuries.

Centuries.

Laughter bubbled up my throat. "I get it now, this is all an elaborate joke." I gestured at Arthur. "You really think I will believe you're older than the goddamn rug?"

"I wish it was," Violet muttered, dangling a spider before her snake.

"It's not a joke," Arthur assured me, but he fidgeted, pushing up his glasses. "I am sure by now you have seen we are all capable of things humans aren't. Is it so incredible to believe immortality exists too?"

Yes, yes it was. I sat in a room with five immortal, all-powerful creatures who were *banished* from their own world.

"What were you all kicked out for, then?"

"It is rude to ask," Jack said, heated gaze settling on mine. "They will tell you when they want to, if they want to."

"How convenient. It wasn't good enough to be criminals in your own world so you came and did it here."

Violet muttered an insult, Arthur turned pale and sweaty and Will and Lillian looked everywhere but me. Only Jack held my eyes, that strange tug beckoning from beneath my skin. Warmth and languid darkness curled around me, coating my tongue, making my breath falter as I entered a battle of wills with the man before me.

"You should trust Jack and Violet," Lillian said. The latter looked ready to pounce across the room, but she continued "They didn't do anything wrong in our world, they were banished because they are twins."

Violet bristled. "Did she really need to know that?"

143

"Yes," Jack said, and even Violet snapped her mouth shut. "Which leads into what we are all here for. So, Arthur, please continue."

The blond muttered something and wrung his hands. "Right . . . so, gods, I don't even remember where I was."

Lillian threw him an affectionate grin. "Our favorite and most terrible druid."

"Right, that's where." He snapped his fingers and turned back to me. "Daniel Harrow runs the Chicago Outfit. Bootlegging, gambling, nasty business, you know the sort. A very powerful druid, and he's amassed a large following over the years for his . . . preachings."

I raised an eyebrow. "Is he Christian?"

At that, everyone laughed. All but Violet and Jack. "Oh god no, he's convinced we should eliminate humans. Sorry, there really is no polite way to put that."

I didn't tell him it was fine, or resort to any usual politeness. "If Jack is so powerful then why doesn't he just stop him?"

A cruel smirk twisted Violet's lips. Arthur turned cherry red. "Delsaran is very powerful, Adeline. It's not that simple."

"Why?"

"We aren't sure of that. It is uncommon for his kind, but he is capable of things even Jack isn't."

"So we need to make a Morrigan," Violet murmured.

Morrigan. I tried to think of where I'd heard that name, but couldn't place it. Lillian filled in my memory. "Remember the party we went to? And I told you about the three Morrigan sisters, Agnes, Nellie and—"

"I remember." More humans that weren't humans.

"Their last name is not really Morrigan," Arthur said. "Just like Jack isn't really Jack or Lillian isn't really—"

"I have been Lillian for a long time," she cut in. Arthur turned pink, nodding his head. "Right. But a Morrigan isn't a name, it is a . . . title, state of being? I'm not really sure how to put it, but since they are the only one in existence they sort of adopted it." He wiped his sweaty palms on his pant legs. "If you know a little about Celtic mythology you may have even heard of them. Humans know the Morrigan as a triple goddess, made of three different women under one name."

I hadn't heard of it. Papa acquired everything from Greek works to tales of the far east, but there was a noticeable lack of European myths in our home library. "So they're goddesses?"

"No, they're fae, but the most powerful among us and very, very old," Arthur continued. "They are powerful because they're triplets. Magic does not follow your rules of nature. Just like glamour-touched individuals can skip generations or never appear at all, there is a phenomenon with multiple births. The amount of power one receives is decided in the womb, just like eye color or athletic ability. But instead of magic being spread between all the children, it amplifies, making each individual more powerful through bonds."

"Multiple births are killed when they are born," Jack said. "They are considered too powerful."

"Which is why our only crime in our world was existing," Violet added. "If that pleases your astute morals."

"But you're alive," I said to Jack, ignoring his sister.

He only offered, "That's a long story," and gestured once more to Arthur.

"The Morrigan sisters have little use for modern feuds, and decided to remain neutral after Delsaran announced his plans for combatting human technology, some twenty years ago or so," Arthur said, sounding much more confident now. "The war was an experiment."

The war. He didn't need to say which one, because every man, woman and child knew of the war, the Great War, the War to End all Wars. Fought with gas and tanks, airplanes and machine guns, if it didn't end when it did . . .

My heart skipped a beat. All of this, everything that happened to Tommy because . . . "The World War was the doing of one pissed off druid?"

Arthur nodded. "Him and his followers have been very influential, very powerful, and a few years of work putting some already tense players in place was all it took."

"But it backfired. Horribly. The war ended and on top of that, we have more technology than we ever did before."

"Precisely," Arthur exclaimed. "Precisely, which is why it was an *experiment*. Pitting human against human wasn't good enough, so their next plan will be much worse."

"And that plan is?"

No one spoke.

No one, except Jack. "Last night, Delsaran warned me I had until Samhain to join his side. We don't know what he has planned and we don't want to find out. We need a way to eliminate him from this world, and the only way to do that is to be more powerful than he is."

"To create our own Morrigan," Arthur supplied.

"But you are only twins," I said, knowing without being told Jack and Violet were the ones that would be responsible with that power.

"That's where you come in," Jack murmured. Arthur didn't feel the need to give his knowledge this time.

The fire crackled and popped, the vines hissed, Violet's snake slithered to the floor and I stared at Jack Warren.

"Because we are connected. From when you saved my life?" It was a guess, and a terrible one at that, because Violet smothered a mocking snigger.

"I saved your life because of that connection." Suddenly, everyone found the ceiling absolutely exquisite.

A deep foreboding settled in my bones. "Connected how?"

Silence. If they all could have faded into the walls, I am sure they would have. It wasn't until Jack uttered his next words that any of them made a sound.

"We call it a parallel bond. For all intents and purposes, it means we are soulmates."

"I WANT A DRINK, does anyone else want a drink?" Lillian stood in a flurry of diamonds and silk, breaking for the edge of the room. Snatching a bottle of the green champagne and something probably safe for humans, she dropped the bottles and a stack of glasses on the center table.

Every person reached for one immediately.

But not me or Jack who stared at one another like we could decipher the other's secrets. We probably could, if exchanging pieces of our souls was possible, sensing him whenever he was in the room, walking each other's dreams . . .

"No, that can't be right."

"Agreed," Violet muttered.

"Well, it does happen," Lillian murmured, filling a glass with brown liquid. She handed it to me. I didn't sip it. "It's so rare that most have forgotten it's possible, but there's been a few stories. For some, it's why they venture to the human world in the first place, to see if they can find their other half. It only happens between a glamour-touched human and a fae, you see."

"We have theories," Arthur added. "Maybe the magic in your family line is connected to his, or it could even date back to our creation, where humans were made by stars and fae by Bogorans, the stars' children. But as Lillian said, it's so incredibly rare to actually see . . ."

They all looked at me. A bond, or parallel as Jack put it, that none of them understood, or perhaps, never thought was real.

"How do you know we actually have this?" I threw the question at Jack, but Violet answered.

"You do," she said. Then, quieter. "I can feel it sometimes."

Out of all of this, that was by far the most disturbing. "Then maybe I'm just connected to you."

She snorted. "You're not, thank the fucking gods. You always sense him, right?" I didn't answer. "Twins have something similar, to an extent. I can sense Jack but only in extremes, and vice versa. But you, you feel him all the time, whenever you like. And since you are paralleled, both of you feel that pesky little desire to complete the power, which, I would like to add, is very uncomfortable for his sister who has to scent you wanting to fuck him all the time."

Red flushed my cheeks. "I don't—"

"It's power and magic, you can shove your fragile sensibilities aside." She waved a hand in the air, as if sweeping away those pesky sensibilities. "I am quite tired of listening to the lot of you ramble on like she's the fucking queen, so here's the skinny of it: Delsaran wants humans dead. We don't want humans dead, because unlike some others we could be a lot worse, and you can keep your judgements to yourself. I am Jack's twin, you are paralleled to Jack, and if you agree to this Bogoran-forsaken mating bond, do the ceremony, etcetera, etcetera, then the three of us make a Morrigan and we can kill the prick in his sleep." She raised her fizzing glass to the air. "Got it?"

No, I did not. One word in her spiel stuck out like a sore thumb, grating against my dwindling sanity. "What do you mean, *mating bond*?"

She smiled with all teeth.

Jack pushed to his feet. "And now would be the time for Adeline and I to continue this discussion in private. Thank you, everyone. Find anywhere else to be."

148

"No, absolutely not." My feet hit the floor, fingers trembling beside my hips. I didn't trust the fae, but anything was safer than being left alone with Jack. "Why the hell is it called a mating bond?"

Will's eyes went wide and Arthur blanched. Violet seemed terribly pleased with herself. "Adeline, I admire your interest, truly, but I highly doubt you want to discuss this with an audience."

I stepped forward, swallowing down the fear clambering up my throat. The tug—the parallel, the bond—writhed between us. "I want that chaperone Violet mentioned."

"I have been around for nearly four hundred years, I can handle some wet dreams," he snapped. "I would also like to reiterate we're not animals, so I don't love the idea of doing this surrounded by my sister and friends."

Heated breaths scorched my throat, hands clenching. "Your word means nothing to me, Jack."

Violet huffed. "Well, that will make it *pretty awkward* when you have to fuck him."

My blood iced over.

I stared at Jack, or not really Jack, but his true form. In an instant the facade broke, revealing his pointed ears, serpent eyes and sharp features, too ethereal to be human. Darkness leaked around him like night suffusing the air. A circle of black started at the edges of his feet, slowly growing wider. The vines slithering nearby scurried away, flowers crumbled and died in their pots. The only thing taking root was belladonna springing from cracks in the floor. Even Violet stood, making her way to the opposite side of the room. I didn't move, frozen and bleating like prey beneath him.

He closed his eyes with a steadying breath. The dark aura dissipated like smoke in the air, his features melting back into human ones. The circle of darkness and poison flowers stopped growing, but remained on the floor. The fringe of the seven-hundred-year-old carpet was burned black.

"Thank you, Violet, for that incredibly delicate and sophisticated announcement." His words were calm. Too calm. No one moved, stiff as statues dotted around the room.

"Now, Miss Colton." He stepped forward. I stepped back. "It is considered a mating bond because my power, and whatever power flows through your veins, would make an especially powerful child. Magic senses this, therefore, the reason you get hot and bothered near me is because magic wants me to put a baby in you. Even better, our mating bond wants us to be wonderful, loving parents together, so once the ritual is complete—which as you may have guessed, means consummating—you instantly become a druid. With your own powers, an enhanced body, and your very own immortality. Congratulations."

Silence congealed the air. Violet coughed, shrugging a shoulder. "Your announcement was far shittier than mine."

My palms turned cold and clammy, heart thrumming against my ribs. "I can't have children. I can't . . ." *Cheat death again.*

Lillian shuffled forward, rubbing a hand down my arm. "Okay, um, I think Jack was probably right and now would be an excellent time to give them some privacy. So, everyone." She waved at the door, then whispered, "If you need me to stay, I can stay."

"Why, so you can spy on me for him again?" I snapped. Harsh, even I knew that, but I was too angry to care. Her face crumpled, but she nodded. I didn't move until the door shut behind them.

"If you think there is any chance in hell I will procreate with you, you have something else coming."

He swallowed, stealing a deep breath before answering. "For your information, there are measures to prevent that sort of thing. But whether we like it or not, in order to make our world-saving Morrigan there is a ritual, and there's no way around it."

I shook my head. "I would rather burn in hell."

His nostrils flared, flame igniting behind his stare. It flickered, matching the fireplace roaring at his back, before dying down to embers. Cold, crumbling ash. He closed his eyes, more tired and defeated than anything.

"We can talk tomorrow. I have things to do."

"I am not staying here. I want to go home."

He looked at me. Truly, looked at me. The bond tightened between us, not demanding or *hot and bothered*, but . . . exhausted.

"You can stay in the Abstruse for now. Knock if you need anything." He twisted his hand and a cluster of foliage beside the fireplace moved aside. A hidden hall stretched long and dark behind it.

Just like that, there was no one left but me and the endless moving walls.

FIFTEEN

UNSURE WHAT TO DO with myself, I finished at least half the bottle of liquor and scanned the teeming bookshelves. The vines had a proclivity for them, hugging the shelves and twisting around the books. It became a battle smacking them away to read the titles. Not that it mattered. They were either in Welsh, so old the English was barely understandable, or written in a strange alphabet I suspected wasn't human. The more I grumbled and pushed the vines to the side, the more laborious it became to pull the books. When one came off the wall and snapped at my wrist, I decided not to read after all.

Despite seeing it only a few hours ago, I couldn't for the life of me find that hidden hallway along the wall again. The one to the Abstruse, not where Jack departed. I was very much avoiding him. Either the vines were sentient and pissed at my intrusion of their bookshelves or one needed magic to access it, because I found nothing even close to an entrance behind the jungle invading the walls.

There were no windows, but a grandfather clock said it was close to eight p.m. I hadn't eaten in over a day, I was exhausted, still wearing nothing but my dirty and torn nightgown and very, very miserable.

I was human, therefore I needed to eat and bathe. Maybe immortality didn't make such things as complicated for all these other creatures, but unless Jack was intent on killing me I needed to leave the study. Spending an evening with Violet Warren seemed more inviting than roaming this hellscape hotel again, but when the clock pushed nine and my stomach grumbled, I gathered my wits and one of the guns Jack left on his desk.

Curious, I popped the chamber and spilled the bullets into my hand. Iron, all of them, I could tell by the weight alone. Reloading the gun, I tore a strip off my nightdress and secured the weapon to my upper thigh. Then I prayed this hotel had a kitchen and served more than poisonous mushrooms or dead mens' fingernails.

Surely, I was a sight to behold. Bedraggled, dirty, bruised, half-naked, but I had no other options and could only hope my bond to Jack meant no other fae would be concerned. Maybe now that I knew the truth, I could use my abilities to see through their illusions all the time, enlightening me on exactly how many people in this hotel were people, and how many were *other*. Both times I'd been in this hotel I saw different things, which meant the illusion only held during certain times and circumstances. I just had to figure out how it worked and how to see through it. Preferably without any immortal creature's help. Better they think I was blind when I wasn't.

While they were clearly keeping me prisoner, I was fairly sure that didn't mean I had to stay confined to Jack's apartments. Even so, I padded along the stones to the foyer silently, opened and closed the door softly behind me, and did the same to the main double doors. Only, on the other side of those stood someone I truly didn't want to see.

Will Porter leaned against the wall, foot propped against the expensive wallpaper while peeling an apple. I froze like prey beneath a predator's stare, hating how accurate that comparison really was. But all he did was shoot me a friendly smile and hold up the apple. "Hungry?"

Did he . . . sense that? Or maybe their powers included extraordinary hearing, and he listened to my stomach grumble across three layers of stone wall. My survival in this situation banked purely on my wit. I didn't have magical powers beyond glamour-breaking, which was unreliable at best. I wasn't immortal, couldn't disappear and reappear. So if I had nothing to fight with but my brain, I needed to acquire all the knowledge I could. Starting with exactly what weapons my enemies had in their arsenal.

With a pleasant smile, I shrugged. "A little. Forgive me for asking, but . . . is that safe to eat?"

He raised an eyebrow, but understanding dawned on his face. "Right, yeah. I'm sure you've heard the no drinking or eating rule a thousand times by now." An awkward chuckle.

I swallowed. "Why is that, anyway?"

"Oh, several reasons. Our food generally doesn't mix well with human guts, but it could also be glamoured to look and taste like something else, or be cursed, enchanted. Other things . . ." He held out the apple. "This is safe though, I promise. Bought it off a cart down the street."

Bought it, or used mind powers or time-freezing powers or whatever else to steal off an unknowing fruit salesman? I took the apple, anyway. "Thank you. That was perfect timing actually, I was just looking for a kitchen."

He shrugged. "I figured, just hoped you liked apples."

I swallowed. "Ah, so, you can tell if I'm hungry?"

His eyebrows came together. He laughed. "Oh, no, I just heard about all your adventures today and figured you hadn't stopped for a meal." He grinned. "I'm a right and proper bastard when I'm hungry, so I can't imagine why they would spring all that on you without a good dinner first."

Okay, so high fae also needed to eat. Good to note. "You seem perfectly pleasant to me, Mr. Porter."

"Like I said before, Will's fine. No one calls me William either, much too formal." He tossed me the rest of the apple. "And actually,

I am a dark incarnation of Beelzebub himself, sent from hell to feed my best mate's mistress."

I stared at him.

His lips twitched around a smile. "Come on, it was a little funny."

I didn't move.

"Right, you're still shell-shocked. All's good." Pushing off the wall, he jerked his chin at the apple. "That going to be enough for you? There is a kitchen here, but it's probably best if I help you navigate it. Charlene is a bit of a bitch when you encroach on her space, if I'm honest."

The thought of going anywhere with the "dark incarnation of Beelzebub" was not very pleasing, but if this fae man was willing to be friendly with me, it was best to shake him for every bit of information I could. Besides, there was some comfort knowing Tommy had worked with him, was friends with him once. Not that Tommy knew what he truly was, but if he could be pleasant enough to my human brother, maybe he would be pleasant enough with me.

Despite that, I pressed my thighs together, feeling for the cool bite of the iron-loaded revolver.

"I don't want to trouble you." Then, thinking better safe than sorry, added, "Were you doing something out here, or . . ."

"Ah, yes, Satan requested I keep watch for now in case his mistress tried to run off again. Seems she doesn't really want to talk to him right now." When I frowned, he shrugged. "Just being honest, love. But it's all with good intentions. You need your space from Jack, but not everyone here is aware of your sparkly, new untouchable status and we wouldn't want a repeat of the other night."

The other night, when I showed up at the hotel when I wasn't supposed to and was dragged off by . . . a goat-man, sentient pig and dryad. Right.

Forgetting any sense of craftiness, I asked, "Is everyone who stays here from your world?"

My stomach chose that moment to grumble. Loudly. We both looked to the source of the offending sound.

"How about we walk and talk?" He offered me his arm. Could fae mind-control via skin-to-skin contact? He was wearing a coat, but—

I sighed. To hell with it. I gave him my arm and he took it with a careless grin.

"Not everyone. Humans stay on floor five and below and everything above is the exact kind of wickedness you're thinking of. Long term, by the way. They all live here. Lillian's apartment complex too. Think you were there for a bit, right?"

I was, not that I'd give anything away. "Was that complex also built on an . . . undercroft?" I asked, unsure if my inflection was for the question or if I got the word correct.

"No, it's just warded and infused. Things got a bit too crowded here." Realizing I had no clue what that meant, he said, "We managed to transfer some of the power here to that site. Not a lot, but enough to recharge all the people that live there, so to speak. And wards are just magical security measures, like an alarm, but you know, magic." He finished the fumbling statement with an awkward grin.

"Sure." I licked my lips, left hand trembling behind my back. "So there's a lot of you, then?"

"Wow, so many questions." A frown slashed my face, but Will looked absolutely delighted. "Of course, I can't blame you, but you are asking an awful lot about things that make my soldier side a teensy bit nervous."

"Your World War service, you mean?"

"Among others. There's also been Scotland, Belgium, France . . . Mongolia once. Don't ask, that's a long story. We join all the wars we can—easiest way to kill yourself off without a body and assume a new identity." He shoved his hand in his pocket, strolling down the hall like this was completely normal conversation. "It's getting trickier and trickier to do that, actually. Even immortality has its pitfalls."

And he was three hundred years old. Granted, that didn't mean he spent all his time in the human world, but surely he'd lived at least a few lifetimes here, pretending he was one of us. Fighting in battles he didn't believe in for the sake of "dying" and starting anew. The same battle Tommy had no choice in joining.

"What about before?" Jack said it was rude to ask why they were banished, but it couldn't hurt to ask about his old life. "In . . . Ildathach?"

"Ironically, also a soldier there. For Lillian." His voice dropped. "I mean, that's how Lillian and I met, but I wouldn't bring that up to her."

We reached the elevator, but at the last moment Will tugged me toward the stairs, claiming he needed to "stretch his legs." Apparently, forty stories of stairwell was the solution to that.

We passed three floors in silence before I said, "He's not letting me go anywhere, is he?"

"What? Oh." He shook his head, halting on a stone landing. I stood several steps above him. "I mean, knowing Jack I'm sure he would let you run off eventually if that's what you wanted, but it really isn't safe out there for you right now. Not to be devil's advocate or anything, but with the way Delsaran's boys have been acting all day, I would be surprised if you made it halfway down the block."

My eyebrows came together. Chicago was at least a day away by train. "Does he already know?"

"About you, definitely. Lillian has been losing her mind all afternoon." The furrow between my eyebrows deepened, and he added, "She's an intelligence gatherer. A spy."

All her talk about listening and learning, coveting the secrets of others, bending the political sway to your liking . . . all a lot more than idle gossip and society's opinion on your marriage. When I accused her of spying on me for Jack, I didn't know how right I was. Anger prickled beneath my skin. Hurt. Any hope I had she was actually my friend fizzled and died right there.

An apologetic smile stretched Will's mouth. "I know, it's a lot."

I nodded, tucking a strand of hair behind my ear. "How would you handle it?"

"Me? I'm just a dumb soldier, so I'd probably curse a lot and drink enough to kill a horse. Pass out in a ditch and do it all again."

I smiled, despite myself. "Maybe I should join up for the next war."

"What the hell do you think we're trying to do, Addie? Have you over for breakfast?"

Of course, that was exactly what they were trying to do . . . if they were telling the truth. None of them seemed especially affectionate toward humans and besides, this could easily be another trick. A way to convince some stupid, completely mortal, young woman to create god-like power for a bootlegger.

But as memories of last night rose, that didn't seem right either. Delsaran, standing on a toppled chair while bloodlust soaked his eyes. Preaching the worthlessness of humans to a crowd.

Will's careless smile melted away. "Either way, you are welcome here. We're not always the easiest lot to handle but say the word and you have friends and allies, promise." He held up his hand, crossing his middle and pointer finger.

"You're not as terrible as I expected." It wasn't even a lie.

"For a dastardly, otherworld criminal, you mean?"

I could have cringed. "I'm sorry about that. I'm sure it's all more complicated than it seems, I just don't have . . ." *A single good experience with your kind.*

"I understand," he said, and I truly think he meant it. "Like I said, if I were you, I'd just drink myself under a table."

I laughed, really laughed and motioned down the stairs. "Onward?"

"Of course, my lady." I wondered how accurate that statement actually was, now that I was Jack's . . . other half.

Now seemed a good time to find out. "What is Jack to you anyway?"

Will tilted his head to the side. "As in . . .?"

"Friend, employer, monarch, deity?"

A smooth, rich laugh rumbled from his throat. "Definitely not a deity. On paper, for the tax and legal reasons you humans love so much, an employer. Very much a friend, even if I want to bash his head in half the time. And technically a monarch, but we are very casual about it."

Naturally, because the monarchy was so casual. I was sure King George felt the same. "Is that a Jack tradition, or a fae one?"

"Oh, that's a Jack thing, for sure. Lillian would have cut off my head." He rushed onto his next sentence. "He was actually a prince back in our world. You asked why him and Violet got banished instead of killed, that's part of it. A bit of nepotism, fortunately for you and I."

Not fortunate for me at all. "Prince of what?"

"You haven't guessed that yet?"

Serpent eyes, belladonna growing wherever he walked. *Medicine is nothing but a well-dosed poison.* I could guess.

"House Valdivia held the mountain territories in Ildathach, but in the human world he's sort of our informal king."

House Valdivia. Delsaran mentioned them, how they would usher in the ruin of fae. Right before the low fae prostrated themselves on the floor and called Jack their king. I suspected Warren wasn't Jack's real last name, but it was jarring. Valdivia sounded so . . . regal.

"It seemed pretty formal to me."

"That's only because you stumbled in on Calamity. Those bastards need different rules. Terribly sorry about that by the way, that was possibly the worst introduction to us imaginable."

"Calamity?"

"It's a temporary truce held once a year so opposing courts can meet, like pirates and parley. Except, Calamity is only attended by low fae, so they tend to be very . . . savage. This is our floor."

He rushed ahead, pulling open the door and making an overly grand gesture to walk through. I smiled in thanks, taking his arm again as we emerged on a landing, overlooking the bustling lobby several floors below. White cloths covered candlelit tables and plush chairs formed a dotted network of gold upholstery. Stiff-backed waiters fluttered around, casting me curious glances but never stopping their endless parade.

I looked down. "I'm not exactly dressed."

"No worries, we're heading straight for the kitchen." The jaws dropped on a dining elderly couple as we sauntered past, no doubt wondering what the homeless woman and well-dressed black man were doing beside their elegant dinner table. They stared at Will a little too sharply for my liking, and I'd unfortunately grown fond of him in the past fifteen minutes, so I stuck my tongue out and waggled my fingers until the woman dropped her fork.

Will chuckled ahead of me. "Maybe you should whip that gun out, really give them a good show."

My face heated. He gestured for me to pass a set of swinging double doors. "Is it the same in your world? How they treat people that look like you?"

"Like what?' He asked, feigning innocence. My face heated even more. "No, not at all. We had too many other things to be discriminatory about, unfortunately. People are terrible everywhere, only now I've found myself on the other side of it."

I chewed my lower lip. "I'm sorry, that's a shame."

"It is, but it could be worse," he said, hovering in a bay behind a second set of doors. Beyond, the sounds of a kitchen exploded to life.

"Where you are from, in the south, I've heard it is a lot less accepting."

I nodded, understanding it was both a question and assessment. "My family minded our own business. We were the strange ones ourselves and my papa didn't raise me to think like that. "

He bounced on his heels, sucking on his teeth. "I knew I liked you." He pushed through the second set of doors.

What met us on the other side was a kitchen, but also not. I flattened myself against the door, wide eyes taking in the many, *many* fae bustling around the room. Vines crept along the walls. Fruits and vegetables and spices grew in droves from the ceiling, hanging over pots and pans floating above blue flames. A woman with pink hair stirred a soup pot while a horned man flicked his wrists at a cluster of self-washing plates. A creature with wispy, white hair, a craggy nose and boils dotting their face stood on a stool and chopped meat opposite a bored high fae man, collecting spices from the ceiling. My jaw fell open, the heat and scents flooding my senses. I was so taken aback I didn't notice the fuzzy, brown . . . thing standing at my feet, hands on hips over a miniature white coat. Large, black eyes settled on us beneath a miniature chef's hat.

Will gave an elegant flourish of his hand and bowed. "Charlene, queen of the kitchen, blessed little brownie darling, how are we this evening?"

The brownie swatted a tiny wooden spoon at him, just missing his nose dipped toward the floor. "Will," it squeaked, "If you don't get yur sorry arse out of my kitchen, I'll be cooking yur head for breakfast."

Will frowned. "Charlene, darling, why must you always be this way? You know I adore you, right?"

"And you're always raiding me fookin' stock!" The brownie, Charlene, released an irritated squeak. "Do'ya know how hard it is to make a marsala for two hundred people without any fookin' mushrooms, boy? You'll be lucky if I don't cut yur cock off and cook that for 'em instead."

Will glanced at me. "Charlene and I go way back."

"And what in the fuck is this?" She waved her spoon at me. "Oy, human girl, the boss know this rotten bastard got you roaming the place? We never got any glamour in the kitchen, you know the rules," she said, waving the spoon back at Will. "I won't be losing me head because you fancy this one, you hear me, boy?"

"Loud and clear, Charlene, loud and clear. This is actually my dear friend, Adeline. If you haven't heard the news yet, she'll be staying with us for a little while. Jack is . . . a bit taken up with her."

Her black, angry eyes turned on me, going wide. "Ah, yur the paralleled girl. Sorry 'bout that. You need anything, sweetheart?"

Shaken by the sudden change in tone, I glanced at Will. He shrugged, gesturing for me to tell her.

"Hungry?" Charlene tried.

Don't drink or eat anything in this hotel. Seeing no other choice, I nodded.

"Well, I've got yur pretty little behind covered there." I think she smiled, but it was hard to tell beneath all the fur. "Come along now, can't have ya blocking the doors."

I turned back to them just as a fae waiter sauntered out, carrying a tray. Like he hit a wall defining this little world and the rest of it, his pointed ears rounded and the sharp edge of his jaw softened as he passed the threshold.

Charlene led us to the back, where a metal table sat with two matching chairs. A standing mirror leaned against it, which she propped against the wall. A door yawned open behind it, overflowing with potatoes and squash piled high from the floor. Back on the farm, it would have taken two seasons to produce that much food. But here it was, piled up like dishrags in the back of a magical kitchen.

"Do you grow your own food?" I asked Charlene. She'd taken the time to snatch a tablecloth and cutlery, which she laid over the rusted table like we were honored guests.

"All meself. Every damn pound." I could have sworn there was pride in her squeaky voice.

"I was a farmer," I said, unsure of myself. "I know a lot about growing, if you ever need help down here."

She released a squealing noise that made me jump. "Workin' down here? Jack's girl? You got much better things to be doin' than that." She shook her head. "Don't you worry yur pretty head 'bout a thing, this kitchen runs tight as a ship. No need to pull yur weight."

I shook my head. "I'm not Jack's—"

"Be right back." She scampered off before I could finish that statement.

Will raised an eyebrow.

"I'm not," I insisted.

He only shrugged, snapping his fingers. A wine bottle appeared from thin air, along with two glasses. "To reiterate, I know we threw a lot at you, but you really should talk to him. Alone, like he said, with an open mind and full stomach. And some liquid fire in your veins." He grinned, pouring me a glass. "I'm not going to argue on his behalf because I think that's useless. Right now you don't know him, but you should try to. I think he definitely wants to know you, so . . . just, attempt it, I guess."

A smile twitched at the corner of my lips. "Very profound, Will."

He laughed, tipping his glass toward me. "I'm a poet and you should never fucking forget it."

SIXTEEN

I GOT DRUNK.

The last time I'd been drunk, I was sixteen. Tommy was having one of his good months, and thought it would be hilarious to make our own hooch in one of the farm's abandoned sheds. He thought Papa would catch on if we kept borrowing yeast, so we took hunks of stale bread and threw them in a bathtub concoction of orange peels, water and grapes we stole off from the Heathertons' vineyard. Six weeks later and we had something close to wine, chunks of stale bread, grape mash, bitter orange and all. I refused to drink it until he did, and it was the worst goddamn thing I'd ever tasted, but it was something silly and fun my brother and I did together. Our secret, our sibling troublemaking, a dumb memory that felt normal compared to everything else that laid between us. Before we knew it, we'd drunk down half the bathtub and Papa found us passed out the next morning. We took turns vomiting between the chores, which Papa doubled for the morning with an angry shake of his head. But when I passed by the shed later that day, he was staring at the bathtub, laughing to himself.

This was not like that time. The wine was smooth, rich, and kept coming with every snap of Will's fingers. We sat in the kitchen of a fancy hotel, drinking out of pristine, freshly steamed wine glasses. I laughed with a stranger who I begrudgingly liked, but could never truly trust. I was twenty and he was three hundred. I was a prisoner and he wasn't even human. And when he dragged my sorry ass back upstairs, I didn't stumble over fresh grass and tilled fields, into a wooden shed where Tommy snored the crickets into silence beside me; instead, a strange apartment that didn't belong to me. Occupied by a man who made my father nothing but drunken memories.

And unfortunately for me, that man was awake.

Will's advice rattled in my skull, but I didn't think now was the time to have that conversation. Especially as something flickered low in my stomach, a recognition before I even entered the room. Like something deep in my bones knew it was getting closer and closer to home.

All the great romances that compared love to magic had clearly never met Jack Warren.

I pushed the door open, thinking I was being quiet but probably wasn't, because his head snapped to the side immediately. He sat with his back to me and a drink clutched in his hand, staring at the crackling fire. One pointed ear twitched. I shivered.

He turned back to the fire, saying nothing, doing nothing. It was a trap, because I needed to ask him to find me that hallway or dictate where I would sleep tonight. Which was an even more dangerous question, because the answer could have been with him.

I haven't fucked you yet.

There was a cold, hard truth in that statement. If only I knew that before yesterday.

But at that moment, none of it mattered. Wine, heat, the absurd bond, it all made my head swim with warmth that dropped low and hard to the pit of my stomach. I could picture him, right now, dropping me to the seven-hundred-year-old rug and tearing off the remains of my nightdress. Heated hands roaming over my ribs and sinking into each divot. His tongue gliding over my hardened nipples, those tattooed fingers slipping between my thighs. My breath getting heavy and hot, desperate and needy as he sank those fingers inside me, pumped them between my flesh, lips gliding over mine while his breath trembled above—

Across the room, he grunted and crossed his legs.

I squeezed my eyes shut.

It was magic. Magic, magic, magic. If it wasn't for the arcane bond pulsing between us, I'd have no desire to touch him at all.

A plush armchair sat empty beside him. Like he expected me. The air grew too hot, the room too small. Maybe Charlene wouldn't mind if I slept in the kitchen. Better yet, I could slip through the kitchen window . . .

"Did Will get to you?"

My pulse thrummed like a rabbit, his honey-sweet voice training my throat. "Yes."

In the most subtle of gestures, he flicked his fingers at the seat beside him, silhouetted against the vibrant fire. I scanned the walls again, but the hallway was still nowhere to be seen. He already knew I was here, there was no sneaking away now. Seeing no other options, I shuffled forward and sank into the seat beside him, sitting as far from him as possible.

He didn't acknowledge my presence, sinking low into his seat with ankles crossed on the hearth. A lowball glass of something dark and cold sat between his fingers, impeccable suit worn like a second skin. He was in human form. I compared him to all the other times I had seen him, mostly in my dreams. He looked so normal now, nothing more than a very handsome man reclined in a leather armchair—it was difficult to reconcile with previous memories.

He took a drawn-out sip of his drink, swirling ice around the glass. "You know where I come from, it's hot as shit."

The fire twisted a rhythmic dance against the stones. The stifling air choked my lungs, but I didn't think it was from the temperature.

I couldn't think of a single thing to say, so I didn't.

"I'm not going to hurt you."

I winced. Again, there was that strange comparison, the two sides of him warring in my brain. There was the Devil—-a tattooed, serpent-eyed man who visited my dreams. At first, I was afraid, but he slowly chipped away at something. I let him dance with me and tell me what flowers to grow and dress me up like his personal doll. To say I enjoyed him then was more complex than a yes or no could answer. If it weren't for everything else I knew of the fae, of the deal my father made as a child and the song he sang each night at the river, I would have said yes. But even in our best moments I knew an important truth—the truth my Papa gave me. When the Devil kills saints he kills slowly.

I wasn't a saint, but I wasn't a sinner either. Yet.

Then, there was Jack Warren. A mirage. Severe and charming and silver tongued, a bootlegger, a socialite, my jailer and a stranger. I'd been taught not to trust any of those.

I nodded, eyes on the ground, hoping that was satisfactory enough of a response.

His fingers pressed hard against the lowball glass, a tiny hairline crack forming above his pinky.

"I am not your enemy, Adeline."

"My father is dead, I'm being held captive and you just told me I'm eternally bound to you. I'm not sure what you want me to say." The words burst forth before I could stop them, the wine too loose with my tongue. I snapped my mouth shut, clenching my teeth.

He shrugged. "You can start with, 'it's nice to finally meet in person.'"

I stared at him, dumbfounded.

"Well, it's not."

"Why is that?"

"Because frankly, Mr. Warren, I want nothing to do with you."

He released a short breath. "You're more creative than that, *annwyl*."

"You are an arrogant, inhuman criminal who consorts with darker powers. Is that sufficient?"

He nodded. "You might be onto something there."

I knew I should shut up. I had enough will to live to realize when I was walking into a trap, but Will gave me too much wine, the room was too hot and suddenly I was so angry I couldn't think. "You made me get on my *knees* before you. My father is dead because of a deal you cut with him. You have quite literally invaded my mind, stalked me and now you are holding me hostage so I can help you *murder* someone."

Somewhere in that monologue, my nails turned white clutching the armrest. He turned his head, cheek pressed against the upholstery. Vertical pupils narrowed to slits.

"Anything else?" He asked.

I swallowed, attempting to push down another tirade but god, that wine was strong. "I'm not sure what I'm supposed to think of you. And I don't understand what you expect after deceiving me. I've known you for two years, fine, but for most of that I thought you were either Satan or a figment of my imagination. And in all that time you never bothered to tell me otherwise. You let me stand there and lose my mind wondering what I imagined and what was reality, all after telling me over and over I could have whatever I wanted. Exactly what you'd say to some silly, stupid girl who means nothing. Because I don't mean anything to you. My entire existence is nothing but a means to an end. It's the only reason I'm still alive."

Jack's stare tunneled beneath my skin. His lips twitched with unsaid words, but he remained silent and I remained fuming. One of those terrible vines snaked across the floor, curling beneath my dirty feet.

Finally, his voice came soft as a dying breeze. "You're different."

"Different from what? When I was asleep and thought you were just a dream?"

He shrugged. "Just different."

Silence pulsed between us.

He shifted back to the fire, slow and indolent. "It's all true."

My mouth snapped shut.

He swallowed, which I strongly suspected was to hide a drunk hiccup. "Except for intentionally deceiving you in *our* dreams. That's not true. The rest though, sure, have it."

"I don't know what else you'd like to call it."

"There are rules, *annwyl*. With our bond. Until you asked me for five hundred dollars, I was not allowed to simply whisk you away or compulse you into telling me how to find you. I was bound by magical law to reveal nothing of myself until you willingly asked me for something, which is considered the first acceptance of the parallel. These are ancient tenets designed to protect humans who find themselves in these bonds. Had they not existed, I would have found you years ago."

The wooden armrest creaked beneath my fingers, but I knew it was true. *Anything you want. Anything at all . . .*

"Is it my turn yet?"

My harsh stare leveled on him. "What?"

"My turn?" He asked, raising a brow. "I'll assume it is. I think you're grieving, angry, and tortured by your less-than-ideal upbringing. I think you want any reason to hate me, because I already told you your father made his choice by going back on a bargain he made. And while I am truly sorry it worked out that way, had he honored the deal in the first place, he would still be alive and well to love you. Nowhere in that bargain did it say I would make you my slave, or drag you down to hell, or forbid you from any pleasures of your former life. You would keep your family and your friends and whatever else you wanted because I understand, Adeline, I truly do, that you didn't ask for this and fate dealt you a strange hand. Twenty years ago I didn't know I'd be entering a war with Delsaran. I only wanted the chance to know you."

He drummed his fingers on the armrest. "I'm glad you had a good night with Will. And that you roamed the hotel without fearing for your life and are maybe just a tiny bit more accepting of who and what we are. Because I thought out of all people, growing up in that town and being shunned your entire life, you would understand what it's like to live in hiding. And I know you don't believe me now—that probably is my fault, and there were much better ways to go about this, but you do have a choice, Adeline. I'm not forcing your hand, telling you what you can or can't do, and whether you decide to help me or not isn't going to change that whatever it is you want, with or without me, is entirely in your hands. I've already taken enough from you, so please find it within yourself to tolerate me long enough that I can give you something instead."

He wiped a hand over his face, closing his eyes. "The hallway is open to your right. I fixed the wards so no one can enter or leave but us without giving permission." He stumbled to his feet, crossing the study with unnatural silence. I remained seated.

"And Addie?" My eyes flicked to his. Half his body already melted into the darkness of the hall. "My favorite nights have been spent listening to you talk about your family, or your flowers, what music you danced to that week or how awful your neighbors could be. When I told you I missed you each month, that wasn't a deception."

He nodded. "Goodnight, Miss Colton."

SEVENTEEN

I WOKE UP IN an elegant cream and satin bed. Early light flooded the windows, the invisible, sourceless breeze fanning the gossamer around the room. I lay completely still, watching the thin material float high and drift back to the floor. Over and over again. Like a rabbit slamming its head into a wall.

As it turned out, the Abstruse came with a private bathroom. My time would probably have been better spent attempting another daring escape, but someone had sealed the windows shut and I could hear Jack moving around in the study. I hadn't bathed in over two days, and certainly smelled like it. That would be awful enough without factoring in the booze I drank last night, which currently seeped from my pores. Deciding that was better than speaking to Jack again, I made my way into the powder room.

Brass faucets turned on of their own accord, filling a clawfoot bathtub large enough for two. Lemon and oleander wafted on the steam and the vines drifted closer on the walls, as if they sought the humidity.

On a gilded vanity lay a pile of folded dresses, another of undergarments, my makeup set, and a jewelry box. Someone had taped a note to the mirror, written in flourishing script:

Sometimes, a woman's most powerful weapons are a good dress and her favorite lipstick.

Here for anything you need.
Lillian

Either Jack lied about the wards or he gave her permission to enter with fresh clothes. Unsure how I felt about that, I sifted through the neat pile while the bath filled. Hopefully, whatever magic turned it on would also turn it off, because I paid it no mind as my fingers drifted through the layers of fabric. Only two of the garments I recognized, the dresses formerly tacked over my windows. The rest were clearly Lillian's or whatever she deemed fit for me. I didn't recognize a single pair of the undergarments, all of my hand-sewn bloomers and garters replaced with tiny swaths of satin and lace. The sort of materials a man would prefer to see.

Shoving those aside, I searched the jewelry box for my mama's pearls. Tommy had already sold most of my jewelry, but among a handful of earrings, pendants and hairpieces I didn't recognize was my mother's necklace, shined and cleaned to perfection.

I gripped the fragile strand in my hand, letting each pearl sift through my fingers. The mother I never met, knew absolutely nothing about because she was gone the moment I was born. Then, twenty years later, my father left this world for the exact same reason.

I undressed and wrapped the pearls around my neck. They lay cool and smooth against my skin, a little reminder all of this was tangible and real. Despite living in a fantasy, my feet were on the ground. I clutched them in my fist as I scrubbed dirt and blood from beneath my nails.

There was always something to do in the mornings. In my childhood, it was waking before the sun to feed the livestock, let the horses into their paddock and begin working in the fields. After that, it was taking care of Tommy and Papa, making sure their clothes were laid out and breakfast and coffee were made. I could count on one hand the amount of times I woke after the sun did. But Papa was gone and Tommy was busy rebuilding. All the years we suffered through, the isolation, the ostracization, all for nothing. A complete and utter waste of twenty years. In the end, I found myself with the Devil anyway.

I entered the study, wearing an old dress and not one of the flashy, expensive things Lillian left me. Any prayers I had that Jack would be off producing alcohol, bribing the fuzz or eating children's souls died with the image of his broad shoulders stretching a gray shirt thin. He had his back to me, sitting at a little dining set I was fairly sure didn't exist yesterday. The scent of coffee, fresh fruit and warm bread basted the room, mixed with the woody crackle of the eternal fireplace. He leaned his head in one hand, annotating a stack of papers precariously perched against a china teapot.

Perhaps it was better to hide. Somewhere in the cracked recesses of my mind *The Charge of the Light Brigade* came to thought. *Then they rode back, but not the six hundred.* Those men hadn't retreated, and look where it got them.

Before I could, Jack's voice rang out, "You can sit, you know. The chair won't swallow you."

I didn't know, and was shamefully glad he gave me instruction rather than making me wander on my own. Then, felt ashamed for thinking that. He wasn't my father or my brother, and he certainly wasn't my husband. I didn't need to take orders from Jack, but found myself sitting across from him anyway.

He didn't look up from his work, only waved one bare, tattooed hand over the spread. "If you don't like anything, I can ring Charlene."

He was in fae form this morning, and I wondered if that was meant to be a warning. My eyes scanned over the food, wondering if it was a trap. If the food was poisoned or drugged, or if he'd wait for me to finish breakfast before telling me I was now indebted to him. Again, I was struck by that reconciliation. Last night, Jack Warren told me everything was my choice, he wanted to get to know me, that he thought I was decent and liked sharing my time. But the Devil was a fae, and these were the things fae did.

I didn't move.

The grandfather clock ticked down in the corner. His pen scratched across the paper and I realized there was no inkpot in sight. Magic, maybe? What a mundane use for it.

He set the pen down. "Would you like something different?"

I shook my head so hard I nearly cracked my neck. "No, no, it's fine, I just . . ." Said nothing, because what would I say, I don't trust your intentions and never will?

He evaluated me, and I truly wished he would stop. I'd spent more personal time with cattle than people, and cattle didn't search your face for every little weakness, each chink in your armour. No doubt, I wore hundreds of them now.

"There's nothing wrong with the food," he said, which only set me more on edge.

"You can eat, Addie." My eyes flicked to his, gold and tired behind a set of wire spectacles I hadn't seen on him before. Arthur had them, but Arthur was once human. Eyeing Jack's cane resting against the table, I wondered how a creature so powerful and mighty needed so much . . . human help.

"You wear reading glasses?" I asked instead.

His eyebrows pinched together, then he sighed. "Oh, right." He snapped and they blinked away. I jumped. "Do me a favor and don't tell anyone about that."

I nodded, wondering why it mattered. Then we stared at each other, and I had more of an urge to vomit than put anything in my stomach.

That harrowing poem wouldn't leave my head, melting into memories of the Woman in White. *Theirs but to do and die.* Those turned to darker places, like exactly what was expected of me and the parallel bond I had with Jack.

It's your choice. Was it though? That was exactly what handsome men told silly women every day, all across the world. Everyone thought they made their own choice when they were manipulated to think that way. *It's your choice.* What fae said to humans before sucking them into bargains or wooing them to their deaths. He wanted me to trust his goodwill, but if it turned out every word from his lips was a pretty lie the consequences would be fatal. Worse, they would impact not just me, but everyone around me. The world. A man who told me I could pray to him asked me to give him god-like power the very next day.

So how did one sheltered, twenty-year-old farmer discern if it was truth or pretty lies? I scanned Jack's sharp jawline, his golden skin and shimmering eyes. Even in his terrifying true form, he was too devastating to describe. But nothing good ever looked like that. The most beautiful flowers were always the most poisonous.

The sprawling study suddenly felt much smaller, the crackling fireplace turning the heated room unbearable.

"Is there something bothering you?"

I shook my head.

He chewed the inside of his cheek. "Perhaps—"

"I don't feel well." I stood, vision darkening with the quick motion. Food. I needed food, but suddenly that no longer seemed important. "Enjoy your breakfast, Mr. Warren."

"Addie?"

I froze.

He drew out a long sigh. "I'd like to have dinner with you this evening."

I nodded. "I will."

I didn't.

ANOTHER DAY PASSED IN silence. When it became clear I wouldn't leave, trays of food appeared on the vanity before the spotless mirror. I picked at them just enough to quell the ache in my stomach. Each time I desired more, I remembered Lillian's famous rule. *Don't eat or drink anything in this hotel.* I still had no idea what the food could do to me, what the wine Jack forced me to drink *did* do to me. I paced the Abstruse, throwing aside the curtains and skimming every warning Papa ever gave me—always wear iron, don't speak to them, never give out your name, etc. But there was nothing in there about food.

When that warning wasn't enough, I thought of the little Baker boys and their sister. How they always asked me for food because there was never enough at home, and their growing bodies were gaunt after long days in the mines. I wondered if they missed me or just missed being fed. I hoped the church ladies gave them donations now that I was gone.

It would be a good time to dance. I always danced when I was sad or angry or just needed to think. But I could only think of that poem, of Papa's endless warnings, then his final death rattle beside the river. Of the brother whose letters were going unreceived, and if he would even notice. About once an hour I tried the windows again, but they were still sealed shut.

THREE DAYS PASSED AND there was a knock at my door. Lillian. I barely listened to her deflated mumbles, asking if I would like to go shopping with her that afternoon. When I didn't reply, those turned to faded inquiries about my well-being and if I would like to chat. In a brief moment of weakness, I considered the offer. We had been friends once, sort of. But then I remembered the dryads who always stood at the edge of the woods. How they would call me their sister, delight each time they saw me. For years they told me how beautiful I was, how they knew I loved ballet, how they would be so honored for me to dance with them. And once or twice I nearly did. But each time their lyrical voices wrapped around me, their offers sounded enticing or my blood ached to dance with them . . . I noticed the mutilated animals they dragged back to their trees.

"Come on, Addie. Please, come out."

I covered my ears.

Dinner never arrived. I didn't notice until the next evening.

FIVE DAYS. IT BECAME abundantly clear Jack sought to starve me out, but I had no appetite anyway. No one entered and I didn't leave.

Until the sixth day, when no food arrived at all. When my head pounded hard enough to erase my thoughts, I took a deep breath and entered the study.

Jack was nowhere to be seen. For a blessed moment I thought I was alone, but a flash of gold caught my eye from a velvet settee. Violet Warren lounged in fae form, stroking the shimmering scales of her snake.

We stared at one another.

A cruel smile lifted her lips. "Are you done being pathetic yet?"

I returned to the Abstruse empty-handed.

EIGHTEEN

WE NEVER WENT TO church, but Papa read the bible. He was a devout Christian, after all. So I knew well that God created the world in six days and on the seventh he rested. Apparently, I would not be granted the same reprieve, because after a week of silence, Lillian *popped* into my bathroom.

I winced in the tub, letting frothy bubbles drift between my fingers. I was too dizzy to do much else, or to care she stood with hands on her hips while I lay naked in the water. Her jasmine scent infiltrated the lemon and oleander wafting the room. In my peripheral vision, her slender hand held out a peach. The pink flesh brought hazy memories of home.

"Eat it. This moment." Her lovely voice held none of its usual cadence, stern and angry.

I shook my head.

She dragged a suede stool beside the tub and sat, cerulean eyes tracing me. "Yes, Adeline." She jutted the damned thing in my face. "You won't starve yourself to death, so either take it of your own will, or we'll revert to harsher means."

I really didn't want to learn what that meant, so I obeyed. Then, for reasons I couldn't explain, murmured, "When my brother left for the war, I stopped eating. I woke up in a field to my papa hand-feeding me peaches."

She was silent for a long moment. Steam permeated the air, the methodical drip of the faucet.

"How does one just stop eating? It's a human need, your body and mind have a drive for it."

I shrugged. "Everything felt so out of my control. But if I stopped speaking, sleeping, eating, I finally had power over something." I took a small bite. "A head doctor told my papa it was selective mutism, with some other irrational behaviors, but I'd grow out of it."

She eyed the half-eaten fruit. "But not all of it?"

"Apparently not." I set the peach on a marble shelf filled with soaps and oils, appetite erased.

"I can relate, in a way. Even fae don't do well with change. Especially fae." She folded her arms on the tub's edge, resting her chin on her wrists. "Immortality is funny like that. When everything is the same for so long, you forget how to adapt."

I cupped bubbles in my palms and watched them float. "You all seem to be doing fine to me."

"Believe me, we have many weaknesses." A tight, humorless smile flipped her lips. "You're Jack's."

"I highly doubt that."

"You would be shocked at the lengths he's gone to find and keep you safe. Though I'm sure that's not any consolation right now." She snapped her fingers. A wrinkled envelope appeared in her hand. "He didn't want me to tell you this yet, but no one can lie in the Abstruse, even in the bathroom. So in the spirit of transparency and friendship, I'm letting you know your brother has been writing. I've been forging letters back to him so he doesn't become suspicious." She held out the letter. "This one is very sweet, I thought it may lift your spirits."

I didn't take the letter. I didn't even look at it. One couldn't lie in the Abstruse, but who knew if that applied to written words. "Thank you."

A tense moment passed with the letter wavering between her fingers. She sighed, setting it on the vanity. "You know, I didn't fake enjoying your company for the sake of spying. I like you, Addie, and am truly your friend."

I cringed. Out loud, it sounded even more pathetic than in my mind. "I know."

"No, you don't." She sighed, gesturing to the soaps. "Can I wash your hair? You look feral. No offense."

I didn't move or speak, so she went ahead without my permission. "Just a forewarning, fae are not nearly as conservative as humans are."

I'd already gathered that as she conversed with me while I was nude.

"A lady should never look anything less than her best. We wear our insides on the outside." Rose-infused soap dripped onto my scalp and her fingers kneaded through the greasy knots. "I always feel much better after a nice bath and some lipstick."

"That's good advice."

"You know what they say—messy bed, messy head." She lathered soap into a stubborn knot. "And we all need a little help sometimes."

I skimmed my fingers over the water. "You have a very different approach than Violet."

She huffed. "You have to ignore her sometimes. Don't get me wrong, I care for Violet deeply, but she's very complex. Not always the easiest to love, and even harder to help."

"I can't imagine what an all-powerful fae woman with goddess looks needs help with."

"Not quite all-powerful. She has them—powers—but she doesn't use them. Ever."

I frowned. "She gave me a poison kiss last week."

"Well, that's not really a power. More her . . . anatomy."

She finished lathering my hair and instructed me to rinse. When I resurfaced above the water I said, "Why doesn't she use her powers?"

"You know, I'm not sure actually. She's very private, hence difficult to help. And Jack would never reveal her secrets." She rested her chin on her arms again. "Truthfully, I think she has a lot of regrets. I know I have plenty, which is why I took my own vow."

"What vow?"

"I will never kill a living thing again, not even a houseplant." She gestured to her arm, where a strange scar puckered her skin. Pale, white lines formed a sort of sigil, but I'd never seen anything like it. "Vows are sacred to fae, just like bargains. I can never break it."

I frowned. "Not even in self-defense? You're a spy, isn't there danger in that?"

She lifted a shoulder. "If it is my time, it will be my time."

I remembered Will's strange comments about her last week. About how Lillian would cut off his head for speaking out of turn. Even knowing what she was, even though fear still pulsed heavy in my blood, the thought of the bouncy, sweet Lillian lopping off appendages was obscene. And that was before seeing the vow marking her skin.

"In the other world, what did you do? Your occupation, I mean."

A sad smile touched her face. "I suppose Will already let the cat out of the bag?"

"No, no he didn't say anything specific." I wasn't sure why I rushed to defend Will, only that it felt like a betrayal of his trust not to do so. Even if his loose tongue was a betrayal in the first place. But he was fae and I was human, so maybe loyalty meant different things to us. They had to.

"This room allows only truths, right?"

I nodded.

"I have an awful one."

"You don't need to tell me."

"You will find out anyway. I'd rather you heard it from me."

I shouldn't have indulged. Indulging was what got me in this situation in the first place. But a stoic mask fell over Lillian's face, a flash of something unrecognizable behind her eyes. It could have been a way to earn my trust, but Lillian was a spy. She was trained to covet secrets, not spill them. In two hundred years, she had to have learned better ways to worm into my brain than revealing something personal.

"Okay." Because this felt like a conversation I should be dressed for, I stepped out of the tub and wrapped a robe around my shoulders. Lillian picked at her cuticles. I settled to the floor, leaning my head against the porcelain tub. Lillian slipped from her stool and sat on the ground in front of me.

Her springy curls crunched as she faced me and leaned her head on the tub. The vibration of her pulse rolled down the porcelain and across my skin. It was strange to think they had pulses, a heart, just like me. So different and yet, the same.

"Ildathach is not like the human world," she began. "Humans can be awful, commit terrible atrocities, but where I come from, there's very little good at all."

She closed her eyes. "I was one of twelve children, the youngest and only girl of the king and queen of the northern islands."

My heartbeat stuttered. Lillian was a princess? How many fae royals got banished to these parts, anyway . . .

"Where we are from, it is tradition that the monarchs have as many children as possible. It's much harder for fae to have children, you see, so they're rare and very special. A match that is centuries old may only produce one or two heirs, so my parents having twelve was considered a miracle. Some believe that's why the parallel bond exists with humans—so fae don't die out completely. They conceive more easily." She swallowed. "But to cut to the chase, the crown doesn't go to the eldest boy like it does in this world. Once both monarchs die, their sons battle to the death for power. Only when all other male heirs are killed can one take a throne."

"That's barbaric," I breathed.

"Quite." She brought a perfect, red nail to her teeth, chewing until the polish cracked. "I was the only girl of twelve children, so I was never really in line for the throne. But my mother was . . ." Her eyes went glassy. "She was what she was, and she had untraditional expectations of me. I was a terrible person. Bitter, arrogant, unfeeling, mostly. So when our parents died, I joined the hunts."

I nodded. "So . . . you were banished because you joined when you weren't allowed to?"

Icy eyes cut into mine. "No. I killed all eleven of them. Every last brother myself."

My stomach bottomed out, frost coating my tongue. I grappled with something to say, but thankfully she continued.

"But, trying to ascend the throne as a woman wasn't an option. Instead of accepting me, the council and court declared me a traitor. I had some supporters, but the rest smelled blood in the water, an opportunity to put their own families on the throne with all the viable heirs of mine gone. Essentially, all I did was allow my family's enemies to take our seat. And the price was all my siblings."

She dug her nails into her arms until little pinpricks of blood erupted.

"Will led my royal guard since I was an infant. Whenever high fae of certain affinities were born, they were taken as infants and raised in barracks as orphan soldiers. I know it doesn't seem like it because we all look the same age, but he's a bit older than me. On her labor bed, my mother made him give a vow to always protect me. Should anything happen to me, he would suffer the same fate. If I died, his vow would kill him too.

"The worst part is, I was so terribly awful to him for years. He despised me, but turning on me meant forfeiting his own life. So when he realized my own court was about to tear me to shreds, he took me to the human world where we met Jack and Violet. They liked Will immediately, of course. How could you not?" A watery smile trembled her lips. "I was only thirty then, which by fae standards is very, *very* young. Violet wanted to kill me, but Jack didn't want any harm to come to Will. He figured I may still be . . . reformed, so to speak. They kept me imprisoned in iron chains for eleven years—completely my fault, Jack gave me every opportunity and I took none of them. But one day he came down, brought me some food and rattled my chains a bit. Told me that I could end my imprisonment by proving myself to him and the others. If I remained his loyal servant, along with taking a vow that stopped me from killing, for exactly one hundred years and one hundred days, then I would have earned his trust and my freedom with it."

"But that was nearly a century ago."

She nodded, slowly. Her eyes bounced everywhere but my huddled form beside her. "A century of Jack humbling me to the point of torture and having no means to harm others changed my mindset. When the one hundred years and one hundred days were over, I retook the vow myself. Forever. So for the rest of my life, I will remain a servant to Jack, one that can do no true harm. It's about the only penance I can offer to Will. To suffer the same fate he did and never return to what I used to be."

Silence trickled down around us. The steamy air suffocated me, like all the words I couldn't offer.

"Is Will still going to die when you do?"

"Yes. Bargains can do no harm once completed or rescinded, but vows are unbreakable once made. No power exists to nullify one. Believe me, I've looked." She paused. "Even so, he was the main supporter of my decision. And as I'm sure you can tell, our relationship has improved exponentially these past two hundred years."

That spoke a lot about Will. But Lillian was a lot of things herself, and despite every ingrained warning in my head, I didn't think evil was one of them.

"So is it awkward that my soulmate made you his slave?"

For some incomprehensible reason, she laughed loud enough to rattle the tub. "Oh, no, don't worry about that. Jack pays me for my work, gives me room and board, and is a very dear friend—more like family than anything. Not that I would, but if I ever decided to leave he wouldn't stop me. We treat that part of the vow as symbolic at this point."

Well, that was one silver lining. "I'm really sorry, Lillian."

She shook her head. "I'm happy where I am now."

"I know, but . . ." I wished I had something more profound to offer, but could only think of, "Thank you for telling me."

"Well, that's what friends do. No secrets, right?"

Hope glimmered in her eyes. I wondered if she was lonely here, despite what she said. Our first conversation resurfaced, when she mentioned there weren't a lot of women "around these parts." Obviously she had Violet, but that seemed like another situation entirely.

Just like with Jack, I wasn't sure what to think. If I trusted Lillian and was wrong, there would be a price to pay. I conjured the image of those dryads. Of the Woman in White sitting in the empty river, delivering sweet promises with only one tiny caveat. Of my father striking a deal he thought he could outplay, then dying because of it.

But then I looked around the walls of the Abstruse. This could be my prison, or it could be my bedroom. There was only so long I could remain stagnant, choosing indecision. It would always come with a risk, but I had to leave eventually. The windows were sealed, the door led to Jack and there was only one other alternative that didn't include putting my faith in a fae. But I was terrified of them because of the consequences; drowning myself in the bathtub to be free of them sort of defeated the purpose.

She didn't have to tell me that story. She didn't have to bring me a peach or wash my hair. She also didn't have to say she truly thought of me as a friend, because if she didn't, the Abstruse wouldn't allow her to. And out of all of them, it wouldn't be the worst thing to have Lillian on my side. I once enjoyed her company. She was my first and only true friend.

"Yeah." I nodded, still unsure of myself. "That's what friends do."

"Are we okay, then?"

I had very little—well, *no*—experience in that department, but Lillian had always been kind to me. And she trusted me with her past, so I could give her the benefit of doubt for now.

"We're okay."

She jerked me into a hug. I wheezed against her tight embrace, patting her back awkwardly as she let go. Thankfully, she didn't seem to mind.

"Excellent. I need someone to go shopping with. Violet despises it."

I laughed, but something else she said stuck out to me, sending skittish energy down my spine. "Did you say bargains can be rescinded?"

"Yes, if both parties agree and are willing. They can be altered as well, under the same conditions."

My thoughts eddied around the Woman in White. If I could find her, maybe I could change our deal. Perhaps even rescind it altogether. Especially now that I was bound to a powerful fae who needed me, and therefore may be willing to help . . .

But the entire reason the Woman in White sought me was because of Jack. It had to be. She told me I cheated and asked for death in return. I'd spent years wondering what that meant, figuring in the end I was supposed to die with my mama but somehow survived.

While that was technically true, it wasn't medicine or luck that revived me. It was Jack's powers. She'd even said that herself—*he thought he could play me.*

So Jack would be no help, but things could still be changed, and that gave me some sense of hope. I just had to make sure that by altering our agreement, no harm came to Tommy. He already survived the war which completed that end of the bargain, but winning in a battle of wits against Death herself seemed an uphill battle. If she was that angry about Jack saving my life, then I highly doubted she would play fair in preserving Tommy's.

That hope deflated faster than it came.

Lillian cocked her head to the side. "What are you thinking about?"

My demise. My brother's demise. I couldn't be sure what Jack would do if he knew the truth, that the mate he was destined to be with could either give him one heir and die or none at all. Lillian thought he had a soft spot for me, but she donned rose-colored glasses when it came to all things Jack Warren. He was her savior, so I understood, but it didn't mean her opinion of him was unbiased. He saved my life as an infant because of our parallel bond and kept me now because of Delsaran. He claimed he wanted to know me, but that was problematic in itself. We hadn't exactly gotten off to a great start, and what would happen if he decided he didn't like me even if I tried, that the bond wasn't worth it?

Mine and Tommy's fates couldn't rely on the chance I could charm an inhuman bootlegger.

Maybe Lillian could help.

"If I tell you something, can you promise not to tell anyone?"

She nodded, sitting up straighter. "Of course. I'll vow it, if you want."

Guilt picked at me. She really wanted me to trust her, understandably after that story she just told, and it wasn't like I gave her the friendliest welcome. I eyed the thick scars on her arm, peeking from beneath her dress sleeve. A few minutes ago I told her we were still friends, and since this was the Abstruse, I meant it.

"That's not necessary," I said. "Just . . . I really need this to be kept quiet, okay?"

"And I swear on the Bogorans it will be." She grinned. "Do you want to tell me or should I extract it?"

My eyebrows furrowed. "Extract?"

"Oh, right, of course." She beamed. "All fae possess three basic powers. Glamour, which you know is illusion. Compulsion, which is bending others to your will. And shading, which is travel." She gestured to the mirror, but I hadn't the faintest clue why. I also ignored the sudden itch that erupted at the mention of *compulsion*. "But some high fae have what we call affinities. They're special gifts that usually run in family lines. Like how Jack and Violet have poison."

"I thought poison was Violet's anatomy?"

"It's a bit complicated. A few millennia ago an ancestor of theirs mated with a basilisk, so some things are anatomical and others are affinity-based." She waved a hand. "Anyway, my affinity is memories."

I didn't know what a basilisk was and I didn't want to. "Memories?"

"Yes, I can see others' memories if I touch them. Or even erase or alter them if I desired to. That's how I knew who you were that first day we met. You brushed my hand and I saw all these images of Jack. I could also smell the parallel bond. That's how Will and Violet figured it out." She chewed her bottom lip, realizing what she just said. "Please, don't be upset."

By the blatant violation of my privacy and mind? No, that honor went to Jack. "It's fine."

She loosed a breath. "Oh, good. But yes, that's a large part of why I'm his spy. It's a useful affinity for that line of work."

And now she wanted me to willingly allow her to sift through my brain. Though, she had ample opportunities many times already. She washed my hair mere minutes ago. "You haven't looked for anything else, have you?"

"Of course not." Her ivory skin turned a deep pink. "That was the only time, I swear. If it makes you feel more comfortable, Jack could teach you to block it."

I shook my head. "It's okay, really. I trust you." I paused. "So, how does this work, I let you touch me and think of the memory?"

She nodded. "That's the easiest way."

I'd add learning the hard way to the list of things I had no desire to know, right next to whatever a basilisk was. "Does it hurt?"

She frowned. "Only if you're unwilling."

Lord above, alright then. I held out a hand. "Go ahead."

"Make sure you think of it exactly as it was. If you alter or embellish it in any way, I won't be able to tell." She took my hand.

I felt nothing. I should have suspected as much, but it was still disarming having no sense of someone else reading my thoughts. I retrieved the memory of the Woman in White, that fateful day beside the river, and dropped my hand.

Her eyes shimmered, frown sinking deeper into her beautiful face. "So that's why you panicked when Violet said it was a mating bond."

I shivered. I didn't mean to, but part of me still didn't believe her affinity was actually that powerful.

"That was a terrible bargain you made."

I shrugged, the gesture swollen with humiliation. "I was eleven."

"No, of course. It's just . . ." Her lips pursed. "Don't listen to me. I'm sorry."

I nodded. "I know what you meant."

"I can help if you want." She drummed her fingers on her cheek, thinking. "Of course, there's always the option of making you infertile. Technically, it's more cheating, but you wouldn't be breaking the bargain if you never had a child. But that's a heavy decision in itself." She frowned. "We should really ask Jack."

"No," I said, too forcefully. She jumped. "I just . . . I don't want him to know about this yet. We have enough issues to sort through, as is."

She nodded with too much enthusiasm. "Of course, no Jack for now. That's fine. It'll just be difficult to worm our way out of this one."

Despite her dreary prognosis, there was some comfort in the word, *we*. With a start, I realized Lillian was the first person I'd ever told. The Woman in White was a secret I carried alone for nine years. Having someone to talk about it with, even if they were clueless themselves, was more relieving than I thought it would be.

"The first step is obviously getting you some birth control. Did you know humans sell that at drug stores now? It's remarkable." She grinned. "We have plenty of magical options as well if we need a back up plan. So for now, there's no need to worry. Nothing will happen to you, I promise."

I breathed a sigh of relief. A weight lifted off my shoulders. It felt as if I'd held it in for years.

"For the long term, we'll have to do some research. Arthur has a magnificent inventory of all non-human creatures. That would be the best place to start."

My lips turned down. "Why would we start there?"

"To figure out what your Woman in White is. I'll be honest, I've never seen a creature like her before."

My thoughts scrambled. I thought it was obvious what she was. "Isn't she Death?"

"Maybe, but I'm not sure. I've never heard of someone being visited by Death like that." Her lips flattened, matching mine.

"But if she's not Death, what could she be?"

"That's what we'll have to find out." She stood, dusting off her dress. "Jack and I have to head over to Arthur's tomorrow, anyway. You should come."

I shook my head. "I don't—"

"You have to leave this room sometime." Her hands fell to her hips, a mother goose expression stealing her features. "If you want my help, I'd like for you to have breakfast with Jack tomorrow. Afterwards, he can bring you to Arthur's and I'll borrow some books from him. Discreetly, of course."

I pinched the bridge of my nose. "It's not help if it comes with conditions."

She bent at the waist and kissed the top of my head. "That's fae for you, darling."

NINETEEN

I'D NEVER BEEN IN battle. My brother had, my new fae companions had, but in that territory I was uneducated. Still, as I slipped into one of my dresses, fixed Mama's pearls and applied my lipstick, it felt awfully similar to preparing for war.

We wear our insides on our outsides. If that were the case, I'd don every piece of armour I had.

Then, attend breakfast . . . with my inhuman mate.

As usual, the dark study glowed under green lamps and the roaring fireplace. A swift breeze slammed the door to the Abstruse shut, as if it were also desperate to get me out. The reality that even the room was tired of me was probably a good sign this was the right choice. With that death knell, I twiddled my fingers in the dark hall and took a deep breath for strength. The monster sipping tea would not harm me. I had a friend and ally in Lillian, and a plan to relieve myself of the curse following my every footstep. My brother was safe and sound in Chicago and for now, I was safe and sound here. If I focused on these things, it almost felt like I was in control of them.

Like the previous week, Jack sat with his back to me. Obviously, he didn't consider me much of a threat. Still, one pointed ear twitched at my arrival, the muscles beneath his broad shoulders tightening. I'd just alerted the predator of my presence. Now all I had to do was make small talk with him.

192

My kitten heels padded over the carpet. The scorch mark from last week still blackened the far edge. Pushing my hair out of my face, I smoothed my dress and sat opposite Jack Warren.

His eyes narrowed.

"Good morning." Fingers trembling, I reached for a steaming teapot in the center of the table. Since Lillian decided this was my punishment, she made it her mission to make the experience as palatable as possible. Literally and figuratively. After asking what I liked to eat in the morning with promises to relay it to Charlene, she mentioned all the *aphrodisiacs* she recommended for our armistice meal. As if we needed any more of those. That's what got me into this mess in the first place.

My selections were Earl Gray, an omelet with *extra* onions and garlic bread. Emphasis on the garlic. The chocolate, pomegranates and figs Lillian recommended sat untouched before my plate.

Jack sipped from a china teacup, evaluating me. "Good morning."

Unsure if that was a question or statement, I smiled shakily and shoveled eggs in my mouth.

He eyed each movement like it personally offended him.

"I heard you will be going to Arthur's today. If it's not too much to ask, I would like to come."

Leaning forward, he scoured my face for god-knew-what. Like it was angry at the absence, the bond roared to life between us. I choked on the eggs in my throat, swallowing them down with a blush. Jack reached over the table for a fig, taking half of it between his teeth in one bite.

"Anything she wants." The words came low, heated . . . dangerous.

I swallowed. A single eyebrow hit his hairline. I debated pitching myself off the roof.

"Does this mean you are feeling well again?" Confusion tore through me, until I remembered the last time we sat at this table.

Eight days ago felt like a lifetime already. A lifetime where I told Jack I felt unwell and hid from him in his own residence.

I gave him a close-lipped smile. "Divine."

His lips pulled into a knowing smirk. The bond rushed straight south, giving me a few thoughts I'd never thought I would have while eating garlic bread.

He sipped his coffee.

I sipped my tea.

"So . . ." I twirled the spoon around the china, fearing if my hands remained unoccupied, I would consider some very inappropriate actions. "You said you wanted the chance to get to know me?"

He leaned back, languorous and arrogant. The dark tattoos at his neck shifted, growing wilder as if responding to the growing heat. "That's typically what mates do."

You don't want to fuck him. It's magic.

"I'd say you already know me quite well. May I ask about you?"

His arms folded over his chest. A long moment passed underneath his stare, activating the primal side of my brain. I couldn't decide if it wanted me to mate or run for my life. "Sure."

Good, now I had to actually think of something. A task made infinitely harder with him sitting like that, knees spread apart only two feet away. God, I'd never even had sex before, where were these thoughts *coming* from?

"Why the bootlegging?" I nearly dropped the garlic bread I was holding. Really—was that *really* the first thought to come to mind?

"It's lucrative."

Waving a hand in the air, I mumbled through a mouthful of bread, "Sure, but can't you simply . . . make money appear? Why go through all of the hassle?"

His head cocked to the side. "Are you asking out of curiosity, or for your brother who's in the FBI?"

Shit, I was awful at this.

"Curiosity." I swallowed. "I can repeat that again in the Abstruse, if needed."

A smile twitched at the corner of his lips. "The money still comes from somewhere. We can't create matter. And if large sums of it go missing, that raises red flags. Since all cash has serial codes, spending it would lead the human government right to our door."

I paused. "So instead of, I don't know, a normal living, you make champagne?"

Serpent eyes narrowed again. "You humans call it absinthe, actually."

"What do you call it?"

"Fae wine."

Wonderful. I was sure the repercussions of that on humankind were completely inconsequential.

"For us, it's nothing more than alcohol. But when humans drink it, it causes hallucinations and euphoria. Once, that was terrifying to your kind, but I suppose it's a new century. Everyone's looking for the hot new fix."

My left eye twitched. "Isn't progress a wonderful thing?"

His smile stretched wider. "Oh, and that's not all, darling. I distill my own gin and whiskey as well. All in the basement of this hotel, actually. You currently sit on the top floor of a fucking gold mine."

I matched his smile. "What a lucky gal I am."

"So the short answer to *why the bootlegging* . . ." He kicked his feet up on the table, as if bringing that word to life. The china rattled. "Running a kingdom is very costly, believe it or not. Especially one that operates as discreetly as ours. I needed the money, humans lose their shit for booze, and now here we are."

I held my teacup in the air. "Hurrah."

Silence prickled between us. I used the opportunity to fire off more questions. "What does *annwyl* mean, anyway?"

"It's Welsh, a term of endearment like darling or sweetheart. Or on occasion, a woman's name."

"Do you speak Welsh in your world?"

"No, we have our own language. But most of the breaks in the veil land you in Wales, so many fae learn it young."

So there would be no vacations to Wales in my future. Noted.

I had another question, but I wasn't sure it was polite to ask. I supposed I already crossed that bridge with the bootlegging question, but this felt dangerous.

I asked anyway. "If you're immortal, does that mean you can't be killed?"

He raised a brow. After a long moment of silence, he said, "We can only be killed by iron weapons or if our bodies are destroyed. That includes no food, sleep, or irreparable damage. Like chopping off my head."

Very good to know. "Is that the same for druids?"

"Druids are more susceptible. You can still fall ill or be killed by normal human means. Your only immunity to death is the fact you don't age."

Great, so even as a druid I would still be inferior to him.

"When did you come to this world?"

"Three hundred years or so ago."

"I thought you were banished for being a twin?"

"When we were born, our mother gave Violet to humans in this world and kept her birth a secret. I found her many years later. When my mother's deception was discovered we were both banished."

I mulled that over. As volatile as Violet could be, her history softened my resolve. How awful to be the child your parents gave up, choosing to keep your sibling instead. I wondered if she held any bitterness toward him over it.

"I have a question for you now." His eyes scoured over me. "What size corset do you wear?"

That was it. I hated him.

"Actually, *sweetheart*, I wasn't done." I smiled with effervescent joy. "How do you feel about attending church with me? Since you're a very devout Catholic, and all."

He grimaced. "You want me to go to mass?"

"Well, not just mass. We'd have to attend Wednesday services as well. In addition to Thursday marriage counseling, Tuesday bible study group, and of course, volunteer at all church-related events." I pouted. "We must think of the sinners, Jack."

Now, his eye twitched. "Anything she wants."

"I have some additional questions." I poured myself more tea, tracking every muscle twitch of his in my peripheral. "Would you consider yourself a well-read man?"

"I read dirty magazines. Does that count?"

"Do you like cats?"

"I fucking despise them."

"Since you live in *this* world now, have you ever considered abolishing your monarchy?"

He picked at his nails. "Democracy is for pussies."

My smile cracked at the corners. "Are you in possession of a single redeeming quality?"

He actually considered it, eyes on the ceiling in thought. After a laborious minute, he decided on, "I'm rich and very attractive."

My face dropped into my palms. I dragged my fingers through my hair, breathing, "I'm supposed to have sex with you."

"Oh, I just remembered one other redeeming quality." He dropped his feet from the table. "I have a massive—"

"Good morning, love birds!" Lillian chimed, popping into existence in a flurry of diamonds and cornflower silk. Her hands flung to her face with fake surprise. "Are you two having breakfast together? My goodness, how *romantic*. That's just so lovely to see, truly."

If I had a gasket, it would blow through the ceiling.

Jack smiled, patting her arm as she kissed his cheek. "What an excellent time for you to arrive. Adeline was just in the midst of telling me how humble, charming and generous she finds me."

I glared at him. He winked.

"See? I told you he'd grow on you." She kissed both my cheeks and held out her hands. "Are we ready to depart? We all know how our faithful druid hates to be left waiting."

I shoved the remaining garlic bread in my mouth. "Lead the way."

ARTHUR LIVED ON THE top floor of a dilapidated building three blocks from the hotel. Because Delsaran's creatures were still vehemently searching for me, Jack and Lillian decided the safest route would be their strange blinking power. The thought of doing that again made my skin crawl, but any other options I threw out were immediately vetoed. To make myself feel a little better, I'd asked how it worked. Jack then rattled off some nonsense about *the shade.*

"It's the space between worlds," he said, snapping, and a book appeared from thin air. "It can only be accessed through your reflection, and only by more powerful high fae. Those beginning to learn always need to start with mirrors, as they're the easiest to access. Which is why you may have noticed every room in this hotel has one. Once you become more proficient, you can reach through anything that reflects your image back to you." He held a polished dinner plate and pressed his fingers through, swallowing his skin to the knuckles. Nothing emerged on the other side of the plate. I checked. Twice.

The porcelain roiled around his hand like liquid until he dropped it to the table. "If you ever want to attempt it, don't. You will get lost in the shade, and once you're stuck there is no getting out, leading to a horrible death. Understood?"

That made me wish I'd never asked, so I took the explanation without further questions. Then he wrapped his hand around mine, winked at me in a three-tier mirror beside the bookshelves, and I plummeted through an ocean of frigid waves. I opened my eyes to chipped tiles.

And promptly vomited on them.

"I swear, by next time it'll be much better!" Lillian said, appearing in my watery vision, dabbing at my face with a pocket square. Someone snapped and the puddle of vomit went into the ether. "It's like drinking. The first time you feel fine, then you vomit a few nights before getting your bearings. Third time's a charm, truly."

When I was finally done retching, I looked around at . . . I wasn't sure. What I guessed was once a living room now held every manner of magical oddity known to man or otherwise. Tables covered every inch of the checkered tiles, creating a labyrinth across the room. Piles of useless items crowded each corner and books were stacked from floor to ceiling against the wall. One of the tables held hundreds of leather-bound journals, while another had a chemistry set and test samples. On another was what I hoped wasn't the remains of a fuzzy animal while one closer to the kitchen held a glass ball, a bowl of burned herbs, a medieval knight's helmet and the most ridiculously ornate chalice I'd seen. Every time my eyes moved something else appeared. Finally, Arthur himself emerged from what I could only guess was a bedroom.

His blonde hair stuck at odd angles and fuschia smears stained his waistcoat. He grinned, clutching a cracked timepiece and pushed his glasses up his nose. "Adeline! I wasn't expecting you."

My face stretched in a tight smile. "I was convinced to come along."

"Wonderful, wonderful, wonderful. We're getting on well, then?" He glanced between me and Jack, grinning. Neither of us said a word.

"Excellent!" he chimed, clapping his hands together. "Right then, very well, wonderful we're all getting along swimmingly."

I nodded. "Like peas in a pod."

"Isn't that just the cat's pajamas?" He smiled so broadly, I felt bad for the lie. "Anyway, it took some digging, but I found those texts you requested, Jack."

A cane clicked along the floor behind me. I became hyperaware of Jack's presence only inches away. "Thank you, Arthur."

"No problem at all, anything for my favorite faerie folk." Digging apparently meant more digging, because he sifted through a haphazard stack of yellowed journals. A whole pile of them toppled to the floor. Lillian smiled where she sat on a table, swinging her legs. "And here we are!"

He produced a notebook with a flourish, balancing precariously on the table to hand it over to Jack. The other took it, leaning his cane and hip on the wall to thumb through the pages.

After a moment of tense silence he sighed, snapping it shut. "I may need a minute to go through this."

Arthur turned maroon. "Of course, the study is quieter if you need."

Jack nodded and made his departure. After telling me I looked divine and kissing both my cheeks, Lillian followed him. That left Arthur and I, who began fiddling with a flask, swirling some blue, glowing material around the glass. I folded my arms and stilled, worrying I'd bump something.

"So . . . is this what druids do all day?"

"Yes and no. Much of this is for Jack, but I keep my own personal records and experiments." He set the flask down, scanning me. "Do human women like tea? It's been so long since I've talked to one, if I'm honest."

A wry smile tugged my lips. "Yes, but only if it comes from one of those flasks."

His eyes widened. "Oh, heavens no. You'd disintegrate or find yourself in 1682. I have clean ones in the kitchen though."

Jesus Christ. "Tea would be lovely, thank you."

"IT'S WONDERFUL HAVING A fresh face around. Spending several centuries with the same people gets a *bit* tedious." Arthur rummaged through every cupboard he had, leaving the doors open behind him. I settled into the only empty seat in the strewn kitchen. "Not that I have any complaints. Our Band of Banished is an excellent little group."

"Band of Banished?"

"Oh, yes, that's what I've taken to calling us. Has a nice ring to it, doesn't it?" He flashed me a smile. "Violet called me an idiot."

"Don't worry, I'm sure she's called me worse."

"That means she likes you." I highly doubted that, but saw no point in refuting it. "Chamomile or English Breakfast?"

A simple choice, and yet, I wondered if there were any social faux pas in making that request. I lifted a shoulder. "Whatever you like best."

"Chamomile it is." He lit the stove and started the tea kettle. I struggled for something to say.

Luckily, Arthur was more than happy to fill the silence. "To think, you may become the first druid in nearly four hundred years. The Guild will be green with envy when they find out I got to you first."

Parallel bonds were supposedly very rare, but I didn't think glamour-touched humans were. From Arthur's explanation the other day, all druids began as humans. "Why four-hundred years?"

"Glamour-touched can only be made into druids by Bogorans. But the last one died over three centuries ago, so we're a dying race ourselves now."

Those creatures again. The *Band of Banished* explained they created fae the other night. According to humans that would make the Bogorans gods, but what kind of gods could be killed off?

Then there was the other thing he said. "I suppose that makes my appearance quite important to you."

"To all druids, and humans of course. You're the first sliver of hope in a long time." He beamed over his shoulder.

Well, that certainly added a whole new layer to everything. It should have been a relief that this was more than handing Jack god-like power, but I wondered if that was a good thing. Surely, I couldn't be the only glamour-touched human out there. For the first druid in nearly four hundred years, there had to be someone much more qualified than me.

I swallowed. "And the Guild?"

"The other druids. We parted ways about two centuries or so ago. I'm what some may call a social outcast."

A tight smile crossed my face. He swiped a bundle of dried sticks from a nearby chair, falling into it with a grunt. "That makes two of us."

"See? You fit in perfectly with our Band of Banished. A most excellent addition." He crossed one long, lean leg over the other. "So, what makes you a pariah?"

My eyes became dinner plates. It was perhaps the most blunt and ill-mannered thing I'd ever been asked. Back in Georgia, it would be social suicide.

But at least it took some of the pressure off of me. I decided to tell him the truth.

"Most people thought I was a devil-worshiper."

He nodded like that was completely reasonable. "If it makes you feel any better, I'm a terrible druid."

The kettle whistled and he jumped to his feet. I helped him rummage through the cabinets, finding nothing but three jars of frog legs, a mice-ravaged flour sack, a honey-pot with the label "Do Not Touch, Live Pixies Inside" and two chipped teacups.

"Why is that?"

"Druids are known for our community leadership. We were the religious chiefs of our day, soothsayers and oral historians. It was our job to keep records and pass down knowledge of the past and future to the humans of our villages, since we are immortal." He poured boiling water into the teacups. One popped as a hairline crack appeared at the bottom. "But long story short, I have severe memory loss."

I frowned. "Is that common?"

"Gods, no." He released an anxious chuckle, sliding the uncracked teacup to me. "I don't really know when it started. But when I was young, my mother always told me I had my head up my ass."

I couldn't help it. A giggle broke free, punctuating the sounds of bubbling from the living room. "I'm sorry, that's terrible."

"But true." He shrugged, smiling like there wasn't a care in the world. "I first noticed it when I would do all the chores for the day, then realize I left the sheep out in the pasture. Then, when I was mid-twenty, I traveled the continent to train with human physicians." He grimaced. "Had a very bad incident fixing a broken arm and that was done.

"From there, I traveled back to Wales, thinking I may do better as a bard after meeting this nice fellow on the road, but you know, I couldn't remember which string on the lute was G." He stirred his tea, staring at the ceiling. Water sloshed over the sides. "Then I spotted some fae, they realized I was glamour-touched and took me to the Bogorans. They blessed me as a druid and sent me off to the Guild. Those were some good times."

I watched tea water swirl around my own cup. "Maybe you only remember happy things."

"Maybe. It also helps that I write everything down. Three times, and I will never forget it." He gestured to the living room. "I'm sure you saw all the journals."

Journals that must date back hundreds of years. Even I had to admit that was something incredible, a thought my puny human brain couldn't process. A living history book sat right in front of me. Seven hundred years . . . what did one even do for seven hundred years?

"I'd love to hear your stories sometime," I said.

His cheeks turned bright red. He stammered on about having to organize his journals, check for discrepancies, but was blessedly saved by Jack and Lillian squeezing into the tiny kitchen. The former leaned against the counter, eyes tracing my every swallow.

"Thank you, Arthur," he said, handing the journal back to the flushed blond.

"Did you find what you need?"

Lillian hopped on the table, swinging her legs and ignoring Arthur's panic. He swiped his teacup from the wood before she knocked it over. "Not quite."

"What are you looking for, exactly?" I wasn't sure why I asked. I truly wanted little to do with this, but Arthur's words weighed heavy on my mind. If druids were all about gaining knowledge, I should probably respect them enough to ask a simple question.

Jack closed his eyes. "How to make a druid without a Bogoran."

At this, Arthur paled. His green eyes widened behind his glasses. "You know that can't be done, right? Not anymore. I assumed you had some other plan."

"If there's a will, there's a way, Arthur." Lillian grinned, tapping him on the nose. "It's just about finding the right resource. Isn't that right, Jack?"

I glanced between them. "Why are we trying to make a druid? I thought I became one with the parallel ritual, or whatever you call it."

Lillian chewed her bottom lip. "Unfortunately, those need to be blessed by Bogorans too. Humans can't simply become something else without an infusion of power, even with the ritual."

I let that settle. So there could be a chance none of this was doable anyway. Something else that should have been a relief, but I wasn't sure how I felt about it.

Arthur glanced at Jack, clutching his teacup between sweaty fingers. "I know what you're thinking and—"

"Yes, but it will know," he cut in. Even Lillian's face soured, a sullen tension swallowing the room. "I'd like to pay it a visit by the end of the week. Get this nasty business done and move forward."

Before I could ask, Lillian leaned to the side, whispering, "You don't want to know. Trust me."

"Actually, Adeline will be coming with me."

We all stared at him. Muscles taut, face a smooth mask, he revealed nothing. Neither about what he planned to bring me to, nor the clear disapproval lining Lillian's and Arthurs's faces. I had half a mind to get up and run from the room, but that did me no favors the first time. Besides, if Jack took me somewhere, it may be another chance to find an escape.

"Where am I going?"

His eyes cut to mine, glinting in the light streaming through dirty windows. "To visit a librarian."

Arthur ran a trembling hand through his hair. "That is certainly one way to put it."

Lillian sat on her hands, as if containing the urge to throttle someone. "We call it *Rihaedon*. It's a word from our language that doesn't translate well to yours, but roughly, yes, it means librarian."

Taking this opportunity to escape suddenly felt like a terrible mistake. "If it has a name, if it's a living thing, why do you keep referring to it as *it*?" I asked.

For a long moment, no one spoke. Lillian hopped down from the table, sighing. "I'll get the skin."

TWENTY

BEFORE HER DEPARTURE, I quietly gave Lillian express permission to enter the Abstruse whenever she wanted. She left four books on the nightstand along with a scribbled note. *There's plenty more where this came from. As you finish them, I'll supply more in English and get through the rest when I can.* I'd planned on spending the night combing through the yellowed pages, but she reappeared in the study later that afternoon.

Jack had said by the end of the week, but Lillian finished her task quickly enough we were ready to go by nightfall. A chorus of concerns rose later that evening as every member of Arthur's *Band of Banished* crowded Jack's study. Surprisingly, the loudest ones came from Violet.

"Are you raving fucking mad?" She lounged across the chaise like she owned it. For the last ten minutes, she'd taken turns cooing to her snake and cursing at Jack.

"Adeline will be fine. She's with me."

"Neither one of you should be going. I'll go." She shot me a pointed look, like this was all my fault.

"You're not going."

"Why not? *Rihaedon* adores me."

Without any knowledge of what this librarian was, I wasn't the least surprised.

Ignoring her, Jack gestured to Lillian, silently clutching a satchel by the mirror. "Is it cleaned?"

Her bottom lip came between her teeth. Like a child relinquishing a toy, she nodded and gave him the bag. "If I may give my opinion, Jack, I really do think Adeline has already struggled enough the past few days. I'm sure you have your reasons but perhaps we should . . . delay them indefinitely."

They all looked at me. Silence descended, and I realized they were waiting for me to weigh in.

That was . . . not something I was used to. Arthur asked me what tea I liked and Lillian asked me to be her friend, but those weren't true decisions, they were preferences. Decisions didn't fall on me. Papa said I could never leave the farm, so I didn't. Tommy said I was moving to New York, so I did. I was raised in a tiny Christian town. Decisions fell on men. Or leaders. Or smart people and not twenty-year-old girls paranoid of their own shadow.

My first thought almost fell from my lips — *I'll let Jack handle it* — but Violet's heated glare fell on me. It would be easy to delegate this to the person more experienced in such matters, but what would they think if I did? I spent an entire week hiding in the Abstruse, angry at Jack for dragging me into this mess only to pass up the first opportunity to do something.

Tommy always told me my gut was smarter than my brain. Right then, my gut bleated like prey while my brain desired answers. Guts were about survival and curiosity killed the cat, but my gut wasn't going to get me out of this one. Hiding away had only gotten me as far as Arthur's apartment. Running away had gotten me as far as a train. Papa was dead and Tommy was being fed fake letters saying I was fine. There was no man in my life to make the heavy hitting decisions. If I wanted out of this, I had to figure it out myself.

"I want to hear what the Librarian has to say."

I anticipated more protests. A formal fae bargain or human written contract to seal the entire thing. At the very least, some haggling on the established criminal's part.

A slow smile took Jack's face. "Whatever she wants."

AN HOUR LATER, JACK held Lillian's satchel in one arm and mine in the other. The study faded from view, replaced with darkness, cool sap pouring over my skin and a sensation of falling. I opened my eyes to the gate of a small cemetery.

Nausea rolled through my stomach. My feet stumbled beneath me, but I didn't vomit. Lillian was right—the next time was better.

For all his cool stoicism earlier, tension rolled off Jack in stormy waves. The hard lines of his face glowed beneath a waning moon, eyes cast to the darkness beyond a set of wrought-iron gates. Gnarled trees twisted from burned grass along the fence, nearly obscuring the gravestones scattering the earth like broken teeth. An old stone church completed the backdrop—cold, dark and crawling with ivy.

A shiver caressed my skin. Nothing about this place looked abnormal, and blissfully, the broken sidewalk we stood on was empty. But it wasn't the emptiness of a calm night or a lonely, quiet street. All the gas lamps were absent flame, like even the lamplighters knew not to touch this place. A throbbing darkness leaked from beneath the gate. I wondered if it was meant to keep intruders out, or something within.

"Would you open it?" Jack gestured at the iron latch. No lock, but I wasn't sure this place needed one.

"Is that why you needed me to come? To open the gate?" The question was supposed to be curious, not malicious, but it came out harsher than intended all the same.

"I could open the gate if I wanted to, but I'd rather have my full abilities for this." A clear, starry sky shimmered behind him, silhouetting his sharp features. "As for why you're here, this was something I wanted you to see."

He offered no more explanation. I sighed and undid the latch. Whatever magic infused it must have been immune to the cool summer night, because the metal was inexplicably warm, nearly burning. The gate swung open of its own accord and we stared at the ten or so gravestones lying beyond. In the center of them all, like the sun surrounded by its little planets, was a ten-foot, marble statue. In a church yard, one would expect figures such as angels or apostles, but the massive stone piece was a writhing display of human bodies, faces contorted in varying states of agony. They climbed over one another, higher and higher, clawing for the sky with desperation.

"I don't know how long the walk will be. Sometimes it's several feet, sometimes several miles, so prepare yourself." He lifted the satchel higher onto his shoulder, leaning into his cane. "If you stay by me and listen to what I say, you'll be fine. Do not speak to it, no matter what it tells you or offers you—I promise it's all lies. Do not wander, do not eat anything, do not *touch* anything, and if I give you a clear instruction, you must follow it. Am I clear?"

I nodded.

"Good." He gestured forward with his hand. "Ladies first."

I released a short breath. "What a gentleman."

Despite my apprehension, an endless chill settled beneath my flesh. I stepped closer to Jack the moment we passed the threshold. The gate closed behind us with a heavy clang.

He side-eyed me, but said nothing. The bond snapped between us, warm and honeyed and demanding attention. My chest tightened, skin flushed until I took another step closer to him. Still not enough to ease the desire, I sighed and looped my arm through his. To my dismay, it felt much better.

We approached the statue. Jack mumbled a handful of words in a foreign language, something dark and smooth. At first nothing changed, but the solid stone now looked different, shimmering and translucent. Without hesitation, Jack pulled me forward until our feet rested where the stone should have been. I blinked and we stood inside a catacomb.

I swiveled. The church, the cemetery, the quiet street with its empty lampposts, all gone. An endless hall ran into darkness in both directions, the pitch black occasionally broken by flickering torches. The walls themselves were made of bones, skulls mostly, but femurs and ribs and clavicles embedded among the fleshless heads too. At first glance they all appeared human, but the occasional tusk or horn or sharp cheekbone said otherwise.

Jack sighed. "Looks like it will be a long one."

My breaths came faster. Boggy mildew filled my nose, the darkness waiting in either direction playing tricks on my imagination. The ceiling pressed down from above, scattering dirt and dust on our heads. Worms writhed through the soil overhead in some reversal of the sky and ground. My heart rate accelerated, a heavy weight filling my lungs.

Jack removed his glove, brushing his thumb across my cheek. Hushed music, cool night air, a starry sky and gentle breeze. I breathed deep, savoring the calm welling deep within me like a filling spring. His hand drifted away.

"I won't let anything happen to you." Placing his hand on the small of my back, he nudged me forward. "Come on. We have a long night."

"WHAT IS THIS THING, anyway?" By my best estimate we'd walked about a mile, but the meandering route of the tunnel made it hard to tell. In some places, the ground lifted or fell with an incline, and twice we came to a fork in the path only to circle back to where we started. Besides the methodical drip of water and the blazing crackle of the wall sconces, it was silent.

"The Librarian is—was—the first druid, according to most records and stories, but no one knows for sure."

Frowning, I squeezed closer to him when the walls narrowed without warning. "It was once human?"

"Possibly." His cane pushed into the damp earth. Beads of sweat formed along his brow. "A few days ago we had mentioned the Bogorans to you, how they were like our gods. They were the first among us, beings of pure power with no corporeal form. If you came across one, they usually appeared as black smoke, sometimes a glittering sky . . . or other things."

We approached a wide puddle. Jack's long legs crossed it with ease. He held out a hand to help me over. "Most people believe they were the descendants of fallen stars. Pure energy that after some time on earth, became something new, corrupted. As far as we know the stars created humans and this world, then the Bogorans created high fae in the humans' image and their own world for them to reside in, but while their creation was stronger, immortal, and possessed abilities humans didn't, they were inherently wrong. Immortality made the fae cruel."

"Humans aren't perfect either."

"No." He gave a thoughtful pause, his face betraying something I couldn't name. "I know you think very little of us, but don't be fooled by what you see in my friends. Most of our kind don't behave the way we do. We've been among humans for a long time."

Lillian spoke a similar sentiment. Proved it with the story of her family's traditions.

"A few of us became greedy," Jack continued. "They saw the power the Bogorans possessed and wanted it for themselves. It was discovered that if you killed one of them, you inherited their power. You can only imagine how well that went—bored, cruel, power-hungry creatures with the abilities of gods. Other fae wanted to level the playing field, and before we knew it, the Bogorans were nearly extinct. Many fled to this world to hide from their own creations. Perhaps it was because they wished to show the stars they could do better, or maybe they felt lonely with nothing to worship them, but the Bogorans created the first druids several thousand years ago. They took glamour-touched humans who possessed enough fae in their blood to handle their magic, transformed them and made them a strange in-between. Not quite human, not quite fae. Subject to illness and trauma just as easily as their human counterparts, but immortal with abilities of their own. And just like the Bogorans hoped, the druids worshiped them."

A torch flickered near his head, casting an eerie glow on his sharp features. "But the last Bogoran died a little over three hundred years ago. As druids cannot create other druids, their line, for all intents and purposes, has died."

Yet, he was still trying to create one. I said as much, and Jack shrugged. "One thing you'll learn, *annwyl*, is anything is possible if you're enough of a stubborn bastard."

I didn't refute it. Jack didn't strike me as the kind of man to chase the wind, even if he was arrogant to a fault. Or maybe just arrogant enough. If he had any doubt it couldn't be done, we'd be trying something else. Not here, slowly making our way through a catacomb.

"And this Librarian was the first one?"

"Supposedly." An unsettling sharpness lined his words. "Whatever it is now, I couldn't tell you."

The path changed, and our conversation died to a hush. The bone walls and packed, muddy floor gave way to smooth, gray stone, each block cut so skillfully they lay atop one another without mortar. A warm breeze barreled down the new corridor, carrying the lingering scent of fire, animal fat and leather. The smokehouse Papa used for tanning came back in vivid memory. I stepped back.

"You remember what I told you?"

I nodded, not finding the words to speak. A primitive fear settled in my bones, an animalistic awareness pumping through my veins. Heat flushed my skin, fingers twitching as I fought the urge to run.

"Don't speak," Jack murmured, nudging me forward. "Don't wander." Another breeze swept past, thicker with stench. "Don't eat anything." Smoke and roasted flesh filled my nose. "And don't touch anything—absolutely anything—you see. Even if given permission."

Orange light filled the end of the hallway, too bright for my eyes to adjust and see beyond it. "If something happens to me, I swear I will haunt you for the rest of my days, Jack Warren."

He released a low sigh. "You already do."

The hall vomited us into a chamber, roughly the size of a ballroom. A stone hearth roared against the back wall, the flames reaching twice my height. Smaller fires scattered the remaining wall space, set into little alcoves designed for the purpose.

But none of that stole my breath.

Atrocities covered the stones through a thick haze of smoke. Skin, human and fae and other things I could never name, pinned like tapestries along the rock. Brown skin, white skin, pink skin, blue skin, the color did not matter, because each one was inked with endless tattoos—neat lines of repeating spaces and letters, written in a language I'd only seen in Jack's study.

Horror coiled deep in my bones, plummeting my stomach to the floor. Smoke billowed around us, the stench of dripping fat and hide. My nerve endings fired in panic, every sense screaming to run, so taken with the disturbing image of all that *flesh* pinned up like butterflies, I nearly missed what lay in the center of the room.

A quiet voice reached us, scratching like leaves along the pavement, like sand drifting through an hourglass. "What a lovely surprise this is."

Jack glanced at me. I ignored him for whatever *thing* called to us. It sat on the finest carpet I'd ever seen, surrounded by crafted rugs, woven blankets and embroidered pillows that sparkled like eyes. A feast fit for a hundred scattered the floor. Silver platters reflected the firelight, holding fruits and cheeses, roasts of chicken and beef and swine, exotic spices arranged in neat mounds and goblets of wine half drunk or knocked onto the floor.

I eyed the mulberry stains. Prayed it was wine.

My gaze honed on the creature at the epicenter. Vaguely, it resembled a naked human. Pale flesh hung off bony legs, splayed like a child sitting on the floor. Wiry arms lifted, the skin hanging off like wings. Only its stomach possessed any meat, a fat belly protruding into its skeleton lap. It hunched forward like the weight pulled it down, staring at me. There was no flesh to fill in its face. The suit of skin resembled something closer to a mask. Behind the stolen flesh it poked at with a needle and ink, I saw nothing but sharp teeth and deep-set eyes in a black void. Dark pupils tracked each twitch of my fingers. Each breath I took and gave back to the room.

Jack tossed the satchel. The strap landed in a half-eaten bird carcass. "No scars, no tattoos, no bruises, no blemishes. Cut up the back and cleaned this afternoon."

My stomach twisted. The creature opened the bag, pulling forth exactly what Jack described. Flawless human skin.

The Librarian hummed. "You've always been so perfect with your possessions, haven't you? How grateful I am." Its fleshless lips pulled into a grin. "What an honor, being called on by Jaevidan of House Valdivia. The Poisoned Son, the Banished King, the fucking Prince of Prohibition!" It threw its arms high, cackling to itself. "How I ache for the day I wear your skin."

It rubbed its stomach affectionately, smearing fresh ink. Jack sucked on his teeth. "Give me a few more years."

"Gladly," it crooned. Jack glanced at me, but I was too deep in my thoughts to acknowledge it.

Jaevidan.

The first time I'd heard his true name.

Unfortunately, this drew the Librarian's attention as well. "Another offering?"

"No." Jack's voice was too sharp, too quick. The thing practically shook with glee.

"Then what?" Deep-set eyeballs scoured me, the skin mask shifting just enough to see shiny, dark flesh beneath it. "A human. I do not recall the last time I saw a living human, though they make for wonderful decor." It gestured to the walls. I didn't look, swallowing bile instead.

It leaned forward. Lumpy fat dumped onto its thighs. "What do you think of my books, mortal?"

"She thinks nothing," Jack said. "I desired a human slave, so I acquired one. And I'm not here for your interest in her. Is the skin a sufficient bargain or not?"

But the Librarian ignored him, its attention caught by something else. I couldn't tell if it was me or the space between Jack and I, but its head swiveled on a toothpick neck, skin flapping like a turkey's gullet. Slowly, its mouth stretched into a grin, so wide the skin shuddered at the corner of its lips.

"You didn't," it breathed. A hoarse laugh crashed through the room. It gripped its stomach, kicking against the floor. "You didn't. You. Fucking. Didn't. Oh, you've outdone yourself this time, boy."

Jack grit his teeth. The sound vibrated through my skull.

"Your arrogance *astounds* me." It kicked its leg to the side, spilling another goblet of wine into the porous stones. "Perhaps that is why I favor you. What an incredible thing it is, to reach beyond the limits of power, but have enough yourself to survive it. We have always been one and the same, haven't we?"

"You speak for yourself, *Rihaedon*. I am not the one trapped in a prison of my own doing."

"But you are, aren't you?" It rasped. Empty eyes turned on me, vicious and reeling. "I must read her."

The Librarian lurched forward, scuttling across the stone on all fours. Brittle nails clicked against the ground and its drooping flesh hissed across the floor. I screamed, jumping back as one of those gnarled hands reached out for me.

A sword pierced down, pinning its hand to the soft stone. Just like all those skins on the walls.

The creature howled, screeching and clawing at the blade Jack buried in it. When it realized Jack wouldn't relent, it used its free hand to claw at his legs, spitting curses in a language I didn't understand.

Ice crept over my skin. My breath came quicker, another step back as the thing released a wail and slumped to the floor. "You bastard scum. You son of a whore. You vile—"

"How can one transform a glamour-touched human into a druid without a Bogoran?"

"It's not fucking possible." It gave a weak laugh, becoming desperate weeps as it prodded the blade protruding from its hand. "My skin. You ruined my beautiful skin."

"It is," Jack hissed. "Tell me or I'll burn the rest."

Harsh sobs died to stark silence. "You wouldn't dare."

Jack leaned down, teeth bared against the creature's ear. "I'll start with the one you're wearing. With you inside it."

The Librarian screeched, empty eyes flicking to me. It smiled with malice. "To change her, you would need to recreate the power of a Bogoran. It would take four things."

"What things?"

217

The Librarian didn't answer. Jack ground the sword in harder. *"What things?"*

"The second Dianomican," It ground out. More silence. Jack twisted the blade. "It has the ritual," the Librarian spat, then smiled. "If you can find it."

"What else?"

"A black mooring, or she will die."

"I don't need to bind her, we're parallels."

Its voice took a mocking sing-song. "You think I don't see that." A scratchy laugh. "Even if she was more fae than human, nothing can withstand the force of gods. Maybe you." It turned a hateful gaze on Jack. "I suppose we will see. Lastly, great power must be bestowed on her. Both dark and light, a blessing *and* a curse."

Jack ripped the sword skyward. The Librarian whimpered, rubbing the back of its hand over its cheek, licking the wound like an animal. It crawled back to the plush circle of furs and feast with a sigh.

"Let's go." Jack grabbed my arm, but I didn't move. The Librarian watched, rooting my feet to the ground. Terror coated my veins, my flesh, freezing me before its beckoning eyes.

"The curse you hold is not powerful enough," it said. "So tell me, just how far are you willing to go, girl?"

Before I could answer, Jack wound his arm around my waist, half carrying me and half hobbling toward the exit on his cane. Savage laughter followed our every step. "You have no idea what powers you fuck with, boy. None. *None.*"

I could still hear its voice when we emerged in the churchyard.

TWENTY-ONE

COOL NIGHT AIR HIT my face like a balm, but the stench of human leather hung heavy in my nose. The fires, the feast . . . I'd known evil existed in this world—I'd known it since I was small, watching the lesser fae devour one another across the river, seeing my brother come home from a brutal and pointless war. But even my darkest nightmares couldn't conjure what I had witnessed beneath the earth.

Stuffing my shaking hands in my jacket I shuffled silently behind Jack as he murmured more faerie words under his breath, swung the wrought-iron gate open, and stepped onto the street. As if the air sensed our dark quest was done, the gas lamps glowed orange and warm.

We looked at one another, but remained still. The bond pulsed between us, a slow and viscous current that hummed beneath my skin. The constant murmur had settled in my flesh, so perpetual and droning I only noticed when it changed, like when your heart decided to skip a beat.

Right then, it swelled heavy and thick, warm and oppressive like a humid summer breeze. Jack lifted a hand to touch me, but his leather-clad fingers drifted away instead.

"It tells lies, *annwyl*."

Maybe, maybe not. All I knew was I never wanted to step foot in that place again. That I understood even more deeply and painfully why Papa tried to hide me. That I'd feared the fae my entire life, but nothing like this. And anger, blinding, unjustified anger toward Jack simply for existing, for being one of *them*.

"What curse did it speak of?"

I gritted my teeth. "Like you said, it tells lies."

He flinched. Any traces of his overly confident nature were gone. His jaw ticced with unsaid words, but in the end, only silence eddied between us.

He held out a hand, voice resolute. "Let's go home."

JUST HOW FAR ARE you willing to go, girl?

I didn't sleep. In the few moments the sandman overtook me, my dreams were filled with a dank catacomb, an apparition of fire and soot wearing a skin suit with a half-scarred face. Then a woman dressed completely in white, washing human flesh in a riverbed.

For about the tenth time I woke with a start, cool sweat dappling my forehead and a sob stuck in my throat. I'd bathed three times when we arrived back at the hotel, but my hair still reeked of fat and smoke.

The gossamer hangings of the Abstruse swirled on a violent breeze. The sheer fabric rippled in stormy waves, streaming over my legs where I sat ramrod in the sheets. Other nights, I'd been too distracted by other things to notice how large the bed was. Three people could have laid side by side with their arms out. In my tiny farmhouse bed, I'd fall off the side if I dared to roll in my sleep. For half my life, I'd occupied the empty bed space at Papa or Tommy's feet, curled beneath the blankets like a puppy with their soft breaths for a lullaby.

This bed was too large. This room. This hotel. This city. Even worse, the world, if it could be inhabited by so many beautiful and terrible things, wide-eyed children playing in the street mere feet above a monster pining for their skin.

It was a strange question. *How far are you willing to go?* How could I possibly know that when it seemed I knew absolutely nothing at all. What I thought I knew of the world was wrong. What I thought I knew of the fae was wrong. I made a fool's bargain at eleven years old thinking myself clever, but really I was so, *so* incredibly stupid. I thought my knowledge was sufficient. I believed Papa was all-knowing. He taught me everything I knew of the fair folk, but he fell victim to magic and the fae all the same. If that could happen to him, what would happen to me, to all the other ignorant humans in this world?

The room that felt so large moments before closed in like a collapsed grave. My breath quickened, my heart beating a staccato as I pulled on the peignoir Lillian left me. It was sheer as the gossamer curtains, and the mid-thigh, rosy negligee I wore beneath left little to the imagination, but Jack was likely asleep and the others never visited at this hour.

Vines snaked across the walls and night lilies bloomed fat and white across every surface. Wisteria petals rained down from the ceiling like soft, purple snowflakes. So beautiful. So magical. So lethal.

I searched Jack's begrudgingly impressive record collection until I found one somber enough for my mood. Within moments the gramophone roared to life. Any vines slithering along the floor cleared, as if sensing my reason for encroaching on their domain. Beneath a shower of poisonous flowers, I lifted my hands high and breathed.

I was myself when I danced. I could speak and be heard in the silence of my feet moving beneath me. I'd long outgrown my pointe slippers, but I danced like I used to anyway. My toes bent at an unnatural angle, my arms floating like feathers in the air. I stretched my neglected muscles in ways they no longer recognized, reveling in the tearing and aching and bruising of my body because at least it amounted to something. Lately, I'd been feeling it for no good reason at all.

"You're very good."

I faltered, missing my beat mid-turn. Jack stood at the end of his hall in nothing but a pair of loose trousers. Made of dark, woolen fabric and laced up the front with leather ties, I knew immediately those clothes were not of this time. Or world.

How I failed to sense him awake and in the room I didn't know, but now that he stood only feet away, the bond rushed forward like a dam had broken. The magic wrapped around me, comforting, soothing—demanding. His bare chest gleamed in the firelight, black tattoos soaking up the flames. One of the children over his heart, the boy, lifted his head with a start. Wide-eyed, he swiveled his head, whispered something in the little girl's ear, and the two went back to clutching one another, huddled close in a violent wind.

Golden, slitted eyes tracked me. Fae form. In a strange way, it was comforting. It was better to fight the enemy you could see.

Then I realized what he was wearing, what I was wearing, and flushed pinker than the negligee he eyed with unsettling interest. The bond also took note and heated, coating my skin with depthless need. My heart skipped a beat. My feet pressed harder into the floor. A deep ache settled low in my stomach, yearning for things my rational mind refused to admit.

Jack turned his head in that sharp, unsettling way the fae did. The bond snapped back, resuming its normal languid undercurrent.

"Did I wake you?"

He shook his head. "No, I couldn't sleep either."

Finally, something we had in common.

I hoped that would be the end of it. He'd return to his room and I would dance alone until I grew tired enough to sleep. Instead he repeated, "You're very good."

"You already knew that."

For once, the first goddamn time since everything went to hell, he looked something close to guilty. It smoothed over in an instant. "Why didn't you continue?"

Apparently, I would be peppered with strange questions tonight. I thought he would know, since he seemed to know everything else about me. The worst part was it was entirely my fault. I'd shared so much with him, so many pieces of myself in the false solitude of my dreams. I'd lied when I said dancing was the only time I could truly speak, and that was what made me fear him most.

The bond simmered to a hush. There was no dagger to my throat, I felt he asked only for the hell of it, and I was under no illusion this was a dream. So I wasn't sure why I said, "We never had the money. My teacher wanted me to attend an academy, but everything went toward the farm and Tommy's health."

"Why not try to make it on your own?"

He already knew why. There was no reason to ask, and no reason why I answered. "I was terrified of the outside, and even if I wasn't, my family needed me. They always came first."

His serpent eyes clouded over. Arms crossed, feet rooted to the floor, he stared past me, beside me, seeing somewhere I couldn't. Just like Tommy always did. I didn't think it was regret for everything with my father, for being the reason I was so afraid, but he couldn't be upset that I didn't show him the same loyalty as my family. Besides, he had Violet and his friends to love him. So it couldn't be loneliness either.

The gramophone finished its song. The record skipped. Petals rained on the lush carpets, the gold-embroidered books, the hotel worth a fortune and the power seeping into every crack in the stone. An apartment with endless hidden halls and bedrooms, yet it was occupied by only one. A cache of powerful magic lay beneath his skin, one his enemies killed and tortured to recreate, yet he looked like a lost child.

I'd never felt sympathy for Jack. I knew at once that rush of thoughts wasn't entirely my own, but something streaked through his magic and mind that crept along the bond. Part of me wished to understand the parallel and everything we could have from it, but another couldn't rationalize something so obscene. Souls weren't meant to be shared. We were too broken for our own.

I didn't want my soul laid bare for him, and I didn't want his soul laid bare for me. But that foreign restlessness ebbed over me again, lonely.

"Do you love your family?" If tonight would be about strange questions, then I may as well ask my own.

I didn't expect him to answer, but he nodded. Slowly. "I love Violet."

That word sounded wrong from his lips. Too human. "But?"

"But . . ." He ran his tongue over his teeth. "You can love someone and not understand them. You can still be strangers."

My thoughts dipped into all those nights with Tommy, watching him tuck away his hearing aids, refusing to read my lips, denouncing everything I felt and understood as insanity or recklessness because for once, we found something too dense for our shared blood to keep afloat.

"What about the rest of your family?"

Instead of answering, he flipped the record. Mikhail Fontine's despondent ballet washed the stones.

He didn't seek permission and I didn't tell him no. Maybe it was the bond, or maybe what happened earlier that night solidified something between us, a tortured secret that created a fresh link in our chain. He donned a pair of leather gloves and took my hands in his. Even with the barrier, our hands fit together like interlocking puzzle pieces. Mind, body and soul. Every muscle of mine made to perfectly complement his. I was born nearly four hundred years after him. He certainly wasn't designed for me.

What kind of unholy power could mold a human in the womb? Or create a man whose touch was poison, who could strike bargains that ended in death when reneged, who could enter my dreams and hear my secrets from a thousand miles away? The sheer magnitude of it was terrifying. The claustrophobia of knowing he could kill me or bend me to his will with little more than a thought. That he only didn't because magic told him not to, he had little use to, or he had too much use for me still. All that lay between us were deception, time, and magic even he didn't entirely understand. Though as my legs shook, as hair stood on the back of my neck and sweat took my brow, I liked the way my hands felt in his. I liked how he turned me in a slow circle, how his body moved silent and smooth like ink pouring off a page. I liked that he led our lullaby dance, but melted into each movement or change I made as we did. Most of all, I liked what he said about his sister, even if it was terrible to find comfort in someone else's loneliness, because at least I wasn't the only one to ever feel that way.

We danced and he responded to each of my movements, slipping into the new steps I made seamlessly. For a brief moment, it felt like someone finally listened to me.

"I had two older brothers," he said. "And parents, obviously, but I'd consider none of us family."

Not just parents and brothers, but royalty. At three o'clock in the morning, dressed in nothing but a negligee with *The Dying Swan* playing, I danced with a faerie prince.

"I'm guessing they were horrid?"

His mouth made a melancholy smile. "Most days, I'm glad it's been so long I can't remember their faces anymore."

I could never imagine feeling that way about my family, even with everything between Tommy and me.

"Do you know why I took you to see the Librarian tonight?"

Smoked flesh tinged my nose. The fire in the back of the room suddenly grew too hot. I swallowed, shaking my head.

"There're two reasons, really." He turned me slowly, not speaking again until our hands found their way back to each other. "First, I wanted you to understand, truly understand the kind of things we're trying to stop.

"It's no exaggeration to say I'm asking the world of you, for you to give your life to what I'm trying to do, so I wanted you to see why. It's not the same to be told—you have to see it. The Librarian is just one of many that were banished to this world. Things like the catacomb can keep those creatures pacified for some time, but not if Delsaran takes power. What was once locked beneath a church, contained and biding its time with offerings, would be free among us. Among humans."

His eyes turned a deeper shade of gold, reflecting back the low firelight. "And there are things much worse than the Librarian, *annwyl*."

If I dwelled on that, I would never sleep again. So I nodded, feeling as much as hearing the music swelling around us. Jack's hand tightened around mine.

We remained silent, drifting across the floor like mournful apparitions.

"You care for humans." I wasn't sure if it was a question or a statement.

"I've lived among them for a long time."

Not necessarily in peace, if his violent reputation said much, but he wasn't like the Librarian, or the redcaps or even Delsaran. Jack was something I didn't quite understand yet.

"What was the second reason?"

The music faded, quiet and mournful. In the ballet, this was the moment the swan succumbed, her fall from grace into the quiet abyss of death. A fitting song for my soulmate to dance with me to. Death and I still had a bargain to keep.

"It's a very selfish one," he said.

I smiled without humor. "I'd expect nothing less of a fae."

Leather slipped over my skin, his hand falling from mine. "I know what I can be. But part of me hoped if you saw a true monster, you would think me a little less of one."

My heart stalled, fingers growing cold.

He bowed his head. "Thank you for the dance, and for accompanying me tonight. You should rest, *annwyl*."

Heavy silence seeped from the walls. He returned to his room. Shamefully, secretly, I wished he'd asked me to dance again.

TWENTY-TWO

"I WANT A BARGAIN."

Jack's human eyes flicked to mine over his spectacles. He clutched a newspaper in one hand and a steaming cup of something that would likely kill me in the other. A disheveled shirt clung to his shoulders with the top three buttons undone, his waistcoat and jacket missing. The bare stretch of skin reared the bond's ugly head, but I had no time for that this morning. I fell into the dining chair across from him, trying and failing to look serious while my stomach grumbled.

He returned to his paper. "I don't strike fae bargains before breakfast."

The urge to shake him hit in a violent wave. "I've thought about what you said, and I want to officially agree to help you. But with rules."

He dropped his cup, leaning his head against his palm. "How boring."

"I'm serious."

"I know you are, darling, and I'm very pleased, but I haven't had my—" He frowned at his cup. "Let's just call it coffee."

"While I'm sure your steaming cup of arsenic is an early morning necessity, we have a lot of ground to cover and I'd like to get started as soon as possible." I pulled the notes I'd worked on for half the night from my blouse. "I have some stipulations, as I'm sure you—"

"Are you going to blackmail me again?"

I blinked. "What? No."

He frowned. "Shame. That was a turn-on."

It was official. If I had to spend an immortal existence with him, I would lose my mind.

"I cover that in my notes," I said, "Everything from our *required intimacy* to the amount of time I will work with you, to some other terms that are non-negotiable."

"Non-negotiable," he repeated, long and slow in a way that made me violent again, but he folded his paper and set it down. "Alright, let's hear it."

Steadying my breath, I stared at my half-crazed scrawl. A wave of deja vu overcame me. To think only a few weeks ago, I sat across from him in a restaurant no less grand than this hotel, also trying to bargain.

Only then, I thought he was nothing but a rakish criminal too charming for his own good. Now, I knew he was an immortal prince of poison banished from his world, attempting to save the human race from a sadistic bootlegger.

Just another Tuesday.

But I held steadily onto my reasons for this proposal in the first place. After our dance, I'd spent the remaining night oscillating between writing a contract, working myself to this decision, and debating everything I'd ever known. Jack needed me to make a Morrigan, a Morrigan could kill Delsaran and Delsaran wanted to kill people. From that perspective the answer seemed easy, it was just everything else that gave me pause. If I did this, I'd have to do it with Jack. And there was no one else here to weigh in, to offer advice or give permission. If I did this, I agreed to it completely on my own, and it would be agreeing to trust him. I tried to think with both my gut and brain on this one.

My brain said I still didn't entirely trust Jack and let's be honest, probably never would, but if I played my cards right I wouldn't be walking in blindly. Children learned from their parents' mistakes and I'd learned plenty from my father's. I could help him and still protect myself and others.

My gut said Jack was many things, but at the end of the day he wanted to help people. The enemy of my enemy is my friend. I'd already made Lillian my friend, I could work for a place like that with Jack too.

I shook my hands, gearing myself up. "To start, everything I am about to say is purely for informational purposes, and is in no way binding. Once we reach a proper agreement, I will repeat my first and last name three times and everything said thereafter will be the established bargain between us."

Steaming drink forgotten, he leaned forward with far too much delight. "By all means, proceed."

"For part one of the *proposed* agreement." I eyed him. He smiled innocently. "I will agree to aid you, within reason and without physical or mental harm, in your mission to find the four items the Librarian told us of on the night of August 6th, 1926 were required to make me become a druid, including and limited to the second Dianomican, a black mooring, a curse and a blessing."

He waved for me to continue.

"During that time, I will live in The Glamour Hotel, in your apartment, with the Abstruse as my private residence, but am allowed to come and go freely with no requirements for how long I must remain in the hotel. This condition expires within one year of the bargain being placed or upon acquiring all four items."

He raised a brow. "Very thorough."

"Part two—within 14 days of acquiring these four items, I will agree to partake in the ritual that will convert me into the magic being your species knows as druids. You will agree to do everything within your power, figuratively or magically, to ensure my survival during this transformation and for six months afterwards. If any side effects I find undesirable appear due to the ritual, you will agree to aid me in relieving them within the limits I just stated."

"So . . . everything within my power?"

"Part three." My cheeks heated, fingers trembling around the notepad. "I agree to partake in a one-time consummation of our parallel bond as long as I am of sound body and mind and able to consent to it. Within one year of this consummation, I agree to help you, within reason, find and assassinate the druid known as Delsaran. This bargain concludes with his death or if the one-year mark has passed."

Jack remained silent.

"No commentary?"

He shrugged.

"Alright." I rustled the paper. "After the conclusion of parts one through three, I will be free to do what I wish, as I wish, with no attempts at imprisonment, deception or trickery, with the remaining years of my immortal lifespan. I will not be required to maintain any kind of intimacy, friendship or relations with you or anyone in your faction. Upon completion of parts one through three, you will contact the druid's guild for me and relay that I wish to join them. From there forward, we go our separate ways and only continue correspondence if we both willfully desire."

Glee faded from his face, his mischievous smile faltering at the corners. I didn't include it to be cruel, only practical. I would agree to help him with this task, but this wasn't a marriage vow. And despite future intimacy, we weren't in a relationship.

Jack didn't want me to think of him as a monster. I didn't, not entirely, but I'd seen enough of the fae to be wary. I couldn't risk him entrapping me if he decided he liked the bond too much.

"What if you don't want to?"

I frowned. "What do you mean?"

"What if you'd rather stay here?" He was serious.

"I—" was completely caught off guard. "I suppose if I'd like to continue working for you, then you won't be required to contact the Guild."

He looked no more satisfied than a moment ago, but nodded. Hesitation hung in the air, congealing into tension.

He couldn't actually expect me to stay, or anticipate me wanting to.

I wasn't sleeping with him because I loved him, or wanted him, or anything beyond the fact our entwined fate made me hot in his presence and we needed the bond to kill Delsaran. It was obvious the parallel bond meant a lot to the fae. It meant we were soulmates, but I was human, twenty, and I'd known Jack for two months and we had gotten along for about ten minutes of it.

Besides, he didn't know about my agreement with the Woman in White, and he never would. Any continued relations between us were irrelevant because I could never marry or carry a child. The one-time consummation was enough of a risk, even with Lillian's assurances. Until the day came my bargain with her was eradicated, I couldn't take more risks than necessary. If that day ever came.

I wondered how Lillian was making out finding birth control. Worse, if birth control pills even worked if your partner wasn't human?

Jack eyed me. "What are you thinking about?"

Your seed.

I took a messy sip of tonic. "Continuing. Additional stipulations I have are during the entire course of all of our bargains you agree to educate me on the fae and help me train my magical abilities."

"Already planned on it."

"And finally, from the day the bargain is made and forevermore, so long as we both shall live, neither you nor anyone within your faction can bring harm to myself or my brother, Thomas Colton."

He frowned, turning something over in his head "You get indefinite protection. Your brother gets a year and when that runs out we'll consider extending it."

I bristled. "Why?"

"Reasons." A long moment passed and I knew I'd get nothing more. He leaned back in his seat, reposed like the haughty prince he was. "Is that it?"

It was, but now I felt as if I had missed something.

"Allow me until tomorrow to think of anything else."

He grinned. "I thought time was of the essence?"

"Hush up and drink your arsenic." I fled for the Abstruse and he laughed quietly behind me.

I'D ASKED FOR A day, but by nightfall I'd done nothing but pace my room, scouring every detail and ruminating on anything I may have missed. Nothing came, so when the clock chimed six, I visited Will in the kitchens for dinner, then waited for Jack to return beside the fireplace.

Usually, someone would have popped in by now—literally—but the apartment had been uncharacteristically silent. It would have been a good time to write to my brother, but when I'd reached for pen and ink, I couldn't think of a single thing to say.

I hoped he was safe, but I'd learned the hard way during the war that writing those sorts of letters only made things worse. Each one you sent off begging for a response, and when you finally received one and wrote another, all you did was spend the space in between wondering if they were dead yet. If that letter declaring safety was sent just hours before a bullet struck, it'd still be weeks before you knew. The unsettling chill of wondering if you wrote to a dead man.

And other than asking for his safety, what else would I say? He trained in Chicago, hunting down bootleggers and gangsters and bringing bad men to heel. I sat before a fireplace, waiting to strike a bargain with one.

Warmth curled the air, fresh with the scent of rain. Without turning, I murmured, "Long day at the office?"

"No, had to stop for hookers and blow on the way home." He fell into the chair beside me.

"How were they?"

"Terrible. None of them looked like you."

I shook my head. "You've got a screw loose, Jack Warren."

"Several." He stretched out his legs and retrieved a hand-rolled cigarette from his pocket. Stuffed with what, who knew, but when he blew the smoke into the air, it smelled earthy.

"I'm assuming that's not safe for human consumption?"

"Why, do you smoke?"

I'd never smoked in my life. It was unladylike, improper, a host of other *un* and *im* and *dis* words. I shrugged. A snap filled the air and Jack's hand filled my vision, waving a cigarette before my eyes. He handed me a lighter. In the grand scheme of his endless power, it was sort of funny he needed one. I breathed in the heady, rich taste of tobacco. I didn't like it, but I didn't hate it. It was nice to have the option to try.

I held the cigarette in front of my face. "I feel like an outlaw."

In my corner vision, he smirked.

I took another drag, then threw the rest of it in the fire. "I'm ready if you are."

"Are you sure?"

No, not even a little bit. But I thought of the Librarian. The Baker boys coming home from the mines, washing their soot-streaked hands before entering the schoolhouse. My brother sitting beside me with our faded book of poems. And perhaps more selfishly, all the life I would miss if it ended too soon. Several weeks ago, my best fate was an insane asylum, but now I had something else. People who needed me, a chance to do something good, to become a druid, and maybe find my own place in the Guild. For the first time in my life, it was a decision I could make myself.

I nodded, repeated my name three times, and sat silent as he produced ink and paper. Pushing my chair closer, I leaned over his shoulder, checking each word he wrote. When he was done and we both approved, he drew a thin dagger over his ring finger and pressed a bloody mark to the page. I did the same.

Perhaps it was a bit like a marriage vow.

LESS THAN AN HOUR after my fate was sealed, Jack called everyone to the study. Will popped in mid-bite of something he no doubt stole from Charlene, Lillian strode through the door smelling of jasmine and Arthur knocked thrice before Jack sighed and repeated he could just come in.

Violet arrived last, her snake following behind on the floor. Red lipstick kissed her mouth and a dazzling, black dress rode dangerously high. She sank onto her usual chaise, refusing to look at anyone but her beloved reptile.

"Adeline has agreed to help us."

Violet released a short breath. "Took long enough."

"The Librarian told us what we needed. It's possible."

Even Violet snapped to attention. Will's nervous stare bounced between us. "I'm assuming it's going to be a bitch?"

"First, we need the second Dianomican."

Lillian nodded, bouncing her legs. "I figured as much. I've been looking for it. All of them, actually." To me, she quietly explained,

"The Dianomican is a very old book that once belonged to the Bogorans. It contains their history and rituals, but when the fae began hunting them they split it into ten pieces, all guarded by different leaders. Since their extinction, the books have been collected and stolen by thousands of owners."

"Because they're cursed," Will muttered under his breath.

Jack sighed. "A black mooring." He looked at me. "They're dark artifacts produced by great sacrifice, capable of binding lives together."

"You know, I used to have one of those," Arthur said. He frowned. "At least I think I did."

Lillian patted his knee and gestured at Jack. "And Adeline needs a blessing and a curse. Strong ones."

"Why not just ask for the sky to turn green while you're at it?" Violet crossed her legs, picking at a bare thread on the couch. "What are the odds of her even surviving the ritual?"

"I think the risk is up to me," I said. Her golden eyes snapped to mine.

"As if you know shit," she snapped. "You realize you would be long dead if he wasn't so obsessed with you? You're nothing but a stupid fucking hu—"

"*Enough.*" Jack snapped. Violet's mouth twisted. Will kept glancing at her, trying to get her attention.

"We are doing this," Jack said. "We are going to attempt it at the least. Unless anyone else has some brilliant plan to kill Delsaran I haven't been made aware of."

No one spoke.

"Good. We start in three days."

Lillian raised a tentative hand. "Um, Jack, my love, why three days?"

He looked at me. "Because I know where to find the first thing on our list."

TWENTY-THR

BEING THE SECRETIVE MAN he was, Jack didn
what we would be getting or how. But two days
disappear immediately after breakfast to do . . . wh
did all day. He lifted a shoulder. "I'm not your enemy
wanted to be." He gestured at the bowl of fruit, the
"Eat and get dressed. There is something I need to d
could use your help with it."

Exhaustion ate my wakefulness after spending th
rather than sleeping. After combing through the f
records, it became clear he was not only tedious wi
detail, but didn't fib when he said he wrote everyth
Unfortunately, nothing was written three times in con
repetitive information instead scattered throughout t
of the entries came with pictures, which moved thing
could glance at a page and see it was not what I se
most were lengthy descriptions. And nothing was
order, neither alphabetical listings, dates nor categori
managed to finish three journals around four in the m
success. Nothing even close to describing the Woman
had six journals to go, not including the ones Lillian h
yet.

The weight of that defeat settled cold and hard as I s
Jack at the breakfast table. I supposed this was our

ally, he'd be occupied with the daily news, paperwork or
ving ledgers, but today he sat at the empty table, waiting. Either
adn't been laid out yet or I woke too late.

sting no time at all, he said, "We'll be assessing your abilities
"

dded, staring longingly at the gilded mirror spitting back our
ions. I'd spent most evenings dining with Will in the kitchens,
ing the sole high fae on the cook staff shade meals through the
n's mirror. Charlene beat Will half to death with her spoon after
ering he smuggled away her supply of imported mangoes. She
n't dare lay a hand on me, but I wondered if this was her
hment.

red at the glass, willing coffee or tea or anything caffeinated to
r. It didn't.

hat abilities?"

ur powers," he stated, as if that explained it all. "In Times
e, you asked if you had any abilities beyond glamour-breaking.
we will find out."

n still human."

t you are glamour-touched, and more importantly, you are
elled to someone powerful. Even without the bond being
d or your transformation, you should be able to access that
of magic."

ook my head. "If I had abilities I think I would know by now."

would you?" I thought there would be more, but he only said,
seen you use it. In very small amounts and not effectively, but I
nse it."

e never used any abilities." A lifetime of fear washed over me,
nge feeling as I wondered if the same magic I loathed ran
gh my veins. But if it was in negligible amounts, maybe I didn't
e. How would I even access it?

238

He folded his hands on the table, staring intently. Now would be the moment for the bond to awaken, but I was too tired to feel my own skin. "All fae have three basic abilities: illusion, compulsion and shade-walking. Illusion, as you know by now, is what we call glamour, and it's the easiest to use. Even the least powerful fae are capable of it." He rooted into his pocket with his free hand, finding a hand-rolled cigarette and matches. "You also know of shade-walking, though this is the most difficult and dangerous, so we won't touch that. And in the middle we have compulsion, which is exactly what it sounds like. Did your brother ever read you the Greeks?"

I nodded.

"Sirens use compulsion at its most powerful," he stated, the words toneless like it was nothing but a party trick. "The more powerful the fae, the more resistant they are to another's compulsion. Humans, animals and plants don't have magic, and therefore are the most susceptible. A few weeks ago, I didn't stop time in Times Square. It was simply a powerful display of compulsion, willing everything around us, even the air, to stop."

Simply. Display. What most considered acts of gods were nothing more than a rap of his cane. "I can't do that."

"Not the way I can, no. But you will." Smoke curled the air, sinfully sweet. I breathed deep, the scent of his poison and breath filling my lungs.

It deeply unsettled me. Compulsion was a euphemism for taking one's free will, and as someone who knew that feeling very well, I wasn't keen on the idea of doing it to others. Especially those powerless and unaware.

I switched the topic. "How about your poison abilities?"

He shook his head. "Those are blood specific. As far as we know, you shouldn't be able to access them yourself, but when it comes to the bond you are resistant in a way most people are not. Usually, if I touch a human it's enough to kill. But with you, it's more similar to—" He waved a gloved hand in the air "—a drug."

I glanced around the room. The den of death—wisteria weeping from the ceiling and belladonna clustered in indigo patches. Not only could he create poison, but it bled from his touch, deadly for all but me. The drug analogy seemed fitting. No wonder I fell into a euphoric head high each time his fingers brushed my cheeks.

I eyed his gloved hands. "Can you control it?"

"Usually, but it's draining. It's much easier to cover up."

Just like glamouring all the fae in New York City, transporting through time and space, and every other unnatural thing he did. It seemed there were no limits to him . . . except for using a cane. And reading glasses. Something clicked in my thoughts.

"It hurts you, doesn't it?"

Surprise flickered his expression, gone quicker than I could follow. "What do you mean?"

"All that magic, or the poison, I don't know which," I said. "It wears your body down, so you use a cane and reading glasses and other aids I'm sure you hide from everyone."

Silence. His face became a blank slate, revealing nothing more than the fact he still breathed. "It's a recent issue." He took another lungful of pungent smoke, the aroma kissing my nose.

I stared him down, scouring those golden eyes for any fissures. "But it's a problematic one now, isn't it?"

"It's not like our kind to spread our powers so thin, or use them even in our sleep. Most are not powerful enough to attempt it, let alone do it and do it for many years. As it is, I have no basis for comparison on whether my *issues* are related."

Most are not powerful enough to attempt *it.* It wasn't conceit, it was truth, but Jack Warren still wasn't infallible. Another piece of the puzzle clicked together, why he—and all other fae—so desperately needed this Morrigan between us. If Jack worsened, there would be no one to protect the low fae. Provide them the constant glamour that allowed them to blend and survive in human society, in a world they had no choice but to be in.

Fae could only be killed by iron or if their bodies were destroyed. But if using all this magic destroyed his body . . .

"Are you dying?"

"No." The little word came too quickly, too forced. "It is nothing I cannot handle. And once we form a Morrigan, it will not be an issue at all."

I said nothing, sensing a thick tension tightening the space between us. The bond decided to appear then, pawing at my chest like a pet demanding attention. His assurances only brought more questions. Did anyone else know, or at least suspect? Surely, Violet did. They had their own connection and she must have sensed something. How would the Morrigan help, by splitting the burden with another person or by enhancing his own power? Would all of his issues cease to be or was the damage already done?

Again, I felt that unsettling weight of responsibility, the feeling I was wholly underqualified for everything Jack expected of me. Arthur and the druids needed me to save their kind from extinction, other people needed me to make this Morrigan, and now Jack may have needed me to keep himself from deteriorating, the consequences of which rippled much farther than a single man. Sweat lined my brow, pulse jumping in my throat. So much relied on the slim chance I could actually survive this.

"Do not mention this to anyone else. It stays between us."

I had more questions, but they all died on my lips with the sharp look he gave me. I nodded. He snapped and a tiny, green succulent appeared on the table. "I want you to attempt compulsion."

My eyebrows furrowed. "Shouldn't I start with glamour, if that's easier?"

"No." He shoved the tiny pot closer. "I want you to start with this."

I waited, hands in lap, but he said nothing. His fae eyes flashed through his glamour, but the rest of him appeared perfectly, pleasantly human. I swallowed. "Some instructions would be helpful."

"Just attempt it."

The command wrapped around me, jolting my spine. Icy prickles ran down my neck with a sudden feeling of urgency. I glared at Jack. He smirked.

Well, this was fine. I stared at the fat, little succulent, willing it to do something. Trying to think of what I could command a plant to do, I figured the simplest route would be something natural, something the plant wouldn't fight me on. If plants could fight. Flora always grew toward the light. There were no windows in the study, but there was a fireplace. Perhaps I could convince the plant it was sunlight.

I stared at its round leaves. *Shift toward the light.* Nothing. Trying the orange blossom in the center, I stared at that and willed it toward the fire. *Your flower is orange. The fire is orange. Don't you want to bend toward it?*

Jack drummed his fingers on the table.

"Maybe I should try something more . . . sentient."

He cocked his head to the side. Snapped.

The vines encasing the bookshelves shuddered and raced closer. They swelled like inflamed arteries, pulsing and diving along the wood and stone until they approached the table. I lifted my feet as one slithered beneath my heel.

"Nevermind, I'll stick with the succulent!"

Jack snapped again and the vines halted, retreating to their beloved books. I clenched and unclenched my fists in my lap.

"Jerk," I mumbled beneath my breath. His lips twitched in the corners.

Okay you stupid, little plant. I'm your master now. Obey.

Still, nothing.

After ten long minutes, I sighed and widened my eyes at Jack, waving my hand over the obstinate plant. He was too busy reading a book and stirring tea to pay me mind.

"May I have some instruction now?"

Without a single glance, he murmured, "You're overthinking it."

"That ain't helpful."

"And neither is instruction." He set the book down. I stared longingly at his tea that probably wasn't. "There is no right way to do this, *annwyl*. It is different for everyone. What works for me or Lillian or Will may be entirely different for you. Unfortunately, the only way to discover how you may access your abilities is by exhausting every method you can."

I closed my eyes, steadying my breath. It felt like a waste of time, but maybe there was a method to his madness. I prayed there was.

He snapped. A steaming plate of breakfast landed on the table, along with a fresh pot of coffee. Why couldn't we have learned how to do that first?

Yanking back his sleeve to reveal a golden wristwatch, he muttered, "Anyway, darling, I have a governor to threaten, so I am afraid you are on your own for the afternoon." He gestured vaguely at the succulent. "Good luck."

BY NIGHTFALL, I WAS fairly sure my eyes bled and I was on the verge of losing my mind. The breakfast from that morning sat half-eaten, growing cold despite the suffocatingly hot room. Lunch and dinner arrived but I didn't touch those at all. Between a cold bowl of lobster bisque and untouched plate of tea sandwiches sat the plant, mocking me with its cheerful greenery.

I took an hour break to scour one of Arthur's journals, which amounted to another waste of my time. Then I was back to the plant, practically begging it to move. By midnight, I'd grown so frustrated I burst into tears.

I slept for only five hours, but I didn't need sleep. I needed to conquer this task. I pushed the curtains of the Abstruse aside and returned to the study where the defiant plant remained a centerpiece between the hardened food dishes. Breakfast arrived again but I hardly noticed.

Noon swept by and I was ready to weep again. It was a plant. It didn't even have conscious thought. Surely, these were inherent abilities to fae, but just because Jack could probably do it in the womb didn't mean I could at all.

And then I was panicking, because so much rested on my ability to make this Morrigan, but none of it mattered if I couldn't manage the most minute of tasks. Worse, maybe that was Jack's reasoning for sitting me here in the first place. He knew I was inadequate—a *succulent* could best me, after all—so while he went off and did real things, he gave me this silly task to keep me occupied.

Lunch came and went but I ignored it, needing to do something, needing to prove myself. My mind raced between ways to manage compulsion, but mostly devolved into self-deprecating insults.

An hour later Jack appeared in the seat across from me, a frown sunk deep into his skin. He snapped and the entire table cleared, the plant included.

I looked up sharply. "I almost had it."

"Why do you do this to yourself?"

I stared at him. "What?"

He snapped again and a bowl of fruit landed in front of me. All my favorites were inside, including several ripe peach slices. "Eat it."

"I'm fine." I stood, searching for the closest living thing I could find, but Jack snapped again and my butt fell into the chair. I scowled at him.

"Compulsion isn't life or death, *annwyl*. That is." He pointed at the bowl of fruit. "And you still weigh next to nothing from your grand week of starvation, so eat it."

"Ironic, since you obviously meant to starve me out."

"Had I known you had this problem, I wouldn't have done that." The words came harsh, clipped. He took a deep breath, lowering his voice. "Please."

My hands remained in my lap. Bile climbed my throat. "I don't have a problem."

"I am just trying to help you—"

"Jack, I appreciate it, but I'm fine." I ran my hands through my hair, pressing my lips into a flat line. "I need to do something worthwhile, so please let me practice."

He eyed me. "You are doing something worthwhile."

A bitter laugh climbed my throat, ugly thoughts forming before I could stop them. "What, having sex with you? Because that's my grand contribution. *That's* what's expected of me, nothing else." My voice cracked on the last word. I could have screamed at the way his face softened.

There it was, the true reason behind my frustration. I was well aware how pathetic it was, and how pathetic I had been. Violet said it herself—*are you done being pathetic yet?* And my brother never needed to, but we knew. He admitted as much in our living room before we left for New York. He said he needed purpose, I said I needed him, and we both knew that wasn't enough. The townsfolk in Fairville would rather their children not go to school than see me as the teacher. I couldn't handle my own dilemma with the Woman in White, but needed Lillian to take out time for me. For a brief moment I had thought I was serving a purpose here, but that was a lie. I only served one purpose, and that was to Jack. That's what my worth amounted to in this world. Sitting in his hotel day after day, waiting for Jack to arrive home from whatever it is he did and didn't tell me about, eventually have sex with him and then nothing. The saddest part, it would probably be the exact same with a human man.

I raked my hands through my hair again, enjoying the little prickle of pain.

"That is not what's expected of you."

I didn't bother to look at him. "I may be stupid, but I'm not that stupid, Jack."

The room went down several degrees. The fireplace danced erratically, but I didn't care much about that either. "I gave you outs, *annwyl*. I told you if you did not wish to do this we would figure out another way, but you agreed, and I assumed you were happy with that agreement. But if you want to renege on the bargain I would be happy to do that too, because this is *not* expected of you and I am *not* forcing you. And if anyone tells you otherwise, I will personally tear out their throat."

I flinched. He continued, "Is this because of me or you?"

My eyes flicked to his, but he wasn't looking at me. His good knee bounced against the floor, his black gloves clenched on his cane.

"Is what?"

He gestured at the untouched fruit. He didn't need to say it, but I knew he meant more than that. My general unpleasantness, locking myself away, falling back into all of my old, terrible habits. But I didn't know the answer to his question, because in truth, it was everything. It was him, and his explosive entry into my life. Everything I still had to sort through with years of knowing him but not really. My entire life imploded in less than a month. I left the only place I'd ever known. Besides the war, this was the longest I'd been away from Tommy. I hid in a grand hotel because too many people wanted me dead. I discovered there was an entire world of magical creatures planning to kill humans, that I was someone's soulmate, and that in a few short months I may become immortal myself. Everything was changing, and it was changing all too fast and all too dramatically and I couldn't keep up with any of it. Because I was weak. I was a scared little girl crying beside the river. I wasn't strong enough for any of this.

"You're not inadequate," Jack whispered. "You just haven't learned anything yet. You have been isolated your entire life, it takes time."

I looked up at him. "I need to get out of this hotel." He frowned, but I cut in. "I know you're busy all day and have little time to keep watch over me, but maybe there's something I could do. I just can't stand sitting here and being use—"

"Done."

I froze. "It was that simple?"

He lifted a shoulder. "I'm not your enemy, *annwyl*. I never wanted to be." He gestured at the bowl of fruit, then the Abstruse. "Eat and get dressed. There is something I need to do tonight, and I could use your help with it."

TWENTY-FOUR

LILLIAN POPPED IN. UPON hearing I would be out for the night she insisted on dressing me, but Jack gave her a task list so long she couldn't find the time to make me her doll. After an hour lamenting the unfairness of it all, she whispered to wear the silver dress and shaded from view.

Standing before the mirror, I put the finishing touches on my lipstick and fluffed my hair. I wore the silver dress as requested, none too happy about the fact it fell directly at my knees. It also had a dangerous neckline, the modest cap sleeves negated by the thick V dipping between my breasts. After donning my pearls and silver gloves I wondered if it was too much, but when I met Jack in the study, his eyes grew three shades darker.

"That's your new favorite dress."

I squinted. "I like my old dresses."

He shook his head, a heated stare roaming from my crown to my feet. "No. That's your new favorite dress."

Deciding to pick my battles, I held out my arm and faced the mirror, but he jerked his chin at the foyer. "I think we should walk tonight."

After weeks of being trapped in the hotel I couldn't be happier. I was curious if Delsaran's men had retreated and the streets were now safer, but feared mentioning the topic would sway Jack's decision. We remained silent in the lift. A gaggle of men tipped their hats and women shot coy smiles at Jack in the lobby. The doorman asked if we would require a car, but Jack hadn't changed his mind in the five minutes it took to exit the hotel, so we continued on the street.

With the end of August, the evening air was unusually cool. The peachy sun dipped low on a rose-colored sky, smog and cigarette smoke curling the air. During my imprisonment, it was almost easy to forget I was no longer in Georgia. But now, instead of wind through the trees and horses nickering in the pasture, horns blared, subway grates wafted steam and metal clanged from the ironworks just down the block. It seemed wherever we went, Jack garnered attention. Men passed us by, eyes wide with recognition as they murmured, "Good evening, Mr. Warren." Women ogled as they passed him, and even the children working their odd jobs on the street called out, asking if the famous Mr. Jack Warren would like his shoes shined or his coat cleaned. It set me on edge, conditioned to recognize attention as a bad thing. In Fairville, my family seldom received the good kind. At home, it'd been better to melt into the shadows.

Jack looped his arm through mine. Heat buzzed between us, our light coats no match for the magic that snaked from his skin to mine. It took me three blocks to work up the means to shake him off, but he interrupted my battle of wills. "I want you to practice using your powers tonight."

I jerked to a stop. "I thought we established I couldn't do that?"

"Compulsion is a tricky ability and requires a lot of training. So that is what we are going to do." He reached into his pocket for a silver cigarette case, lighting one as he withdrew it. "If it was nothing more than controlling the minds of others, I would not have bothered with my human front and business, nor would Delsaran with slowly swaying the fate of humans." His arm unlooped from mine and we faced one another. "It works so long as you are within close proximity of your target, and for the less powerful, you must look them in the eyes."

"So, me?"

"For now." He glanced around, paranoia jumping on his skin. It raised the hair on the back of my neck. "But again, the problem is it only works in someone's presence. Therefore, you can not compulse someone and expect a long-term outcome. I could not, for example, ask a police officer to ignore a distillery in my basement, because the moment he left, he would return to his normal thoughts and storm right back inside. You must learn how to sway a conversation, compulse someone into little truths and thoughts that lead them where you want so they reach a final conclusion themselves, and stick with it. It is as much an art form as magic."

"Sounds like manipulation and coercion to me."

"I do many terrible things for some halfway decent reasons." A chill swept through the air with the sun's final descent. His breath condensed between us in wisps, lips far too close for my sensibilities. He looked charming as ever tonight in a black suit cut for his body, a fresh silver chain hanging from his waistcoat and a dark gray newspaper cap over his dark hair. His golden eyes searched me, our bodies too close, our breath mingling in the air.

"I thought you were the good guys?"

His mouth tilted up in a smirk. "Oh, we're all quite bad. It's more fun that way."

Well . . . that was certainly a lot more of a turn-on than it should have been. I swallowed the heat clambering up my throat, keeping my thoughts in reality. "I'm better off attempting grand feats of magic before the art of clever conversation."

"You know more than you think." His hand came between us, the back of his thumb brushing my cheek. "You are smart, *annwyl*. You are crafty, and you have a glorious will to survive in less-than-ideal situations, so you have my confidence."

If only *I* had a shred of that confidence. "What is it you have me doing exactly?"

"You will ask a ballerina for her slippers."

"Why?"

He grinned, eyes bright beneath the awakening streetlamps. The Devil returned. "Because the ribbons are a black mooring."

AS FRENZIED NIGHTLIFE TOOK to the streets, we approached a theater lit with a dazzling marquee. Yellow, flashing lights illuminated *The Republic Theater* above glass doors teeming with guests. A sign out front announced a private charity showing of Giselle hosted by local philanthropist, Yevgeny Bernthal. Glimmering Rolls Royce's and Bugatti's rolled to a stop before the velvet-roped entrances, where valets in tuxedos and tall hats took their cars around the corner. Women in fur coats and diamonds, men in Italian leather and crafted suits. They all entered arm in arm like royalty gracing a palace with their presence. Though the silver dress Lillian provided was stunning—the shimmering fabric no doubt equal to Tommy's monthly salary—I felt wholly underdressed.

"You are unsettlingly beautiful tonight," Jack whispered. The low words caressed my ears, sending heat down my spine. I wondered if he could sense my unease or if I was just too poor at masking my emotions.

"I believe the word you are looking for is beguiling."

He grinned. "And I would have it no other way."

We approached the crowd. Without us needing to display an invitation, a red-faced usher approached and tipped his hat. "How are you this evening, Mr. Warren?"

I paid the usher no attention, stewing in my anxiety until Jack said something, held my arm and I caught the end of, "—my dear friend,

Miss Colton. Any requests she may have I would like fulfilled, understood?"

A discreet exchange of money, then our morally questionable usher led us through a lobby packed shoulder-to-shoulder. A crystal bar spanned the back of the room, but no alcohol framed the mirror. While women in cloche hats and shimmering dresses sipped virgin cocktails, the usher led us to another door manned by two large men and a second vermillion rope. We were waved through without so much as a word. Money truly did rule the world.

Behind that door lay a second bar, much less crowded. While mostly men occupied this room, several women dotted the velvet chaises and upholstered booths. One sat at a table all to herself, ankles folded, a violet sash around her chest and a twinkling tiara upon her head. Cigar smoke made a thick haze and scattered the light of green lamps and flickering candles. Jack led me forward as my feet stumbled on the Persian carpet.

"Unfortunately, I must subject you to small talk before the show." He placed a gloved hand on the small of my back and heat rushed to dangerous places. "These people are vipers. Keep your wits about you."

My last wits currently resided in a potted desert plant, but I nodded. I examined the crowned woman again, wondering who she was. Jack caught the movement and smiled. "Would you like one?"

I side-eyed him. "A royal companion?"

He leaned in, leaving no space between our bodies. "A tiara."

Chills erupted on my skin, thoughts skittering to unholy places. "It would seem rather gaudy for a farmer."

"But you are not that anymore, *annwyl*. You are mine."

I pressed my lips together. "A mistress to the Prince of Prohibition?"

He bent down, ever so slightly, human eyes scouring mine. Darkness pooled between us. Unyielding need. My breath hitched, muscles taut as he placed a breathless kiss to the corner of my lips. "A *princess* to the Prince of Prohibition."

"Mr. Warren, I was afraid you wouldn't make an appearance tonight."

Jack stepped away. I forgot I had a working pulse. An older gentleman with a vivacious blonde on his arm stepped forward, nodding at my escort. The woman's narrowed eyes fell on me, no doubt assessing.

"I always appear for a good cause." Jack shook the man's hand, then kissed the top of the woman's scarlet glove. Gesturing to me, he said, "Mr. and Mrs. Bernthal, I would like you to meet my paramour, Miss Adeline Colton."

My tongue turned to lead. Through my buzzing consciousness, I lifted a hand for Mr. Bernthal to kiss and kissed the cheeks of his curvaceous and much younger wife. The low dip of my gown suddenly felt like a child playing with her mama's clothes.

"A paramour? I thought I would never see the day," she said. Green tinged the words, her gaze growing contemptuous.

Her husband patted the back of her hand. "Mr. Warren has always been a cavalier man. Only a matter of time before a fine woman would capture his attention."

Apparently, I did not meet the expectation of what kind of woman that would be.

Her gaze left me, hungry eyes roaming Jack. "Hm."

I had little claim to Jack. I made that abundantly clear in our bargain, and most other interactions with him, but I suddenly had the urge to throttle her.

Politeness would probably be the safer route. "Thank you for having me tonight, Mr. Bernthal. I have to say, you could not have chosen a better venue for tonight's charity. This theater is stunning."

"Oh, and she comes with a southern drawl. How quaint." Mrs. Bernthal's lips tilted up, her eyes matching the action. "Is this your first time attending theater, Miss Colton?"

It was, unless you counted the plays Fairville's church group sometimes produced. Tommy liked to attend them and dragged me along. They took place in the town center, beside the well. The men spent days constructing a wooden dais for the children dressed as angels and prophets to perform on.

"Actually, Miss Colton is a performer herself. Ballet." Jack's simmering stare landed on the woman, but I felt she misinterpreted it.

"An excellent achievement. Ballet is quite the respectable and dedicated art form, if I do say so myself," Mr. Bernthal said. It would have been fine enough, had he not added, "Unlike those jazz performers up in Harlem. Before we know it, class and etiquette will cease to exist, should they have their way."

I swallowed. "I—"

"I believe the vainglorious customs of New York's elite will subsist quite well. Do not worry yourself, Mr. Bernthal," Jack said. It took me several moments to realize it was an insult.

Vipers, indeed.

But Mr. Bernthal only laughed, wagging his finger at Jack. "I always liked you." He gestured toward the bar. "Speaking of, I needed to chat with you about the request you sent several weeks ago. Why don't the ladies find something to eat before the show begins?"

I eyed Mrs. Bernthal, who showed no hint of emotion except for her eyes. They scowled.

A painful smile took my expression. "It would be my pleasure."

TWENTY-FIVE

AFTER AN HOUR OF Mrs. Bernthal intensely interrogating me on how I wooed Jack, he arrived at our table with the bribed usher from earlier. A younger man in a tuxedo—obviously, still training—fidgeted beside him.

The young man led us through the dwindling crowd to a private opera box. Thick, gold curtains parted the arched entry. Red velvet stretched the plush seats with a crystal ashtray raised on a mahogany table between. The only thing between our bodies and a dizzying fall was a brass railing, freshly waxed and shining beneath the lights. Above us, a fresco rivaling the Sistine Chapel took my breath.

The inside of Jack's hotel should have prepared me, but I'd never seen anything more grand, more deliberate and exquisite in every single detail.

"It's like a palace," I breathed.

His lips curled in one corner, but I couldn't tell if it was mocking or he found me endearing. Surely, whatever ancient castle he had in the fae world made this all look like a broom closet.

"I thought you would like it."

Mocking or endearing, I still didn't know. I was curious about what he discussed with Mr. Bernthal, but doubted he would relinquish information on *man talk*, so asked instead, "Who will perform *Giselle* tonight?"

"The Russian ballet company. World tour."

My guts hit the floor. "You mean . . . Anna Pavlova is performing?"

He rested his head in his hand, legs crossed in his plush seat. "Why, have you heard of her?"

No, she'd only been my idol since I was eleven years old. Her pictures only covered every bare wall space of the ballet studio I learned at. I'd only had some very private and pathetic fantasies of her inviting me to Moscow to perform.

I cleared my throat. "Once or twice."

"Good, because you need to steal her shoes."

The lights died, the curtain went up and thunderous applause echoed around the amphitheater. The opening strings drowned my high-pitched, "What?"

"*Annwyl*, sit down, the show's starting." He waved to my seat, then the usher standing sentinel behind the curtain. "What's your name, son?"

"Gilbert, sir."

"Gilbert, you wouldn't happen to have anything a bit stronger than tonic stocked for special visitors, would you?"

"Sir, I'm—I'm not sure what you—"

"Hooch. Jag juice. White lightning. You got me, Gilbert?"

He turned three shades of strawberry. "I can inquire with the manager for you, Mr. Warren."

"You are the fucking bee's knees, Gilbert."

I sank into my seat, glaring. "That poor boy looked ready to piss himself."

Jack frowned. "I'm fairly sure he did."

"Are you always this insufferable?"

"Most days," he murmured, checking we were alone. The first of the ballerinas floated onto the stage. "After the show ends, I have provided additional charity funds so you may have a private meeting with Anna in her dressing room. As men, human or otherwise, are not allowed, you will have to go alone. Whatever you do, do not ask for anything outright, that's how you fuck it all to hell. Other than that, you're welcome."

I blanched. "You're welcome?"

"Yes, you're welcome, because not only do we find the first of the Librarian's objects—in record time, I might add—but you get a private meeting with Anna Pavlova . . . unless it was a different dancer you often dreamed about, telling you you are the most exquisite ballerina she has ever seen?"

I tore off a silk glove and smacked his arm with it.

DESPITE MY LOOMING TASK, tears ran down my cheeks with the final curtain and round of applause. Everything I'd heard of Anna's dancing was understated at best—she was true magic, floating across the stage and bending her body in ways I could only wish to. Had Jack told me she wasn't human, I would have believed it in a heartbeat.

During intermission, Jack delivered more instruction, and some explanation. Unfortunately, I'd given him the idea for this heist when we danced in the study to The Dying Swan. He'd heard rumors the famed ballerina was gifted the slippers by a powerful fae, and once she came onstage, he was sure of it. They appeared like nothing more than white stage shoes to me, but Jack said enough power ebbed from them to make his hair stand on edge.

We'd have to cut the ribbons off, which made me angry enough to ignore him for an entire hour. Just before the final score, he told me Anna should not be aware of what the shoes were, just that they were special to her, so to frame our conversation carefully.

Gilbert succeeded in finding us jag juice, the last of which I downed with zero decorum. If I had to steal from my childhood hero, I would be drunk while I did it.

"Remember what I told you," Jack murmured, his lips a hair's breadth from my ear.

I nodded and he nudged me forward. A hulking security man waved me past a red-roped passage and down a hall near the stage. Dancers drifted in and out of dressing rooms, wiping makeup off their faces with their tutus bobbing around them. They were so beautiful, so elegant even in the way they walked and waved their hands while speaking to one another. An ugly sliver of envy uncoiled in my chest. Once, this had been my dream.

A gold placard featuring Anna's name glowed before my face. I knocked on the door.

"Come in."

Her dressing room was no larger than a closet, her vanity and costume rack taking up half the space. Mrs. Pavlova herself was a slight woman, a fragile bird lying in a riotous nest of tulle and lace and ribbons.

She smiled. "Hello." The simple word held a thick Russian accent.

I froze on the spot. "Hi."

"You are Adeline, yes?"

Dear god, she knew my name. Sweat lined my brow, my lips bobbing like a fish. She smiled wider, gesturing for me to sit. "Your husband says you are a great lover of ballet."

"Jack is not my husband."

"I am sorry, you must speak a little slower. I am afraid my English is not perfect."

"Mr. Warren is a friend," I said, slower, controlling my breathing.

"He must be a very good friend." She winked, reminding me of Lillian, which further reminded me why I was here in the first place.

"We've known one another a long time." Not entirely a lie, which according to Jack made compulsions stronger. The more truth to it, the more likely someone was to believe it. "He arranged this meeting as a gift."

"Oh?"

"A birthday gift." I had the sudden urge to beat myself over the head. "You see, it's my last one." Also technically not a lie, if I stopped aging, but it wasn't as if I could tell her that.

Mrs. Pavlova frowned. "What do you mean?"

Rule number two of compulsion: never go back on something you said. "I've been infected with a terrible illness."

She leaned back.

"It's not contagious," I rushed, so loudly she jumped in her seat. "Um, no, it's very rare. Only—only blonde women can get it."

She raised a brow. "Blonde?"

I nodded, gravely. "Yes, it's something with the—with the color."

She nodded. "I see."

"I have six months to live, maybe less." *Stupid, stupid, stupid.* "So Mr. Warren wanted to give me a very special farewell gift."

"That is terrible. I am so sorry."

God, I was awful. I was terrible. I hated myself. Why didn't they have a charm school in Fairville?

"I have accepted it." I smoothed out my skirt with a smile. "And I must say, this is a dream come true for me. I have danced since I was young and I've always admired you."

She faced the mirror, resuming her tirade against her stage makeup. "Oh? Are you with a company?"

She didn't look at me. I could still see her eyes, but only in the mirror. Did that still count? Goddammit. "I was to join one, but with my illness . . ."

"Of course, I understand." Her weak smile reflected back in the mirror. "You could always still try. I was very sick when I was young too."

"I know." Then, realizing I sounded like a stalker, added, "I read about it in the papers. It's part of why I admire you so much. I feel we are alike."

Her smile waned.

"If it's not too much to ask . . ." She turned. I debated smacking myself. *Whatever you do, don't ask for something outright.* "Could I have something from you? Perhaps an autograph?"

"Oh! Of course." She stood, rooting around her dressing room. "Do you have a pen, Miss Adeline?"

I blanched. "No."

The waning smile turned flat. "I think my friend should. If you excuse me one moment I can find it."

"Thank you very much." She stood, no taller than I was sitting, and left with the dressing room door still open. Barefoot.

Her white ballet slippers remained beneath her vanity.

I had two options.

Wait in the dressing room with magic I was fairly sure I did not possess at this point, all to manipulate my idol into handing over a prized possession.

Or, steal them.

Dammit.

I grabbed the shoes, tying the ribbons tightly to my garter and letting them hang in the space between my legs. A shock went through me, reverberating along my skin. The shoes brushed my stockings and I jolted, but there was no time. Checking the coast was clear, I ducked into the hall and desperately tried to walk like I hadn't just stolen from the greatest ballerina to ever live. The red rope came into view, the hulking guard and the emptying lobby just beyond. Jack stood with his back to me, smoking.

"Miss Adeline?"

I froze, mid-stride, turning with augmenting horror. Anna Pavlov stood in the center of the hall, frowning. "I found a pen, Miss Adeline."

"You did?" I stuttered.

She nodded, brow raised. "Did you still want an autograph or . . . ?"

Her eyes bored directly into mine. Jack said I had magic. I could will her to go look for ink, to go use the powder room instead of returning to her dressing room, to decide to find her hotel immediately and fetch her things in the morning.

I stared deep into her eyes.

They bounced side to side. "Are you well, Miss Adeline?"

Fabric swung between my legs, which I held at an awkward angle to accommodate the slippers. Another jolt went through me, a fiery pain that sang along my veins. Sweat broke on my brow and my hands flexed and unflexed. Anna's friend popped out of her dressing room and the security officer lingered behind me.

I did the only thing there was to do.

I faked a seizure.

"O Bozhe!"

"We need a doctor!"

Faces swarmed above me and I kept squirming. If I could have *compelled* some goddamn foam into my mouth I would have done it. Jack's voice rang above the concerned ballerinas, security and then he pushed his way through.

I pretended to faint. The sound of six horrified ballerinas shrieked through the remnants of my dignity.

"I have medicine for her. In the car," Jack said. "No worries, ladies, this happens all the time." He scooped me up bridal style, the head of his cane digging into my ass cheek. More exclamations sounded as he limped me through the lobby, people asking if I was alright or offering to call a physician. I squeezed my legs together to hold the shoes in place, gritting my teeth through the pain. Ice coated my inner thighs, so cold it left an agonizing burn. Jack leaned down and brushed his lips over my brow, barely a touch, but warm ecstasy swelled deep in my chest, honey coursing through my blood.

A pop went off. Broken glass. Through the thin film of my eyelids, something flashed.

Jack cursed under his breath. Cool night air hit my face.

A valet asked if we needed a car and he waved them off. Garbage and piss met my nose as he set me down, my eyes opening to a garbage-littered alley.

The first thing I did was lift my dress, fingers fumbling around the ribbons tied to my garter. The thin material of my stockings had rubbed away where the shoes touched, two red and raw spots burning on the inside of each thigh. I grunted, throwing the cursed things to the ground and breathing hard through my nose.

Jack stared at my lace undergarments, head cocked to the side.

I dropped my dress.

His eyes snapped to mine, lips trembling with a captive smile. I took a deep breath, pointing my finger at him. "Don't even think about it, Jack Warren."

He shook his head, pressing his lips together. "Think about what?"

I stepped forward. "A single smile." Step. "A single laugh. Step. "A single thing besides complete and utter silence—"

He latched his arm around my waist and tugged me against him. The last thing I saw before the shade was his grin reflected in a dirty puddle.

AIR PASSED MY CLENCHED teeth as a cool cloth pressed to one of the burns between my legs. The fire crackled against my bare feet and one of the vines slithered past. Wrapped in the thick green was a little clay pot containing aloe vera. It dropped the potted plant to the stone and remained still.

I waited for it to do something. Snap at my wrists or snatch the pot away. It did neither. I patted the end of it, murmuring, "Well . . . that was very kind. Thank you."

Satisfied, the vine slithered away.

Shaking my head, I snapped an aloe leaf and slathered the sap along my wounds. It still burned terribly, but the pain subsided enough to breathe again.

"You should really let me look at that."

I jumped, pushing the hem of my nightgown down. Jack had gone to bed nearly an hour ago, or so I thought, because he now leaned against the wall, observing me.

A slow shiver danced across my skin. He fell into one of the armchairs beside me, peering down to where I splayed on the floor. The beautiful silver dress wrinkled around my spread legs, my feet turning pink from their proximity to the fire.

"It's nothing. I'm fine." I stood, thighs at odd angles and trembling. I wasn't fooling anyone, but prayed he would let it go. I didn't want him to know just how badly the black mooring reacted to me, just how horribly I'd screwed this up.

If he did, it would only prove what I said earlier.

I hadn't taken a single step when he said, "Magical burns don't heal like normal ones, Adeline."

I hated the way he said my full name. Like I was a child that needed scolding, though I knew that was exactly how I was acting. But rational thought wasn't with me tonight. "Thank you, but I already said I'm fine. Goodnight, Jack."

"It shouldn't have done that to you."

I turned. His cane rested between his legs, the metal pommel catching the firelight. He observed it like it held the secrets of the universe.

My stomach bottomed out. "Come again?"

"A black mooring is powerful magic. Very few of these artifacts exist in your world, but still, I have never heard of one . . ." His voice trailed. I realized he wasn't looking at his cane, but a set of tiny shoes perched in his lap, the white fabric nearly engulfed by his thick thighs.

Just as I suspected, though I wasn't sure why he was surprised. My epic decision to partner with Jack suddenly felt so foolish, a contrived destiny I convinced myself of to gain a sense of purpose. Things went wrong when I was involved. I knew it, Jack knew it, Violet knew it, Tommy knew it.

"I'm sorry."

"About?"

"That I screwed it up." I sank back to the floor, picking at the carpet.

The crackling fire filled the silence. He sighed, murmuring, "We have to deal with these things as they come."

I blew out a heated breath, sending a floppy lock of hair back onto my head. "Why ask for my help at all? If these were so simple to get, why not shade in and out of her dressing room or compulse her or anything else?" I knew I should shut up. I had asked Jack to take me from the hotel, to give me a chance, but I wanted to know. If my help here was genuine, or he was just trying to make me feel better.

"Did you do it?"

"Do what?"

"Compulse her."

"No." There were about a million more things I wanted to say, but I kept them locked away.

He stared at me. Somewhere in our conversation his human form melted away, his snake eyes roaming up and down my face. I shivered. The tattoos along his hands danced, the fire on his right roaring into a starless night.

"You did good, *annwyl*."

"What?"

"You did good," he said. "It all went to hell, but you figured out a way. It was embarrassing, immoral, painful," he jerked his chin at my legs, "Yet, you did it anyway."

"In the most inept way imaginable."

"But you managed, didn't you?"

I said nothing.

"This was the easiest task. By far. It was practically a joke." Disappointment echoed in my chest, but I said nothing.

"This was nothing but preparation for the real thing," he continued. "A test run. From here, it only gets more dangerous; there will be more sacrifices than a few burns and some humiliation, and you will probably regret that bargain you made with me but you will keep trying, *annwyl*, because this is what you wanted, so you are going to take it. And I am letting you, but what you agreed to help me do cannot be taken lightly, nor can the bond between us, and I need you to understand that as much as I'd love to, I can't always be there to save you. You will have to do it yourself sometimes. The hard way."

Pain lanced along my skin. The vine slithered back, curling around my ankle with a gentle squeeze.

"I'm not like you," I said. "I'm not powerful. I'm not worldly. I haven't seen centuries pass with my own eyes. I don't understand how you can possibly look at me any differently than your sister does. I'm nothing but a stupid fucking human."

"You're Adeline Ruth Colton." He pushed to his feet, stepping past my legs. The vines followed him out. "Today you learned something, and tomorrow you will be a little stronger."

TWENTY-SIX

"NO."

"It's only a few hours."

"Absolutely not."

Over breakfast that morning, Jack asked me to do the unthinkable: spend the day with his sister.

"You said you wanted to help, and this is how you can help. I need Violet away from the hotel for the next few hours."

I'd been wrong to think he wouldn't reveal what he discussed with Mr. Bernthal, though I desperately wished he hadn't. Violet sorely distrusted the man, but he may have pertinent information to find the next item on our list—unknowingly of course, since he was human. The only catch, he desired something in return. That something in return was a year-long contract where Jack supplied liquor to his string of speakeasies. Philanthropist, my ass.

The deal was to be brokered today, but since Violet adamantly opposed it, he wanted her distracted. And himself, because the timing couldn't have been worse. It was a new moon.

Even now, sitting ten feet apart with his hands bound in his lap, the bond snapped so viciously between us that I kept my legs crossed for the past hour, afraid if I got up I'd lose any sense of control. Jack, being the completely rational man he was, had quite literally asked Charlene to bind his hands with iron chains and leave him on the couch. The new moon meant the veil was at its thinnest. When the veil was at its thinnest, magic was at its most potent in this world. When magic was at its most potent, our parallel bond desperately wanted us to fuck.

"I would rather sleep with you now and watch the world burn as a result."

He chewed his lower lip, glancing skyward, "Please do not mention sleeping with me again."

At that, magic pulsed so heavy between us I forgot to breathe. My muscles ached, my skin catching on fire, an animalistic side of my brain screaming obscene things. I squeezed my thighs harder together, taking a deep breath. "Just leave me with Lillian."

"Lillian will go with you," he said through gritted teeth. The words were low, set with a deep growl. God, I wanted— "But Violet is the only one I trust to protect you. And again, I need her away from the hotel."

It was like getting thrown in a cold bath. "Just say you want me dead, Jack."

"She's the most powerful, whether she will admit it or not." I wasn't sure what difference it made, since she refused to use her abilities. "So please, I am begging you, Adeline. I will get on my knees for you."

I shot to my feet, covering my ears. "Are you insane? You can't say *beg*."

AN HOUR LATER, I clutched my purse to my chest and shifted on the sidewalk. The arrival of September brought a chill to the air. Out of all the clothes Lillian bought me, I wore the only dress that covered my ankles, an autumn jacket of burgundy and a felt hat I'd had for years, stitched myself back in Georgia. In my mad rush to get as far from Jack as possible, I was fairly sure lipstick coated my teeth and I had a run up the back of my stockings. The doorman, who was actually a satyr, raised a brow.

"You don't get it. You're not parallelled," I said.

He shrugged, stuffing a cigarette in his mouth.

A white Rolls Royce screeched to a stop on the curb. Lillian leaned out the back, red hair blazing with a brillant grin. Violet sat in the driver's seat, a silk scarf around her neck. A scowl cursed her lips.

"Get in the car, human. We're getting zozzled."

"I'M JUST SO EXCITED we're having a girl's day together."

"Please shut up."

"Yes, Violet." Lillian sank back into her seat, fidgeting. Despite the crisp air, Violet had the top of the car down. The biting wind nearly took my hat and burned my face. She careened through the city streets, leaning on her horn more than she allowed the car to be silent. I spent every moment pressing harder and harder against the door, praying the passenger side would pop open and I'd be killed instantly.

"We are going to a bar," Violet said. "We are drinking. We are not speaking. And the moment my brother sends word you can return, I am dumping your ass in his fireplace."

Lillian leaned forward again. "Violet, come on, we can't kill our favorite human."

Violet shot me a look that said she most definitely could.

"I haven't had a night out on the town in ages."

Violet made a hard turn onto Broadway. "It's eleven a.m."

"Or morning," Lillian corrected. She grinned. "Adeline, have you ever been to a speakeasy? It's just *so* fun and—"

"We are not talking," Violet snapped. She jerked us to a screeching stop in front of a warehouse, letting the engine idle. I looked around, wondering where exactly this bar was supposed to be, when I noticed Violet staring at me.

Her eyes narrowed, chin bobbing up and down. "Not yet," she murmured with omen, cut the engine, and stepped onto the sidewalk.

Taking a breath of courage, I joined the two women loitering on the cement. Violet adjusted her gloves, pulled a cigarette from her purse and lit it between her teeth.

I swallowed. "Are we really going to a bar?"

Violet's eyes flicked up. Her serpent ones. "Is there a problem with that?"

Lillian gave me the tiniest nod of encouragement.

"It's just . . ." Violet glared harder. "I didn't think women were supposed to go to bars. There's drinking and fornication and—" she raised a brow. "—you know, unseemly things," I finished.

She threw her cigarette to the ground. "Good girls are boring. I'd rather be a whore."

She turned on her heel and stomped down the sidewalk. I watched her go, slack-jawed.

Lillian shot me an apologetic smile. "I also like sex."

My flesh jumped with that forbidden word. Her eyes widened. "Oh, I'm so sorry. I forgot it's that time of the month for you." She looped her arm through mine. "Don't worry, darling, we'll get you so splifficated you'll forget your daddy even exists."

"My father's dead," I told her for the tenth time.

"Gosh, chicky, you know I didn't mean *that* daddy."

We picked our way through a labyrinth of rotting rafters, finding Violet before a thick, rusted door. She rapped her knuckles three times and a panel slid open, a gruff voice asking, "Password?"

"Oh, would you just open the fucking door, Garrett?"

He mumbled some choice words and the door opened to a dark hallway. Lillian pulled me along, practically skipping. The smell of smoke and sweat hit like a brick wall. Garrett was a beastly man who took up half the hall, and Lillian and I had to go single-file to shuffle past him. Beyond lay a room of pure, unadulterated debauchery.

We were the only women in the joint besides a single brunette, breasts fully on display and splayed over a man's lap. His pinstripe suit wrapped around her and his cigar smoke coiled her nipples. The men at his table dealt cards, while the remaining men in the room turned red faces on us in unison. Every single one clutched a tumbler of dark brown liquid.

Violet sauntered forward, hands swinging at her side and chin tipped to the ceiling. Claiming the last empty table, Lillian skipped after her and I shuffled forward, eyes to the ground.

"I haven't been here in a while. It's turned into a shithole." Violet grinned at a scowling man, shoving another cigarette between her teeth. "What's your poison and how much of it until you pass out?"

I realized she was talking to me. "I'm not sure."

"I don't know why I'm still shocked by how pitiful you are." She shook her hair out and released a puff of smoke. "I like gin, Lillian likes whiskey, get whatever the fuck you want and tell the man it will go on my tab."

I didn't move. "I don't think I've ever heard a woman swear as much as you."

"That's because you have never known anyone fun." She fluttered her hand at me. "Go on. Now."

Sighing, I wormed my way through the worn chairs scattering the rotted wood. Billiard balls smacked in the background and low chatter formed an endless hum. Only three men sat at the bar, because there were only three stools. The bar itself was flimsy plywood, rattling ominously each time someone set down a drink.

I leaned against the wood, giving my best smile to the ancient man tending bar. White caterpillar eyebrows scrunched over a wrinkled scowl. He was missing three teeth and the rest were rotting and black at the gums. His shirt hung open, liver spots peppered with tufts of wiry, white hair.

"What?" He barked.

"Hello, how are you today?" I asked. All three men sitting turned to look at me. I swallowed. "Um, my friends would like one gin and one whiskey, please. It will go on the dark-haired lady's tab."

The bartender leaned forward on his elbows. His rancid breath crossed my nose. "This isn't an establishment for women. Go find a girl's club."

I chewed my bottom lip. "Actually, I think my friend has been here—"

"I don't give a shit, lady. I'm tending bar today, and I say no women. Go back to the Mason-Dixon line," he said, the last bit with a terrible impression of my accent.

A long breath passed my nose. "There was a woman when we came in, sir."

He released a hacking laugh. Spittle hit my cheek. "You want to take your top off and work? By all means, go ahead. Just wash the cow shit off first."

"Noted." I turned on one heel, performing my shameful walk back to the table.

I hadn't sat down yet when Violet hissed, "What in the ever-loving fuck was that?"

Sighing, I threw my hand in the air. "I don't know, Violet. Why don't you go ask yourself?"

"I'm not talking about him. I'm talking about *you*." She gave me a look I reserved for manure and bugs. "That was fucking pathetic. Try again."

"Why don't we just—"

"Go. Try. Again."

I implored Lillian for help. She gave me a tight-lipped smile that said she sympathized, but wasn't on my side.

Move to New York, it will be a fresh start. Make friends, it will be good for you. Come on Addie, it's just one party, you most definitely won't get sucked into a turf war between non-human gangsters. It's just one day, darling, my sister isn't that bad.

"What?" The bartender snapped.

"Look." I reached into my purse, pulling a wad of emergency cash Jack gave me. "We're already here, we can pay, just serve us some drinks, please."

He leaned forward until we were nose to nose. "What part of *no* do you not understand, bitch? This ain't Chumley's. Get out."

Tears pricked the back of my eyes. I tried staring into his, using that stupid compulsion power Jack thought I had, but it was to no avail. He turned a darker shade of red. Finally, I pressed my lips together, nodded, and retreated back to the table again.

"Sit the fuck down."

As usual, I did as I was told.

Violet leaned forward, hands splayed on the dirty tabletop. "What did that man call you?"

I shook my head.

"What did that man call you?"

Water blurred the edges of my sight. Of course, every man within five feet now watched, holding in their laughter. "Nothing you haven't called me before, Violet."

"I don't count. You're fucking my brother. I can call you whatever I want."

"I'm not—"

"God, you know what I meant." She breathed a melodramatic sigh. "This isn't Georgia, darling, you *ain't on the farm* anymore. How the fuck do you expect to do anything with Delsaran if you can't stand up to some toothless fucking git in a shithole bar? He works behind a piece of plywood, Addie. *Plywood.*" She snapped in my face. "It's time to throw out whatever bullshit they taught you in Sunday school and grow a fucking pair. Be a woman. Go demand a drink."

Hot, acrid anger bubbled to life. "You hate me, Violet. Why do you care?"

"I don't hate you, I think you're pathetic," she snapped. "I think you're weak. I think you listened to whatever your darling papa and sweet brother told you even though they both ruined your life. I think you're a smart girl playing stupid because you'd rather bark like a dog when thrown a bone than make a decision for yourself. And if you're going to act like that you'll get us all killed, so do the bare goddamn minimum for once in your pathetic fucking life."

Ruby tinged my vision. My throat constricted and sweat lined the inside of my gloves. I ripped them off and threw them on the table. "Fuck you."

My heels squeaked on the floor. A man howled as I stormed past. *Today you learned something and tomorrow you'll be a little stronger.* Fuck this. Fuck Violet. Fuck the entire world I was trying to save. Fuck Anna Pavlova. Fuck Jack for telling me my one accomplishment was child's play. Fuck him for telling me I needed to save myself. Fuck my family for never allowing me to. Fuck myself for never trying to. Fuck World War One and prohibition and succulents and Calvin Coolidge and *fuck that goddamn bartender.*

"Are we really doing this again, lady?"

I slammed my hands on the counter. "Do you know who my daddy is?"

His eyes bounced in his skull, a slow smile forming around wretched teeth. "What?"

"I said, do you know who my daddy is?"

The bartender laughed. My vision turned a lovely shade of scarlet. "No, I don't know who your fucking daddy is."

"Who stocks your liquor?"

"That's none of your business."

"I see a bottle of absinthe down there. That all come from Jack Warren?"

His smile faded. "What's that to you?"

I leaned on the plywood until we were nose to nose. It creaked beneath my shaking palms. "If you buy your hooch off of him, you must have heard a thing or two about his reputation."

"Everyone's heard of Jack Warren."

"Tell me," I hissed. "Tell me exactly what you've heard happens to people that piss that man off."

He crossed his arms. The patrons around us became unusually interested in the plywood. I fingered slow circles over it, sighing. "It's a shame, really. I can tell you're a hard-working man, good values. Jack will be so disappointed when I go home tonight, crawl into bed, and sob about how much I smell like cow shit."

My eyes went wide, blinking innocently. "Now, I'm going to ask you one more time. Who the fuck do you think my daddy is?"

"NO, LILLIAN, FOR GOD'S sake it goes like this. *Oh, all the men make all the laws, which makes the women fret, but wait and see those laws, when we at last our suffrage get.*"

I laughed so hard gin bubbled out my nose. Lillian turned a deep cherry next to me. "I could have sworn there was at least one swear word in there!"

"That's probably how Violet sings it and she's pulling your leg," I said, wiping tears from my eyes. I hiccuped. "Violet, I swear on the lord above, I've never heard you speak a sentence without the word fuck in it."

"It's a beautiful word," she sang. A row of empty glasses decorated her elbow. "The most beautiful in the English language, in my humble opinion."

"Oh, yeah? And why is that Miss Violet?" Roger—it may have Robert—leaned forward. He sat with his chair spun around, his tie fashioned around his head. Lillian was in the process of undoing all his clothes.

"It's so versatile." Violet waved an elegant hand at him, grinning. "How many words in the English tongue can you think of that are a noun, verb, adjective, *and* adverb. *Fuck.* My favorite insult, conversation filler, exclamation, intensifier and my favorite fucking thing to do. To fuck," she said, raising her glass. I clinked mine against her's, pinky out, sloshing gin over the side.

One of Roger Robert's friends flicked my hair. Violet scowled at him. "Hands off, that's technically my sister-in-law."

He grinned like a cat. "I don't see a ring on her finger."

"She doesn't need a fucking ring."

I shook my head. "I got something better."

"Yeah?"

"Tell me, do you believe in soulmates, Raymond?" Lillian procured her lipstick and drew a heart on Roger Robert Raymond's cheek.

"Only women believe in that shit."

"*Ooooo,*" the three of us sang.

"Toss him." Violet said.

"Straight to the bin," I echoed.

"But look at Riley's face, so soft and sweet." Lillian pouted, squishing Roger Robert Raymond Riley's cheeks together.

"I like you," he said, rubbing his nose against Lillian's.

She smiled. "You'll keep my interest for a day or two."

"Adeline, my least favorite person, come here." I slid my chair closer to Violet with a horrible screeching noise. The bartender scowled across the room. "I have to tell you, darling, you are entirely less insufferable today."

I put a hand to my heart. "Violet, that may be the kindest thing you've ever said to me."

She held my face in her hands, eyes swarmed with endless affection. "Don't ever get used to it, you wonderful bitch."

"I want to dance! I want to dance!" Ignoring Richard, Lillian climbed on the table and threw her hands above her head, smacking a low-hanging lightbulb. "I'm a fucking suffragette! Women can vote now, you bastards! Fuck the patriarchy! I love America!"

"You can't vote, Lillian, you're not American," I hollered.

Her red eyes turned on me, hands over her chest. "I *vote* with my *heart*, Adeline. *God.*"

"Alright, girls, I'm over this flaming bag of shit." Violet rubbed her temples, hiccuping loudly. "How the fuck do we get home?"

"We can shade!" Lillian exclaimed.

I paled. "I'm not shading with you."

"We can drive!"

"I'm not driving with you either."

"I'll call my soldier," Violet said. She stood on wobbly feet, cupping her hands around her mouth. "Bartender, you awful, horrendous man, is this shithole in possession of a telephone?"

He grit his teeth. "There's one two blocks away."

"Wonderful." Violet braced a hand on the table, blinking at me. "Alright, human, get over here. I can't fucking walk."

TWENTY-SEVEN

"YOU THREE ARE IN *deep* shit."

Violet threw her arms around Will from the back seat, nuzzling her face into his neck, "William, darling, why must you always have a stick up your ass?"

I blanched. "I think what she means to say is—"

"Yeah, yeah," Will said. He winked. The car bumped far too much for my liking along the pot-holed road. There were better routes to take, but I suspected Will wanted to punish us.

Lillian woke beside Violet, blinking at the fading dusk. "Where's Remington?"

"We ditched him at the bar," I said.

"We did?" She pouted. "I was going to fuck him."

"We did you a favor," Violet snapped. "That man was vile. I would never let him touch you."

"It was true love," Lillian said, dream-like, and fell back asleep.

"Jack is going to be pissed," Will sang. It was joking, but the side-eye he gave me was not.

I beamed.

"I'M A SUFFRAGETTE," LILLIAN mumbled. Violet had one arm and I had the other. The looks we got in the hotel lobby were nothing short of horrified.

"Yes, yes, of course you are, darling," Violet hummed, patting her head. After wishing us luck, Will took off in his car.

We heaved Lillian into the elevator and set her up in the study. The room was empty, the fire roaring and vines crawling, but no Jack. Violet put her hands on her hips. "Oh where, oh where, could my big brother be?"

"You're twins."

"He was born two minutes earlier."

I closed my eyes, swaying on the spot. A tug prodded at my chest, snaking through the floors to my other half.

Perhaps Violet sensed it too, because she pulled me back onto the lift. One moment the gold brocade of the elevator was before me, then Violet kicked in a door. A room of men smoking around a table blinked in unison.

Jack was at the head of it.

"Hello, Jack," she called. The six other men glanced around, one being Mr. Bernthal. As far as I could tell, they were all human.

I grabbed Violet's arm, but to no avail. She leaned against the wall, grinning. "I'm done babysitting. How has your day been?"

Jack gave her a tight-lipped smile, head tipped to the side. "Wonderful. I will see you both upstairs in a little while."

"Now what are we doing?" She leaned on the table, peering down at a bold-lettered contract. "Really, Jack? I thought we decided against this."

One of the men raised an eyebrow, snuffing his cigar into an ashtray. I backed toward the door.

Jack's gaze narrowed, nostrils flaring. "Are you drunk?"

"Oh, horribly," Violet said. She swung around, noticed me hovering in the doorway and yanked me forward. "If you can believe it, I actually had a tolerable day with this one. All her idea by the way. The drinking, I mean." Violet winked. "Gentlemen, have you all met my brother's . . . whatever the fuck she is?"

Jack sucked in a heated breath. *"Violet."*

"This is Miss Adeline Colton," she said, shoving me against the table. My stomach dug into the wood. "She was brought here against her will from bumfuck, Georgia and technically speaking, we were holding her captive." She threw her arm around my shoulders. "And while my brother decided to go behind my back and write up this contract I said was a *terrible* idea—no offense, gentlemen—Addie and I spent the day teaching her not to be a dimwit before getting splifficated. By the way, Jack, your secretary is currently passed out on the settee. And I ran up a fairly ridiculous tab. Anyway, Addie had quite a bit to drink and she's feeling a bit loose if you know what I mean, so if I were you, I'd tear up this entire thing and get her sweet little ass up—"

Jack rapped his cane on the floor. All six men slumped face down on the table.

I yelped. His fae form flickered to life, simmering eyes falling on Violet. "What the fuck?"

"What?" She blinked innocently, but her vicious smile ruined it.

"I asked you to keep an eye on her. Not get hammered and—"

"Yes, yes, you asked me to babysit your twenty-year-old, doe-eyed power reservoir." She walked her fingers toward the strewn contract on the wood. "Why must you always be such a shit?"

"Get out."

"Have it your way. Enjoy your evening." Fingers wiggling, she shot me a grin and sauntered out the door. I turned to follow her, instantly sober, when Jack said, "Not you."

I froze on the threshold. He still held his fae form, furiously clutching his cane. As much as I hated to admit it, I wished Violet would return to be the target of his ire.

"Do you have any idea how stupid that was?"

The six human men breathed softly against the table, their breath fogging against the polished wood. Cigar smoke curled the air with a dense fog. Jack's golden eyes cut through the smog like stars.

Very stupid. Even more stupid when one considered I thought I had a breakthrough with Violet, but it seemed I was nothing more than a pawn to infuriate Jack. A silly trap I fell right into in my desperate attempt to appease her. And I actually thought I'd done something worthwhile today, standing up for myself and not acting like an utter doormat for once.

Suddenly, I was sick of it. Sick of everything, especially when the bond reared its ugly head, snapping and lashing between us. The honey-coated energy of his presence wrapped around me like a song, like smooth liquor and a crackling fire. My skin itched to touch him, my tongue craved his taste, and suddenly I was so angry about it all, I forgot Jack was mad at me first.

"We had a good day," I said.

He went so still I thought he froze himself too. "You do realize Delsaran still has men looking for you? And the two people capable of providing protection convinced you to get *splifficated* with them?"

"You were otherwise occupied."

"So you should have held them accountable. Lillian, at the very least."

"Maybe I didn't want to," I said. My feet shuffled forward, drawn like a moth to flame. "Maybe after a lifetime of discipline and rules, contracts that run my life and you pulling all the strings, I wanted to have one day where I could be normal with friends. Aren't you the one who told me to start handling myself, anyway?"

A tic went off in his jaw, clenched so hard I swore a tooth snapped. "You're acting like a child."

"You're acting like a tyrant." I waved my hand at the contract. "Screwing over Violet, screwing over me, ordering Lillian around like a slave when all she wants is your approval. Do you actually want our help or do you just want everyone to ask 'how high?' when you scream 'jump'?"

"Clearly, I want your help, which has the basic requirement of you remaining alive."

"I've had no life." It was a truth I kept buried, a thought I'd dutifully ignored, but now that it was in the open I couldn't stop the rest from boiling over. "I have been a prisoner since the day I was born, first by my father, then my brother and now this. I was never allowed friends. I was never allowed to make my own decisions. I was never allowed a moment of peace without someone delivering me warnings or telling me everything I was doing wrong. I wanted to go to school, and I wanted to meet people, and I wanted to become a dancer and travel and make friends and find a man I actually wanted to be with and now *this.*" I flicked my hand between us, the simmering bond needing no name.

"When I'm in a room with you, I can't breathe." The words hardly mattered, because my feet slid closer to him anyway, reeled in by that incessant tug. "I can't sit in my own skin. You gave me a choice but it really isn't one, let's be honest, because I want you so bad and I don't even know why. Because I don't want you, Jack. I fucking don't."

Silence ebbed between us, his attention raptly on my trembling face. He swiped his thumb over his bottom lip. Shrugged. "And what would you like me to do about it?"

Blood boiled in my veins. "What?"

"What would you like me to do about it?" He repeated, slower, pushing to his feet. He stood so close each breath pressed my chest against his. "You want me to woo you, make you want me? You want flowers, poetry, you want me to get down on one knee, Adeline? Will that satisfy you?"

I pushed to my toes, baring my teeth. "That's a start."

"And then what?" he murmured. "What will you want from me then, darling?"

Low heat roared beneath my skin, my stomach tightening with each whispered word. "Some reprieve would be nice."

"Reprieve?"

"I told you, I can't fucking breathe," I whispered. "All this magic begging me to touch you, and I can't do anything to take the edge off."

Golden eyes shot above my head, arm coiling around my waist. Only when darkness and a poisonous breeze surrounded me did I realize there was a mirror on the wall.

The fire crackled and belladonna bloomed. I stepped back, only for him to crush me against his chest again. My toes brushed the floor as he pushed me back. A mess of red hair snored softly from the settee.

"Lillian, there's six men downstairs who need their memories wiped."

She gave a weak thumbs-up and rolled over. Jack half-marched, half-carried me to the Abstruse, slammed the door behind him and shoved me onto the bed.

He dropped to his knees. My eyes became saucers. "What are you—"

"Taking the edge off." He tore off his gloves. Smooth, tattooless skin—he was back in human form. I barely had time to ask what he meant when he ran his hands up my shins, igniting my skin beneath the thin fabric.

"Jack . . ."

"Tell me to stop anytime." He waited, his thumbs doing slow circles over my knees. I stayed silent. His hands drifted higher, reached the clasps of my garter belt and undid each one with a snap. My stockings slipped down my thighs.

I inhaled a sharp breath. He rarely ever touched me, not without some barrier between our skin, but each time was electrifying. Sparks broke across my body, a languid heat unfurling low in my stomach. Simple, lovely memories unfurled with each stroke, a warm breeze and satin sheets.

He pulled my stockings to my ankles. Unfastened my heels and threw them aside. I slipped lower on the bed, my toes brushing his thighs where he kneeled in worship on the floor. He continued touching—intoxicating little strokes of his fingers across my skin, hands running up and down the length of my legs, then he pressed his lips to the inside of my knee.

My blood raced, my face flushing so hot I forgot to breathe. He roamed higher. Another kiss to the inside of my thigh. A little higher. Higher.

"I thought we couldn't . . ." I didn't have it in me to finish that thought.

"We're not." The words danced over my skin. My hands shook so hard I clutched the comforter. He continued his ascent, only hesitating when he reached my burn, brushing the wound so lightly, I hardly felt it all. The hem of my dress moved with his lips until he had it around my waist. Only the thin satin of my undergarments hid something very private from him.

His eyes flicked up. He waited. I should have refused him, I should have put a stop to this, but desperate need evaporated all my thoughts. I didn't want him to stop. I didn't want his hands or lips to leave. Ecstasy pounded through my blood and all I could think was, *more*.

He tugged my panties off and stuffed them in his pocket. A cherry blush ran up my throat, my thighs closing, but he pushed them apart. A cool breeze rattled the Abstruse's curtains and I was suddenly aware I was half naked, spread wide in front of a man. A man that clutched my hips, staring longingly between my legs.

A low sound came from the back of his throat, eyes fluttering closed. "Tell me to stop, *annwyl*."

My breath hitched. I said nothing.

He kissed along the opposite thigh, hands riding dangerously close to the crease of my hips. I hadn't the faintest clue where this was going, both hoping and fearing he only wanted to look. All his clothing remained on.

He didn't stop this time. His lips pressed that dangerous crease at my thigh, hot breath meeting the hotter wetness between my legs. Alarm rang through me, a sudden thought that he still wouldn't give up this game. My lips parted, a stuttered mess forming words. "What are you going to do?"

Hooded eyes met mine, darkening by the second. "What do you think I'm going to do?"

I swallowed, nerves firing strange signals. "I don't—I don't know, you're not going to kiss me down there, are you?"

One dark eyebrow formed an arch. "Do you want me to kiss you there?"

Yes. No. Was that something people did? The extent of my sexual education was watching animals on the farm, and I'd never seen any of them do *that*. It felt wrong, but there was something so awfully dirty about it, I wanted to know if he'd do it anyway.

"Is that something fae do?" I asked.

A devilish smile took his lips. He leaned in, thumbs stroking the curve of my ass, and ran his tongue up my center.

An entire lungful of air blew past my lips, hands clenching the sheets until my knuckles turned white. That was—that was definitely—

I couldn't complete the thought because he did it again. A noise I'd have nightmares about for weeks passed my teeth, but it only encouraged him, thumbs spreading me apart so he could lick deeper, suck harder. Before I could stop myself I dug my fingers into his hair, rolling my hips against his face. He made a noise resembling a growl and pushed a finger deep inside me.

I gasped, vision dark. He murmured something in a language I didn't recognize, asked, "How many times, *annwyl?*"

I could barely push the word out. "What?"

"How many times have you touched yourself?"

My tight walls should have given that away. I shook my head, mouthing what I couldn't form.

Glamour shattered and his eyes went serpentine. I panted, moaning loudly when he pushed deeper inside me. "You are going to be the fucking death of me, Adeline."

I felt the same. All my thoughts, feelings and memories reduced to a single point of contact. I squirmed against the sheets, a pathetic, needy noise whimpering in my throat. He obliged my need, fingering me harder, pressing his lips back to that forbidden spot. I could have lived and died like that. I would forgo any future happiness just to keep him there. My stomach tightened. I flushed hotter. My breath grew so frantic black tinged my vision. My nails dug into his scalp, the silkiness of his hair the greatest high. A shockwave rolled through my body and I lost the means to breathe.

He pinned me down as I shook, moaning and whining and half-sobbing against the sheets. An image burned my vision of a starry night. A rolling green pasture and leaves black with dusk swaying above my head. A dark moon graced the sky, a low voice, whispering, "*Annwyl . . .*"

I jerked back to reality faster than I left it. Jack moaned against my cunt, the vibrations rolling across my skin. He looked up with those arcane eyes and shoved me back on the bed.

He was on top of me before I could blink. I wasn't thinking, just moving—shoving his jacket off, tearing buttons at his collar. He kissed my neck, my chest, wild and desperate, only stopping to pull my dress over my head. He tore the lacy bandeau beneath in two and kissed my breasts, sucking my nipples until my back arched off the bed. I forgot where we were, what we were doing, any rules we were supposed to follow. The only thing I recognized was the fire beneath my skin, Jack's body hovering over mine, the way he worshiped me with his hands, his tongue, his teeth. How I would die if he stopped.

I clawed his back, his hair, unsure what I asked for as I panted, "Please, please, please . . ."

He went rigid above me. His fingers dug between my ribs, so hard I already felt bruises forming. I made an anguished noise, tugging at his hair, begging him to keep going. Hot breaths hit my chest. He shook his head, mumbling, "I'm sorry. I shouldn't have . . . I thought I could . . . "

I reached for him again, but he was already on the far side of the room, tugging his clothes into place. He was gone before I could understand what just happened.

TWENTY-EIGHT

JACK WAS NOWHERE TO be seen the next day. Or the next day. Or the next. The new moon came and passed and he still didn't appear. I'd just about lost my mind combing through Arthur's journals, attempting to find a single passage about the Woman in White. When not doing that, I spent hours on end staring at a potted tree, willing it to angle toward me. Any attempts at glamour were a massive failure. Will found me in the kitchen several times, asking about my week between dodging Charlene's wooden spoon. I wanted to ask if he'd help me with glamour and compulsion, but then I'd have to admit I didn't know where Jack was, and I'd also have to admit I wanted to know where he could be. I had far too much shame for that, so I lied through waning smiles and retreated to the empty apartment alone. The bond snapped between us. Lips brushed my hairline, a quiet voice whispering, "I'm here, *annwyl*."

Furious, hurt, confused—I was either one of the three or all them at once. Punctuated by the occasional humiliation and shame, it was a cocktail for a pity-party with no end in sight. How I went from screaming at Jack to naked beneath him was a mystery I didn't want to solve. I could blame it on the bond, but even I knew that was only part of it.

Then there was everything to dwell on that I had screamed at him. *I've had no life*. What a way to a miserable epiphany.

287

I was about ready to chuck the innocent plant into the fire when Lillian's delighted voice rang through the living room. "Adeline! Perfect, just the human I was searching for."

She stood before the mirror, dressed to the nines in a dazzling seafoam gown and matching headband, fitted with white feathers and diamonds. She sashayed closer, tilting my chin and turning my head to the side. "What are you doing, darling? You need to get ready."

"For?"

She winked. "We're going to a party."

NEARLY AN HOUR PASSED before Lillian was satisfied. My protests fell on deaf ears, and before I knew it I stood before the study's three-tier mirror in a knee-length dress of garnet and gold. The scalloped lace hem rubbed my stockings and slim black heels clicked together. When I'd reached for my cloche hat, Lillian slapped my hand away and tied a jewel-speckled headband around my forehead. Glittering diamond tassels hung by my ears and brushed my shoulders.

"Absolutely divine," she exclaimed.

"Will you tell me where we're going yet?"

"I'll let Jack explain."

My stomach bottomed out, and not from Lillian shading us from the room. We landed in a deserted alleyway before a freshly cleaned window pane. Every other window along the gray, brick building was shattered. A wooden door hung loose on its frame, the words *Silver Tongue* crudely carved in with a knife.

I glanced around. "Lillian, where the hell are we?"

"We have to retrieve the others first." She grinned, rapping her knuckles on the weathered wood. I was afraid the door would come clean off the hinges.

"I don't think that door leads anywhere."

"Patience, darling."

After a moment of huffing warm air into my gloves the door changed, shifting to a proper position on polished hinges. The crudely carved name glowed with liquid silver. Magic hummed from the threshold. It cracked open just enough for a low voice to whisper through, "I am always hungry, I must always be fed. The finger I touch will soon turn red."

"Fire," Lillian said. Whoever stood on the other side grunted and the door opened all the way. Beyond laid nothing but a dark hall.

"Come along, we don't want to be late." She looped her arm through mine. Darkness closed in like a shroud, my breaths growing uneven as my eyes attempted to adjust. I stumbled blind, only guided by Lillian's encouraging tugs.

Magic tainted the air, heady and strong, just like when Jack led me into the Librarian's lair. I was about to turn back when Lillian chimed, "Here we are." A lock clicked and a second door opened.

There was no feasible way the cavernous room fit into the dilapidated building outside without the means of magic. The walls and ceiling were made of brambles, a rich, smooth wood that looked closer to glass than anything once living. A crystal bar took up an entire wall with every manner of fae mixing cocktails behind it. A fire roared in the center of the room, flappers with wings and high fae in suits dancing around it to a band of nymphs playing in a dark corner. Curtains of rich, rippling fabric and wooden dividers with moving paintings carved out private spaces. My hair stood on edge with all the power buzzing the air, the many sets of inhuman eyes that landed on me with curiosity.

I gripped Lillian's arm. "Where are we?"

"The Silver Tongue Speakeasy, of course. Most famous on the eastern sea border. Among our kind, at least."

I figured that, since I was yet to see another human. A group of high fae men puffed magenta smoke, one nodding their chin at me.

"And why are we here?"

"I told you, gathering the others," she said, leading us to a massive scarlet curtain, the gold border brushing the floor. "Usually, this is where we discuss business since Jack doesn't love us all popping in and out of his private residence all the time. We've been there more recently because of the newest occupant." She winked. "But now that things have calmed down a bit, we can meet here more often."

Or because Jack was avoiding me, and would rather be here than the apartment. I slipped my arm from hers, following her lead as she tugged the maroon curtain aside. A space far too big for what I saw outside of it lay behind. An ornate table stood in the center with a velvet booth forming a half-circle around it. Fat candles dripped wax along the walls and floors, some embedded in the brambles and others hovering below the ceiling. Between the fabric and lowlight, it cast everything in an eerie, ruby glow. Including Violet, Arthur, Will and Jack seated around the table.

"The red room," Lillian said. "Always reserved for us." She dropped into an overstuffed armchair in the corner, crossing her long legs. Will and Arthur looked like they were on their ninth or tenth round of fae wine, Violet fed her snake with a bored expression, and Jack stared at me.

After three days of no contact, one would think he could at least muster a hello. The bond was certainly angry about it, frantic and snapping between us enough to make me squirm. But he only waved a hand at the empty space across from him, urging me to sit. Will threw his arm around my shoulder the moment my bottom hit the fabric.

"You look lovely tonight," he said. Jack's teeth ground together across from me. "I'm glad you could make it. Lillian was gone so long we thought you both got lost in the shade."

"She wouldn't let me leave looking like anything less than the Queen of Sheba." Just because I could tell it annoyed Jack, I edged closer to Will. "What do you think, is there a resemblance?"

"You look less disastrous than usual," Violet murmured, not bothering to turn from her snake. It snapped at a squirming spider she held before its face. "Give her the run down and let's get out of here." The tone was bored, but her serpent eyes snapped to Will, heated with annoyance.

I frowned. "This isn't the party?"

"The party is on Long Island," Jack said, breaking three days of silence. He refused to look at me. "I discovered the last owner of the second Dianomican."

"How does the last owner help us?"

"Because he may know who stole it from him." Jack's voice tightened, his broad shoulders tense beneath his suit. "He's known for throwing extravagant parties on his estate every weekend. We are going to crash it and see if he's willing to speak with us."

"Sounds like someone else I know."

He ignored the undertone, but none of the others did. Even Violet glanced between us curiously.

"Is that it?" I asked, breaking the tense silence.

"No." Jack's lips twitched in the corner, as if there was something he desperately wanted to say. "The man we are going to see is a druid who nowadays goes by Henry Foster. Very old, very powerful, which is how he acquired a piece of the book in the first place. His specialty is in divinations. He's one of the best there is."

I scanned the room, wondering if any of their expressions would explain so I didn't have to ask. They all remained tense and silent. "So he already knows we're coming?"

Arthur released a choked laugh, grinning like a fool. Violet glared at him until he stopped.

"I have no idea, and it shouldn't matter because we are only going to talk. The problem is, he's a very devoted supporter of Delsaran."

Ice crept through my veins. "Perhaps I shouldn't go then."

"You are glamour-touched and you are paralleled to me, so you will be fine. But I would prefer if you avoided him as much as possible, so while we are at his estate I want you to stay with Will and Arthur while Lillian, Violet and I go and find him."

I bristled. "Why bring me along at all if I'll only get in the way?"

I knew the answer. I knew before he opened his mouth so I wasn't sure why I asked. Maybe I was a masochist, because my blood boiled as much as I knew it would when he said, "It's too far away. I don't want to stretch the bond."

"You mean you're worried your human battery won't be doing its job. Can't have Jack Warren being anything less than his best, can we?"

He tilted his head to the side, eyes flashing in the low light. "Perhaps, or perhaps the aforementioned human battery was a bit concerned the other day about her breathing problems, which would not be relieved with distance—in case she was curious."

I snapped my mouth shut. Lillian looked between us, clapping her hands together. "Okay, Jack and Violet with me and Addie, you'll be going with Will and Arthur. Let's go find a mirror now, shall we?"

WILL LEANED IN CLOSE, whispering, "Trouble in paradise?" The car jostled so much I nearly put his teeth through his lip with the top of my skull.

A proclivity for divination apparently came with consequences, because Lillian explained that Henry Foster was not only rich, powerful and famous, but highly paranoid and prone to fits of hysteria. Therefore, his entire estate—acres along the Long Island Sound rumored to cost over a million dollars—was warded against all forms of magic, including shading. Jack and Lillian were both strong enough to break it, but as this was a visit of good faith we decided that would be bad form. A line of cars driven by glassy-eyed chauffeurs waited at a set of iron gates, ferrying partygoers along the private road to and from the house.

Though the chauffeur hadn't expressed any interest in us, Will still spoke in low whispers. Arthur sat in the front, playing with his broken timepiece and pretending not to listen.

"It's complicated," I said.

"It always is."

Despite Henry Foster's opinion on humans, a fair amount worked for him and even more visited his house. Our car arrived just a moment before the one carrying the other three, stopping in a circular driveway before a stone mansion crawling with ivy. Golden light poured from the twenty-something windows and a marble balcony teemed with smokers. People littered the yard like lawn ornaments, sipping bubbly from crystal flutes between puffs of cigarettes. As I stepped onto the pavement, I got a glance of the backyard, where humans and everything else danced, drank and ate nearly shoulder to shoulder, covering every square inch of Mr. Foster's yard down to a sandy private beach.

"Divination, you said?"

Will exited the car behind me, leaning close with a conspiratorial look. "They say he helped fix the World Series a few years ago."

"Why bother? Just bet on the winning team."

"Where's the fun in that?" He lit a cigarette. "Do you know how boring immortality can get?"

I shivered against the autumn breeze. "Not yet."

Arthur stumbled from the passenger seat, bidding our chauffeur a goodnight. The vacant-eyed boy only stared forward and drove away.

Will frowned. "I think that lad needs to lay off the dope."

"Ours didn't look much better." Violet appeared behind him, golden snake wrapped around her shoulders. "Do you think they will have something for Harold to eat?"

My eyebrows met in the middle. "Harold?"

"Harold. My snake." The viper hissed, flickering his tongue like I'd offended him.

"You named your snake Harold?"

Her face twisted like I wore a dunce cap. "I didn't name him anything. His name is Harold." The black fringe of her dress swayed as she turned for the backyard. I had a sneaking, horrifying suspicion Harold wasn't always a snake.

Jack came beside me and Will found somewhere else to be. He leaned hard on his cane, holding out a pocket square.

"Take this. Keep it on you."

"Why?"

"So if anyone gets too close they'll scent me on you."

Sometimes, I hated the sudden reminders none of them were human.

"Next time, just piss on my leg," I said. I hated that he cracked a smile at that. I hated the relief I felt even more.

"Stay with Will and Arthur, and don't eat or drink anything."

"I know the drill by now."

He nodded, scanning the yard like he sought something—or maybe he didn't want to look at me.

I swallowed, fingering the edge of my jacket. "Is your leg bothering you?"

"What?"

"You're leaning on it hard. I haven't seen you do that in a while."

His attention snapped back to me. "I'm fine. We'll meet back here in two hours."

He snatched Lillian and they followed Violet onto the lawn. Will appeared beside me, throwing an arm around my shoulders. "Just let him brood for a bit, love. That's what I do."

I released a short breath. "You don't have to sleep with him."

"And thank god for that." He turned, spotting Arthur stealing petals off a freshly-pruned rosebush. "If you ever get worried, just remember we still keep that one around."

I stifled my giggle, looping my arm through his. Arthur joined us, red in the face, puffing about the rare variety of rosebuds Mr. Foster had and all the experiments he could use them in. We made our way to the backyard, fighting for space on the overtaken patio. Despite the autumn air, women flounced around in sleeveless dresses. Men in bathing attire drank with their feet dipped in a sparkling inground pool. Violins sang from a raised dais, each performer in a black tuxedo. Fresh fruit, imported cheese, shrimp cocktails and clams on the halfshell made a table just for picking, while an entire boar turned on a spit as the main course. Beside it, a pair of women fought loudly. Their husbands desperately tried to pull them apart and everyone pretended not to watch behind covered smiles. It felt like two worlds colliding, the classy venue and provisions with the mindless drunks half-dressed and gossiping. Beautiful and exquisite on the surface, but a darkness surged beneath the surface.

"I don't like this place." I plucked a champagne flute from a passing waiter, needing to give my hands something to do.

Will nodded. "It has a strange energy, doesn't it?" Arthur was too occupied counting his rose petals to comment.

The three of us agreed to find the beach, where at the very least it was much less crowded. A group of men raced in the sand, each carrying a barefoot woman on their back, cheeks red and eyes dazed as they taunted one another from their steeds. A couple kissed feverishly in the tide, the man slipping his wedding ring in his pocket before she opened her eyes. An older gentleman with missing shoes, hat and tie snored loudly in the sand.

"You'd think none of these people have ever drank before."

"Probably not this stuff," Will said, snatching my glass and holding it to the moonlight. "The strangest thing is it looks and smells just like normal champagne."

"Could it be?"

"I'm not sure."

Arthur took the glass from Will and sniffed. His eyes narrowed, then he dipped a pinky in and licked it. "Hm."

Will's expression soured. "What does 'hm' mean?"

"Hm." Arthur repeated, having another taste.

I took the glass from his fingers, tossing the rest in the sand. "Whatever it is, I don't think you should be drinking it, Arthur."

"There's something off about it, but I just—I can't quite put my finger on it. I know I have tasted this before, but I cannot remember . . ." He frowned, turning back to the party. "I should take a sample home."

"How about we wait out front until the others are done? I don't think there's much for us here anyway."

"Agreed," I said, shivering. It wasn't from the cold this time.

Being the lovely men they were, both Will and Arthur put arm around me, rubbing my back to chase the chill away. Jack should probably take more notes from them and less from the Devil. I smiled, gripping Will's shoulder as I stumbled in my heels across the sand. Another icy breeze barreled off the water and my entire body shook. My teeth chattered in my skull, suddenly too cold to continue forward.

Adeline.

I stopped. Dark sand stretched down the beach, but outside of a few drunkards was completely empty. People drank and laughed on the lawn and the party still raged at the house. The exact same as a moment before, but something felt different.

Adeline . . . Ruth . . . Colton.

"You alright there, love?" Will's dark eyes swam into view, his mouth turned down in a frown.

I shook my head. "I think I'm hearing things."

"Definitely time to leave," Arthur said, taking my arm.

ADELINE.

I swiveled. A clear night sky spanned above the water, a crescent moon reflected in the rocky waves. A weathered dock stuck into the Sound like a thorn, a little speed boat bobbing beside it. The group of drunk racers ambled past, talking and laughing, obscuring the view. When the last of them passed the dock, a woman sat on the weathered boards.

Her white dress was so long it floated on the waves, catching her feet as she hummed and kicked her legs. Long, white hair tumbled down her back beneath a veil. She held a dress in her hands. Seafoam green.

Adeline . . . The woman shook her head, running her fingers over the dazzling fabric. Blood dripped down the bosom. The dress melted into a man's jacket, the dark fabric torn to shreds.

She looked up. Smiled with a row of sharp, glistening teeth.

I stepped back. All the air left my lungs, my heart pounding in my chest. Someone shook me, men's voices saying words I couldn't understand.

Would you like to make another bargain, Adeline?

"They're going to die," I said.

Will shook his head. "What? Who's going to die, what are you talking about?"

Tick tock, annwyl.

I shoved past Will, past Arthur, and ran for the house. They shouted behind me but I kept sprinting, pushing through the thickening crowd.

"*Addie,* where are you going?"

There was no time to explain. There may have been no time at all. A woman glowered and I shoved her aside, a man scowling as I grabbed him by the jacket and threw him out of my way. The lovely violin music turned haunting, the discordant notes screeching in my ears. I passed the gorgeous buffet table, now littered with rotten fruit and droning flies. People drank and laughed around the pool, oblivious to the sharp bones littering the bottom. One of the glassy-eyed waiters turned sharply, his face no longer that of a young man, but a rotted corpse.

"Addie! What—"

"We have to find them. Do you know where they went?" I grabbed Will's shoulders, shaking him so hard his eyes bounced in his head. Arthur appeared beside him, heaving with strained breaths. "Don't you see what's happening? We have to find them *now.*"

"It looks the same as five minutes ago. What's gotten into you?"

A lifetime of doubt washed over me. Every woman in Fairville tittering behind their fans, every man joking about who'd marry the town loon. The pastor saying I let the devil in my heart, my own brother convinced I was unwell. Violet's snubs, Jack's warnings, the endless criticism I gave myself. Every mocking comment, every sniggering insult, every demand I go to church or see a doctor or get my head out of blatant fantasies. Every single time I'd been told I was insane, stupid, wrong, only for the truth to appear with a pair of golden eyes. Every time I doubted myself when I shouldn't have.

I ran for the house. Alone.

The gilded handles on the veranda door were rusted and spotted with age. The white stone now chipped with molding paint. I tore open the doors and stepped inside. The party continued behind me, but inside the house, it was completely silent.

A frayed rug ran beneath my feet. Furniture that must have once been beautiful had torn upholstery and deep scratch marks. A fine layer of dust coated the room, the air chilled like an empty graveyard.

A grandfather clock chimed. I jumped. Someone laughed.

I whirled around, releasing a breath. Golden eyes smiled above me.

"Jack, what the hell?" I breathed.

"What are you doing?"

"Looking for *you*," I snapped. "God, I thought something had happened. Where are Lillian and Violet? We need to leave."

He kept smiling, shaking his head. "Why do we need to leave? Everything's fine."

"Look at this place." I threw my arms wide. "It's time. If you haven't gotten what you need, we'll find another way. Let's go. Now."

He stepped forward, entirely too close. I waited for the bond to snap but even that must have been smothered by this place. He ran his hand down my arm, tilting his head down to face me. "Calm down, darling. I've got it all under control."

"You don't understand, I saw —"

"Adeline." His fingers came beneath my chin, tilting my face toward his. "Relax, okay? Enjoy the party, we'll finish up soon."

"Enjoy the party?"

"Enjoy the party," he repeated. His nose brushed mine, his lips just inches away. "Have something to eat, drink some wine, dance a little with Arthur and Will, then I'll take you home later and we can —" he winked.

I froze. His fingers brushed my face, lips teasing mine only a hair's breadth away.

"Where's your cane?"

He blinked, smiling like this was a joke. "My cane?"

"Your cane," I breathed, glancing at his empty hand. "Your leg was bothering you. You've been leaning on it hard today."

He shook his head. "Addie—"

I stepped back. "What's my nickname?"

He laughed. "Addie?"

"In Welsh. What do you always call me?"

We stared at one another. I didn't move.

"You're not Jack," I whispered, unsure if it was in my head or out loud.

The smile melted off his face, eyes flattening. "Stop fucking around, Adeline."

"You're not Jack." I took another step back. He rolled his eyes, following my path. "You're not Jack, where's Jack, *where the fuck is Jack?*"

My back hit one of the molding couches. He didn't stop. "Everything is fine, darling, can we please get back to the party?"

"Who *are* you?"

He scowled. I reached for my hair, one of the long, sharp pins Lillian used to fasten my headband.

He rushed forward and I swung down, not looking, not breathing, but he released a howl of pain, loosening his grip on my arm. He screamed, clawing at the silver pin stuck in his eye.

"*Adeline.*"

I ran as he swiped for me again, missing the yellowed claws erupting from his hand by inches. The veranda door was right there, Will and Arthur on the other side of it, but Jack, Violet and Lillian were still somewhere in this house. I had a second, only one, to make a decision.

The sharp sound of bones cracking snapped behind me. I ran for the stairs.

"*You fucking bitch.*"

I took the stairs two at a time, making a hard left at the top down a dark hall. The mansion was huge, doors and halls and everything else making a labyrinth across the second floor. Heavy footsteps thudded behind me, pounding across the worn carpet pimpled with scorch marks. I saw nothing but peeling wallpaper, paintings hanging by one corner and shattered glass glittering in the carpet. The footsteps grew closer, punctuated by a chittering sound. I slipped into the next hall, flattening against the wallpaper.

"Adeline." It was Jack's voice, but not, the sound tainted, the lyrical accent gone. "Come on, darling, I just want to talk."

I steadied my breaths, scanning the dark corridor. There was nothing. Nothing but rotting floors and exposed beams and broken windows.

Broken windows.

Broken windows.

"Addie, are you listening to me?" I slid across the floor on my knees, wrapping the hem of my dress around the largest shard jutting from the frame. "I want you to listen to my voice. Just listen and breathe, darling. Everything is fine. You know how much I love you, don't you?"

I gripped the glass over the fabric, wrenching it back and forth, trying to wiggle it free. "I love you, Adeline. I love you so much. Please, just come back and talk to me. I just want to talk."

I pushed the glass back and forth. It wriggled, growing looser, but whatever glue or magic held it in the frame wouldn't break free. My breath came in stuttered gasps, my heart slamming against my ribs. A whimpering noise sounded in my throat as the sharp edge cut through the fabric and into my hands. Blood ran down my wrists and I cried silently, praying, begging, asking anything watching over to get it free.

The footsteps stopped. A deep inhalation of breath. "I know where you are now, Addie."

The footsteps grew louder, frenzied. I screamed, throwing all my weight against the window frame until the glass broke free. Blood ran down my arms like war paint, sweat poured down my face, a screeching cry rang in my throat and rancid breath breathed down the back of my neck.

I froze. Something hot and wet dripped onto my hair, heavy breathing sounding behind me.

I threw myself back, holding the shard of glass above my head. Darkness, spit and the smell of rotting meat came down on me. My back hit the floor, all the breath rushing from my lungs but I held my arms straight, pushing and digging as the shard of glass hit sinew and flesh and a vicious scream exploded my ears drums.

Claws scratched at my face, my arms, my chest, but I kept pushing. Kept shoving that piece of glass harder and harder like I was reaching for the sky, for the hand of god. My cheek split open and I screamed. And screamed. And screamed.

The noise never stopped, but the claws retreated. Something howled behind me, a keening cry that frosted my veins. Blurry tears shadowed my vision. My head felt light, but I stumbled to my feet, retreating back down the hall.

Adeline . . .

I walked, dragging my hand along the ruined walls to remain upright. Blood pooled around me like a dress floating on the water. A trail of death growing with each step I took.

Adeline . . . Ruth . . . Colton . . .

I swallowed, hitting my face to keep myself awake, but ragged flesh met my fingers instead. My cheek, what did it do to my face . . .

Do you want to make a bargain?

But there was something else. A tug. So simple, so tiny and weak, but the little warmth grew in my chest, a guiding light showing me the way home. All I had to do was walk. Just a little farther. Everything . . . everything would be fine.

I shuffled down the stairs, tripping on the last step. My face smacked the ruined rug.

That bond tugged at my chest, nudging me forward. Tears blurred my vision, blood running between my fingers splayed on the floor. But that tug kept pulling, the warmth kept pulsing, beckoning, begging me to come find it.

I was back. Back in that starry field, a dark moon hovering above me. The rolling hills stretched as far as the eye could see. The leaves swayed on a playful wind, winking the stars in and out of view. I was happy. The joy was infectious, leaking from my bare feet into the ground, making the grass dance with me and the wind lift my hair. I was happy. I was okay . . .

"Jack," I murmured against the floor. The little nudge grew hotter, the tug in my chest more demanding. "Jack," I half-sobbed against the carpet. "Please," I whispered. "I'm sorry . . ."

The bond snapped between us. Lips brushed my hairline, a quiet voice whispering, "I'm here, *annwyl*."

TWENTY-NINE

A ROOM I DIDN'T recognize swam into focus. Like the rest of Jack's residence, it was overwhelmingly hot with a fire crackling in the wall. Vines laced the walls like arteries. Wisteria coated the ceiling, leaving the stone no longer visible. Besides an oak armoire and dresser, the only furniture was the dark bed I lay in. People spoke in low murmurs beyond an open door, but I was too exhausted to move.

I lifted a hand, expecting open, weeping wounds, but the skin was smooth. Shiny and pink in some places, but mostly healed. I frowned, turning my hand over, but nothing changed. Fog rolled through my brain and my vision blurred. God, I was tired.

The low voices grew louder, the beginning of an argument. I pushed the covers off my legs, wiggling my toes to make sure they still worked. Memories scattered in my brain like a hand waving through smoke. I remembered fighting with Jack, what we did in the Abstruse. Three days of sullen silence, Lillian arriving and doing my makeup, a car ride, a party, then a feeling that something was deeply wrong. Anything else was . . . hollow.

I pressed my feet to the floor, steadying myself against the bed frame. A vine slithered closer, wrought with little white flowers. It wrapped around my ankle, squeezing gently.

"I'm fine," I said. I went to pat it, but grew so dizzy halfway down I straightened again. "Thank you. I could really use some water though."

The vine released my ankle, slithering back into the main room.

Any chatter died to a hush.

Willing my legs to move, I shuffled forward on the carpet, growing dizzier by the second. I stumbled, making my way around the bed frame. A warm hand caught my elbow and held me up.

I blinked, staring into a pair of golden eyes.

A flash of teeth entered my vision, rancid breath and a silver pin.

"You shouldn't be up yet."

I waved him off, choosing to lean against the bed instead. His hands hovered around me like he expected me to drop, but I only slumped to sit on the sheets, leaning my head against a bedpost.

"*Annwyl*, let's go back to bed."

"Jack," I mumbled, vision swimming, "I'm not sure what happened, but I'm pretty sure you owe me. So let me sit here for a moment, please."

He nodded, expression guarded. Was he still angry at me? Was he ever? I got seventy-two hours of absolutely nothing, so I wasn't sure what he was thinking. I wasn't sure why I cared, but I was angry. And not just because he ignored me for half a week after we . . . whatever you wanted to call it, but something else I couldn't name. It slipped with the smoky memories drifting from my conscious thought. I was angry because . . . because I thought something happened to him and . . .

"I need water," I whispered, sand lining my throat and scratching each word. He blinked from the room and returned with a glass before I took a full breath.

"Here," he murmured, tipping the glass against my lips. Half of it dribbled down my neck. "*Annwyl*, you are the most brilliantly stubborn woman I know, but please, let's lie down in bed for a while."

I nearly asked him to leave, but I was so tired, and the bond snapped between us, the warmth welcome for once. It made me a

305

little stronger, my muscles ache a little less and pushed some of the fog from my brain. I nodded, eyes closed and lips still dribbling water. He lifted and deposited me back at the head of the bed. A moment later the door slammed shut, and he crawled in beside me.

I lay in bed with a man. I'd never done that in my life, and I hardly counted when I sat on the edge of it while he kneeled in front of me. He shrugged out of his jacket and kicked off his shoes. I wormed my way beneath the covers, a depthless chill rolling through my bones despite the heat. His arm came around me and his forehead pressed against mine.

"Rest a little longer and I will explain everything, okay?"

Come on, darling, I just want to talk.

I nodded, already half asleep.

JACK WAS ASLEEP WHEN I awoke again. Darkness streamed through a single window, nothing but a few lit candles providing low light. Judging by the melted stubs, it'd been a few hours since our first conversation.

A crepe, ivory nightgown hung off my shoulders. I had no idea where it came from and didn't want to. Mouth parched and head pounding, I reached for the half-empty water glass on the dresser. Jack's eyes snapped open.

Fae eyes. Fae everything. It was rare to see him without any glamour at all. The sharp points of his ears peeked through his messy hair, the sharp bones of his face washed with the remnants of sleep. Dark tattoos swirled and danced on his bare torso, up his thick neck. Over his throat, a pack of crows soared through an open sky.

"Did I wake you?" He shook his head. I was surprised he understood the gravelly question.

He reached behind him for the water glass. I downed it in one sip and he snapped, instantly refilling it. Glancing around, it became clear we were in his bedroom and not the Abstruse. I lay in his bed. He wore nothing but trousers.

For a moment, I wondered if we completed the ritual and I'd forgotten. But that didn't seem right either. If I was anything more than human, I doubted I'd feel like this.

His bare hand brushed my arm, his lovely poison seeping beneath my skin. The pain faded, and with it, my wandering thoughts. I sank back to the sheets. My head hit the pillow he occupied, our faces mere inches apart.

"I am an asshole."

I snorted, eyes fluttering closed. "Did Lillian tell you to say that?"

"No, I came up with that myself." I spared a glance at him. He clutched an ink-coated paper between his fingers, most of the sentences crossed out. *I'm afraid of losing control too* and *I should have known better* and *I know you are not happy here, and I wish I could fix it* beneath thick black lines. At the bottom, *I am an asshole* was circled three times.

He snapped and the paper disappeared. Silence encased the room.

I am not your enemy. I never wanted to be. I never wanted him to be either. In our dreams, he was a friend. A confidant, someone to dance with and speak to outside of my constrained world. I took the deception of that harshly, everything harshly, because Jack was right. I had a problem. But I wasn't afraid of losing control—I was afraid I'd never have any.

Maybe Jack wasn't my enemy, but if he wasn't, who was? Papa, Tommy . . . myself. Several days ago, I screamed at him that I never had a life, and that was the most terrifying thought of all. With no life, I was nothing. I had no idea who I was or what I wanted. I knew I wanted children but couldn't have any. I knew I loved my family, but they were as imperfect as I was. I knew I was incapable of handling so many things around me. That Jack said he would contact the Guild after my transformation, but I still wasn't sure of that. It seemed like nothing more than the next appropriate step, not what I actually desired. I didn't know what I desired.

His thumb stroked my cheek, tucking my hair behind my ear. "What are you thinking about?"

"Why have you been fighting so hard for me?"

Slitted pupils narrowed, his lips tucking down. "What do you mean?"

"Violet doesn't think I should be here. Will, Arthur and Lillian are more polite about it, but they know I'm useless on my own. I make all your lives harder."

"None of us are without our faults, *annwyl*."

Yes, but my faults seemed tremendous by comparison. Maybe. Lillian had her bloody past. She said Violet was a difficult person to understand, harder to help, and Jack said that in his own way once about her. Arthur had memory loss and social anxiety. Will couldn't seem to stay out of trouble. And Jack was . . . Jack. But I still saw so many good things in them, more than I ever thought I could see in the fae.

"I'm sorry," I whispered.

He nodded. "You said that last night, too."

A memory. My face on the carpet, fingers digging into the ruined threads. A vision of a starry sky and field, much like the one tattooed on Jack's hand. I'd begged for him, and I'd said I was sorry, because I was. Sorry our friendship fell apart when I discovered what he was. Sorry I couldn't be the powerful mate he wanted me to be, especially now that he may be dying. Sorry I lashed out when I was scared. Sorry I was always scared.

"You always used to comfort me at night."

It wasn't a statement, but a question. Not everyone would understand that, but Jack was something more. We were bonded. He knew me. I didn't have to spell it out for him or dance to be heard.

His arm came around me, lips brushing my hair, breaths slowing as we fell back asleep.

JACK WAS GONE IN the early morning. I reached for my robe beside the bed and padded into the living room, the bond telling me I'd find him there.

The vines went wild as I emerged. Lillian slept draped across one of the chaise lounges, Will slumped in an armchair beside her. Arthur read a book before the fire. Only Jack noticed my presence, though I suspected he knew I was awake before I entered the room.

His golden eyes scanned my body, slowly. Satisfied with his assessment, he nodded toward an empty chaise, gently shaking Will awake. The latter's eyes bulged out of his head when he saw me.

"*Veermag,* you should have been asleep for another two days."

"Do I want to know what that means?"

"Very bad word in fae," Jack said, followed by a half-hearted wink. He sat beside me, donning his gloves and pushing my hair back from my face. "Will, could you—"

"Already on it." He kneeled in front of me, gripping my face and turning it side to side. "You know, you heal remarkably well for a human."

I always had. Bruises faded within a day, cuts and scratches disappeared before a week could pass. Papa always said it was because his bargain kept me healthy, but Jack never mentioned anything like that in the deal he struck with my father. Even still, the stinging, pink wounds along my hands and face shouldn't have been closed yet, if at all.

Unless I'd been asleep longer than I thought. That theory went out the window when Jack said, "Will's affinity is healing."

"Oh." That would have been good to know.

"It's a bit of a secret, as it's very rare," Will said, giving Jack a side-long glance, then me.

I thought of what Lillian said about his past. How infants born with special affinities were taken from their parents and raised as soldiers. "I won't tell anyone."

He nodded, stroking his thumb over a raw spot along my face. "There's a lot of side effects, just so you are aware. Most people need a few days to sleep it all off . . ." He frowned, dropping his hand. "Right now, I'm not sure there is much else I can do. It looks the best it can, considering the circumstances."

"Speaking of those circumstances." I glanced around. Lillian still slept, but Arthur had set his book down on the side table, watching intently. "Where's Violet?"

"The shade."

I frowned. "I thought Violet couldn't shade?"

"She can, she doesn't because of her vow. But Lillian brought her there and left her in a pocket we sometimes use. With Henry Foster."

Ice crept through my veins. "That thing—"

"Wasn't Mr. Foster, but a creature from Ildathach," Arthur said. He frowned, rubbing his wrists in his lap. "I knew I'd remembered where I tasted that champagne before. Phooka venom."

I glanced between them. "What's a phooka?"

"Shapeshifters. Masters at glamour that produce very powerful illusions."

"And one was at Mr. Foster's party?"

"Precisely."

"Which still doesn't explain what it was doing there. Or why Adeline was the only one that could see through the glamour," Jack said. They all looked at me, including Lillian, who rose from the couch with all the grace of someone who'd been awake for hours.

Memories flooded back. The unsettling party with dark magic thrumming beneath the surface. Our walk to the beach. The Woman in White.

"I don't know." If the Woman in White broke the glamour for me, then I suspected the reasons weren't good. Fae never did anything for free.

I wasn't sure announcing that to the entire room was the best idea. For all I knew, the two things were simply coincidence and there was another reason for my ability to see through the phooka's illusion. My bargain with her was to remain a secret for now. At least until Lillian or I could discover more.

"I'll retrieve Violet," Lillian said, already standing beside the mirror. She blipped from existence and we waited in tense silence.

"What happened?" I asked. The wounds along my palms throbbed, flesh remembering the shard of glass ripping my skin.

Jack shifted against the upholstery. "We met the phooka, thinking it was Henry Foster. It slipped us venom and it functioned like a sleeping draught. We still don't know what its intentions were, but it had the three of us with Mr. Foster hidden in the basement."

"I thought you were impervious to venom?"

"Not this kind."

I swallowed. "Did I kill it?"

"No, just wounded it enough to weaken the glamour. I woke up and—" He turned away. "We have been busy making sure you recovered, so Violet has been guarding Foster until you woke up. Hopefully, we can get more answers now."

They waited until I was healed to interrogate the druid. That seemed . . . impractical, considering all we were doing. But as I looked around at their tight faces, I realized they were worried. Genuinely worried. Either my wounds were worse than I'd realized, or they'd grown fond of me.

Lillian and Violet returned, a bound and gagged man standing between them. Dark, gray hair sprouted from his head, parted in the middle with random pieces stuck at odd ends. His dark eyes widened, incoherent as he attempted to scream through the gag. Jack tensed and snapped his fingers. The man silenced instantly, following Lillian to the couch without a fight.

She tore the gag from his mouth. He sputtered a few choice words and coughed, shaking the binds at his hand. His head shook with violent fervor, cheeks turning red. "I don't know what the meaning of this—"

"Oh, shut up," Violet barked, shoving him to the cushions. She found me and gave a slight nod of acknowledgement. Harold slithered out from a cluster of vines, wrapping around her leg and twisting up around her shoulders.

Jack nodded. "Henry Foster."

Mr. Foster scowled. "It's been a while."

"Not long enough," Jack said, leaning back. Despite his cool expression, his cane vibrated against the floor. "You've always attempted to swindle magic beyond your limits, but this was a new level of idiocy, even for you."

"As if you are one to talk." He sneered in my direction. "Glamour-touched, I'm assuming?"

I guessed Jack hid our parallel bond, if Mr. Foster hadn't noticed it yet. "That is none of your business."

"Neither am I." Mr. Foster scowled, holding out his hands. "Release me."

"After a few questions." Lillian settled beside him on the settee. "You can tell us or I can take your memories. Your choice, Henry."

Mr. Foster's cheeks turned a mottled red, his bound hands clenched into fists. "I don't think I owe you anything after what you did to my house."

"After what *we* did?" Will spat. His legs twitched, like he was ready to jump us and strangle the druid. "You would have either been glamoured forever or someone's next meal if we hadn't stepped in."

His eyebrows came together. Powerful illusions indeed, if even Mr. Foster didn't realize what happened to his home. He shook his head. "What are you talking about?"

"It appears a phooka has taken up residence at your estate," Jack said. "Any idea why that may be?"

His eyes flashed, the little emotion smoothed into indifference within a blink. "You must be mistaken."

"It nearly killed us, so we are certainly not," Violet said. Harold poked his head through the curtain of her hair, hissing.

"I think I would know—"

"One would think your arrogance has limits, but apparently that is infallible as well," Jack said, tone even, but a vicious edge lined the words. "So, while we are here, first the phooka, then my other questions. Which you will answer one way or another." He gestured at Lillian.

She gripped Mr. Foster's face. "Wait. Stop."

He took a deep breath, shaking Lillian's fingers away. "I don't know, genuinely. But Daniel Harrow had expressed some dissatisfaction with me, a few days prior."

A moment passed before I remembered Delsaran now went by Daniel Harrow.

"Dissatisfaction about what?"

"He wanted me to perform a scrying through the shade. I refused."

"A scrying for what?"

His lips snapped shut. Lillian placed her head on his shoulder, fingering his collar.

Sweat lined his brow. Again, he looked to each of us for reprieve, but we had none to offer. Me most of all. There was a whiff of sympathy when I saw him bound and dragged from the shade, but this was a man who supported Delsaran. A man who wanted to see humans eliminated for no other reason than more power. Even worse, he once was one.

"He wanted to see something from the past."

"That's not possible," Jack said.

"It is when using the shade." Perspiration poured down his cheeks like rain. "Time is not linear within the shade. With all of the alternate realities, the possibilities . . ." He cleared his throat. "Theoretically, one could use divination to seek out the past. Not to change it, but garner information."

"What did he want to know?"

Mr. Foster's eyes fell on me, pleading. "I was like you once, human. Delsaran will kill me if—"

The glamour around Jack disintegrated. His serpent eyes found Mr. Foster, the dark tattoos vibrating along his skin. Power leached around him, coating the floor in hazy darkness. The vines closest to us slithered away, the surrounding plants withering to brown. The floor blackened, melting beneath the surge of poison.

Will jerked me back from the circle of death. I fell against his chest, breathing heavily.

"But I will kill you now," Jack said, voice tainted with a bone-chilling tone. The corruption inched closer to Mr. Foster. "Therefore, I suggest you take your chances with your master down the line. So, I will ask you one more time, Henry, what was Delsaran looking for?"

Mr. Foster pulled his feet up before the crawling circle met his toes. A sharp cry left his throat. "He wanted to know about a bargain you struck twenty years ago."

The circle stopped. The entire time, Jack had barely lifted a finger.

I shook so hard it became difficult to stand. Will guided me to a chair, gingerly pushing me down.

Jack grinned. "Oh?"

Mr. Foster nodded. "Yes, yes, a bargain. I don't know much more, just that he thought it may have something to do with—" His eyes fell on me. "He knows you cavort with humans, that you are willing to dirty your bloodline—"

A knife whistled past, embedding in the thick cushion behind Mr. Foster's head. A thin line of red bubbled on his cheek.

Violet shrugged beside the fireplace. "My hand slipped."

"A human saved your life, Henry." Lillian laid a hand on his shoulder, gesturing at me. "She was the only one that could see through the phooka's illusion. She fought it single-handedly with nothing but a shard of glass. None of us would be sitting in this room without a human's help. One of only twenty sun cycles, no less."

His throat bobbed. At the party, Will had asked me if I understood how boring immortality could be. A light-hearted joke, but it didn't feel so anymore with Mr. Foster cowering on the sofa. He was human once. Somewhere along the way immortality tainted him, just as Jack had said happened to the Bogorans' creations, the fae. Could time truly make us something so terrible—people without sympathy, emotions, memories of what it had once been like before power and endless life flowed through our veins. Would the same one day happen to me?

It hadn't happened to Arthur. Or Lillian, or Will. Maybe Violet a bit, but . . . not Jack. Not completely.

"He knows what you have. Your bond," Mr. Foster said, quiet as death. "He wants to know how you got it."

"Because he saved my life," I said. "He saved my life so I could have a chance, because he's decent enough to remember our bond exists because humans and fae are more alike than not. Delsaran doesn't need a crystal ball or tea leaves to learn that. Neither do you."

Will squeezed my shoulder, nodding in approval.

"I saved your life. Now you owe me something. That's how magic works," I said.

Mr. Foster scowled. "That's how fae bargains work, which neither of us are."

"I won't threaten you," I said, softly. Jack's eyes narrowed. "You already said Delsaran will kill you, so you have nothing to lose, but you could have something to gain if you're willing to tell us something."

Lillian shook her head. "Addie—"

"What do you want?" I cut in. "A life for a life, that's the first part of our deal. I saved yours, so you won't tell Delsaran what you know of mine on the penalty of death. I have a question for you, so if there's something you want in return then ask it now. If you look around this room, I think you'll see that's the best offer you will receive."

Jack pushed to his feet. "Absolutely not. Adeline—"

"Let's hear what he wants first," I said.

Mr. Foster's expression twisted, but he didn't outright refuse. Animosity tainted the air like smoke, thick and unfurling the longer we sat in silence.

"I'd like to read your fortune."

"Done." I gripped Will's shoulder and pulled myself to stand. "Could one of the fae in the room seal the bargain?"

Jack grit his teeth, shaking his head. "I am not allowing that."

"Do you have any other suggestions?" I asked.

"Torture," Violet murmured.

"Lillian can take his memories. And she will, right now." Jack nodded at the redhead, who frowned with resolve.

"But he can alter or hide them. Or lie if we torture him," I said to Violet. "Even throwing him the Abstruse doesn't guarantee he will talk to us. A bargain is binding. If he has what we need, then he will have to tell us. The truth, and nothing but it." I looked at our captive. "And any information he gleans will never leave this room. He can rot with the knowledge of my fortune forever, unable to ever convey it. Isn't that right, Mr. Foster?"

He looked none too happy about that, but nodded. I gestured for Will, who seemed the most agreeable to anything I suggested. Jack murmured in their native tongue, words I couldn't understand but knew spoke threats. Will only shook his head. "She's right. Let's just get this over and done with."

Before the others could protest, magic whooshed between us. The bargain was struck.

"Who stole the second Dianomican from you?" I asked.

Mr. Foster's lips twitched in the corners. After a long moment, he ground out, "Lorvellian."

Antipathy charged the air. I gestured to Jack. "Is that sufficient?"

He nodded, glowering at the druid.

"My fortune, then?"

Mr. Foster showed a row of glistening teeth. Blood roared in my ears, but I sat across from him on the floor where he instructed. Lillian unbound his hands and he pulled a deck of cards from his pocket.

"Tarot," he explained, placing them on the coffee table. "A simple spread, past, present and future. That is all I wish to know."

I waved a hand at the cards, urging him to continue.

He shuffled them, power crackling around his fingers. Goosebumps pimpled my arms, breath scattering as he flipped the first card. "The past." A second. "The present." A third. "And your future."

Three intricate drawings faced me. The titles beneath them revealed nothing of what they meant.

"The Hierophant," he said, pointing to the first. "It tells a past of tradition and rules. There was a religion or code you followed rigidly, a set of beliefs you followed blindly. But it was all for nothing, because it led to this." He pointed to the second card. "The Devil."

I almost laughed. "It represents a seduction, a bond you can't break. Something material in this world that will do nothing but taint you, should you hold onto it." He glanced between me and Jack. The latter bounced his foot on the carpet, dark eyes promising hell.

"And lastly, the wheel of fortune. Your future."

I stared at the card. A wooden wheel spun on its axis, random items at the end of each spoke—a heart, a set of daggers, a baby, a tree, among others too faded on the old paper to decipher.

"The wheel of fortune represents cycles. An endless loop you can't break free of."

I swallowed. "What does that mean for my future?"

But Mr. Foster only frowned, staring at the card. He rubbed his thumb across his chin, eyes narrowed, pulse quickening in his neck.

Lillian chewed her bottom lip. "What does that mean, Henry?"

Sharp eyes flicked up, glittering like he'd just discovered the last piece of a puzzle. He didn't seek me, but Jack, a slow smile spreading across his face. "May you enjoy everything you have sowed."

A hot breeze circled around me, suffocating my breath. Jack stood, a hideous sneer showing his teeth. "Lillian, wipe his memories and release him."

Mr. Foster jumped to his feet. "We had a bargain."

"Exactly." Jack stepped forward. "In exchange for information you could read Adeline's fortune, along with a life for a life. Nothing in there about keeping your memories of the last few days. Should have bargained better."

He waved at Lillian. "Do it downstairs, please."

Violet grabbed Mr. Foster by the collar. He screamed the entire way to the elevator.

THIRTY

THE NEXT THREE NIGHTS I spent in Jack's bedroom, some unspoken agreement between us. Our days went as they usually did, breakfast together as he did paperwork and I read Arthur's journals. When he asked why I had them, I said I was looking for a creature I once saw beside the river. Not a lie, but not a truth either. Guilt ate me over it, but I stood with my decision to keep this from him until later notice. He had enough to deal with, and Lillian already procured me human birth control, along with several fae elixirs and instructions when to use them. Something I was grateful for each night I went to sleep next to Jack. We barely touched, but the thought was always tempting.

Despite the side effects Will warned of, I felt completely normal by the end of the week. He told me solemnly he did the best he could, apologizing profusely as he ran his fingers over my face again and again. I realized why the morning after meeting Mr. Foster—a thin scar marred my cheek, starting below my eye and ending at the corner of my lips. The left side of my face. Tommy and I had matching battle scars now.

It seemed more fate than coincidence, and I still wondered why the Woman in White appeared that night. What it all meant, especially as it tied into the fortune Mr. Foster delivered. The wheel of fortune meant cycles, but outside of my past and present readings, he offered no other clarification. Cycles could mean anything, but it couldn't be mere coincidence I received a scar where my brother was wounded the same night I saw the woman. If there was a loop I'd be stuck in, it started and ended with Death.

Something I'd rather not think about. Not today or any other day, especially as I spent another twenty-four hours roaming the apartment in silence. Jack was noticeably absent when I woke up this morning, so I attempted more compulsion practices and reading.

I was ready to slam my head into a wall when a vine slithered past. I patted it mindlessly, frowning when something crinkled beneath my fingers. It loosened its hold around a stamped envelope. I broke the seal.

8 p.m. Wear your favorite dress.

I shook my head. He probably wanted me to rob another ballerina.

DESPITE MY BETTER JUDGMENT, I combed through the vast array of dresses Lillian procured me. The simplest one still lay at the bottom of the laundry pile from my girl's day with her and Violet. The silver dress only reminded me of the ballet, which I would rather not think about.

I went with one of sky-blue satin and silver embroidery. I finished my lipstick, fashioned a matching silver headband and donned my pearls. I looked like a dancer. I looked like a flapper. I looked like a gangster's wife.

Ignoring that last thought, I made for the study when a knock hit the Abstruse's door. Familiar warmth bloomed in my chest, the scent of fresh rain and oleander. The bond jerked and thrashed but I willed it to shut up. It was not in control. I was.

They say "fake it until you make it" and I was intent on doing that.

Stealing a calming breath, I opened the door.

Jack stood silently in his best suit, clutching a bouquet of roses. "Miss Colton."

I raised a brow. "You leave for the day and we're already back to formalities?"

His human form stared back at me, gears turning behind his eyes. I realized this may have been an official peace offering I just blew to hell, but it would take more than a few roses to sort through our tumultuous bond.

"Perhaps I should have prefaced this better," he said. "I've been thinking a lot about what you said. After the speakeasy the other day."

I said a lot of things, then said very little with his face between my legs. Then we didn't speak, I was nearly killed, and now we silently sleep in the same bed together every night. Sighing, I opened the door, gesturing for him to step inside. Partially to be polite, mostly because one could not lie in the Abstruse.

He set the roses on the dresser, a perfect crystal vase appearing beneath his fingertips. Such beautiful magic. So simple, yet so complex with each glimmering fragment catching the light. And he did it all with so little effort.

I sat before the vanity, touching up my makeup. It felt more comfortable to have something to do. "And?"

"You were right."

The lipstick froze halfway to my face.

"There are many things I have taken from you, since long before we met. It was never my intention, but I do take some responsibility."

Of all things, I expected that least. I hid my surprise by focusing on my lips. "You can't be held accountable for what my father did. It was unfair to place that on you."

"I could have done better." He stood beside me, leaning his hip on the vanity drawers. I ignored him for the mirror. "I don't want you to feel trapped here, Adeline. Or at the very least, like you've sacrificed every piece of your life, all those experiences you wanted to have. It's the entire reason we're here, doing this. So you and many others have a chance to lead the lives you wish."

It was a good answer, a perfect one, but I still had so many doubts. I could never seem to figure Jack out. One moment he treated me like a plaything, the next an equal. A criminal, a banished prince, yet he made his life's mission helping my kind. He offered safety and second chances to so many, then had a man dragged to his basement and his memories wiped.

A chill erupted on my skin. "I appreciate it, thank you."

His foot tapped the carpet, a methodical rap that skittered across my nerves. "That was my preface."

"And the rest?"

He licked his lips, a foreign timidness edging his eyes. "I'd like to take you out on a date."

My eyebrows furrowed. "A date?"

"Yes, and this is twofold." He shifted, avoiding my heavy stare. "I am aware the situation with the bond and our . . . later duties to it aren't particularly romantic. But that does not mean you do not deserve at least one normal human experience, so I'd like to attempt to—" He flourished his hand in the air, a nervous smile breaking free "—woo you."

"Woo me?"

"With flowers, maybe. I will be honest, the only poems I know are not suitable for women. I can get down on one knee if you truly want, though it's not as suave with a cane."

Snorting, I shook my head. "You don't have to do that, Jack. We already said our apologies."

"That's the second part. Believe it or not, I like you very much, Miss Colton." He smiled. "So before we are eternally bound by fate and magic for our immortal lives, I would like to . . . date you." His snake eyes flashed, smoothed back by glamour in a blink. His facade had cracked. He was genuinely nervous.

It was so . . . normal. Really, nothing about it was normal, but the flowers, the knock on my door, the use of our family names, the way he squirmed like a teenager asking a pretty girl to dance . . .

A smile tugged my lips. The man who just created crystal from thin air was nervous I'd turn him down.

I cocked my head to the side. "Well, I still think you're a bit of an asshole, Mr. Warren."

He released a short breath of air, an awkward grin as he turned to the side. "I suppose I deserve that."

I held out my hand. "But I'd like that date."

"DO YOU PLAN ON telling me where we're going?"

"That will ruin all the fun."

New York zoomed past, a blur of lights as we sped toward Harlem. When I'd brought up the shade, Jack said we would do this the normal way. Hence, driving.

People dallied on the sidewalk, smoking cigarettes and sipping from flasks. The crowd was mostly young, smooth faces in their father's suits and an array of stockings rolled to the knees. Feathers and jewels and fringe flashed beneath a dazzling marquee, *The Cotton Club* flashing in silver lights. Jack rolled the car to a stop, tossed the keys off to a valet and came around to open my door. I placed my hand in his. "*Very* dashing."

He grinned. "I can be, on occasion."

I smiled, looping my arm through his. The bond didn't snap this time, but settled into a languid warmth, something smooth and lovely. His rain-soaked scent washed over me. I breathed deeply. It didn't feel like I was suffocating at all.

"Do you think it punishes us?" I asked.

His eyes flashed. "What do you mean?"

"The bond," I clarified. "It's not so . . . intense right now."

He shrugged, pulling me onto the sidewalk. The crowd formed a line. Music filtered from behind the dark doors where five jittery men manned the entrance. Through the walls it was hard to hear, but my feet itched with the vibrating drums, the low bass that swirled across the sidewalk.

"I think it prefers when we're happy," he finally said. "But it is strange magic. So few have experienced it, let alone understood it. It's something we will have to figure out with time."

Together. The unsaid word wavered in the air. Whether we liked it or not, the parallel bound us. It decided, for whatever reason, Jack and I were meant to find one another. I had enough things deciding my fate, but as he led us to the top of the line, nodding at a doorman, I wondered if this one wasn't too bad.

It wasn't a choice, not really, but he was giving me something. He was putting in effort where none was needed. He didn't have to date me. We already had something much stronger.

Without a word, the man opened the door and gestured for us to step through. A round of scattered applause, heavy laughter and the fading notes of a piano. I bounced from foot to foot, hardly containing my excitement.

The corner of Jack's lips lifted. He leaned down, murmuring against my ear, "I want to warn you beforehand, the man who owns this joint is a proper bastard, but we have a tentative deal going and this place has the best lineup in the city."

"Are we supposed to meet him?"

"I'd prefer to keep you far away." I frowned. He responded with a tight-lipped smile. "As I said, a proper bastard. And he adores blondes."

"Sounds like you two have much in common."

He sucked in a breath as if preparing a great tangent, but settled with, "No." I laughed and he added, "I tried to bring Will here, once. He was kicked out immediately."

Any laughter died in my throat. "Oh. Maybe we should leave, then. If it's that sort of place."

Malice flashed in his eyes. "Don't worry, darling. I already have a plan for that." He winked. "But there is someone I want you to see. I think you will appreciate it."

I let him guide me down the hall, the opening notes of a new song firing through the room. "Any clue as to who this mystery person is?"

A massive room yawned open. A crowd too thick to move through covered the floor, people cheering and waving bottles of beer. Lights illuminated a massive stage, teeming with dancers in feathers and glitter surrounding a six-man band, each player a young black man. Jack nudged me forward, pointing at the stage. "Him."

The man he referred to sat at a piano, smiling at the crowd. The tails of his crisp tuxedo hung off the bench, his fingers twitching above the keys, as if impatient to play. Jack leaned down. "That man, Addie, is the fucking future."

I smothered my laugh with my hand. "I thought divination was a druid skill?"

"You don't need divination. Just listen."

We stilled. A hush died over the crowd, even the drunken dancers paying their reverence in silence. The first notes struck, soft keys on the piano. The drums hit. The bass plucked. Slowly, sinfully, the music rose in the air, building on each artful note. The band joined one by one, playing off the pianist's lead, sound swelling as his fingers first danced over the keys, then flew. The pulsing crowd cheered, the dancers forming their first steps. The frenetic music washed over me—wild, loud, fast, *beautiful*.

My feet shimmied against the floor, my limbs quivering with the desire to move, dance, join the fray and bask in the energy.

"Are they fae?" I asked.

Jack laughed. "No, darling." He pointed at the pianist. "His name is Duke Ellington. As human as they come, but that's magic, isn't it?"

"I've never heard anything like it."

"They call it jazz." Jack beamed, taking my hands. "Do you want to dance?"

Everyone moved, all but us glued to our corner of silence by the hall. Their movements were wild, frenzied, absolutely joyous in the way they kicked their legs and swung their arms. It held none of the finesse of ballet, but all the passion. Women twirled their skirts and men lifted them by their waists. They laughed and hollered, threw their hands in the air and shook as if in a fever. Chaotic energy leaked from their pores, the band ferocious and lively above them.

I nodded.

Grabbing my hands, he led us deep into the thicket, leaving his cane propped against the wall. His movements were fluid, expression pain-free unlike the night at the Long Island estate. A brief moment of doubt arose, that he only chose to indulge me because our bond made him stronger. I cast it to the side. Whatever Jack's intentions, I wanted to enjoy tonight for myself.

It was something I'd never truly done. Outside of my obligations to my family, farm life was hard. I'd worked my entire life, whether it was to keep the farm afloat or to appease my family's demands. I never dreamed of dancing at a speakeasy, or wearing a short dress and rolled stockings, because I was taught it was unseemly. But none of those people were here. I was, the band was, and Jack Warren was.

The moves were fast, difficult to follow. It took several tries and observing the other dancers to get it right. But when I finally did, I was free. Mr. Ellington and his band played with their souls, the music washing over me like a spell. The energy around us took me higher, filled my chest until I was practically floating on the ceiling.

Jack couldn't keep up, but that was fine. He leaned down, brushing his lips across my temple and told me he was sitting down, but he wanted me to keep dancing. That he loved to watch.

He found a corner booth with men who clearly recognized him. They offered him a drink, which he declined. He waved an airy hand in my direction, winking, and sat with his elbows on his knees in deep concentration. His eyes flashed, a spark of curiosity threaded with want. They were human eyes, but every emotion was entirely, passionately fae.

When he caught me dancing in the past I stopped. Too shy, too embarrassed, too private. Dancing was how I spoke, and I never wanted to speak to him. But he brought me here tonight, not just to smooth things over between us, but because he knew I'd appreciate it. Love it. His eyes met mine across the room, flickering gold in the dim light. He wanted me to speak, but more importantly, he wanted to listen.

So I spoke.

A new song began, even quicker than the first. I fell into the rhythm, the fervor of it. Joy effervesced from my soul and sang beneath my skin. I was passionate, I was wild—I was everything I wanted to be but never could. There were no limits here. Even the steps I had mimicked melted into other forms, my limbs finding new ways to twist and my feet discovering new patterns to turn in. There was no Delsaran, no brother I still had yet to see, no bond taking my every breath. All that remained was my body, Jack's enchanting smile, and the music Mr. Ellington brought to life behind me.

Sweat dripped down my face and breaths heaved in my chest. I had no sense of time or place, no clue how many minutes or hours had passed when Jack sauntered next to me, threading his arm around my waist like it had always belonged there. Dancers replaced one another like clockwork, some returning with fresh drinks and faces and others bowing out for the night. I never dreamed of stopping, couldn't even if I tried, but even the musicians must have been feeling tired, because a slower, quiet song started from their instruments, washing over the room like a lullaby.

Jack smoothed back my hair, tucking an unruly strand behind my ear. "I knew it."

I beamed up at him. "Knew what?"

The corner of his lips tugged up, a whisper of a grin. "That you would be the best one out there."

Pink flushed my cheeks. I shook my head, but he added, "Not a single person here could look away from you. It was like you were magic."

Denial formed on the tip of my tongue, but the melody hit its stride and Jack pulled me against his chest. The bond curled between us, sweet as honey and fresh like falling rain. My breaths met his, our movements matched wordlessly. Maybe magic and humans weren't so different—vicious when hurt, but beautiful when loved.

But hope had disappointed me before. People had too. Happiness was earned in blood and cruelty, and never returned the way we wanted it to. A bargain with Death had taught me that.

But those thoughts were for another night. For now, with the enchanting music and Jack's hand tucked in mine, I was just a girl on a date. We danced around one another like we did in my dreams. We were the last ones to leave.

THIRTY-ONE

THE FOLLOWING DAY JACK invited me to a boxing match, of all places. Lillian squirmed like a child beside me, her words a low singsong. "How was your night?"

The wooden bench beneath us creaked and moaned with the stampeding crowd. Smoke curled the air, bookies making their rounds and calling out for bets. Will had mentioned in our dinner conversations he liked to box—*it keeps me out of trouble*—and tonight was his championship fight. I'd shown my surprise to Jack earlier, asking why Will still participated while our hunt for Delsaran was underway. When the world was at risk. He'd shrugged, sipping his cup of arsenic. "Because he loves it. It gives him a reason to keep fighting."

All of his friends came to see him, so I tagged along. The small arena stank of sweat, alcohol and cigars. Men waved their hats in the air, gray suits melting in the fog of smoke beneath the dim lights. In the center of the room, a raised stage glowed beneath oppressive lights, illuminating the fraying ropes and past stains. The dark splotches on the bleached fabric made my stomach turn.

"That good? At a loss for words?" Lillian's face came entirely too close to mine. I folded my hands in my lap, straightened my back and gave her my best impression of prim and proper. "A lady never tells."

She vibrated against the wood, clenching her hands and squealing. "I am so, *so* happy. Jack was *so* nervous, and he honestly thought you'd still be so angry with him, but I told him. I said, 'Jack Warren, if you give a single damn you will man up and you will—'"

"Where did you go?" Violet asked. At Jack's request she left Harold at home, much to her chagrin. She leaned back, feet crossed in front of her and back propped against the raised bench behind us. A group of men behind us scowled in annoyance.

"Dancing," I said. Keeping it simple would be best, since not answering Violet surely came with consequences.

She nodded, pulling a cigarette case from her bag. Thick vapor curled around her gloves. "Good. He's not always an idiot then."

That response seemed very un-Violet-like, but was a welcome surprise. Maybe our little outing at the bar was more successful than I thought.

Lillian prattled on about how happy she was Jack and I were getting along, that she'd love for all of us to go on holiday once this nasty business with Delsaran was over, and that she had been scouring wedding dresses. I leaned forward, catching the outline of Jack's shoulders beside the ring. A thick cigar bobbed between his teeth, a gray flat cap hiding his dark hair. He stuffed his hands in his wool coat, eyes narrowed on the two men he spoke to. One of them nodded and took off, the other counting billets with fumbling fingers.

I frowned. "Do I want to know what's happening down there?"

Lillian stopped mid-sentence, blinking. Her focus followed my line of sight. "Oh, no worries, darling. It's just a bit of the side business."

"Side business?"

"Gambling makes nearly as much as the hooch," Violet said. A cloud of smoke erupted above her bored expression.

Shaking my head, I murmured, "Why am I surprised anymore?"

"Any bets tonight, ladies?" A silver-haired bookie stopped in our aisle, calling out numbers. Violet sighed and produced a bill. "Twenty dollars on Will Porter."

"Twenty dollars on Porter! You hear that gentlemen, the ladies are betting big tonight! Let's keep this pot growing."

My eyes widened. "You sure have a lot of faith in him."

A secretive smile curled her lips. Arthur poked up from the bench beneath us, waving a bill in the air. "Excuse me, sir. May I place two dollars on Dave Larrin."

"*Arthur*," Lillian hissed. He jumped, glasses askew.

Lillian stared at him, face pinched.

"What? Harrin has more experience, holds several titles . . . he actually invented a new—"

Violet leaned forward and flicked his ear. He yelped, waving his money at the bookie. "Actually, sir, make that two dollars on Porter."

I smothered my giggle and placed my own bet. Chatter, men hawking bets, and lightbulbs from the press cameras shattered the air. Heat trickled down my neck from the stuffed room. Beside me, Lillian waved a fan at her face.

Commotion broke out near the entrance. Two beastly men barred the doorway, yelling at someone hidden by the shadowed night. Several heads turned, but most paid no attention, the noise blending into the cacophony already filling the room. A shout of alarm rang across the arena and silver flashed. Someone pushed through the bouncers, waving a badge in the air.

Violet jerked upright. "Fuck, it's the fuzz."

I scanned the room. "The bookies know to run for it, right?"

She grabbed my arm in one hand and Lillian's in the other. "Sure, but not the three hundred bottles of gin in the basement."

Shouting erupted as everyone realized who just barged through the door. Down by the ring, Jack fought the swollen crowd to the entrance, gesturing at random men swarming around him. He scanned the dark walls until he found me, frowning. His eyes shifted to Violet and he nodded. Arthur trotted behind us with a book under his arm, offering to take me back to the hotel while Violet and Lillian helped Jack handle the situation. The entry door remained dark and silent. The beastly men yelled at the man with a badge, nothing more than streaks of his fair hair poking through the shifting crowd. Only one police officer. That couldn't be right.

I dug my heels into the ground, yanking Violet to a stop halfway down the stairs. "Why is there only one man?"

The men around us realized the same thing. A small group still shouted on the floor, but those occupying the bleachers stopped their mad dash for the exit. A fistfight broke out and the press went wild snapping photos.

Violet shook her head. "No fucking idea. Can anyone see where Jack went?"

I surveyed the floor, but he was nowhere in sight. Even the bond had gone cold.

More punches were thrown, then the cop backed away, bloody hands in the air. The crowd cleared just enough to offer a glimpse of his face. Blonde, dark eyes, half his skin smooth and clear and the other riddled with burns.

My heart stopped.

The jeering crowd died to a hush, the breaking camera bulbs and rising murmurs. The lights seemed to dim around me, all my focus on the man spitting blood on the cement floor. Warm, brown eyes flicked up to mine. My brother's eyes.

I pushed past Violet before she could stop me. Lillian shouted something immediately swallowed by the blood roaring in my ears. I hit the floor, shouldering my way through the throng. Only the burly men remained in my way, a wall of muscle and bulk. I was ready to crawl between their legs when Tommy pushed past and grabbed my arm. "Adeline."

"*Move.*" I shoved the bouncer aside. He must have recognized me through Jack because he did so without hesitation. Blood leaked down Tommy's face from a cut at his temple.

"Tommy, what are you doing here?" But he wasn't listening, hand latched around my bicep as he dragged me away from the ring. No one stopped him this time. He marched me down a dim hall and shoved his way through a rusted door. Behind it, a men's locker room flickered in dreary light.

He whipped me around, gripping my shoulders and surveying me for . . . I had no idea. His breath came in ragged gasps and his wild stare bounced around the room. I attempted a step back, but he held me firmly in place.

Licking my lips, I broke the silence. "I thought you were still in Chicago."

"What are you doing here?" Fury laced every syllable. I wilted beneath his grip.

"*Adeline*." If possible, I shrank down further. "We're leaving. Right now. And you are going to explain *everything*."

That knocked the stupor from my skull. I shook my head, finally breaking free. "Tommy, it's fine. I promise. Go home and I'll meet you at the apartment in a few—"

"I have been looking for you for weeks. Where have you *been*?"

I faltered, words forming and dying on my lips. "I thought you were training in Chicago."

"I left early because of this." He snatched a newspaper from inside his jacket and held it up. *Society Talk*. The very gossip paper I once blackmailed Jack with. The front headline glared in thick black, but I ignored it for the photo beneath—Jack carrying me bridal style from the ballet theater while I faked unconsciousness.

I remembered the shattering glass, the flash of light and Jack cursing beneath his breath.

Horror raced down my spine.

"A seizure?" He was still angry, but concern edged the biting words.

"There was no seizure. I faked it, it's a long story."

That did nothing to deter his wrath. "I received no letters for weeks." His breaths came heavy, red crawling up his throat. "Then all of a sudden this paper lands on my desk. My sister being carried off by Jack fucking Warren with a headline about him saving his new bride. I came home three weeks ago, Addie. *Three weeks.* And I haven't seen you once at the apartment. I have been pulling every resource at my fucking disposal attempting to find you and now you're saying it's fine? Just go home and you'll see me in a few hours? We are leaving *now.*"

Sighing, I snatched a handkerchief from my purse and dabbed at the wound leaking from his forehead. "I know you're angry and you have every right to be, but please, just give me a moment to explain—"

He hissed, rearing back his head and snatched my wrist. Right-sided Tommy. Scarred face, angry eyes, the person less a brother and more a stranger. At that moment, he was the only man I saw.

"I know what they are," he said, the words so low, so cold, they could have been spoken by a dead man.

I shook my head.

"I know everything now." He snatched my other wrist, tugging me closer. "You were right, you were always right. I don't think you're insane. I know what happened with Dad and the Devil and I'll apologize for all of that later, but they've tainted you, Addie. That's what they do. We need to get away from here right now and I promise you'll understand—"

"Addie?"

Will emerged from a hidden door, eyebrows furrowed. He stood bare-chested in his boxing attire, cloth wrapped around his hands and wrists. He leaned his head to the side, trying to peer around me. "Everything alright in here, love?"

Tommy whirled around. Confusion fled Will's face and he let out a breath. "Oh, Tommy. Sorry, didn't recognize you for a moment

334

there." Noticing all the blood, he added, "You doing okay, lad? You look a bit roughed up."

"Yeah, everything's jake," Tommy said, a bitter laugh squeezing his throat. Will was his friend from the war, but any recognition of that bond fled Tommy's eyes. He didn't loosen his hold on me, but edged us slowly toward the door. With his body turned at an angle, a medallion slipped from his waistcoat to thump against his chest. Though painted white with a red cross in the center, I knew immediately it was made from iron.

Will looked at me, a question flickering across his face. I shook my head. Tommy scowled between us like a wild animal. I placed a hand on his shoulder the same moment Will said, "I'm not sure what's happening, but if you—"

"This is a family matter," Tommy snapped.

Will nodded, hands out like he approached a wild beast. "I get that, I do. But I think you're scaring Adeline so maybe we should all calm down for a moment."

"I said, *it's a family matter.*"

"You certainly just made it one."

The bond flooded my senses, sharp and prickling against my flesh. The rusted door smacked against its frame. Jack leaned against it, hands stuffed in his coat and shoulders loose, but rage leaked from him in heated waves.

Tommy looked between the two men, more like a cornered animal than a human. "What the fuck are you doing here?"

My teeth clenched. "*Tommy.*"

I'd been demoted to furniture, for all the attention any of them paid me. Jack produced a cigarette. His voice remained calm, but his hands trembled through the smoke. "I believe I should be asking you that, actually."

Tommy nodded, feral expression turning crazed. "I came for Adeline, and now we're leaving. I apologize for all the commotion, Mr. Warren." Still, he didn't move. None of them did.

Jack stiffened, noticing the same medallion I did. His lips curled up in a sneer. "I hate always being right."

"Maybe I could get some explanation," I said, attempting to pull my arm from Tommy. No luck. My skin ached with developing bruises.

"Jack, let me speak to him. Alone." I glanced at Will, who took the hint and exited through the back. Jack didn't move.

"*Jack.*"

He finally tore his eyes off my brother, scowling. "I will be directly on the other side of this door. You have ten minutes."

Metal clanged behind him. Tommy's furious glare turned back on me. "He's not your husband, Adeline. He's not your anything, and we're leaving."

"Jack doesn't make decisions for me." Not entirely the truth, but I could hardly explain the entire situation now. "What do you mean you know everything?"

"Now's not the time." He fled my side, scouring the walls for exits neither Will nor Jack took. "But you need to listen to me. You're not safe, neither of us are. I have tickets for Chicago and all your things are packed. If we leave now, we can make the ten p.m. train."

What seemed a lifetime ago, that was all I ever wanted. I blackmailed the famous Jack Warren for the chance to run away. But just a few months had changed everything. Humans were in danger and I had agreed to help protect them. I discovered the truth surrounding my entire life. I had friends. A mating bond I only just began exploring.

"I'm not leaving, Tommy."

His tirade froze, fingers wrapped around a rusted window frame. "Yes, you are, Adeline."

"No." In another life, I could never imagine denying Tommy anything. His word was gospel, his say final. He was one of the two men in my life I always obeyed. But Tommy was wrong. Our entire lives he was wrong, and that may not have been his fault but I still wouldn't follow him blindly anymore. I made the decision to help Jack. The only true choice I was ever given.

He threw his hands on my shoulders, staring deep into my eyes. "They warped your mind, Adeline."

"They didn't warp my mind!" I released a heated breath, willing back frustrated tears. "You said my mind was warped by the Devil once. Then mental illness. Neither of those things were true and I need you to trust me now."

"The Devil," he said.

I shook my head. "What?"

"The Devil. That was true." He nodded at the door Jack stood behind.

I sighed. "He's not the Devil, Tommy."

"He may as well be." He pulled me closer. Blood ran into his teeth, turning his grimace crimson. "I know you think you understand everything, Addie, but you don't. You're young, you were sheltered, and you're an innocent, pretty girl being manipulated by someone who's convinced you he's good, but he's not. I swear to fucking God he's not, and you're not safe, and once we are on a train to Chicago I can tell you everything, but we don't have the time."

"Is that what you think of me?"

His lips pressed into a flat line.

"I'm nothing but a stupid, little girl to you. Aren't I?"

He shook his head. "Addie, we don't have—"

"Would you listen to me for once?" My scream echoed off the lockers, haunting as it bounced back into my ears. "That's all you do. That's all you ever do anymore, talk and talk and not listen to a damn word out of my mouth."

"You want me to listen to you, fine." He threw his hands in the air. "What is your evidence? Because I have plenty, Addie. An entire fucking filing cabinet."

I shook my head, tears spilling over my cheeks. "I don't know what happened to you, Tommy. I really don't."

His face scrunched in pain. Anger. "Life. I'm sorry you haven't experienced it yet."

We stared at each other. The schism growing between us for years caved in, a vast chasm no longer passable.

Jack rapped on the door. "Addie, you alright?"

I remained silent. Tommy's skin grew red beneath the blood. "I'm coming back for you."

"No, you ain't."

He nodded, clenching his teeth. "When this all goes to hell, you know where to find me." His hand fell from my shoulder. He pushed through the back door.

The child in me wanted to stay there, knowing Tommy would never really leave me behind. But the adult knew otherwise. When he walked through that door, it was the end. He wasn't coming back.

He didn't.

THIRTY-TWO

I HARDLY SPOKE THE rest of the night, silent and sullen beside Lillian and Violet. Will won against Dave Larrin. Arthur offered to take me back to the hotel, but I murmured that I'd rather wait for Jack. The clock pushed midnight as I sat alone among the empty seats, smoking a cigarette Violet provided. Jack counted cash on the floor with a group of human men. I tried not to fall apart.

It was better to be here. As soon as we arrived back at the apartment, as soon as darkness surrounded me, I'd no longer be able to contain myself.

Jack must have recognized that, because the electricity shut off, the others left, and he joined me on the dirty bench, long legs outstretched on the row beneath us. Silver light washed our clothes from the dusty window behind our heads.

"Thought you didn't smoke?" Though as he said it, he handed me a silver cigarette case and matches.

Sighing, I waved out the flame and puffed on the end. "I'll live forever anyway. What does it fucking matter?"

He raised a brow. "Thought you didn't curse either?"

"You tainted me." I took another long drag, forcing myself not to cringe. My brother said as much mere hours ago.

"I'm sorry," he murmured. I couldn't tell if he meant for Tommy, for tainting me, or both.

"What was it you said? That we may love someone and still find them a stranger."

"Seems uncharacteristically poetic for me."

I snorted, closing my eyes and pressing a hand to my forehead. "Tell me everything will be alright in the end."

He went rigid beside me. Something fractured behind his eyes, left edges I didn't recognize.

"That doesn't instill confidence, Jack Warren."

He shook his head, and the remnants of whatever crossed his mind, with it. "Everything will be fine, *annwyl*. I promise."

Nodding, I blew smoke into the dark room. It seemed neither of us could be entirely sure of that. A rising tide lifts all ships, but a swell also sinks them. At least if I circled the drain to hell, I wouldn't be alone.

He lit his own cigarette and slipped his hand into mine. The black leather encased my fingers, warm and soft and molded to the shape of him perfectly. It wasn't the same as being touched, but it was all I could have for now, and I welcomed it.

The embers between our joined fingers glowed in the dark. Twin flames igniting the silent smoke, roiling with everything we didn't say.

"HE'LL COME AROUND," WILL said. We sat in our usual corner of the kitchen while the dinner rush flurried around us. On a Saturday night, the hotel's restaurant descended into a state of disarray. The kitchen, worse. We'd wanted to leave nearly an hour ago, but feared interrupting the tide of workers would result in losing an appendage.

Charlene gave him a warning wag of her finger, storming past with a bushel of potatoes in her furry arms. I smiled and she smiled back, nodding once before giving Will a final silent reprimand. He grinned with all the unimpeachable honor of a thief, sliding a paper-wrapped bundle of dried steak deeper into his pocket.

"I don't know if he will." I sighed, running my hands through my hair. Lillian trimmed it for me this morning and the fresh strands stuck at odd angles. Paired with the thick bags above my cheeks and hollow stare I wore all day, I must have looked crazed.

When I awoke this morning, Jack was already gone for the day. Breakfast steamed on the table, along with a note giving instructions for practicing glamour and stating we needed to talk when he returned in the evening. After Lillian popped in, I attempted the glamour only once before realizing I wasn't in the right headspace. Seeking to distract myself, I sat with one of Arthur's journals, but spent most of the day staring at the fire instead. Three hours later I had enough and found Will in the kitchen, as if he anticipated my arrival.

These damn fae were reading my mind. Or I wore my heart on my sleeve more than I cared to admit.

"When I was a guard for Lillian, back in my prime," He winked, "I'd spent my entire life training to be in the royal guard. We were selected from birth and raised in our division since the day we could walk. I've never met my own parents. My life was sworn to Lillian before I could even speak a vow. It was all I'd ever known."

Yet, here I was complaining of my woes. "I am so sorry, Will. We don't need to talk about Tommy."

He waved a dismissive hand. "It's a life long gone now. What I mean to say is, all I'd ever known was what I was told and what I had seen. There were ideals so ingrained in me they shaped me into who I am, and many still do. So when I fled with Lillian, it was like . . . watching my entire world destroyed, all in an instant. It ruined me for years."

I nodded.

"Think of how you felt when you first arrived here. You were every bit as terrified and distrustful, but you've come around, mostly." He swirled his glass of fae wine in anxious circles. "Thomas was a very good soldier. He followed every order, observed every rule and regulation and he adapted quickly. He talked about you all the time. For a while, I actually thought you were his daughter."

Swallowing, I focused on the sauce-stained floors instead of Will's words. Tommy gave everything to come home to me, and I gave my future to bring him back. All for nothing, because I betrayed him in the end. The Woman in White made her bargain well.

"People don't take change well. Massive change, less." He tipped his glass toward me. "Everything he's ever known went away in an instant. Give him time to adjust on his own. He'll remember what's important in the end."

"That's just the thing though, how *does* he know?" I swiped my hands through my hair again, ripping at the roots. Lillian would collapse if she saw. "He left for Chicago convinced I was a head case and came back speaking of the fae. Who told—"

"There you are."

The kitchen mirror flashed and Violet appeared beside us, red in the face. Warning bells went off in my head.

Will jumped to his feet. "What's wrong?"

"Not you, you," she said, snapping at me. My heart plummeted to the floor. Before I could protest my innocence she grabbed my neck, shading us back through the mirror.

We appeared in a dark service hall just outside the lobby. She released my throat, stepped back and raked her eyes over me.

"Since when do you shade?"

"What the hell happened to you?" She asked instead.

My frumpled dress hung off my shoulders, wrinkled and sweat-stained from clenching it all day. The rest needed no further explanation.

"Nevermind, just act normal, please." She combed her fingers through my hair and pinched color into my cheeks. I slapped her hands away as she shoved me toward the door, pushing me through and blinking from sight.

The bustling room took over my senses. Golden light washed the marble floors and bellmen streamed past for the hall. No one ever lingered for long in the lobby, always looking for some place to be.. Now, patrons lingered on the edges of the room, drunk and curious eyes pointed at the squabble happening in the center.

Jack clutched his cane with renewed furiosity. Around him stood seven men with badges on their coats.

I rushed forward, forgetting any decorum as I stumbled into a trot. Jack turned several feet away, expression drawn.

Smiling at each officer, then Jack, I slowed my breath and said, "Violet sent for me. Everything jake?"

"I'll assume you're Miss Adeline Colton," the nearest officer said. His black coat seemed to drain the light, a thick, gray mustache crowding his upper lip. "Agent Rodney, it's a pleasure, m'am."

"Oh, the pleasure's all mine." I glanced between him and Jack. "Apologies if we have met, sir, but may I ask how you know me?"

The other men eyed me with a spectrum of incredulousness and animosity. *Traitor* played on loop in my head. Nothing about them seemed extraordinary, except for Agent Rodney and one of the younger fellows behind him. They wore matching medallions next to their badges, the white symbol with a red cross. The medallion Tommy wore last night.

"Just a wellness check is all." He surveyed the room with distaste. My lips snapped closed, afraid wine stained my teeth and breath.

"It appears there has been a missing person report put out for you," Jack said. Body stiff, he stuffed one hand in his pocket and nodded his head at me. "Clearly, you can see she is alive, well and willing."

343

Willing, dear lord did that have many a connotation. I smiled painfully. "If this is about my brother, we spoke last night. He hadn't realized I stayed with a friend while he was in Chicago."

"A friend," Agent Rodney repeated, the two words drawn into the length of a speech. "Which friend may I ask?"

"Lillian Carter," I said as Jack muttered, "Me."

For God's sake. I folded my hands behind my back to hide the tremors. "Miss Carter and I have been staying in Mr. Warren's hotel, is what he means."

"And why is that?"

I laughed, meaning for it to be light and carefree but it sounded maniacal. "I mean, look at the place. If you could get a few nights for free don't you think you would take the opportunity?"

"Not if my life depended on it." Anger swelled down the bond in stormy waves. I stepped closer to Jack to quell it.

"Well, if this was about me you can see I'm perfectly alive and well and willing, as Jack—I mean, Mr. Warren, put it." I placed a hand on Jack's upper arm. "If that's all, then I think you can take your leave. I'm sure you have more important things to attend to."

The agent had been busy sizing Jack up, but all his attention snapped back to me. "That's not all, Miss Colton."

I nodded. "Oh?"

"We'd like to have a look around the place," Agent Rodney said. "The basement, specifically."

While I poured every ounce of willpower into schooling my face, Jack stepped forward. "Why would that be?"

The agent sucked on his teeth. "I'm not at liberty to say."

"And I am not at liberty to show you anything without the proper documentation. This is a hotel, not a crime scene. I have guests to cater to. They've paid good money and I won't have you interrupting anyone's stay."

Agent Rodney nodded. "I can make documentation happen."

The air stilled. Tension swelled between the three of us like heat crackling before the lightning. A vicious smile spread Jack's lips wide. "I wouldn't be so sure."

The young, medallion sporting officer stepped back. The others glanced around uneasily. "Even you have your limits, Mr. Warren. Don't think we're unaware of some of the . . . opportunities you've offered to the police. In exchange for their cooperation, I mean."

Jack cocked his head to the side. "You think I speak of the police?"

Now, even Agent Rodney hesitated. Malice coated his skin as he faced me. "Also don't think we're unaware of your relationship with a *much* younger, easily impressionable woman."

Red crawled up my throat, my heart thumping inside my chest. The smooth-faced agent clutched his medallion, mumbling the lord's prayer beneath his breath.

Jack took notice. "I would watch yourself, man. As I'm sure you know by now, I have friends in high places."

He smirked. "And how high would that be, Mr. Warren?"

Jack leaned in. Dark energy charged the air, a vicious undercurrent that pebbled my skin.

His voice came low and dangerous. "God."

That was enough for the young officer, who nodded his head and walked from the lobby. A moment passed in frozen animosity, then one by one the remaining agents followed him. Agent Rodney left last.

"If you change your mind, give me a call," he said, placing a business card in my numb hand. The lobby resumed its normal hustle and bustle. The show was over.

THIRTY-THREE

"WE HAVE A PROBLEM," Lillian sang, tone too light for the impending doom. The six of us sat around the red room of the Silvertongue Speakeasy. A dryad delivered five flutes of fae wine and stumbled back behind the curtain. As this particular establishment stocked nothing safe for humans, I went dry.

Or not, as Will produced a flask from his jacket and handed it to me.

"We have several problems," Violet said. Instead of the booth, she chose to lay across the table like a fatigued decoration. As I reached over her for the flask, Harold hissed and snapped at my hand.

Jack snarled at the snake. If possible, it gave him a haughty glare and returned to its roost among the vines. Instead of candles, soft, blue will-o-wisps hung over our heads, resting peacefully in overgrowth that hadn't been here last time. Fat, white flowers grew in droves, vaguely scented like dogwood blossoms with a whiff of something I couldn't name. When I went to touch one, Jack carefully pulled my hand away.

Petals floated like snowflakes into Violet's hair. She waved a hand until Arthur placed a crystal stem glass between her fingers. "Do we think Delsaran tipped them off?"

"Tipped who off?"

"The knights," Arthur said, ominously. He fiddled with his glasses, cleaning the lens on his shirt for the hundredth time in the ten minutes we sat here.

"The Knights of Templar," Lillian said. The vines formed a seat for her against the far curtain. She reclined in the bramble throne, long legs crossed, appearing every bit the striking princess she used to be. All she was missing was a crown.

"As in, the crusades? Those Knights of Templar?" I asked. Tommy found us a book on them once. They were a fringe group of the Catholic Church in the Middle Ages. Extremists who fought in the holy wars and assassinated those who opposed Christianity. But they disappeared hundreds of years ago, disbanded and never seen again. Some even claimed they were a myth, a story told to children at bedtime.

"That would be the one," Arthur said, fiddling with his spectacles again. "Sorry, devout Christians make me nervous."

Violet sighed. "Everything makes you nervous." Propped up on her elbows, she stared at me. "They're very real, very irritating, and very good at fucking everything up."

"They died out centuries ago," I said.

"No," Jack murmured, staring at his wine like he could implore it for answers. "That's just the story they tell."

"After the crusades they were given a new mission," Lillian said, sipping her wine. "They were devoted to their faith, extremely so. In the Holy Wars, they thought Muslims and Jews were the enemies of religion. Then they discovered a much worse foe."

I looked around. "Pagans?"

"Fae," Jack said. "Their mission changed. They went underground, seeking the key to immortality so they could carry on their Holy War on even footing."

"Did they find it?"

"Oh, yes," Will murmured.

"But how?"

"Fuck, if we know," Violet said. "It isn't as if many encounter them and walk away unscathed."

I shook my head. "Those men were in the FBI."

"A secret sect," Jack said. "I've long had my suspicions, but it's never been a problem. They have a history of infiltrating ruling powers. Government, economics . . . police."

I thought of the medallion hanging around Tommy's neck. "That can't be right."

"No offense to your darling brother, but we're not making this up," Violet snapped. "Now, not only do we have Delsaran breathing down our necks, but the Knights are very aware of all things Colton." They all looked at me.

Blood rushed past my ears. Tommy . . . Tommy wouldn't. Would he? Model soldier, model son, model man, of course he would. He'd found his own faith in Fairville, and that was after a lifetime of hearing the fae came from hell. That they were devil creatures preying on the little sister he spoke of all throughout the war.

My hands turned sweaty and cold. Jack laid his gloved ones over mine.

"You knew," I said. When we made our bargain, he wouldn't promise protection to Tommy for more than a year. Because he knew.

"I suspected they ran their own section of the investigation bureau. And with your brother's knowledge and history with fae, it was only a matter of time before they found him."

I ripped my hands away. "We could have helped him."

"I think it was already too late," Will said. Violet sat upright, folding her legs beneath her. Will reached across the table for me. "Believe me, none of us are happy about this, but likely he was taken in as soon as he got to Chicago. Maybe even before."

"*No.*" I heard their words, understanding them but refusing to believe. Refusing to believe Tommy could be swindled into something like this. Because if it was true, when I changed, when I worked with Jack, when I sided with them—

Will was wrong. Tommy would never come back.

It was the final nail in our coffin. The slam of a hammer announcing the death of my family. Mama was dead, Papa was dead, and now, I was dead to the only person I had left.

One of the will-o-wisps above my head fizzled, a faint keening noise as its soft light flickered, then drained away.

Will stood, hands on the table. Arthur paled and even Lillian sat straight. Only Jack and Violet didn't move, sharing a look.

I didn't care. Not that I may have just used magic, that my grief may have *killed* something. Agony poured through my veins in place of blood. Fire sang beneath my skin. The devil-folk, the war, these knights. Why was it always my family?

Would you like to make a bargain?

A pathetic cry passed my clenched teeth. Jack removed his glove, reaching out for me. "*Annwyl.*"

"*Don't.*" I slid away before his fingers could brush me, before he could calm me with poison and magic. He didn't get to take that away too.

"We'll find a solution," Lillian said softly. "You know me, know my vows. I would never harm Thomas. We'll find a way."

Will slowly sank back to his seat, still fixed on the will-o-wisp above me. Violet wrung her hands together, appearing nervous for the first time since we met.

Arthur scratched at his temple. "On that note, I do have an announcement to make. I have done a little sleuthing." He grinned sheepishly. None of us responded. "Um, well, I know where Lorvellian is."

Violet held her hands inches from his throat. "You tell us this *now*?"

"I just remembered this morning!" His cheeks turned a motley of pink. "And like I said, Christians make me antsy so I wanted to wait until—"

Jack breathed deep. "Arthur."

"Yes, right." He pushed his glasses up his nose. "Interestingly enough, he owns a bank. In the five points."

Will sighed. "Should have known."

I vaguely recognized the name, then remembered in one fell swoop. Lorvellian was the fae Henry Foster told us stole the second Dianomican from him. "Is that in New York?"

"Just downtown," Jack murmured, facing Arthur. "Are you sure?"

"Very. Even had an old colleague confirm it. He has a checking account with them."

"If there's any place he'd keep the book, it would be there," Lillian said.

Will threw his hands in the air. "What good does that do us? We can't stumble into a wyvern's roost and—"

"What's a wyvern?" I interrupted.

They all went quiet.

"It's like . . . well, it's a dragon," Lillian said.

My toes went numb. "Excuse me?"

"It's a dragon, but it has two legs instead of four and—"

"It's a dragon," Will snapped. "He's a bloody fucking dragon. And the bank is his fucking den. And we're not getting the fucking book."

My eyes widened. "Will?"

"He doesn't like wyverns," Jack mumbled. He downed the rest of his glass. Fresh bubbly replenished instantaneously and he downed that too. "And it's going to be a problem."

Lillian kicked her legs. "You know all those fun bedtime stories about dragons and their treasure hoards? They're quite accurate, actually."

"Accurate?" Will snapped. "I'm sure tales told to human children leave out a few, *very* important details."

"Which we can handle," Lillian said, calm as a summer breeze. She gave him a gentle smile. "Isn't that right, Will?"

He crossed his arms, falling back in the booth.

"If the bank is his roost, it will be warded against magic. All magic, even shading," Violet said.

"That's the least of our problems," Jack said. "If the bank operates for humans, we can't exactly rob it with the Knights watching our every move."

Color drained from my face. "You can't actually mean to hold up a bank?"

"How else would we get a bloody fucking magical book from a bloody fucking wyvern," Will said. His dark cheeks flushed, fingers trembling against his coat. "The problem is you can't rob a wyvern den. That's how you get *eaten*."

"Actually," Arthur said, holding a finger in the air. Will turned on him and he shriveled. "Um, well, I did a little more research and—" He produced a rolled paper from his jacket, spreading it on the table to the chagrin of Violet. Neat, black lines formed the layout of a building.

Lillian hopped down from her perch. "Arthur, you brilliant, star-sent Druid. How did you get this?"

"Even dragons need permits from city hall." He flushed pink from fingers to hair, tapping strange markings along the top corners. "I recognize these sigils. They're wards, but not against magic. They're more like alarms. If anyone performs magic within the building, Lorvellian knows."

"Traps!" Will exclaimed. "He *wants* someone to be stupid enough to rob him."

Jack pulled the parchment closer. "This is good. Very good. Well done, Arthur."

I looked over the layout. A massive square designated as the lobby took the forefront, cornered on three sides by teller stations. Beyond that, I hardly recognized half the words detailing cash drawers, vault locations, special access points and even a safe room. Noticeably, there were almost no security measures. Not surprising if a dragon kept watch over it all.

"We still have the Knights to contend with," Violet said. The room instantly sobered.

Not just the Knights. Tommy. My brother. "Who are they watching?"

Violet raised a brow. "All of us?"

"They still function as a human organization, yes?" I asked. Jack nodded beside me, still absorbed by the parchment. "They questioned Jack about the basement."

"Which reminds me, Violet. I'm placing you in charge of moving the operation to our second location. I want nothing left behind."

Violet nodded. Since everyone else seemed surprised by this secret second location, I figured I wouldn't be told either. It didn't matter. "They're watching Jack. Probably Will and Arthur too."

Lillian shook her head. "We don't know that, darling."

"You are a secretary. You are his sister," I said, gesturing at Violet. "I am the stupid human swept up in it all. Secret or not, they still have regular authorities to report to. They couldn't sweep the basement without the proper papers. Therefore, if they're going to survey anyone as a front, it will be the men."

Sensing the direction of my plan, Will nodded enthusiastically. "I think she's onto something."

Jack side-eyed me. "No."

My jaw clenched, breath whistling past my teeth. "No one pays attention to us. We're just the women."

Violet clucked her tongue. "Speak for yourself."

352

"You three need alibis. They'll take any excuse to bring you in and I'm fairly sure Violet just said anyone who encounters them doesn't live much longer afterwards."

"No," Jack said, louder this time. "If anyone handles this, it will be me. I'm not asking any of you to risk this."

That made me pause. Even Violet's eyes softened. Lillian sighed, sliding the layout closer. "Adeline has a point, you know. If an alarm goes off with any magic, it only gives us one opportunity to use it. And Jack, darling, you know I adore you beyond anything, but magic is your biggest strength." She gestured across the table. "Violet doesn't use her powers, so she's well-equipped without it. If it's just us, we can find the book and I'll use our one shot to shade away."

"And me."

Even knowing these people, even with everything behind us, there was something deeply unsettling about five powerful immortals taking instant notice of me.

"Lillian doesn't kill and Violet doesn't use magic," I said. "That won't be enough. Even without the dragon, two people couldn't possibly rob a bank of this size."

Jack shook his head. "No one's sticking it up. They'll sneak in."

"Through what entrance?" I pressed my finger hard enough into the table to hurt. "There's only one way in or out. The front door."

Arthur raised a tentative hand. "This is wonderful, truly, but I have to say, it's all moot when you consider it. Violet and Lillian are easily recognizable, as are you, Addie. Your brother has the Knights watching you too. And I think three women robbing a bank will catch some interest, don't you think?"

Lillian cocked her head to the side, sucking on her teeth. "Not if we're dressed like men."

"I'll consider Lillian and Violet," Jack said, rolling up the parchment. "This conversation is done until further notice."

An unrecognized feeling filled me, hot and violent. All my life I'd been nothing but a wall ornament, something to protect and covet. A burden on those around me. Jack said I could do magic, but I couldn't. Lillian said I could be strong, but I wasn't. Arthur said I was smart and Will said I was loved, but Violet told me I was weak. Pathetic. She was the only one man enough to tell me the truth.

I no longer wanted to be that fragile thing on the wall. The woman in the wings, waiting for someone else to tell me it was my turn to be involved. I was tired of sitting in that apartment, sick of staring at plants all day, and I was truly, sickeningly done with being afraid. I never put trust in myself, but I knew I was right about this. I wasn't going to stand by and be too weak to fight for it.

"Lillian refuses to harm others," I repeated. "Violet will apparently be busy fighting a dragon. Or security. Or any number of people in the bank who happened to be armed. And to add to that, I'm the only one among you with extensive gun experience."

Jack rolled his head on his neck, exasperated. "Using a gun and being proficient are very different."

"I was a farmer," I snapped. "I can shoot a squirrel from eighty yards."

"A squirrel isn't a human."

"You're right, it's a smaller target."

Golden skin rippled with collapsing glamour. His serpent eyes flashed, teeth bared as he turned in his seat. "Adeline. There is no way, not even a sliver of a chance after the other night—"

"I won't do it without Addie," Violet said. Surprise flickered through me. She nodded. "I can handle Lorvellian, but Lillian will need protection from everything else in order to crack the safe. She can't very well blow it up with bullets hitting her back."

"Blow it up?"

Lillian shrugged. "There was one summer in the 1880's I got bored and taught myself to safe-crack." She made an exploding gesture with her hands. "Nitroglycerin. Fascinating stuff."

Violet rolled her eyes. "You three need to be somewhere public while a bank is robbed. Many witnesses. Lillian will blow the place sky-high and I have to duel a fucking wyvern. And what will Adeline do in the meantime? Compulse plants?"

I nodded, hands loosening.

"If she wants to use the gun, let her use the fucking gun." She shifted back in her seat. "So don't worry your sweet little heads. Go out, relax—"

Lillian grinned. "Have a drink. Maybe get something to eat."

"—gossip a little, enjoy your day. We don't want you boys to worry about the important stuff." Her serpent eyes flashed. "The women will handle everything."

THIRTY-FOUR

IN THE ABSTRUSE, LILLIAN adjusted her waistcoat in the mirror. A tin of Lucky Jim's pomade rested on my vanity beside Mama's pearls. A buttoned shirt hung loose off my shoulders with a gray waistcoat, a black tie slung around my neck. Matching men's trousers covered my legs and air sluiced through my thighs with each step. I wore socks instead of stockings, dress shoes instead of heels, and when I finished slicking my hair back on my head, I donned a bowler instead of a headband.

"Very dapper," Lillian said, grinning and skipping in her men's clothes. She gave her hips a shake. "We look like a couple of drugstore cowboys."

"Skinny ones," Jack said from the door. Lillian beamed and I turned red. Facing the mirror, I attempted to fix the messy knot barely holding my tie together.

In the reflection, Jack gave a subtle nod of his head and Lillian found somewhere else to be. Sighing, I focused on my neck when Jack's hands clasped my waist, spun me in place and he flicked my fingers away from the tie.

The ceiling seemed especially lovely today. The walls and floors too. I gave them the attention they were due, smoothing my breaths as his fingers brushed my throat. "You have to get it even first," he murmured, flipping my collar and adjusting the fabric.

"Let's put you in a garter and stockings. See how well you manage."

The corner of his lips lifted. "I'm not sure I could pass as a girl."

"What about me, then? Do I make a handsome man?"

He finished the knot, stuffing the tail of the tie underneath my waistcoat. He patted it down, then brushed his fingers beneath my chin. "No, you make a beautiful woman."

Clasping my hands behind my back, I pulled my lower lip between my teeth and avoided his stare. He placed his hand beneath my chin again, tilting my face up.

"I know you're not happy about this," I said.

"I'm not."

The remaining night at the Silvertongue had devolved into argument after argument, making plans and revising them until dawn broke the sky. When we returned to the apartment, Jack retreated straight to his bedroom and I lingered in the study. When he emerged several hours later, we didn't speak a word of what was decided, nor in the four days that followed. Even though we reverted back to our normal routine—as normal as it could be, all things considered—tension suffocated us each morning at breakfast, each night when we went to sleep.

"I needed to do something. I want to try."

"I know."

Apprehension and acceptance warred on his face. He wasn't happy about this, but he would allow me to go anyway. Or maybe there was no permission needed. He was the Poison Prince, the King of the Banished, but he'd wielded very little authority over me. I wasn't his equal, not truly, but if Papa or Tommy ever disagreed, it was their creed I obeyed. Jack never lauded his gender or power over my head. Or maybe I'd just grown stronger since then.

Maybe he didn't care, but that didn't seem right either. A lot rested on my safety, but the look he wore ran too deep, not something reserved for a valuable asset or possession. He worried for *me*.

"I'll be fine."

He nodded, running his tongue over his teeth. "I know that too."

I wondered if he'd ever lost anyone. With centuries under his belt, he must have, but the fae weren't like us. Their emotions and humanity waned with the passing of time—he'd admitted that himself—but Jack wasn't entirely like them. Some alien result from a non-human residing among humans for too long. Whoever he'd lost in the past affected him, made him worry in a way that wasn't common among fae. He hadn't lost that piece of himself yet.

"Thank you," I said.

"For?"

"Allowing me to make mistakes."

His face smoothed over, acceptance taking root. "Always, *annwyl*."

A moment passed. Like the tension broiling between us didn't exist, he grinned. "Wish we had a camera. Your first major crime."

"Maybe the press will arrive on scene. Or I'll get my first mug shot."

"You never forget your first."

"That's what I've heard."

A serpentine smile stretched his face, and just like that he was back to normal, which for him meant crime across worlds and general marauding. It was unfortunate how much it had grown on me. He stepped closer and all the air whooshed out of my lungs. Heat curled beneath my skin as his expression turned humorless.

"What?" I asked.

He shook his head, slowly. His eyes touched places that made me burn. "Nothing, just admiring the sight of you in my clothes."

My mouth dried to a crisp. "Your clothes?"

"Well, Lillian took them in." He cocked his head to the side, something uncivilized roiling in his gaze. "In a lot of places, apparently."

I was suddenly aware of how loosely the trousers fit. Pink flushed me head to toe. "There seems to be no skill Lillian doesn't possess."

His lips turned up and he offered me an arm. Our eyes met in the mirror and he winked. "Let me know if you need help out of them."

We shaded, and for once I was grateful the endless darkness and silence hid my quiet laugh.

THE PLAN WAS SIMPLE. Too simple.

Jack contracted a driver he'd used several times in the past. For what, I didn't wish to know, satisfied with the knowledge Jack trusted him and he was the proud owner of a Bugatti Grand Prix, which could apparently reach speeds of 125 miles per hour. When I called that bunk Jack said he clocked it himself. While driving it.

If it weren't for the task at hand, there'd be some humor in an immortal who could teleport at will being excited by fast vehicles.

The floor in the back of the car had been outfitted with a glistening, freshly cleaned mirror. The three of us sat with our heels on the seat to avoid scuffing it, much to the disdain of the driver. When I asked him his name, he said, "Driver." So there was that.

He must have had some indication the people he worked for weren't exactly human, but Driver never mentioned it. In fact, all he did was smoke and grunt while Violet handed me a box of iron bullets to load. Lillian would go without, as it was her powers that would get us out, and "guns make magic especially finicky." Instead, she had two daggers strapped to her forearms, a short sword down her back, and a leather bag with a special payload. Nitroglycerin. She had a bag of fucking dynamite.

For Violet and I, we each had a Winchester pistol on our hips that I swore were from the last century. Violet had her usual twin swords and an extra dagger *just in case,* and the grand reveal: we had our own Thompson submachine guns.

I'd only ever shot rifles and shotguns, but now didn't seem the time to mention that. As I loaded iron into the drum magazines and two spares, Violet gave the final rundown. I could recite the plan in my sleep by now, but my nerves were grateful for the reminder.

Driver would deliver us directly in front of the bank at 7:15 a.m., when doors opened to the public. The hope was there would be as few people as possible. We were here for the book, not to inflict damage, something Jack repeated several hundred times while Violet scowled. The guns were mostly for intimidation, and should be used "as needed." Namely, if someone began shooting at us. Or a dragon appeared.

We would enter the bank in exactly this order: Violet, who would incapacitate the two guards at the door. Me, who would instruct the tellers and any patrons to get down and tie their hands. Then Lillian, who would hopefully enter with the satchel of highly sensitive explosives after there was no risk of bullets flying. Violet would remain in the lobby to keep an eye out for Lorvellian, escapees or the police. I would follow Lillian to the safe and provide protection and watch while she blew the thing to Europe. When the explosion went off—which, according to Lillian, would be heard in Brooklyn—Violet would make her way back to the safe while Driver circled several blocks away. We'd recover the book before Lorellian or the police realized what happened, and Lillian would use her compact mirror to shade us back to the getaway car. Driver would get us to a second car closer to the hotel, since Lillian was surrounded by too much technology to shade the three of us all the way back from the bank. We'd shatter the mirror so nothing could follow in car one, change back into our lady clothes in the backseat, dump the men's attire at the local iron forge where any physical or magical trace would be destroyed, use the mirror in car two to shade back to the hotel, and later rendezvous with the boys, who would be sipping bloody marys at the Cheshire Room while we robbed a bank.

Easy.

"Are you getting cold feet, darling?" Lillian asked, the same moment Violet hissed, "Get a goddamn grip." One of the iron bullets fell from my trembling fingers and tumbled beside the latter's thigh. I scooped it up and shook my head. "First time nerves."

"You're stealing a book, not losing your fucking maidenhead." Violet sighed, running her hand through her pomade-slicked hair. She shook her head and placed a bowler low on her brow. "Don't fuck this up, human."

I slammed the drum into the Thompson. "No promises, demon."

She actually smiled at that. We arrived at the Five Points, only minutes away from our destination. Crisp, stone buildings clashed with dusty roads, dirty faces and the remnants of the last militias to rule this city. After the death of Bill the Butcher and the dissolution of the Dead Rabbits, most of the war-torn streets had been taken over by government buildings and offices. Still, the residue of crime and poverty lingered in the last ramshackle housing units, the young boys rising early for factory work and clothes full of moth holes hanging on laundry lines. Punctuating the despair were the justice building, the courthouses, and several other marble monstrosities raised to the sky like gaudy Pantheons. It was difficult to say if the end of that era was a blessing or a curse to those who lived here, but with Prohibition and the six years that followed, it didn't feel like New York made much progress.

Probably made me a bit of a hypocrite, but I cast that thought aside as the bank came into view. Just like its neighbors, it was polished, white stone faintly resembling the temples of Rome or Greece. A freshly swept sidewalk gleamed in the sunrise while several men slipped inside. Two thick, mahogany doors boasted stained glass and gold handles. Any windows along the building were thick with iron bars.

I took a deep breath, mumbling the plan over and over like a prayer. In and out. Not even a dramatic escape, as we would exit through the shade before anyone realized we left the building. If all went according to plan, the dragon—the fucking dragon—wouldn't know of our daring robbery until we were long gone. The hardest part would be getting in, which was mostly up to Violet. For all her faults I'd give her one thing—if there was anyone I wanted beside me in a shootout, it was definitely her. After that, all I had to do was hand out twine, follow Lillian down a hall and grab the book out of the safe. Less than ten minutes and we would be on our way. It took me longer to eat breakfast.

I handed Violet her guns and Lillian pushed the straps of her bag higher on her petite shoulders. Driver pulled up to the sidewalk and knocked on a wooden crucifix twice. "Godspeed to the flappers."

"Thanks," I mumbled.

Lillian twitched beside me. "Alright, here we go. And ladies, remember, this is nothing but a soup job, all we want is the book. We're only throwing lead if necessary. " She gave Violet a pointed look. The two had very different opinions on violence.

I cocked my head to the side. "Technically it'd be throwing iron."

Violet snorted and wrapped a dark bandana around her face. Lillian and I did the same. Then she held up the Thompson, admired it, and gave the trigger a gentle kiss. "Alright, girls, let's go rob a fucking bank."

THIRTY-FIVE

"EVERYBODY ON THE FUCKING ground."

A chorus of screams went off. I instantly regretted every single one of my life's decisions. Violet had the security officers out cold before I even reached the door, and much to Lillian's chagrin, had yelled out for everyone to get on their knees and released a spray of bullets into the ceiling. It was like watching a hyena lose its mind. At the least, we timed the endeavor well, because only three people stood in the lobby being served by tired, old bank tellers, of which there were eleven. Every person in there besides us was an older man, and looked very much ready to shit their pants.

I tied the unconscious guards' hands behind their backs and made my way to the crowd. A teller fumbled with his telephone, cursing each time he dropped it. I pointed my gun at him, willing my nausea to subside and dropped my voice. "Are you deaf? Grab some fucking air."

His hands shot above his head like he had propellers attached. I tied him up first, reminding myself over and over we weren't going to hurt anyone, we just wanted the book, and we were getting the book to save the world so technically, we were doing charity right now. That was a good word for it. Charity.

Beside me, a man's nose exploded with blood as Violet hit him with the butt of her gun. She pointed her fingers at me, then gestured to a back hall, wide eyes vicious and bloodshot. I nodded, waved Lillian inside and swung the Thompson and spare drum I carried around as she walked ahead. Fourteen sets of weary eyes tracked us into the darkness.

There were few windows, and we'd arrived before any of the tellers had time to check the safe and turn the lights on. Some were electrical and others gas, but it hardly mattered since I couldn't find a switch and Lillian saw well in the dark. I was the one with the submachine gun, but I digress.

Thankfully, the main safe stood beneath a heavily fortified window. Golden light cut through the bars like butter melting around a hot knife. It was enough to see in, and that was all I cared about. The hallway was a dead end with no other doors, halls or exits off of it besides the barred window. One way to the safe and one way out, unless of course, you weren't human.

"Alright, so far we're hitting on all eight," Lillian murmured, more to herself than me, and I realized she was more nervous than the three of us combined. She dumped her bag and began sorting through the contents, retrieving a rolled canvas first. She undid the leather ties and unveiled a set of delicate silver tools. "Diamond dusted," she said, holding up a drill. "State of the art."

"Good, let's put it to use." Stale air clogged the hall and dust motes floated in the watery light. Beyond our little lit corner shadows caught the walls, playing tricks on my eyes. We'd only taken two turns, but none of the lobby's light reached this far. The dark hallway yawned open like the mouth of a beast.

Lillian kept chattering—soothing for her, but my teeth set on edge. Each swirl of dust had me swiveling the tommy gun, my pathetic human ears perking at every noise between Lillian's endless babble. Like she said, it was all going according to plan. I just needed to remain calm.

She cranked the handle on the drill and the quiet hum of churning metal filled my ears. "Once we get this through, I'll need you to mold some grease for me while I make the nitro."

I blanched. "Shouldn't that have been done at home?"

"I didn't trust Violet to not go trigger-happy." She finished the drilling and blew the dust away, spitting into a rag and wiping as much as possible. "Don't want that to explode on us."

"What?"

"The dust," she mumbled. I stared at the little particles floating through the air and cringed.

"Don't worry, I've done this a few times."

I blew out an exhale. "How many times?"

"Many," she said, then under her breath, "Once successfully."

There was no time for that. Lillian handed me a glob of lye and fat, or "grease" as she called it, and instructed me to knead it until it was tough, forming it into the shape of a thin cup. Meanwhile, with *delicate* precision, she uncorked several flasks of foul chemicals and mixed them into one. Once that was all done, I gripped my gun like it was a dismembered appendage while she stuffed grease into the hole, and slowly drained her chemical concoction into the pit. Several spools of twine later and we were halfway down the hall, crouched against the wall. The end of the explosive shook in one of her hands, a book of matches in the other.

"You may want to cover your ears."

I raised my hands just before she ignited it. The last thing I saw was fire racing down the twine, faster than any Bugatti, and an explosion of light.

My head cracked against the wall. A high-pitched whine rang in my ears and tears exploded behind my eyes. Slowly, the world melted back into color and sound, but a deep ache throbbed behind my temple. Lillian waved her hands in front of me, frantically screaming. "I'm sorry! I'm sorry! Way too much nitro, but the door's open at least. We're still hitting on all eight."

I stumbled to my feet. Despite the explosion, I kept a firm grip on the gun. My brother would have been proud.

No time for those thoughts either. Violet materialized from the shadows, eyes flicking in every direction. Fae could see far better than humans, and I had no desire to learn what made her pale. "Let's just get the fucking book," she said, throwing one arm around my shoulders and dragging me to the safe. Lillian skipped behind, singing about how she was really good at this, and maybe she should do bank heists more often.

Rotten sulfur and a metal tang permeated the air. Smoke and dust filled the entry, waved away by Violet while I wretched and coughed. Through the tears in my eyes I noticed something . . . extremely disheartening. Nothing but three, smooth steel walls and a mountain of cash shimmered in the haze.

"There's no book here." Then, louder. "There's nothing but fucking money."

"Untwist your bloomers, girl, that was only the first half." Violet unsheathed a knife, and to my horror, cut a long slice down her arm. More to my horror, she wrenched my wrist away and did the same.

I hissed in pain, growing woozy as beads of red dripped down my palm. I swayed on my feet, growing nauseous as Lillian made her own wound and we all clasped bloody hands.

"If you faint, I will leave you here to die," Violet said. Somehow that snapped me out of it. Fire lanced up my arm and Violet closed her eyes, murmuring, *"Creache omert sliuah. Terach."*

Light filled the hazy safe. For a moment, I thought the nitroglycerin came back for vengeance, but no sound accompanied the golden glow, sprouting from where blood dripped from our three clasped hands. Light burned away at the metal like flame eating a page. Violet laughed, serpent eyes glowing brighter than the power consuming the floor. "See you on the other side, bitch."

DARKNESS, LIQUID PULSING AGAINST my skin like we traveled through the shade, then my back hit something hard and noise exploded like a thousand wind chimes. The ache behind my skull throbbed harder, purple welts formed along my skin and I gasped for air. When I found the strength to open my eyes, fire erupted around me.

No, not an eruption. My bleary eyes exploded the oppressive lights into bursts of orange and yellow. A vaulted ceiling towered over me, thick with golden buttresses molded into glorious and horrifying scenes. A dragon bursting from the earth. A dragon unleashing fire upon a throne. A dragon dismembering a crowd of screaming humans with teeth and claws. A lot of fucking dragons.

Sconces adorned the wall and ceiling in a halo of fire, but that was only half of the glow. It hadn't been wind chimes I'd heard I lay on a hill, easily twenty feet tall, made of shiny, gold coins. I shifted and several clanged, skittering down the horde in a landslide of wealth. The entire floor was covered in hills and valleys of glowing gold, forming shimmering waves around the cavernous room. Archways of gold columns lined a far wall, and beyond those, gold as far as the eye could see.

It wasn't just gold, either. Rubies the size of my fist pockmarked the hills like inflamed cysts. Diamonds reflecting the yellow light, sapphires of the deepest blue and automobile-sized geodes cracked lengthwise, sitting like entryways to crystal caves. Some of the gold formed objects—goblets, jewelry, several crowns and most notable of all, a throne perched on a shifting pile of coins, preparing to tumble to its new resting place.

Because there was nothing else to say, I, being a woman of reason and class, murmured, "Holy fucking shit."

The tommy gun and spare drum smacked the gold beside me, just missing my head. I jumped and looked up, but only a gruesome fresco stared back at me.

Where the hell were Lillian and Violet?

I stumbled to my feet, sending more gold down the slide. The sound echoed around the room, expanding as it bounced off the walls.

Nevermind, they had to be here somewhere. I hoped. Finding the book was first priority. The sea of treasure stared back at me, and I prayed to God the book wasn't buried in it.

Clearly, Lorvellian was an intelligent reptile. He had to be if he built this room, the bank, all of it. If he stole a precious book he'd want to keep it in good condition, and throwing it among a pile of jewels and gold hardly seemed the way to do that. Besides, if he had such a keen interest in the Dianomican, then maybe he hoarded other valuable books as well. Perhaps this treasure crypt had a library.

That seemed as good a plan as any. I threw the gun's shoulder strap around me and slid on my behind to the bottom of my hill. Which was terrible of course, because now I had to climb another one. The golden coins may as well have been drifting sand, sinking beneath my hands and feet with each step, turning a single pace into three. By the time I reached the archways, sweat poured down my face and my breath came in heaving gasps. As soon as this was over, I was taking up a new exercise regimen.

Beyond the archways, there was nothing but more gold. A chandelier the size of Jack's study swayed from the ceiling, lit with honey flames. Like the buttresses, the metal had been carved into gruesome scenes. I knew very little about wyverns, but nothing about this place came off as cozy.

More archways lined a far wall, but beyond those the dark stone floor came into view. Convincing myself that was the most logical route to a library, and I was not just avoiding having to climb gold anymore, I gravitated to the dark alcove like a moth to flame.

I peeled the jacket off my shoulders and tied the arms around my waist. Somewhere along the way my hat went missing, but it was too late now. Beyond the entry was a sight so beautiful I feared it was a fever dream. An actual library.

The room formed a circle, only about ten feet across. Shelves lined the walls and stacked upon one another, like the inside of a turret. One that reached so high, when I craned my head back the wall of books disappeared into darkness. A gold ladder stretched up from tracks embedded in the stone floor.

I was about to touch it, determined to check every goddamn book in that library when a strange thought occurred to me. Why would a dragon need a ladder?

And where the hell *were* Lillian and Violet?

No, something was wrong. The same eerie sense I had at Henry Foster's estate crawled over my skin. This was all too . . . easy. The robbery was supposed to be easy, we designed it that way, but no one mentioned the goddamn dragon lair we'd teleport to. And now, just landing among the lifeless treasure trove — ladder exactly where I needed one. A convenient library as I sought out a book.

I snatched my hand from the rungs. Dread coursed down my spine, plunging me into a purgatory between action and thought. If the book was anywhere it would be here, but the other girls were still missing, and now that the thought formed, I couldn't help feeling something was terribly wrong.

I stepped back. Nevermind the book for now. The search would go much faster with Violet and Lillian, anyway. I should find them first, make sure they were safe.

A gust of air billowed through the door, sending the torches into a hypnotic dance. My breath came in shallow gasps, the hair raising along my arms with the sense I was no longer alone. My back faced the arched alcove. The only exit.

Clicks reverberated against the stone floor. A beastly snuffle, then a long breath and a blast of heat. The hair over the back of my head blew upwards, freed from the pomade by a rush of searing air. My fingers twitched by my sides, oxygen stagnant in my lungs as my breath stopped. Another blast of scorching air and I closed my eyes, trying not to whine.

A tearing sound filled my skull and the clicks retreated from the alcove. I took my first breath in what seemed like ages, daring to open my eyes. The shimmering ladder and a row of faded books stared back at me. I stared at the thick side rail and attempted not to faint.

The smooth surface reflected the image of what lay behind me, and he was . . . I would think of a word later.

Black scales covered the beast, shimmering red when the firelight caught them just right. A tail at least twenty paces long swished among the gold coins, the end a bulbous knob covered in thick barbs the size of my forearm. Two membranous wings crumpled as he shifted on taloned hands attached to the end of each. A thick head wrenched side to side, crowned with five massive horns as black teeth gnashed and carved into the remains of what I prayed was an animal.

Suffice to say, I'd just met Lorvellian.

Maybe he was a nice wyvern.

He let out a bellowing screech that shook the chandelier. Gold coins scattered and tumbled to the ground. I used the noise to grab the ladder, and without thinking climbed as high as I could.

The noise died to a hush. I froze, squeezing my eyes tight.

Okay, I'd been in worse situations. Actually, not at all, but I needed some confidence and if lying did it then I would tell myself many,

many lies. I incapacitated a phooka with nothing but a shard of glass. As I currently had a fucking submachine gun loaded with iron, I'd say I was in much better form this time. I was completely alone and trapped in the lair of a fire-breathing dinosaur, but I'd endured dinner parties with Fairville's church group, so I could survive this.

An animal brayed, squealing and stomping the ground before the sounds turned to more ripping and gnashing. In the ladder's reflection, the beast reclined on a bed of gold, gnawing on a bone, surrounded by blood spray and sinew. Any higher, and I'd be above the alcove and lose the reflection. But if I couldn't see it, then it couldn't see me. Hopefully.

A spray of gold erupted in the chamber and I climbed five more rungs. The sconces dwindled here, only three to the ten lining the turret's floor. Above my head, the sconces got fewer and fewer, until only one flickered in the darkness, far, far above my head.

Now would probably be the time to make a plan. There was a possibility the ladder led all the way to the main floor of the bank, but as I entered the room by magic I couldn't be sure. Best case, Lorvellian would leave and I could find a way out without sneaking around him, but who knew how long that would be. Already, sweat poured off my skin. My skinny arms shook as I held tight to the ladder. The tommy gun and spare drum hung off my back, daring me to cave to gravity. How long would I have to remain here until the dragon left, minutes? Hours? Days?

Between the loaded gun and spare drum, I had two hundred bullets. Violet had the others, but she was nowhere to be found so those were gone for the time being. I thought of the scales sheathing the dragon and wondered if it mattered. There was no doubt in my mind a blade would never penetrate his skin. An iron bullet, maybe, but that was putting a lot of eggs in one very tiny basket.

I couldn't hold on forever, which meant I had to make a choice — up or down.

The wyvern roared in the main cavern, shaking dust motes off the books. Up. Definitely up.

The next hour was the longest, and possibly most painful of my life. I was grateful for the ever increasing distance between myself and Lorvellian, because I was soon choking on the air I breathed. Having no indication how Lorvellian hunted, I decided the safest route was to be wary of any and all senses. The high fae had enhanced scent, sight and hearing. I wouldn't take the chance of Lorvellian possessing any of those.

I only climbed when he made noise. Despite the increasingly darkening chamber, I searched above and below each time I moved, checking for scales and teeth. There was nothing I could do about scent and I simply tried not to dwell on it.

No matter how far I moved, the ceiling only seemed farther away. I'd lost track of how many shelves I passed. The floor of the turret was nothing but a pinprick. My arms rattled against the metal and I pressed my forehead to the gold, taking a deep breath. I could do this. I could do this. I could—

A faint hum rattled against my skin, warm and soothing like a summer breeze, scented like the fresh rain and oleander that followed Jack. I breathed out a trembling sigh, thanking god or the stars or whoever. Silence stretched around me, the scent and hum remaining, but no Jack. I was still alone.

I swallowed, willing my burgeoning tears to retreat. Hopelessness ached in my chest, then despair, then anger. Blinding, beautiful anger. I placed another hand on the rung.

My father protected me, but he never prepared me.

One more rung.

My brother loved me, but he forgot to believe in me.

Another.

Jack told me I would have to save myself. He was not a hero, no knight in shining armour, but I was no damsel in distress and that was okay. Because he was mine. He was mine and our bond was ours and I told him I could do this, so I would. I would climb. I would rise. I would believe in myself for once in my fucking life. *I would not die here.*

Anger reinvigorated me, adrenaline coursed through my blood and I rose higher and higher. Each step was a task, each release of my hand the moment between life and death, but I pushed. I pushed and I sobbed and I grunted through every fresh spark of pain until finally, that lone torch at the very top flickered before me.

The hum got louder.

A stone ceiling creaked inches above my head, no trap door or opening in sight. I could have wailed, but that hum rattled my bones, chattering my teeth. The scent of rain and death grew so strong it strangled my lungs. And within the torch's dim light, I noticed a book.

It was the only one on the top shelf. Plain, with nothing but dark leather and flat metal etched into the spine, the title in a language I didn't recognize, but a moment later I realized it wasn't a language at all. They were runes.

The silver flashed and the hum grew stronger, nearly knocking me off the ladder. There was no way to truly know, no definitive sign it was the book I searched for, but I knew.

Gasping, I reached one trembling hand toward the leather. My fingers brushed the surface, and the hum instantly stopped.

The second Dianomican.

Choked laughter clawed up my throat. I found it. I honest to God found it. My skin was too dry to produce more perspiration, my muscles ached and my soul felt half to the grave, but I had the book. Now all I had to do was escape.

I pulled the book to my chest, swaying far enough from the ladder to stuff it in my waistcoat. But then the metal flashed, searing light into my eyes and blinding me. The humming began with renewed vigor, shaking my hands and body and threatening to topple me. I held on for dear life, blinking and blinking away the tears startling my eyes. My left foot slipped and my one hand bracing the rung grew damp. The metal slid beneath my fingers and I screamed. Images lingered before my eyes, watery and dark. My sight returned just in time to see my fingers slide to my middle knuckles, then to nothing but my finger pads.

I fell.

THIRTY-SIX

TIME STILLED. A SINGLE, beautiful moment passed where I remained in suspension, the rung hovering before my eyes and gravity not quite catching yet. Then my stomach sank with the free fall and I tumbled down, down, down.

I gripped the book close to my chest, screaming. The ceiling rushed farther away, hundreds of shelves flashing away in an instant. The book fell from my fingers and hovered above my chest, the metal glow illuminating the world as it rushed past. Blood roared in my ears and cries echoed in my throat, but the light grew brighter, smoother, *molten.*

I stared at the silver lettering. My eyes reflected back at me, bursting with fear.

The torches grew in number.

The floor rushed closer.

I focused on the metallic sheen. The dark leather surrounding it. My lips opened wide in the reflection, the ruptured arteries in my eyes. The silver moved in a single fluid motion, then the leather twisted and expanded into darkness. I watched my reflection, still screaming. Ten torches surrounded the turret and grains of stone brushed my back.

Everything went dark.

Liquefied.

Noise rushed past me, the feeling of water congealing and coursing over my skin. Endless black swirled against my skin and the feeling of free-falling dropped my chest. But I wasn't falling any more. I was in the shade.

I could have celebrated the fact I'd actually used magic, but all the warnings about shade travel entered the last remaining nerves in my brain. I had to think of somewhere to go. *Now.*

Lillian's compact.

I closed my eyes and pictured it. The smooth metal exterior, the intricate latch and the shimmering mirror beneath. I filled my mind with nothing but images of the compact, of Lillian holding it, of my own reflection staring back as she hovered it before my face. But then a horrifying thought occurred—if something happened to her, if Lorvellian found her first, then there was a chance the compact was gone forever. A chance the tiny mirror now resided deep inside the wyvern's gullet.

Thoughts of the dragon filled my mind, then the cavernous room and shimmering treasure trove. Images flitted past before I could stop them—Lorvellian tearing into flesh, the glistening rubies and golden throne toppling to the floor. Waves of golden coins undulating around its black scales, reflecting red from the blood splattering them.

My back hit something hard.

Breath whooshed from my lungs and exploding metal chimed in my ears. The gun hit the soft flesh of my belly and I sputtered. When I finally opened my eyes, gold coins surrounded me in every direction.

But directly above, was the still face of a dragon.

Yellow claws pierced the gold hills on either side of my face. Membranous wings stretched like massive curtains, sheltering me from the room. Lorvellian's dark eyes scoured me, black smoke billowing from his nostrils and streaming toward the ceiling. His maw opened wide, a deafening screech rattled the air and hundreds of blackened teeth bared down.

For all our weaknesses, there was something truly remarkable that happened when a human wanted to survive. All rational thoughts fled my brain. There was no sound, no color, no process of calculation as my hands folded around the tommy gun and aimed up. My finger squeezed the trigger and released a sound that could only come from hell.

Dozens of bullets sprayed the air. Lorvellian screeched, acrid blood leaking from his mouth and sizzling as it hit the coins. Five talons swept toward my face and I rolled down the mountain of gold.

A roar like a freight train trembled the walls. There was no time to think, no time to scan my surroundings. I grabbed the book where it fell on the ground beside me and ran.

Past the alcove leading to the library were more interconnected halls and doors. Unfortunately, they were large enough for a dragon to follow, but if I stayed among the gold I would never outrun him. I probably couldn't now. My lungs heated, constricting as I pushed my legs harder and faster than ever before. Coins clanged against the walls and another deafening roar bellowed along the walls.

Each doorway opened to another monstrous treasure trove or lined turret filled with objects I saw no use for: crystal balls, pelts, glittering jewels, among others. Besides the library there were no other ladders. No way up and no way out. If Lorvellian entered and exited by magic, I was dead.

Talons clicked along the floor, rushing closer. A blast of heat singed my back where the gun bounced against my spine. My arms pumped beside my body, the jacket tied around my waist coming loose and fluttering behind. Stones cracked and a monstrous howl erupted in my ears.

Entering the shade once was a nearly impossible feat, let alone finding my wait out of it. Attempting it twice with no training or clue how I managed the first time was a terrible risk, but my options were growing fewer. My legs slowed as my energy depleted, my swollen lungs barely taking enough breath. I couldn't outrun the dragon forever and I highly doubted I could kill it. There was only one way out of here, and it may cost my life.

I slowed to a stop, dropping to my knees and wrenching the book from my waistcoat. Lorvellian was nowhere in sight, but I could still hear him, the scraping strides dying to a hush. Either he thought I spontaneously died or he matched my pace. He was enjoying this. He wanted to hunt.

I settled the Thompson into my lap and pointed it down the hall, legs splayed in front of me to keep some balance. Not that it mattered—with the amount of rounds this thing blew in a minute, aiming wasn't a necessity. I grasped the book in one hand and the trigger in my other. In my peripheral, I could just see the darkened end of the hall. I focused on the silver lettering of the book.

It lay flat and dull this time, the hum absent and the leather unremarkable beneath my fingers. Maybe the book had finite powers and I just used the last of its reservoir. Or maybe what happened before was a one-in-a-million stroke of luck, but I had little time. The clicks grew louder, a snort of fumes and ash and a grumbling I could have sworn sounded like laughter. Sizzling droplets hit the ground, and I looked up and into the eyes of a wyvern.

He crowded the entire end of the hall. Black eyes shifted into a molten ruby. Dark blood sprayed from its maw and face, streaming onto the floor in rivulets. His jaws opened wide, a little spark igniting in the back of his throat. I breathed deep and focused on the book, but I couldn't so much as catch my own reflection.

Smooth, gold coins pebbled the floor. The spark in Lorvellian's gullet grew larger, roaring to flame He stalked closer, the heat of his body radiating down the floor. I stared at one of the coins, catching the fuzzy outlines of my eyes. The image was barely discernible, but

I could imagine the size of my pupils, the rich, brown color, the almond shape as I stared at my reflection on the coin's surface. The image grew stronger, the yellowed gold around it turning to liquid. I breathed faster, Lorvellian stalked closer and the liquid rushed like waves in a storm.

I could feel it—sap coursing over my skin, the smooth silkiness of the shade's air. Darkness closed my vision but I was still here, still in the hall. The heat was nearly unbearable now, my trembling fingers turning a deep shade of red. The fire in Lorvellian's throat swelled to the size of a car, a blast of flames and—

Darkness fell around me. The consequences would be severe if I was wrong, but I needed to find Lillian and Violet. If something happened to them. Casting any memories of the mirror lining the getaway car, I once again focused on Lillian's compact, the silver metal, the outline of her red curls framing the image . . .

I hit the floor of the safe.

Three, smooth steel walls reflected back at me. The mountain of cash was half burned. Lillian shook on her knees, fluttering around Violet who convulsed against the floor.

"Addie?" Her eyes went wide and she grabbed my arm, ripping me to the ground. "What just happened?"

I looked around. Everything looked exactly the same, except the burning hole in the floor was gone and Violet was mid-seizure. Her golden eyes rolled back in her head, foam forming at the edge of her lips. Darkness seeped around her in a circle Lillian avoided the edge of.

"I have the book," I said, throwing it to the ground. "What's wrong with Violet?"

Lillian snatched the Dianomican from the floor. "How did you find this? You were only gone for a moment!"

I shook my head. "I was gone for—nevermind, what's wrong with Violet?"

Lillian raked her hands through hair, destroying the delicate pomade. "I don't know, I've never seen this before. You disappeared and she just started shaking." Her fingers fluttered over Violet's arm. As soon as they made contact she cried out, wrenching back her now-blackened fingertips.

I grabbed her hand and pushed it into her lap. "How do we get her out of here?"

"I don't know, but I think the—"

Come out with your hands up. We have the building surrounded.

I stood on shaking legs, the strap of the Thompson dropping from my shoulder and clattering on the floor. The voice was dull, barely discernible through the flames crackling on cash and dense walls of the safe.

"Please tell me that wasn't the fucking police."

"Shit, shit, *shit*." Lillian reached for Violet again, only to come back with more necrotic wounds. The latter hadn't stopped shaking, the circle of black slowly enlarging around her. "I've never seen this before. I didn't think this could happen to fae, I—"

I tuned her out. I had a hunch, a horrible one that could be disastrous but it was all we had right now. "Get your compact out."

"We can't leave without Violet."

"Just do it, Lillian." I stared at Violet on the floor, my stomach churning. Jack had a poisonous touch too, but it didn't affect me as deeply because we were paralleled. I was human and much less resistant to powers than Lillian, so if I was wrong I could easily die, but we were running very, *very* low on options.

Screeching reverberated through the safe and the faint sound of flapping wings. Lillian paled.

"And that's the dragon," I said. "Dragon and police, get the compact and let's go."

She frowned, shaking so violently she dropped the compact as soon as it came from her pocket. I feared the mirror cracked, but she opened it with trembling hands and our faces glistened back. She grabbed my hand as the reflection started to swirl. I took a deep breath.

"The moment I touch Violet," I said.

She nodded, taking a shaky breath. My fingers trembled above Violet's hand, too many thoughts swirling through my brain. My skin met hers and I screamed in pain, but didn't let go. Darkness encased us and my feet hit the sidewalk.

The sun blazed down, not a cloud in the sky. The city street was quiet, no other pedestrians in sight. The car idled in front of us with the mirror's glint reflecting through the window, but Driver was nowhere to be seen.

Awareness pricked my skin. I looked up. Seven sets of eyes landed on me—six cops and Driver between them, hands cuffed behind his back.

For a moment, the only sound was chirping birds, a crisp autumn breeze and leaves scattering the sidewalk.

A bullet tinged off the driver's side. Lillian cursed, wrenching the back door open. My burned fingers ached, but the wounds were only red and raw, not black like Lillian's. I threw a silent, unconscious Violet in the back and Lillian fell into the driver's seat. A second bullet hit the headlight and glass exploded onto the road. Cops yelled for one another, drawing their weapons and forming the beginning of a barricade. Violet lay across the backseat and I'd have to cross the car to get to the passenger side. I kicked the door shut, jumped on the step bar, grabbed the top railing and pounded the driver door. "*Go.*"

Lillian floored the gas and I lurched to the side, still hanging off the side of the car and swaying violently. After an hour hanging off a ladder my arms screamed in agony, but I pressed closer to the door and hung on for dear life. The cops shouted, jumping out of the way as Lillian barrelled past them.

Sirens sounded immediately, the screech of wheels as they turned and followed us in high-speed pursuit. Lillian stomped on the gas, sending us to speeds that had my brain rattling in my skull.

"Fuck," she screamed over the wind. "Fuck, fuck, *fuck*."

I would have done the same had I not been breathlessly holding on. We hit an alleyway and I pressed against the metal, screaming as gravel-lined bricks raced inches away from my back. The spare drum hanging off my waist hit an electrical box and scattered bullets across the road.

She made a hard left at the end of the road, veering us onto a busy street. Two cars honked and swerved out of the way and a group of women with parasols screeched in the passing wind. Two police cars appeared behind us, one of the cops leaning out the passenger window with a rifle.

"Duck down!" Lillian screamed, but it was too late. She swerved the car and a bullet hit the back window, only inches from my waist. More cars veered out of the way and I flattened against the metal, attempting to make myself as thin a target as possible. A bullet whooshed past my back, tearing the fabric of my billowing waistcoat. Cold air rushed against my skin and I released one hand from the rail. The Thompson was gone, left behind in the safe. But I still had the little hand pistol.

The car rattled so hard I feared I'd be thrown off. Lillian swerved through the increasing traffic, cursing before putting us in a dizzying tailspin, and crossed the dividend. The world spun in nauseating colors and sound, then she floored the gas on the opposite side of the road, taking us back toward the bank.

I pulled the pistol from my holster just in time. We passed the two cop cars, the gunman leaning out the side with his own weapon pointed at me. I raised the pistol and fired off a shot, poisoned fingers burning against the trigger. I missed by several feet, but it was enough to force him down. The cars made sharp turns behind us and weaved through the lanes.

"Did you just shoot at the police?" Lillian screamed out the window.

"They shot first!"

Bullets sprayed the back of the car. The little pistol only held six rounds and I had already used one of them. Lillian stopped swerving, just long enough for me to aim. I lowered the gun and fired a round at the front wheel of the closest car.

Popping rubber resounded across the road and the car swung to the side, rolled on a metal rim and came to a standstill. But there was no time to celebrate, because the second car was still in hot pursuit and Violet went ram-rod straight in the backseat.

Our eyes met through the glass window, both sets wide and fixed on one another. Sweat dripped down her forehead and her skin was pale. She pulled herself up with a trembling hand and screamed. "*Jack.*"

Another bullet passed through the back window, just missing Violet's erect body and burying itself in the glove compartment. I aimed for the tires again but missed. An enraged voice called out, "What the fuck is happening?"

My blood singed, skin heating as the bond roared to life. Lillian swerved and I swayed dangerously to the side, catching a pair of golden eyes, wide with horror, staring at me through the window.

"Why is she on the *outside of the fucking car*?"

"Because shit went wrong, Jack. Shit went *very wrong.*"

"Jack," Violet moaned. She reached for the front seat and he grabbed her hand, shaking her. "What's wrong?"

"Something with the magic. She tried to bypass the wards with blood so they wouldn't trigger and I think it—"

Too many bullets to count sprayed the trunk. One missed me by inches, or so I thought because a thin line of blood bubbled along my arm.

It's just a graze. It's just a graze. It's just a graze. I raised the pistol and fired, but missed once again. The cops gained speed and the traffic thickened, slowing us down.

Jack grabbed Lillian by her sweat-stained waistcoat, wrenching her away from the wheel. They switched spots in a blink, but it was enough time to send the car into a tailspin. The passenger mirror broke into hundreds of pieces against another vehicle's door. I held on to the rail with both hands and the pistol slipped from my grip.

"Get them out of here," Jack said.

"I've been driving a car, you'll be lucky if I can shade one of them!"

Violet still shook, wide, fevered eyes bouncing around the cabin. "Get Violet to Will, now. I'll shade with Jack."

Violet moaned and Lillian nodded. The two blinked from sight and Jack's serpent eyes met mine through the side mirror, furious.

I shimmied to the back of the vehicle, rolling into the backseat moments before another spray of bullets hit. Jack ducked his head down and I curled into a ball against the glass mirror.

I screamed over the roaring wind, "You're not supposed to be here."

"If Violet could reach me, it meant something was very fucking wrong." He swerved around a cluster of horn-blaring cars.

I gripped his headrest and shook it. "Just shade us out now, let the car crash."

"So the cops can report everyone in the car disappeared? The Knights will be on us in five minutes."

Fuck, I didn't even think of that. "Where are we going?"

"The second getaway car. Unless you have a better plan."

I looked behind us. The police were even closer now. A second getaway hardly mattered if they followed us, but I had no better plan.

He cursed under his breath and veered right, taking us off the main road and dipping into another alley. It threw the cops off enough that they lost distance, but we veered onto a new road and they were already on us again. Streets, billboards, open-mouthed people at busy intersections and swerving cars passed in a hazy blur. My heart pounded in my chest, my thoughts eddying between how black and white stripes would favor my skin tone and if we could actually pull this off. We swung into another alley and Jack slammed the brakes, throwing his door open and gesturing for me to do the same. He grabbed me around the waist and faced the side mirror, but something stopped him. The thick edge of the Dianomican peeked out from my waistcoat, vibrating against both our chests as he pulled me to him.

"Is that—"

We fell into the shade before he could finish. Darkness blanketed us, but within a blink a new roof hovered over our heads. We were parked in a different alley and all the mirrors and windows were intact. The second getaway.

Jack took a steadying breath, fury rolling off him in his waves. We were both in the backseat, staring forward. "Let's just go home."

I nodded, freezing as police sirens wailed too close. Jack cursed and closed his eyes, whispering something in his native language. "Maybe not."

A police car rolled into the alley with keening sirens. The headlights illuminated the shaded road. Jack looked normal enough, but I was still in men's clothes. Men's clothes coated in blood and torn by passing bullets. The graze against my arm bubbled with blood, leaking into what remained of Jack's shirt.

There was no time to shade again. The car rolled closer, a cop with a megaphone screaming to remain still.

"Just let me do all the talking," he said. "Stay in the car, cover that wound on your arm . . ."

A second car entered the opposite end of the alley, blocking us in. My breath came quicker, an idea forming in my head. "Lay across the seat."

"What?"

He was too shocked to react as I grabbed him by the waistcoat and shoved him down. Then I ripped off my waistcoat and shirt, sending buttons flying across the cabin. I threw those in the front and shimmied out of my trousers. They were men's clothes on the outside, but I still had women's undergarments underneath.

Jack's eyes went wide, feral, his skin heating where my thigh brushed his arm. I climbed on top of him and straddled his waist, ripping into his waistcoat and shirt that fit far better on him than me. Then I undid his belt buckle and pants, pushing them down enough to see the gray boxers underneath. All at once the bond snapped, roaring between us in a tidal wave. I forgot where I was, what we were doing. The touch of his bare skin against my knees intoxicated me, sending reminders of the last time I was half undressed before him, the feeling of his tongue sliding inside me. Shivers coasted down my spine and his eyes flashed with crumbling glamour. He propped his head against the car door and grabbed my waist, pulling me down on his rock-hard erection.

"*Annwyl,*" he moaned. My mouth went dry, the feeling of his cock pressed against me the only thing my mind could comprehend. His boxers and my lace panties separated us and I was desperate, grinding against him for any sense of feeling.

He grabbed the strap of my bralette and pulled me down, taking my lips in one heated movement. His tongue slid across mine and I moaned against him. The window above his head fogged, the car shaking as he thrusted against me, tugging at my underwear. I ran my hands down his chest, panting, moaning, biting his lower lip until he made that heady groan I loved and pressed closer until even air didn't separate us.

The car door opened. Jack's head fell back, giving him an upside-down view of the two cops standing outside the door, pistols pointed in our faces. My eyes widened, skin going cold despite the heat rolling off the man beneath me. The cops paled, eyes oscillating between me, my exposed breasts and Jack's savage scowl as he stared up at both of them.

"Put your hands in the air?"

Jack hissed, grabbed the car door handle above his head and slammed it shut.

THIRTY-SEVEN

"WE'RE DEEPLY SORRY ABOUT the . . . interruption," the captain said. Jack stood before him, a cigarette bobbing between his lips. I leaned against one of the police cars wrapped in a blanket. Jack had enough time to glamour away the men's clothes and make an illusionary dress for me, but it was only strong enough to appear that way, so I was still technically naked in the cold November air. I'd shaken enough one of the officers offered me an emergency blanket they kept in the trunk.

Usually Jack garnered all the attention in a room, but five out of the seven officers studied me, all but the captain and a squirming man beside him listening to Jack twist all their words back at them. What began as interrogations turned into tickets for undressing me in public, which somehow turned into the entire unit profusely apologizing for the mix-up. While he worked his literal and figurative magic I ignored the curious and leering stares of the other officers. Between the newspaper clipping, my brother's reports and finding us now, I'm sure they were dying to find out how much I knew. How easy it would be to break me down if they could separate me from Jack.

Thankfully, Jack hadn't allowed that. He finished his conversation and placed a hand on the small of my back, guiding me back to our vehicle. As he opened my door for me another car entered the alley, bouncing as it traversed the uneven, pot-holed terrain. He shut my door and circled around to the driver's side. The cops approached the new vehicle, instructing them to move out of the way. Someone waved a badge from the driver's side and they pulled over.

Jack revved the engine and I kept my eyes down. The last thing I wanted was to give the new arrivals any reason to question us too. I shook in the cold and Jack reached down, removing one glove to caress my thigh. It had a dual effect, both warming my chilled skin and something much deeper.

Four men exited the new car. We rolled past them. I recognized the driver immediately, Agent Rodney who had questioned me at the hotel. His gray hair shimmered in the mid-afternoon, the red and white medallion peeking from the top of his waistcoat. Two of the men I didn't recognize, but it was the fourth that froze my blood.

Tommy exited the passenger door, leaning against the brick wall. He scanned the car, Jack, and his eyes settled on me. No surprise, not even a flicker of recognition or shock as our eyes aligned through the glass. Neither of us moved. My chest cracked open, a hairline fracture all my emotions rushed for at once, but in the end I kept them locked away, hidden behind my breastbone. The invisible wound closed and I looked away. For once, my brother had to come second.

I didn't look back as we pulled onto the street.

I DRESSED AS SOON as we reached the hotel. Lillian popped in briefly to report Violet was doing much better, currently resting at Will's apartment where he could monitor her the next few days. In as few words as possible, I explained what happened with Lorvellian, keeping some of the more gruesome details to myself before Jack could blow his top. I'd tell him about both of my shading experiences later. Neither had an answer for the distortion in time I seemed to experience, but neither seemed concerned either. I supposed that's what centuries of power and magic did to the fae psyche.

Like he sensed our discussion, a fae man arrived with a letter, which detailed the extensive plans Lorvellian had to hunt us and the excruciating things he would do when we were found. My skin paled, blood running cold, but Jack only rolled his eyes and said he'd "add it to the rest." *The rest* was a toppling pile of papers hidden beneath his desk, presumably more death threats.

The second Dianomican lay silent and cold on the coffee table. Since our little endeavor together, it hadn't shown the faintest flicker of magic. Had I seen it anywhere else, I would presume it was an exceptionally crafted, but very ordinary book. Lillian circled the table warily, finally declared she would take it to Arthur and see what he could find, and blinked from the room. That left Jack and me in stark silence, sitting beside one another on the settee, giving the wall thousand-yard stares.

"Well that was fucking shit." His head rolled against the cushion to face me. "Want to get drunk?"

"IT STILL LOOKS LIKE a dog," I said.

"Shit, you're right," he mumbled. I laughed. He adjusted his hands, and the blackened leaves hovering between them. We lay side by side on the floor in a nest of blankets and pillows fit for royalty. The fire crackled at our feet. For the past hour, he'd been attempting to use crumbled leaves and glamour to form a floating, miniature tiger between his palms. I took voracious joy in his lack of artistry.

He scrapped the whole thing and began again. "So you just . . . entered? One moment you saw some movement and the next, in the shade?"

"Essentially," I said, propping myself on one elbow and taking a long sip of my wine. "Is that not how it's supposed to work? Whenever I do it with someone else it feels like one moment I'm in this world and the next I'm just not."

"It's different for everyone, but I have never heard of that before." He formed the legs first, darker and lighter leaf fragments forming monochrome stripes. "For example, I need to step in, if that makes sense. Or reach a piece of my physical body toward the mirror. Then it feels like being sucked inside."

"That's horrifying."

"The shade is horrifying, darling." He grinned, flicking his eyes toward me. The tiger's legs shattered and debris billowed into the rug. "On the fucking fates."

I tried to stifle my laughter, releasing a horrible snort instead. His grin grew wider and I waved at him. "Shouldn't something like that be simple for you?"

"In my defense, I have only seen a tiger once and it was a hundred and seventy years ago." He gathered all the leaf fragments in the air and snapped them from existence. "How about you give it a try?"

"Absolutely not. It's far more entertaining watching you."

He propped himself up to face me. "Because I'm terrible?"

"Awful," I said around a grin.

"A spectacular disaster," he agreed, still smiling. He took another sip of his own drink, some dark liquor I thought may be safe for humans, but he flicked my hand away when I went to try it. That was about four drinks ago.

"I don't get it," I said.

"Why I can't make a tiger?"

"No," I said, slapping his arm. I was too tipsy to invoke any true damage. "Shading is supposed to be the most difficult. I can't even compulse your house decor, so how I was able to —" I waved my hands in the air dramatically. "Do you think it was because I had the book?"

"Possibly." He sipped his drink again, more pensive this time. "Still doesn't seem right, but we are in uncharted territory."

"Ain't that the truth." I pushed to my knees, finishing my glass. Jack snapped and it instantly refilled. He lay on his back, arms behind his head, and stared at me. Maybe it was the alcohol, but his eyes glimmered a little brighter, the corner of his lips a permanent upward slant. I couldn't help but remember the feeling of his bare chest beneath my hands, the warmth of his lips caressing mine. My cheeks flushed and I glanced away, praying he didn't catch a flicker of that through the bond.

"I am drunk," I declared.

"Hello, drunk," he murmured. The low tone made me flush hotter. My drunken brain was tempted to kiss him again, but the rational side intervened first. The last time we attempted such a thing, we'd almost been unable to stop. Tonight, we had both been drinking and that was clouding my better judgment. And we weren't in this position because he was my lover, but for one reason only. The same reason I put in our contract outside of our one-time obligation—we required nothing else of one another.

The lines were blurring, and not just from the alcohol. I knew he cared about my well-being, and truthfully, I cared for his. I may always have my lurking fear, but in moments like these all I could picture were our nights shared in dreams, then our nights shared in reality.

But that was a dangerous line of thinking. There was too much hanging in the balance—the fate of my kind and the curse hovering over my head, not to mention the need he had for the Morrigan to make him stronger. Becoming further entangled with Jack outside of business held too much risk at the moment.

But I could indulge a little. We were stuck together for the time being, anyway. "So now there's nothing left but the curse and blessing."

He nodded, instantly somber. "I know where to get the blessing. It's the curse I'm still working on."

"I find it hard to believe receiving a blessing is less difficult than a curse."

"Not entirely." He swirled the liquor around his glass. "There are plenty of curse options, but I'm trying to mitigate some of the expected damage."

"How do you mean?"

"I don't want anything to truly hurt you."

My heart fluttered in my chest. I willed it to silence. "If it can be helped, you mean."

His rapt attention fell on me. "No, ever."

I chewed my bottom lip, avoiding his heavy look. Sipped my wine. "Let's talk of something else. I already had a shit day."

"Mine wasn't too bad. Mostly, I drank with Will and Arthur."

"Lucky you," I drawled. He laughed, inching closer to me. I fell back on my side, ignoring how lovely the heat from his body felt pressing close to mine.

His hand landed on the rug between us. I traced my fingers over his, over the black ink across his knuckles. "What was your world like?"

"I thought we were aiming for lighter topics?"

"It couldn't have been all bad." My eyes flicked to his, and they refuted the six words I just said. "You don't have to tell me."

"No, it's not that. It is . . ." He shrugged, following my tracings as I finished the first line of letters at his pinky, circling back to his index finger. "It was very long ago."

"When did you come here?" I wasn't sure why I asked so many questions, why the answers mattered to me. But Jack already knew so much about my life, from everything he witnessed to what I told him in my dreams. I was curious and the wine loosened my tongue. He was so unique. I wanted to know what made him that way.

"Very young, as far as fae go." He closed his eyes. "It was the 1600's, so do with that what you will."

Hundreds of years. Hundreds. "Have you visited many places in this world?"

"Many."

"What was your favorite?"

He gave a noncommittal shrug, then a small smile. "Depends on the century."

"I despise you," I said, slapping the top of his fingers. His smile stretched wider, showing several teeth. "I've never been anywhere but Georgia and here. Meanwhile, you've probably plodded across the entire world, biding your time."

"And you will have the same opportunity." He flipped my hand upside down, lacing his fingers through mine.

If we survived this. As soon as I helped him kill another living being. Even knowing what Delsaran was, it felt an undeserved reward for such a gruesome task.

"I must seem so young to you." The words slipped out before I could stop them, but it was too late to take them back. "All those years, all those places you've seen, everything you must know by now. I must be an infant in comparison."

"Yes and no. Immortality makes one stagnant." He paused, his fingers squeezing mine. "That is part of why I like humans so much. You have finite time, so there is no room for complicity. Humans move so quickly, every few decades it is a completely new world. To survive here is constant adaptation. I am always learning, same as you. Besides, I think of you as an old soul."

"I like that." I slipped my fingers from his and tucked them beneath my waist. The feeling was too comfortable, warm and tempting. I stood, stretching my arms above my head. "And coming from a four-hundred-year-old man, I'd say that was quite the compliment."

He smirked. "Would you like more of them?"

"I would, but you're too old for me."

A pillow smacked me in the chest. I gasped, feigning shock, but his unruly grin had me bursting into giggles.

I slumped back to the ground. "So, is this what you do all day when there're no all-powerful druids to kill?"

"Why, are you enjoying yourself?'

"It's not the worst thing." I shot him a lazy grin. "But, really, what do you like to do? It can't all be drunken nights with women and crime."

"Drunken nights with *woman* and crime are very satisfying to me."

I rolled my eyes, but heat blossomed behind my ribs. "I'm serious, there has to be something you like."

"Hm." He rolled onto his side. "It's a secret."

I grinned. "Well, now I'm only more intrigued."

"Promise not to tell anyone."

I placed a hand over my heart. "I promise to tell absolutely everyone. Including *Society Talk*."

He blew out a short breath, capturing a smile between his sharp teeth. "I like going to the movie theater."

I sat up, incredibly intrigued. "Really?"

He nodded. "Absolutely love it."

"But you can do *magic*."

"It's not as exciting after several centuries."

"Huh." I sank back to the floor, clutching a pillow to my chest. "You know, that is the last thing I thought you would say."

A lazy smile fell on me. "What do you like to do?"

I hiccuped, pressing the back of my hand to my mouth. "Um, well. Definitely not the movies. I've never actually seen one—"

I gasped as he wrenched my pillow away, rolling on top of me and pinning my arms to the floor. "You have never seen a movie?"

"No—what are you doing?" I burst into a fit of alcohol-induced laughs as he rubbed his nose against mine. "Addie, I am four hundred fucking years old and I see a movie once a week. What the hell have you been doing with your life?"

"I don't know—oh god, you're crushing me."

He pushed up, no longer flattened against my chest. "We are going to see one. Right now."

I paused. "What? It's ten p.m. I'm drunk, you're drunk, we can't just—"

"Right now," he declared, pushing to his feet. "Get your coat on. Do your lipstick or whatever else women do, you have five minutes."

"*Five minutes*? Jack, I'm not—"

"No, I will not be denied this." He pointed at the Abstruse, then the mirror. "Five minutes, or I'm taking you in your house clothes."

THIRTY-EIGHT

MY TOES TOUCHED THE rain-soaked sidewalk, my burgundy coat fluttering around me. Jack's arm held tightly around my waist, his face entirely too close as he leaned in. "You lost your hat."

I turned, watching the red and white flowers tumble halfway down the block. "Oh, shoot. I suppose I'll be improper tonight."

"That's my favorite way to have you." He nuzzled into my neck, kissed my cheekbone and pushed away. His hand slipped down my arm and wrapped around my fingers. Next thing I knew, he tugged me over wet pavement into the bustling street.

Umbrellas flickered toward the sky and headlights caught the rain. I laughed, holding a hand above my head but was soaked within moments anyway. Jack threw his jacket around me and ushered us around several street corners, stopping before an enormous building, tiered like a cake and stretching to the sky. A marquee flashed with golden letters, pronouncing the color of his eyes as we rushed inside.

I paused in the entryway, taking in the overwhelming sights and sounds. If I thought the theater looked like a palace, it was nothing compared to this. The monstrosity was called the Paramount, and the designer truly took that name to heart with each opulent detail.

Marble floors ran beneath our feet and gold embellishments laced the walls. An absurdly large crowd swarmed the gilded ticket booths for this hour, people caught between throwing nickels at the ushers and gawking at the performances dotting the lobby. In one corner, a woman sang on a velvet-wrapped dais while in another, a group of circus men breathed fire before a group of bewildered children. Men in tuxedos ferried drinks and food on silver trays, couples argued about which picture to see and through foggy glass, a cigar room exploded with smoke and laughter. I grinned at Jack. "This is insanity."

"They don't call them movie palaces for nothing." He smiled back, clearly satisfied with himself, and pushed aside grumbling patrons for the ticket booth. It was obvious who recognized him and who didn't, judging by who profusely apologized or told him to get back in line. The teller turned three shades of scarlet when we appeared and I couldn't help but laugh. Jack gave him ten cents and we were on our way.

The woman left her dais and was immediately replaced by a five-man. The firebreathers on the other side made way for a woman in a sparkly suit, dangling from a spinning hoop suspended in the air. I stopped to watch her, but Jack pushed me forward like an ecstatic child.

"We missed the vignettes they play in the beginning, but we are just in time for the first showing, and they usually do another performance before the second film comes on. And before you ask, yes, we are staying here well into the early hours of the morning because you need the full experience, and I will accept nothing less."

"Whatever he wants," I said, grinning. Wine fogged my brain, but it was slowly clearing away. Jack delivered our tickets to an exhausted usher, who showed us our seats in the dark theater. I could barely see my hand in front of my face but Jack moved without thought, helping me into my seat. Lights scattered the floor and surrounded a stage with a full opera pit beneath. Above them, the largest screen known to mankind stretched from the platform to a vaulted ceiling. The auditorium itself easily held several thousand, with children running between the aisles, a balcony teeming with people and endless rows of plush seats, all filled by dark silhouettes. Jack took my hand in his, a flash of his teeth glimmering in the low lights. I only then realized he had left his cane at home.

I smiled back, laying my head on his shoulder.

The screen flickered to life and applause filled the theater. Grainy numbers counted down to zero, then a monochrome title—*Nosferatu, a symphony of horror.* I shifted closer to Jack as the credits began, nothing more than a succession of pictures, one after another. I wondered if the whole movie would be lapsed still-shots, actors moving in jerky motions from one picture to the next.

The opening credits ended and I gasped. It began with an overview of a bustling town from the peak of a church tower. People scurried along on the street before it faded to a man fixing his bowtie in a mirror. There was nothing jerky or awkward about it. They were actually moving, as if we were watching reality in sepia tones.

"It looks so real. How did they do that?" I whispered.

Jack placed a hand on my knee, rubbing little circles over my dress. "Just wait. This is a good one."

The orchestra took up the background music. They must have had every object imaginable down there, because they included sounds as they appeared in the film—tolling bells, smacking doors, rattling china and everything in between. Before long, even the energetic children found their seats, absorbed by the mirage of movement and sound. No one spoke, neither in the theater nor in the film, but there was no need. Everything was conveyed through movements and music, facial expressions and body language. Just like ballet.

Nosferatu himself appeared in a doorway and I jumped, grasping Jack's arms. His shoulder shook with silent laughter beneath my cheek. The orchestra's music swelled, discordant and horrifying as Nosferatu stalked his prey. My pulse raced, palms sweaty, but I couldn't look away.

Jack leaned down, brushing his lips against my ear. "Adeline, don't tell me you are actually *scared* right now."

"Of course I am, look at him. He's terrifying," I whispered back.

Jack brought the back of his hand to his lips, smothering a laugh. "You saw more terrifying things on your way to breakfast this morning."

"Charlene is only scary when she breaks her spoon out. And her sous chef is a bit frightening, but this is something else."

He slid lower in his seat, beaming at me. "You're not serious, are you?"

I narrowed my eyes at him. "I bet this was all a part of your plan. Take me to the horror showing so I'm scared enough to jump in your lap."

The next scene was a woman in bed. The doors to her balcony blew open in an ominous wind. She rose, slowly, and ambled forward as if in a trance.

"Oh no, don't do that," I whispered.

Jack stretched his arm around my shoulders, tugging me closer. "You are exactly right. I, the four hundred-year-old inhuman creature from another world, assumed my human partner—one who has encountered a phooka and wyvern—would be so terrified of Nosferatu she would be eating out of the palm of my hand."

"It was a highly effective plan," I breathed.

We watched the rest of the movie in silence. By the end I was practically in his lap, but he didn't have a single complaint. In fact, after they showed several short advertisements—*commercials,* Jack explained—a comedy vignette about two brothers in a toy shop, and the second movie began, I tried returning to my seat. He held me firmly in place, one arm around my waist and the other stroking my hair. Halfway through the second film I realized he wasn't watching at all, but noting all of my reactions with a smile on his face.

So I laughed extra loud at all the jokes, gasped at the dramatic scenes and swooned when the two lovers finally kissed. If movies made him happy, then I would give them my full attention. He did that for me, watching me dance at the Cotton Club, so I'd do it for him too.

It was just past two a.m. when the showing was done. Rain came down in thick sheets. Orange and yellow leaves blew past in a frigid wind, but I asked Jack if we could walk home anyway. He was more than happy to indulge me, grasping my hand as I babbled on.

"I definitely liked the second one better. What was it called, again?"

"For Heaven's Sake."

"It was so enchanting. I liked the funny bits, but the romance was the best part."

He rolled his eyes with a small laugh. "Of course you liked the romance."

"Let me guess, you are more of a horror fan?"

"War, horror, crime, thrillers," he said, counting each one off on his fingers.

I grinned. "As if you don't get enough of that on a daily basis."

"Nothing beats the real thing." He gripped my waist, helping me over a large puddle. I stumbled on the landing, planting a hand on his chest.

My soaked hair flopped into my eyes and he brushed it back. A dark alley surrounded us, smoke drifting from the rooftops and raindrops chiming against steaming pipes. A steady tide of water streamed from broken gutters and iron fire escapes above our heads. Through foggy windows, candles burned to stubs in residents' windows.

"Did you have a good night?" I asked.

His lips pitched up. A small nod. His hands never left my waist.

"I still can't believe you're a closet cinephile. Don't get me wrong, I love it, but to think the infamous Jack Warren spends all his nickels at the movie palace."

He squinted his eyes and flicked water in my direction. I laughed, shaking the extra droplets from my hair like a dog.

"Like I said earlier, immortality gets stagnant."

I smiled, adjusting his soaked collar. His tie was a lost cause, so drenched the knot hung loose halfway down his chest. "Well, magic fascinates me. It all fascinates me, so it's incredible to think our trite little human inventions would do the same to you."

"That's why I like it so much." His hands tightened on my waist, thumbs doing lovely little circles against my hip bones. "Humans do not have powers or immortality, nothing that the fae need to survive. But not only do you survive, you make music and write plays and invent new ways to make day-to-day tasks easier. You are all so . . . imaginative." He grinned, tapping my forehead. "You cannot use glamour to make clothes, so you began with needle and thread and moved to sewing machines. Or you did not have the ability to shade, so you domesticated horses, then turned to cars. Humans cannot steal memories or use divination, so you invented the camera. Then you took the camera, refined it to take hundreds of photos in a minute, and all of a sudden we can sit in a theater and watch people tell a story from another time. If that's not magic, I'm not sure what is."

A torrent of rain came down, spraying the pavement in a tidal wave. The sound beat against the bricks and balconies like a symphony, accompanied by the wind. Our hair ran into our faces and our skin was pale with cold, but an inexplicable warmth expanded in my chest, a lovely hearth flickering to life. A tug.

"I'm glad it was you," I whispered.

He nodded. "If you want, it can always be."

A million thoughts flooded my head, but I heard none of them.

He kissed me.

402

I waited for a sunlit field, swaying peonies and a warm breeze playing on my skin. Those things never came, but the rain did. The chill settling along my muscles, water sluicing down my face, a frigid wind and the smell of smoke, but most of all, Jack's warm hands cupping my cheeks. The soft feel of his lips over mine, the taste of him filling my mouth. I pushed to my toes, raking my hands through his silky hair. His heavy breaths matched mine, our chests beating hard against one another.

"*Annwyl*," he breathed. Warmth grew, spreading through my veins and evaporating in my blood. His hands tightened around me, body flush with mine and my toes lifted off the pavement. I felt lighter than air, effervescent, *alive*. I took his top lip between my teeth and the feeling swelled to the sky.

"Addie?" His lips stopped moving, his hands firm on my waist but still as stone. I opened my eyes and gasped, wiggling my toes in the air.

I was . . . floating.

Just a few inches off the ground, but the pavement lay beneath my feet and open air, putting me at eye-level with Jack. I laughed, grasping his jacket as I suddenly moved upward. My toes brushed his knees, my wide eyes stuck on the ground.

"What are you doing?" I asked.

He grinned. "I'm not doing anything. This is all you."

I held onto his hands for dear life, but I couldn't stop laughing. "Goodness, how do I get down?"

He gave my hands a gentle tug, but instead of me coming down, he drifted up.

"Shit." He released one hand and pawed at open space, tilting back as he scrambled mid-air. I laughed, grabbing his waistcoat and yanking him against me. We hovered near the top of a doorframe, then slowly drifted up, up, up.

He wrapped his arms around my waist and squeezed. "I suppose we will go with it, then." And he kissed me again.

And again.

And again.

I laughed in between breaths, beaming in the spaces his lips left mine. We drifted past the first set of balconies, the second, the third. I saw knick-knacks in windows, people tucked safely into their beds. Children reading stories beside waning candles and lovers tight in each other's arms. The rain came down, refracted by the light of all those warm, little homes. Jack softened the kiss just enough to whisper, "You were all I ever wanted."

We stopped drifting.

We dropped.

A scream lurched in my throat, but Jack grabbed my face and looked directly into my eyes. Cool liquid and darkness rushed past and we landed on the ground with a quiet thump.

I bumped my head against his, palming his chest as I breathed hard on top of him. He was flat against the road, wide eyes meeting mine.

We both laughed so hard, the rain stopped before Jack could shade us home.

THIRTY-NINE

FOLLOWING MORNING, I woke with possibly the worst hangover of my entire life. Jack wordlessly handed me a foul concoction of things I didn't wish to know, but when I sipped the tonic it tasted like strawberries. When I narrowed my eyes and asked if he glamoured the taste, he stuffed his hands in his pockets and found the ceiling exquisite.

Lillian popped in around noon and asked if we wanted to visit Violet, who was still resting at Will's. Despite the persistent headache I wanted to see if she had been doing better, so I declined Jack's offer to stay behind. The shade rushed past the three of us and we landed in a spotless living room.

When I said spotless, I truly meant spotless. The checkered tiles of Will's den were free of any scuffs, the grout boasting a fresh shine. All the furniture was polished and free from dust, arranged in perfect right angles. The mirror we shaded through refracted the midday light into a fire hazard on the perfectly plumped sofa. The only living thing was a single potted fern. I watched with fascination as a brown leaf broke from the stem and disappeared the moment it hit the floor.

"Hello, can everyone please remove their shoes?" Will rushed in from an adjoined kitchen, hands outstretched like we came to rob the place. I shot a questioning look at Jack, who only shook his head and gestured at my feet.

"Thank you, thank you. And Lillian, please I know you like to fix your makeup, but do you think you could powder in the hall?"

Lillian snapped her compact shut, shoving it in her purse. "Anything for you, Will."

"Where is Violet?"

"The bedroom," Will said. I could have sworn there was a suppressed shudder, but he said nothing as Jack drifted past him. I decided to give the twins a moment alone. "Your home is lovely, Will."

"Oh, thank you. I'm very particular about my space." He pushed past me, picking a piece of lint off a throw pillow.

"You do an excellent job." I smiled, gesturing around. "You know, it actually reminds me a bit of Arthur's apartment."

Feral eyes snapped to me. "Please, tell me that was a joke."

I giggled, not having time to answer before there was a steady knock on the door. Will hung his head. "Arthur, for the love of the fucking gods it's been two-hundred years. You don't need to knock."

Arthur poked his head in, body still obscured by the door. "Oh, Adeline. What a lovely surprise."

I gave him a little wave, peering around him for Lillian in the hall, but she was nowhere in sight. "Did you see Lillian out there?"

"Oh, right. I think she said she needed to shade out for a moment." He turned so hard he knocked his cheek on the door, sending his glasses askew. Will looked ready to combust beside me.

"Just come in," he said, defeated. He grabbed Arthur's arms, stopping him on a perfect, square tile before the sofa. The druid grinned, oblivious to the high fae patting the stains off his suit.

"Arthur, this is your tile. You are one of my best mates and I appreciate you endlessly, but I will have a fucking stroke if you move from your tile. So I am begging you, until you visit Violet, stay on your Bogoran-forsaken tile."

Arthur nodded. "Of course. And what a lovely tile to be on." He turned in a circle, nearly taking Will's head off with his swinging arms.

Jack stepped out of the bedroom, nodding at the door. "Addie, she wants to talk to you."

Surprise flickered through me, but I nodded. Will was in the middle of sweeping the floor space around Arthur as I knocked on the bedroom door.

"On the fucking fates, not you too. Just come in."

I shut the door behind me, sinking into a chair next to the bed. Will's bedroom was as immaculate as the rest of his home, except for the very annoyed fae woman reclined on his sheets. The nightstand beside her teemed over with elixirs, half-eaten food and several books, all with snapped spines. She dog-eared a page on the one she currently held, snake eyes falling on me.

"How are you feeling?"

She lifted a shoulder. "I'm not dead."

I nodded. "That's always a silver lining."

"You are fucking telling me." She rolled onto her side, placing her hands beneath her head. "I feel fine but Will won't let me go home yet. I swear he's worse than Lillian sometimes."

"He's just worried. We were all surprised." I paused. "Speaking of that, did he ever confirm what happened?"

She sighed. "Like Lillian said, I tried to bypass the wards with blood, but ended up poisoning myself instead. Guess you are not the only one who is an idiot, sometimes."

My lips tilted up in a half-smile. "You know, I have been meaning to mention something to you." She frowned, but waved an airy hand at me. "In the bank, you told me if I fainted, you would leave me to die. And all I am saying is, you totally fainted and I saved your ass."

Her eyes narrowed, mouth set in a hard line. Then the corner of her lips twitched, trembling as she held in a laugh. "I fucking hate you."

"I fucking hate you too, Violet."

"Good, glad we are on the same page." She grinned, flopping back to the bed. "Alright, I need you to be useful for once. Will has me on a steady diet of medicine and shit, but I know he keeps liquor stocked in the kitchen."

Ah, so that was what she needed me for. At least she was feeling back to herself. "Anything in particular?"

"Whatever has the most alcohol in it."

I patted her leg, quietly padding into the living room where the three men spoke in low whispers. They paid me no mind as I snuck into Will's cabinets, found the highest-proof gin I could, and returned to the bedroom.

She reached out for it, but I held it away. "The reaction you had to the ward wouldn't have anything to do with you shading the other day, would it?"

She rolled her eyes, but remained silent. I found an empty teacup on the windowsill and poured her a drink, depositing the stolen bottle under the bed. After a long sip, she sighed.

"I don't use my powers."

"I know. I thought you vowed it."

"As a personal philosophy, yes, but not a formal vow. Not like Lillian." Her serpent eyes flicked to mine, evaluating. "May I give you a piece of advice?"

I stilled. Never in a million years did I think Violet would ask for permission to give her opinion, especially to me. I nodded, warily, refilling her cup after she downed her drink.

"Do you think my brother has happiness?"

"Um . . ." This felt like a trap, it had to be. Surely, she would launch into some tirade about how I would make Jack miserable for the remainder of his existence. But her question prickled my insides, a tiny thorn embedded in my skin. I knew Jack was lonely. Exhausted, run down from everything he did and the effects on his body. But he never indicated anything else.

"When we become a Morrigan, your entire being will change. Not just in becoming a druid, but the sheer amount of power you will possess. It is something fae thousands of years older than you have never experienced." Her serpent eyes fell to her drink, staring deep through the transparent liquor. "Power changes you. Jack can tell you that, Lillian can tell you that, and I, most of all, can tell you that."

"People like Delsaran and Henry Foster let it corrupt them, but none of you." I leaned my head to the side. "That ain't who I want to be, and I have no doubt you will keep me in check. All of you managed to retain your humanity, despite everything."

"It's not just that," she sighed, stretching out her legs. "This is not the life Jack wanted. He never wanted to be a prince in Ildathach and that did not change here, but he has a power the rest of us need. He protects the low fae and allows us to live in this world in secrecy, but it is with great sacrifice. I'm sure you have figured that out by now."

Nodding, I murmured, "I know, but the Morrigan will help him."

She looked at me like I was a window to something only she could see. Or perhaps, a mirror. "Jack is my favorite person in this world and the last one. You have Tommy, but I have him."

I shook my head, but she continued, "Despite anything that has happened between you two, he will always be your brother. And I want you to understand I feel the same before saying this." She picked at her nails, chewing her bottom lip. "We have all made choices that led us here, including you. But every choice we make has a consequence. Nothing in this world comes free, and what we are trying to do, the kind of power we are reaching for, is expensive, Adeline. It does not come fucking cheap." She glanced at me. "So before we finish the last of our tasks, I want you to ask yourself, truly fucking ask yourself, if this is a price you are willing to pay."

Her heavy words trembled in the air, playing off the humming radiator and birds chirping outside the window. In the living room, the men burst into raucous laughter.

Just how far are you willing to go, girl?

"Do you know what the price is?"

Her eyes narrowed. "Your Woman in White does."

A trickle of fear ran down my spine. I glanced at the living room door, but the low chatter continued without pause. "Did Lillian tell you?"

"No."

"Then how—"

"Do you want to know why I never use my powers?"

I nodded, unsure of myself.

"Because I have the most, but it comes with a price no one is willing to pay."

I stared into her serpent eyes, dark and ancient. I once described her as a wrathful goddess. Now I wondered how far off I had been.

"Just keep that in mind," she said, handing me her cup. "And do make yourself useful and wash that before Will has my head."

I nodded, pushing to a stand. Before I could exit, her low voice called out, "She's a wraith."

I froze, hand latched on the door. "What?"

"Your Woman in White. She's a wraith, created by the last Bogoran itself over three hundred years ago."

I turned, slowly. "How do you know that?"

"Because Jack and I were there."

A chill seeped between us, heavy and throbbing in the silent room. Darkness curled around me like an omen. A curse. "What happened to the last Bogoran, Violet?"

This time, she didn't look away. "We killed it."

I SPENT THE REMAINDER of the afternoon in a daze, trying again and again to placate Lillian when she gave me a tongue-lashing for providing Violet alcohol. After a few hours the woman of the hour joined us in the living room, showing no indication whatsoever of our private conversation. Jack kept trying to steal my attention, but I needed a moment to think.

It felt like Violet was telling me something. Something important. I played over all of our past interactions, but at this point, there were too many to count. Worse, her words to me that infamous night in the hotel kept running through my head. *I warned you to stay asleep.*

Jack shaded us home in the evening, asking if I would like to have dinner together. I declined, feigning a headache and a request to go bathe alone.

In the darkness of the Abstruse, I wondered if I was overthinking everything. Violet and I reached a place of mutual respect, or so I thought. This could have been something else, a way to mess with mine and Jack's heads. Or it could have been nothing at all. Violet was strange on a good day.

The more I mulled it over, the more it seemed like a confession. I'd heard of criminals so overwrought with guilt they confided in others or turned themselves in. She once described the death of the Bogorans as a genocide, so killing the last one could have laid heavy on her conscious. It fit into the reasons why she never used her powers, if she only had them because of an awful deed.

Still, she knew what the Woman in White was. That she had been visiting me.

It would be better to get answers before jumping to any conclusions. I conjured something to say to Jack, but when I entered the study, he was nowhere to be found.

Despite infinite powers, there was no simpler way to contact someone than a telephone. Thankfully, Arthur possessed one, and

411

the number was written in a contact book in Jack's desk. I dialed the operator, gave them Arthur's information and waited with bated breaths as the line rang.

"Hello?" A porcelain plate crashed in the background, along with a steady stream of water.

"Hi, Arthur. It's Adeline. I hope I'm not interrupting dinner."

"Oh, no, I was simply attempting to transform a plate into steel." Another crash, and a quiet curse. "Did you require something?"

"Yes, please." I glanced around the study. Nothing but the ever-moving vines, but I couldn't help the feeling of being watched. "Do you have any books about wraiths?"

"Wraiths?" He paused, drawing a short breath. "I may, but they are very uncommon. Was there something specific you needed to know?"

A pulsing headache formed behind my eyes, a real one. "To start, what are they?"

"The druids aren't entirely sure, but generally they are known as agents of death, such as grim reapers, if you have heard those tales."

"I have."

"Oh, wonderful." Another plate shattered in the background. "Less phoenix feathers . . ." he mumbled. Pen scratched against paper. "Anyway, wraiths are fragments of souls. Once blended together, they form dark entities, capable of curses, hauntings, the usual. Does that help you any?"

"Did you say soul fragments?"

"Yes, from many different souls. As the fae say, connections draw power."

Right, so I knew the Woman in White was a wraith, but not why the Bogoran created her, or what that had to do with me and Jack. Unless she was angry Jack and Violet killed her maker, but why involve me? Why tell me I cheated? All that did was produce more questions.

"And you said they are agents of death, in what way?"

"Well, first you have to understand what human death is, and that gets very complicated. Have you ever heard of the term *beansidhe*?"

I shook my head, the throbbing pulse growing stronger. I rubbed a thumb into my temple. "Um, no."

"There are three of them at any given time, usually women, and they are not just death, but . . . well, as said, it is complicated." He sighed, muttering something about hexes. "Wraiths harvest souls for them, and do so in the hope to one day be freed."

Lightning struck inside my skull. I gritted my teeth against the sudden pain. "They're slaves?"

"In the way all souls who cannot move on from this world are."

"How are they freed?"

"That we don't know."

The headache swelled. I captured a pained grunt behind closed teeth. "Right, thank you, Arthur. I think that is all I need."

"Any time." A pause. "Is everything okay over there?"

I chewed my lower lip, fighting tears springing to my eyes. "Yes, fine. Goodnight."

"Goodnight, Addie."

The line went dead. I placed a hand to the back of my head, taking a breath. Scorching heat met my fingers.

I blinked at the fuzzy room. The firelight bloomed too large, the vines slithering along the walls too loud. Color and sound blurred together, mixing like peach juice and bathwater, blood and an icy river.

Adeline.

I shook my head. Nothing but the vines and books, the roaring fire, but the voice grew louder. *Adeeelineeee.*

"Fine," I said, aloud. "I get it, now. You are a wraith and you are angry at Jack for some reason, but we can resolve this."

Adeline . . . Ruth . . . Colton.

413

"What do you want from me?" I stood, smacking my hands on the desk. Tinny laughter followed the sound.

A swath of white filled my corner vision, but nothing was there. More laughter, chiming like bells. *You are the thirteenth. The last one.*

"What does that mean?" Fire exploded in my head. I brought my hands to my eyes, sobbing, "Fuck."

"Addie?"

Peeling my hands away, I stared at the dark figure standing before the mirror. Golden eyes scoured me, narrowing. "I stopped by Will's to see if he had something for your head. Is everything okay?"

I wasn't looking at him, but behind him. A reflection in the mirror shimmered with no companion in this room. White hair, white eyes, and a long, white veil gathering near her feet.

"I heard you needed a curse. All you had to do was ask."

She smiled. I screamed.

FORTY

I HIT THE GROUND. Jack grabbed my face, frantic words swimming beneath my consciousness. *Annwyl, annwyl, ANNWYL.*

"He looks exactly the same." The Woman in White ran a sharp nail down his cheek, but his frantic eyes remained on me, lips moving in my darkening vision. "I would say I'm sorry for this, but I'm not."

Jack's face no longer filled my view, but an open field, a star-kissed sky. Someone jerked my hands above my head, raw and bleeding from rope bindings. I thrashed and screamed, kicking at the villagers, begging my husband to come find me. Dirt-streaked faces spit at my skin, chanting, *Witch, witch, witch.*

They hung me from a cross. I sobbed, praying for someone to listen. *Where is he, where is he, he was supposed to come find me.* But fire licked my toes, caressing my ankles and swirling up my shins. I screamed, and screamed, but only fire came from my throat—

I was in a river, a little girl playing with tadpoles. My tattered dress hung around me, soaked with mud. A group of boys from the village surrounded me, taking turns poking at my hair with sticks. I batted them away, tears running down my face, when one of them dared me to jump in. *But I can't swim.*

The largest boy nudged me forward, laughing the entire time. *Do it, freak.*

My head sank beneath the water. I waved my arms, kicked my legs, but only spun in endless circles. I gasped for air, but only breathed water. Everything was dark, I was choking, choking and —

Lying in bed, sick with fever. Wrinkles and liver spots coated my arms, pale blue and withering away. Someone held my hand, their quiet breath racing across my cheeks. A man's voice curled around me, his fingers smoothing back my hair. *You can go, my love.*

A shuddering breath passed my lips. *I do not wish to leave you,* I said.

He kissed my cheek, wiping away my tears. *Wherever you go, I will always find you.* Darkness closed in, the last memory his hand on my face —

A knife to my throat, blood spraying —

I knew you were seeing him, he screamed, squeezing my neck, *I knew —*

Does this taste funny to anyone else? I set down my teacup, pressing a hand to my head. *Where is —*

A horse kicking my head —

A bullet tearing through my chest —

An umbilical cord wrapped around my neck.

YOU CHEATED.

I opened my eyes. The Woman in White held my dress, dragging me through the liquid darkness of the shade. I clawed at the ground, but there was nothing to grasp but endless black. *What are you doing?*

You wanted to live forever. Now you can.

Let go of me!

She squatted beside me, wrenching my face between her ghastly claws. *Did he think his actions wouldn't have consequences?*

I sobbed, tearing at her hands, but she only dug in harder. *He did this to us.*

Who, what did they do?

She tore her hand away. My reflection came back in her milky irises, my wide eyes and bloody cheeks.

You are such a stupid little girl.

What do you want? I screamed

Me? She laughed. *I want to be free. But if you live forever . . .* She cocked her head to the side. *You will just have to become something else instead.*

Become what?

She smiled. *You will not remember this, but I will, Adeline. I will remember what you cannot, but know you won't become a druid. No, you will become something . . .much . . .*

Much . . .

Better.

PART THREE

WHEEL OF FORTUNE

FORTY-ONE

I WOKE UP IN the bath.

A white nightgown floated around me. I clutched the edge of it, watching a scarlet plume curl from the edge. It burst into a geyser of red, turning the bath water into a pool of blood. I screamed, kicking and thrashing, when an arm tugged me closer, wiping water off my face.

"Adeline, can you hear me?"

The dim lights of the Abstruse bathroom shimmered. Jack had me on the floor, braced against his chest and sopping wet. I lifted my hands, but only glistening water droplets coated my fingers. The bath itself was clear of any color.

"It was the fucking wraith." Violet swam into focus, golden eyes hovering beside Jack's. I blinked again and more faces materialized.

"What's a wraith?" I asked.

They all glanced at one another, but I hardly noticed. Fire shot down my spine, filled my throat, burning me from the inside out. I screamed, but as quickly as it came, the feeling retreated.

Will touched my face, a grimace spreading his mouth wide. "There's nothing I can do."

Jack swallowed, glancing at me. Pain flickered across my skin, hands around my throat squeezing the life from me—but there was nothing there. I clenched my teeth, sobbing, and Jack pressed his lips to mine.

"I'm going to take you to someone who can help you."

He kissed me again, deep and lovely. All my pain ebbed away.

"I'm so sorry, *annwyl*."

"For what?" The words drifted from my lips, but my vision darkened before I heard the response.

WATER SLOSHED AGAINST THE side of a boat, rocking me into a lullaby. I thought I was dreaming again, but when I opened my eyes, a rainy sunrise flickered back in a haze of gray.

I smacked my hand against the bottom of a wooden row boat, but a leather glove took my arm and pulled me down. Golden eyes blinked back at me, raindrops scattering his eyelashes. "Just lay down."

"Where are we?"

"The east river."

I blinked dewy mist away. A thick, wool blanket coated me head to toe, the rain beading on top of it. A flickering lantern adorned the front of the boat, shaking in the breeze. Jack lay across the bottom with me. Behind his head, gray buildings and curling smoke drifted by.

"Why?"

"It's the only way to get where we need to go." He lifted his head, just enough to glance at something down the river. "Once we get under the bridge, we'll be there."

"Be where?" But pain exploded in my head, the feeling of blood running into my eyes.

"Sh, Addie, it's okay, look at me." He tore off a glove, pressing a calloused palm to my cheek. I melted into the feeling, the pain subsiding enough to breathe, but ever-present.

"Did I get my curse?"

"Yes."

"What is it?"

His audible swallow mixed with the racing river, the autumn wind barreling through the sky. "None of us are entirely sure. A wraith gave you some memories of her past lives, but I cannot say why or what the result is. But there is power beneath your skin."

Shivering, I murmured, "I don't have any memories. I don't even remember last night."

"Lillian took them away. We thought it may help you, but there seems to be . . . residual pieces."

"But we don't know what my actual curse is?"

He chewed the inside of his cheek. Fury, disappointment, fear and a few other things crossed his expression. Slowly, he shook his head.

I placed my hand over the one he held on my cheek. Memories swirled in my brain like fog writhing against glass, obscuring what lay behind it. They were there—flashes of things, bits and pieces of scenes, but nothing tangible. Only one thing broke through the haze. *He did this to us.*

"What did you do?" I whispered.

He remained silent. The boat swayed side-to-side, the frigid mist a relief against my inflamed cheeks. Metal clanged from the shores, the factories beginning their work for the day. Seagulls squawked overhead and fishermen loaded into their boats, yelling to one another about tides. An eternity passed before Jack sat up, tucking a strand of hair behind my ear. "It is about to get very dark."

A stone pillar came into view, then my first glance of the bridge overhead. Beams stretched toward the heavens and bird nests poked from the rafters. The wood and stone monstrosity slowly took over my vision, the underbelly swallowing the slate sky.

"Three," Jack murmured. I gripped his hand. "Two."

The last sliver of sky faded away, the river carrying us directly beneath the bridge.

"One," he whispered.

Endless black surrounded us. The little lantern at the head of our boat flickered, the color whitening like molten silver. I sat up, swiveling my head in every direction. We floated through a depthless night sky, nothing but darkness above, below and around us.

Shuffling forward, I gripped the edge and peered over the side of the boat. The bow cut through liquid like ink, the silver flame reflecting the little waves ebbing away from the wood. Within moments they flattened again into a sea of onyx glass.

I held my hand in front of me. Unless close to the flame, it was swallowed by darkness. "Is this the shade?"

"No." His arms came around me, pulling my back against his chest. "It is hard to explain."

We remained like that. Whenever a new bout of pain washed over me, he kissed my shoulder, my cheeks, my hair until it subsided, washing us in silence once again. I stared into the endless void of black. It didn't feel like the shade. There was something comforting about it—the darkness of peaceful rest, blanketing and carrying us home.

The silver flame grew brighter. The boat changed direction, and I realized it wasn't our flame, but a second light bobbing in the distance. It grew in intensity as we neared, a beacon leading us to on. I squinted, covering my eyes with a hand when the boat hit a hard surface and rocked back. The silver flame illuminated a set of steps. A stone walkway rose from the ebony sea and at the end of it, a brilliant silver glow like someone pulled the moon down from the sky.

I pushed away from Jack and took the stairs. Puddles of inky darkness reflected the ethereal glow. Each step filled my bones with light, an overwhelming sense of serenity. Jack followed close behind, footsteps splashing in the puddles.

It was hard to see now. The light glowed so bright and everything around us was so dark. But I couldn't stop, drifting like a ship bobbing closer to shore. When luminescence surrounded me, nearly blinding, the light retreated to a single pinpoint. A tiny voice called, "Jaevidan, is that you?"

Jack stood beside me, bowing at the waist. "Thank you for receiving us, Estheria."

"No, thank you for visiting. It has been too long since I have seen your lovely face." The light swelled again, chiming, "And who might your companion be?"

When my eyes adjusted, I could see it was not a light at all, but . . . a child, no older than four or five. She perched on a massive silver throne, bare, chubby feet dangling in the air. Glittering, silver ringlets fell down her shoulders and silver skin sparkled like diamonds. A dress like liquid starlight flowed around her, and a crown of twinkling lights made intricate patterns on her head. Joy. Pure, effervescent and beautiful joy filled me. She leaned her head to the side with a smile, every dark thought erased from my head. I no longer understood long-forgotten words—grief, anger, fear. Only love and her radiating light.

Tears ran down my cheeks, scattering her light into tiny rainbows. I sank to my knees, shaking. "Are you an angel?"

Jack shook his head. "She is a fallen star, *annwyl*."

Her smile broadened, glittering teeth around a twinkling laugh. "Jaevidan, did I not teach you better? How could you bring a guest and forget to tell her what I am."

He bowed his head. "Forgive me, Estheria."

"I could never be upset with you for long." She gestured to me with a plump hand. "What is your name, daughter?"

I swallowed thick tears, grasping for words. "Adeline."

"Oh, how beautiful." She pressed her hands together with vibrant glee. "Would you come closer so I may look at you?"

I glanced at Jack, who gave a solemn nod.

I pushed to trembling feet, shuffling forward. I fell at the seat of her throne, gazing up into her glittering face. She grinned, placing a hand on my cheek. "Just as I thought, stunning in every way. You chose your lover well, Jaevidan."

"She is very special to me."

"I can tell. What a wonderful thing it is." But her brilliant smile faded, melting into childish confusion. "Oh, no. You have . . . sadness. So much sadness." Tears brimmed her diamond eyes, glittering on silver lashes. She looked at Jack. "Jaevidan, why does she have so much sadness?"

He folded his hands behind his back, chewing the inside of his cheek. "Your children of flesh and dust are not like you, Estheria. Darkness roots deeper in them."

"Oh." She pressed a hand to her heart, wiping away a falling tear. "I understand, but this is something no mother ever wishes on her children." She took my hands in hers, tiny and glittering in my palms. "My daughter of flesh and dust, I wish to help you. Is this why you came to me?"

I grasped for words, but Jack filled in. "Adeline was cursed. It was something we needed to help your other children, but I am afraid it may have hurt her too deeply. The Morrigan we seek to make also requires a blessing. I know I am not one of yours, but if your blessing could help her . . ." He stopped. "I will give you anything in return."

"Oh, my lovely Jaevidan." She frowned, gesturing for him to come closer. "You may not be a son of flesh and dust, but you are a child of the Bogorans, my nephew of glamour and blood. They were my family, as are you. I still weep for them every day." She brushed a silver tear away, turning back to me. "Only the most precious of souls would accept a curse for their brothers and sisters. You have truly made me proud, daughter, and I will always offer you my blessings."

I nodded, swallowing a fresh wave of tears. "Thank you."

Her angelic face melted into a watery grin. "This is what mothers do, but I must ask something of you first. This sadness . . ." She pressed a chubby palm to my heart. "Perhaps it will always fill you, but I ask you to remember all the light whenever it becomes consuming. The joy you felt when Thomas came home to you. The memories of your father, whose soul has sung me such beautiful music since joining us in the dark. All the friendships you have built with my nieces and nephews of glamour and blood. Most of all, Jaevidan." She beamed. "He loves you, daughter. He loves you so much. It is one of the most pure and endless things I have ever felt."

A trembling breath fell out of me. I turned to Jack. "You do?"

He blinked, glancing at Estheria, then me. His lips pressed in a flat line, head dipped in a subtle nod.

The star looked between us with a knowing smile. "But of course, my children are strange. Powerful feelings may scare them, but we must not run from them, daughter. Or you, nephew. They are your most precious form of magic."

Jack held my eyes, and I his. The bond could not reach here, but I didn't need it to know what swelled between us, what he tried to convey to me. Tearing my gaze from him, I spoke to the star. "I will cherish it. I promise."

"Good." Her hands fell from mine. "Before I give you my blessing, there is one more gift I think you should receive. After all, I have missed many birthdays." She giggled at her joke, reaching up for the crown of light. "Though before I do this, I must ask Jaevidan for his permission. There is something I wish to give her, and I think you know what it is, but as it belongs to you it is your choice and yours only."

Jack nodded. "I know. She may have it."

"And she will use them wisely." The star plucked a single light from her crown, glimmering in the silver glow. In the palm of her hand it melted into a single diamond, dangling from a delicate chain.

She beckoned for me to come closer. I thought it would go around my neck, but she laid it over my hair like a tiara, the single diamond falling between my eyes.

"Contained within this light are memories. Jaevidan's memories." I frowned, bringing my hand to the diamond, but she gently pulled them away. "This is something very precious, so it must be used with care. Only after Jaevidan has allowed you to see them. You will know when he is ready.

"But a dangerous path lies ahead for you, my daughter of flesh and dust. Many troubles, much sacrifice, some even my light may not be able to reach. But these memories will remind you of what is important. They will be the light that guides you home. Do you understand?"

I nodded.

She smiled, so brilliantly and lovingly that her skin took an endless shine. "With that said, I offer you my blessing now." She raised a hand in the air, her shimmering palm filling with light. "My name is Estheria of the Valaxes. I am the eighth fallen star. With this light bestowed on Adeline, my daughter of flesh and dust, I give my brightest blessing." She pressed the light to my cupped hands. It faded into my skin, warm and gentle and cherished.

I bowed my head. "Thank you."

"Always remember," she murmured. To Jack, "As should you, Jaevidan. And please, you must visit more often."

"I promise I will."

"You fill me with light. Now, go on. I know you children have much to do." Jack bowed one last time, gesturing for the boat. I stood to follow him, but Estheria reached out, pulling me closer.

Her tiny lips whispered against my ear. "He will do anything for you."

I nodded. "I know."

"It is a wonderful and terrible responsibility." She pushed away enough to look in my eyes, face set. "You will hear many things, Adeline, awful things, and you will question all you know. But you must always trust in Jaevidan. Find answers in his memories. This is the only way to remain in the light."

I fingered the delicate chain in my hair. "I promise."

She bowed her head. "Now follow him home."

I blinked.

We were no longer surrounded by darkness. Seagulls swooped overhead and a fishing boat ambled past. The underbelly of the bridge floated away, revealing a slate gray sky once more. Jack and I lay still in the rowboat, not a word between us. I cried the entire way home.

FORTY-TWO

WHEN WE SHADED INTO the study, everyone sat among the settees. Jack and I hovered before the mirrors, his hand firmly around mine.

The vines rushed closer with our presence, but Jack shooed them away. I looked over the faces of my friends—my closest friends—because that's what they had become. I wanted to say something profound, something worthy of standing by Jack's side, of holding their attention, but the only thing I could think of was, "It's done."

One by one they rose. First, Will, who edged closer and wrapped me in an all-consuming hug. He planted a hand on the back of my head, rocking us back and forth before kissing my cheek. He nodded at Jack and walked away.

Then Lillian, who dabbed at an endless stream of tears, throwing her arms around both our necks and squeezing us in closer. "Thank you for everything," she whispered, kissed both our cheeks and shaded from view.

Arthur. He stood before me, fumbling his fingers on the buttons of his waistcoat. "I am coated in pixie dust, but know I am embracing you in spirit."

I smiled. "In my head, it is the best embrace in the world."

"Excellent. That is exactly the way I intended it." He shook Jack's hand. "It is, and has always been an honor working for you."

Jack nodded. "Thank you, Arthur."

Lastly, Violet. Harold coiled around her neck, slipping into her hair. A heartbeat passed where the three of us stood alone in silence.

She looked at me. "Honestly, I never thought you would pull this off."

My lips lifted in a half-smile. "I'll take it."

She nodded, instantly somber. "When shit goes south, and it fucking will, you know where to find me."

"I know."

Flicking my hair, she turned to Jack and threw her arms around his neck, squeezing him tightly. "I love you."

He squeezed her back. "I love you too."

She followed Arthur into the foyer. That left the two of us completely alone.

The second Dianomican lay on the coffee table, the black mooring beside it. I held my curse and my blessing. There was only one thing left to do now.

My fingers reached for the chain around my head. I slipped it off, tucking the gift inside the folds of my skirt. Jack watched my every movement. In my dreams, those looks excited me, then they terrified me. Now, I wasn't sure how I felt, but it was none of those previous things, instead something heavier and deeper than words could describe.

"What now?" I asked.

He shrugged, the gesture swollen with tension. "I have been studying the second Dianomican. It's all fairly straightforward."

I nodded. "Oh, good." Needing to rest, I found my way to a velvet settee. The cursed book stared at me. It looked exactly like any other book, but I wasn't that foolish girl making a bargain beside the river anymore. I knew just how dangerous magic could be, how it could look and act much like anything else. The fae sporting a human glamour beside me was a constant reminder.

"What happened with the curse?" I asked.

He was silent for so long, I thought he would never answer. "Have you ever done something for the right reasons, but you are still unsure if you made the best choice?"

"Yes." I looked around the faded study, the crackling fireplace and vine-encased walls.

"I made a choice once, a long time ago. It led me to you." Golden eyes flickered to me, repelling the light. "But I may have unintentionally harmed you in the process."

I dug deep for the memories, but none came. The last thing I remembered was my intentions to call Arthur, shortly after learning Jack and Violet had . . . that they may have killed the last Bogoran together. But after that, nothing. Darkness, and nothing more.

I waited for pain to come, the strange feelings I had all morning, but none arrived. The star had truly blessed me. Only time would tell how well.

"Mistakes make us human," I said.

He nodded. "That they do."

All my doubts and fears resurfaced. A lifetime of them. Everything from Papa's whispered words to Tommy's warnings, the ominous story from Violet and everything in between. Once we crossed this threshold, there would be no turning back. I struck my bargain with Jack, but he would renege the moment I asked. This . . . this was the true test. This was the final hurdle. After giving myself to Jack, I placed my fate in things I didn't understand.

The star told me to follow Jack, that he would always keep me in the light. But I'd given myself to blind faith before. Even Henry Foster knew that with my past. I had a choice to make now, the most important one I ever would. Walk away, or follow Jaevidan Valdivia, the Poison Son, King of the Banished, the Prince of Prohibition, into the dark.

"I am afraid," I whispered.

He placed his hand in mine. "I am too."

Somehow, that was all the confirmation I needed. I knew right then I had already made the decision long ago.

I stood, taking the second Dianomican in my hands. Power leaked into my skin, chilling and wrong. I handed the book to him. "Can I have a moment to myself first?"

"Of course."

I made my way to the Abstruse. Darkness flickered through the window, the last remnants of light fading from dusk. The curtains danced in a sourceless breeze. I ran my hands over them, savoring the feeling of silk, of the air caressing my skin.

Sometimes, a woman's most powerful weapons are a good dress and her favorite lipstick. So I bathed, using all the expensive oils and soaps. I applied soft, pink lipstick and wrapped my pearls around my neck. Staring at the closet, I leafed through all the beautiful, hand-crafted clothes, the lacy night things Lillian provided and the dresses brought here from Georgia. At the bottom of the pile was a white, satin lingerie set. At home, I watched countless women get baptized in the river, always in billowing white dresses. If that is what one wears when gaining eternal life, then why not.

I slipped into a matching negligee and a floral robe to cover everything underneath. Glancing in the mirror, I realized it may be the last time I saw myself as a human.

I ran my hands over my face, memorizing each slope and curve, every sharp line. I wondered if I would remember this moment hundreds of years from now, or if this face would change, the image one day swallowed by time.

I wondered if I would recognize myself in the morning.

Theirs but to do and die. Maybe death wasn't always a bad thing though. Pieces left us, and something new grew in its place.

Holding onto that thought, I entered the study.

Jack had pushed all the furniture against the walls, drawing sigils on the floor. A large circle of white chalk ran over the carpet and stones, with arrows crossed like a compass rose. At the head of each sat white candles, the flames a strange silver color. He was halfway around the perimeter, the book in one hand and drawing runes with the other.

I stepped carefully over his lines, plopping down to the floor in the center. His eyes flicked to mine, a little smile lifting his lips. "Terribly romantic, isn't it?"

I nodded. "I always wanted to lose my virginity in a dark sex ritual."

"You and every other blushing young woman." I cracked a smile, tracing the patterns he drew on the floor. Lines pulsed in the silver candlelight, little movements like they were brought to life on the floor.

"Anything I should know?"

"Do you want to be surprised?"

I shrugged, a sudden nervousness itching beneath my skin. "Just wondering if you desired some help."

"Thank you, but I got it." He smiled. "Do you need a drink?"

I raised a brow. "Do you?"

"Oh, no, definitely not. This is another Thursday for me." I laughed, retrieving myself a flute of champagne and one for him too. I returned to the center circle, taking little sips and trying to slow my heart. Considering everything I had done the past few months, it was a bit comical this rattled my nerves. Then again, Violet lashed at me for being nervous about robbing a bank, saying I wasn't losing my maidenhead.

"I'm guessing you have some more experience in this department."

He didn't glance up from the book. "The ritual? No. Sex, yes."

I nodded, pressing my lips together. It seemed incredibly silly, but I suddenly prayed I wouldn't be awful at it. Insecurities swelled to the surface, the thought of everything he had done before me, all those experiences. Undoubtedly, he'd been with many beautiful fae women. The kind with hair like starlight or perfect, lithe figures. I pulled the robe tighter around myself, feeling a bit stupid for dressing up. It would all come off anyway.

He looked at me, sharply. I chewed the inside of my cheek, holding his stare but feeling the restless need to look away. "*Annwyl?*"

I swallowed. "Yes?"

"You are the most beautiful woman I have ever seen."

I smiled. "You're pretty dapper yourself, Mr. Warren."

He winked, finishing the circle of runes and fetching several items from his desk. He sank to his knees in the center of the circle with me, smoothing back my hair. "We can wait."

I shook my head. There were some things in life you needed to prepare for. Others, it didn't matter how much time you gave yourself, the only way to be ready was to plunge in feet first. Part of me would always be afraid, but if I let it delay me now, then I'd regret all the moments I passed on.

The star said feelings were terrifying, but they were nothing compared to truths. I spent my entire life afraid of everything, the fae, magic, my family's safety, the thoughts and feelings of people around me. Then Jack and everything he was to me, the people in his life who became the people in mine, and whatever our futures held. But the words I breathed between us were the most terrifying of all. "I want you."

He ran his thumb over my cheek. The gloves were gone, along with his jacket, tie and shoes. He was in human form—just another layer that hid what lay beneath.

He spread the book open beside us. Strangely, the words were written in English. The ritual took up an entire page, detailing all the sigils Jack drew, the candles, instructions for using the black mooring among other details and words to be recited. Weddings were a ritual. There were words to recite, traditions to repeat. Once I swore I would never get married, and I stood by that. I had something better, after all.

Jack uncorked a small vial shimmering with dark ink. "Close your eyes." I did so, and his thumbs ran smooth liquid over each of my eyelids. His fingers drifted over my face, making intricate lines that swirled down my neck. He tucked his thumbs beneath the collar of my robe, pulled tightly around my chest. "I need to remove this, okay?"

I nodded.

He gently pushed the satin away, letting it slip off my shoulders to the floor. He paused, a sharp stare as he roamed over me. A shiver caressed my skin, but it wasn't from fear this time.

A deep breath, then he continued the intricate patterns on my shoulders, beneath my collarbones. I spared a look down, watching the lines tumble and swirl on my skin like his tattoos. His hands drifted over the swells of my breasts. "This too."

I lifted the thin straps of my negligee, careful not to smudge the lines he made. They fell against my arms and I stopped, overcome with fidgeting energy. He kissed my ink-whorled cheeks, my hairline, and pulled the straps down, along with the lace bralette beneath. My nipples peaked in the cool air, heat flushing beneath my skin.

Jack made thick lines, eyes scouring my exposed chest like this was the most important task in the world. A quiet breath passed his lips, a subtle grunt as he shifted his legs. He pushed the negligee down until it gathered at my waist. Something flickered in his dark stare, then he ripped it in two and tossed the ruined fabric aside.

"Lillian will have your head for that."

He shook his head, lips twitching like he had something to say, but only continued making the lines, hands trembling the longer we went on. When he reached my navel the movements grew quicker, less

433

precise and more rushed. His heavy breaths came between us, stroking my bare skin as I kneeled naked before him.

"So many fucking sigils," he breathed. He grabbed the straps of my panties and tore those too, pulling the fabric tight against me as he wrenched them away. I shivered, hands fluttering near my thighs and what lay beneath them, but he took my wrists in his and clasped them behind my back.

He stopped painting. Stopped breathing. His glamour broke, but only in the eyes. His narrowed pupils roamed over me, the pulsing vein in my throat to my heaving chest. They dipped down my stomach . . . lower. He wedged a knee between my thighs, parting them. My breath came faster, goosebumps littering my skin. Golden eyes flicked to mine, then sought between my spread knees.

The bond strengthened between us, hot and demanding. Poison leaked from his skin to mine, seeping into my veins. My lips kept parting, fumbling around words I couldn't form. His free hand drifted beneath my chin, lifting my eyes to his.

"*Annwyl*." A heavy breath fell past his lips, tainted in sin and death. "You know I would do anything for you, right?"

I nodded.

"I only have one rule." His fingers dropped from my face, dipping between my legs. He ran them over the center of me, streaking wetness across my skin. I forgot to breathe, knees clenching his muscled thigh as lightning shot up my spine. "This is mine, and mine only."

Right then, I would have given him anything. Sensing that, his lips lifted in a knowing smirk and he dropped my wrists. I released a panting breath, going rigid as he finished the sigils.

I forgot I was undressed and he wasn't. Forgot any earlier worries or fears. He gently pushed me onto my back, bending my knees and butterflying them apart. He removed his waistcoat, his shirt. The silver pocket chain bounced silver light across his chest. He drew several sigils beneath his collarbones, then one between the deep V ending beneath his waistband. I sat up, wishing to trace the dark lines myself, but a tender nudge sent me back against the rug. "I still need to . . ." He closed his eyes, knuckles white around his belt. I shifted closer, pressing one bare knee against his hip. "Fuck."

He dropped down, placing an arm on either side of my head. I chewed my lip, feeling like I was distracting him from something, but he ran his lips up the column of my throat.

My fingers fumbled against his belt, a desperate breath as I pulled it through the loops. The dark gray button came undone and I moaned, hands roaming over his chest. The sigils smeared beneath my touch, but they didn't matter. Rain and oleander, the heat rolling off his skin, it filled the bond and my soul, too consuming to remember he had a task.

A sharp grunt left his throat. He grabbed my wrists, wrenching them above my head. The glamour fully broke, his swirling tattoos golden in the firelight. "I have one more sigil. I need you to say a few words, then I am tying you up and fucking you until you forget your name. But I need you to be still, darling. Can you do that for me?"

I heard exactly seven words in that spiel, starting with fucking and ending with name. He pushed up and a pathetic whimper left my pouted lips. His eyes roamed over me, a hand down his face. "You're fucking killing me."

The last sigil he drew on his throat, lines jagged and bent at odd angles. He reached over my head for a set of white ribbons and removed the rest of his clothing. His thick erection hung between his legs, and something savage sparked in my blood. He pulled me to straddle his lap and tied the ribbon around both our backs, making a thick knot at our sides. My chest went flush with his, frenetic energy spilling into my blood and making me grind wet heat against him. A low groan sounded in his throat and he grabbed my hair, wrenching my head back. Violent eyes met mine. *"Creoche glin ilirash.* Repeat it."

435

The words fell over me, thrumming in the pulsing air. I knew at once they were from his native tongue, something few human throats had ever breathed. I echoed the statement. Power pulsed around us, so strong the taste tainted the space between us. His hands roamed my thighs, eyes dark with promises of what was to come. Heat swelled low in my stomach, each word coming shakier than the last. Each breath strained my back against the ribbon and my breasts taut against his chest. The bond became something else. Vicious, impatient, *alive*. The candles flickered, the roaring fire breaching the confines of its home. The vines snapped at the perimeter of the circle. The last words left my lips and all at once, the candles blew to withering smoke.

Jack ran a hand down my face, kissing me softly. "*Yn y bywyd hwn ac o hyn ymlaen.*"

He pushed inside me.

I cried out, back arching against the ribbon. A twinge of pain as he pushed deeper, as his thickness stretched me to the limit, then power—raw, aching power shot through my veins. I dug my hands into his hair, breaths ragged as I looked to the place our bodies met. He lifted my hips and pulled out, rocking back in with a slowness that made me feral. I pulled at the dark locks coating his head and ground down on him, desperate, frantic, needing to feel him deep inside me again.

A low growl sounded in his throat and he laid me on the ground, the ribbon tied around our backs keeping him close. His fingers grasped my jaw, his dark eyes consuming me. He pulled out. Slowly, so fucking slowly. "I've waited a long time to do this, *annwyl*. I'm savoring every fucking second."

My knees shook against his hips, a needy whine filling my throat. He rocked in and my eyes rolled back in my head. He felt so good. God, how could anything feel that fucking good? His shaky breath danced across my neck, eyes darting down to where he claimed what was his, over and over again. He gripped my waist hard enough to bruise but I didn't care, rolling my hips against his measured movements and pushing him as deep as he could go.

His eyes fluttered closed and he cupped my face with both hands. "Am I hurting you?"

It dawned on me that that was why he started like this. It was my first time and he was worried. I shook my head, running my hands down his face. "Fuck me like you want to, Jack."

Darkness flickered over his face, something deep and primal and *fae*. He kissed me with months—years—of endless want, taking my lower lip between his teeth. Power coated my bones, something foreign and unfamiliar crawling beneath my skin. But it was nothing compared to the feeling of him inside me. He shoved himself in until we were hip to hip, a low sound in his throat at my dirty moan. Stars exploded in my vision and his taste coated my tongue. Heat pooled beneath my skin, wetness between my thighs and I was moving with him, matching every breath and movement, screaming his name over and over until that heat shot lower. My breaths grew quicker, an all-consuming feeling melting between my legs. He growled and pushed to his knees, seating me on top of him again.

I grabbed his shoulders, rocking against him, needing to keep that feeling. He grabbed my face and forced my gaze to his, "I want you to look at me when you come."

My lips parted. He dipped a thumb between them, streaking the wetness over my skin. "Good girl," he murmured, pushing deeper. "That's it, *annwyl*. Just like that."

I sank lower onto him. Heat swelled, too strong to name. I needed him touching me, I needed him in me, I needed nothing but his scent and taste coating my tongue. I bit my lip, movements harder and faster and breaths frenzied. He reached between us and stroked me, the feeling something indescribable, so achingly good I immediately broke. I cried out, nails digging into his shoulders and face buried in his neck. It felt so good it almost hurt, but he was relentless, pounding into me deeper, harder, until I was nothing but a shaking, sobbing mess on top of him.

"You're so good. You're so fucking good, *annwyl*." He kissed my face, my neck, hands coasting up and down my skin. I was limp and useless in his arms, trembling and overcome as he used me to bring his own release. He grabbed my hair and pulled my head back, dark eyes meeting mine before he pushed in as far as he would go. His tongue slipped against mine and he moaned—loud and dirty and low before he was spilling himself inside me.

I felt each twitch of his hips, each pulse of his cock filling me with his release. Our breaths coated the air, sweat on our skin and wild heartbeats. The candles flickered to life again, a warm, natural yellow. I lifted a hand behind his back, turning it over once, twice. Something shimmered beneath my skin, a little glow separate from the high of what we just did. My body felt like it was on fire, renewed, something deep and primal lurking beneath flesh.

Jack wrapped his arms around me, kissing my neck and growling low in my ear, "You're mine now. You know that right?"

I turned my head, brushing my nose against his. His darkened eyes scoured my face, pupils widening and narrowing with vicious approval. "Am I different?"

He shook his head. "You're perfect." He kissed the tip of my nose, then brushed his lips over mine. "Did you hear what I said?"

"I'm yours?"

His eyes flickered back and forth between human and fae. "Say that one more time."

Heavy warmth settled deep in my stomach. My body . . . that wasn't the only thing that changed. Ink smudged him all over from when he kissed my face. A definitive sign of what we just completed. Not long ago, I told him this very action would mean nothing to us. It was a business transaction, a means to an end. After, I would find my place with the Guild or return home. But everything changed, and this time, I wasn't afraid of it.

I streaked my thumb over his cheekbone. "I'm yours."

He had me on my back faster than I could blink. He was still inside me, already hard again. "I was going to take you to the bedroom, just so you know."

I laughed, spreading my arms wide. "Why, when you have such a perfectly good floor?"

He kissed me. "I had the same exact thought."

FORTY-THREE

I BLINKED AGAINST THE golden firelight, sweat coating my hairline. We never made it to the bedroom, but Jack found it in himself to drag out the blankets we previously used for our floor nest. He didn't stop, kissing and fucking and worshipping me well into the early hours of the morning. I drifted to sleep sometime around two a.m.. The grandfather clock beside the bookshelves said it was now four.

His even breaths hit the back of my neck, his golden arm tight around my waist. Murmured words left his lips, all in a language I didn't speak. I doubted I'd ever visit Ildathach, but I wondered if he would teach me his native tongue anyway. We had all the time in the world now and I wanted to learn, even if I could only use it with Jack and the others. That made it even more special.

Between Jack's body heat, the fire and the blankets, it was incredibly hot. I removed his arm from my waist and stood, stretching my limbs. I felt . . . different. Stronger, leaner, maybe even a little taller. I brought my hands to my face, feeling for all those soft curves and sweeping edges. The bones in my face felt deeper, more pronounced. My hands fell away, trembling.

I forced myself to drink some water before drifting to the massive three-tier mirror. Ink smudged me head to toe so it was difficult to tell, but I was undoubtedly changed. All in small, subtle ways.

Nothing that made me completely indiscernible, but to myself, I looked like a stranger.

I ran my fingers through my short hair, now shinier and smoother. My brown eyes were a shade darker, golden flecks catching the light. The freckles dotting my nose and cheeks were more prominent, the bones just a little sharper. I lifted my hand before my face again. My skin shimmered with the slightest glow, nothing some good makeup couldn't recreate, but it was my natural pallor now. More, something thrummed just beneath my skin. A feeling of restlessness. A feeling of power.

"I never took you for the vain type."

My eyes bounced to Jack, who lay on his side, grinning. He was changed too. It carried the same subtlety, his thick muscles suddenly thicker, his golden skin a little brighter. His sharp eyes focused on me, predatory and all-seeing. Each of his movements came sharp and strong. He had always seemed that way to me, but now that he was restored the difference was stark.

I rolled my eyes with a little smile, trying to think of a quip to return, but only said, "It's strange."

His grin melted into something serious, his serpent eyes no longer predatory, but *starving*. He pushed the blanket back from his hips. "Come here."

I drifted closer, not stopping until I stood naked before him. He was on his knees faster than I could blink, grabbing my hips and wrenching me closer. I fell forward until my knees brushed the ground, straddling him. He kissed each of my ribs, nuzzling his face against the lines beneath my breasts. More ink coated his face. "Maybe I should wash this all off."

He snapped and the ink left every inch of my skin. "Problem solved."

I grinned, running my hands through his hair. "I can't believe you just passed on the opportunity to rinse me off."

He groaned, kissing the underside of my breast. "That bath is only big enough for one."

"I'm even more surprised you haven't already replaced it."

"An issue I plan to remedy as soon as possible." He pulled my hips down until I brushed his cock, already hard and throbbing beneath me. Wetness gathered between my legs, heat swelling. His tongue brushed over my nipple, biting down softly then smoothing over the little sting. I moaned, digging my nails into his scalp, kneading at his skin while he lapped at mine.

"Fuck, you taste so good." He moved from my nipples to my neck, drifting up my pulsing vein to my jawline, before tugging softly on my earlobe. "I want to be inside you," he breathed.

Shivers danced down my arms. I pouted with a little smile. "You haven't gotten your fill yet tonight?"

"Never, but especially not when you look at me like that." He flipped me onto my back, pulling apart my legs. A low noise hummed in the back of his throat, jaw set. "You are so fucking beautiful."

I bit my lower lip, containing a flattered little grin. He dropped his face between my thighs and the smile turned into a heady moan.

He ran his tongue up my center, not stopping until he reached that glorious little spot at the top. When he found it he did slow circles, pressing one finger inside me while I moaned and writhed beneath him.

"So fucking perfect," he growled. The low vibrations skimmed across my center, not stopping until they faded down my thighs. I dug my hands into his hair, forgetting everything I had worried about moments before, forgetting everything but the feeling of him licking me like a man dying of thirst. He thrust his tongue inside me, moving his fingers to my favorite spot instead. Heat built low in the pit of my stomach, not stopping until I broke against his mouth.

He wiped his mouth with the back of his hand, a little motion I barely caught with my eyes rolled back in my head. In another blink he was on top of me, wrapping my legs around his hips and pushing slowly inside me.

"You should let me do that to you sometime," I said.

"Do what?" He nipped at my breasts, shoving himself into the hilt. My moan swallowed my next words, and it was another few minutes before I remembered them again.

"Taste you like that."

His movements grew frenzied, his eyes three shades darker. He ran his thumb around my lips, staring intently. "You keep talking like that, *annwyl*, and I won't have time to make you finish again."

I grinned. His thumb pressed against my mouth, silencing me, but I parted my lips, running my tongue from the base to the very tip.

His eyes rolled back in his head, hand fisting the blanket beneath me. My devious grin widened and I did it again, taking his entire thumb in my mouth this time. I ran circles around him with my tongue, closing my eyes and moaning as I licked him. His rhythmic pace faltered, body taut above me. When I opened my eyes, his wide ones stared down at me.

"I think I'll do this." I grabbed his hand, wrapping my lips around the tips of his pointer and middle finger, slowly making my way down to the bases. When his fingers brushed the back of my throat I grinned, eyes on him the entire time.

He went preternaturally still. "Then what?"

I closed my eyes and *sucked*. His palm flattened against my throat, moving with the vibrations as I moaned.

His fingers slipped from my mouth, wrapping gently around my neck. He didn't squeeze, but the intent was there, the dangerous intent behind his eyes. He slammed into me and the smile melted off my face. He did it again and I gripped his arm, nails digging into his skin.

He lifted one slender leg and threw it over his shoulder, rocking into me as he pressed a burning kiss to my ankle, then one a little lower. Fire sang beneath my skin, his hand on my throat squeezing gently. His hips rolled into me, free hand skimming up my thigh and over my knee, anchoring me to him. He threw my other leg on his shoulder and fucked me hard enough to shift us off the blankets and onto the stone floor.

"The things you do to me are going to be a problem."

I laughed. "Why is that?"

"I can't get anything done with you like this." He pulled out and flipped me over, wrapping an arm around my waist and dragging me up until I was on my knees. My back was flush with his chest, his knees nudging mine apart. He buried his face in my neck, grabbing his cock and running it along me. "You're a fucking poison, *annwyl*."

I shivered, lifting my arms above my head and around his neck. I craned my neck back until I rested my head on his shoulder, staring into his heated gaze. "I suppose you like all the changes."

"I like *you*." His lips ran along my jaw, fevered breaths heating my skin. "You were beautiful yesterday and you are beautiful right now."

"Was this supposed to happen?" It was hard to think with his hand dipped between our legs, nudging himself against me. I was so wet I ached with it, but I wanted to know. "Was I supposed to change?"

"No. I don't know." He kissed my cheekbones, breathing hard against my ear. "You don't smell like a druid, honestly."

Fear dropped my stomach. "What do you mean?"

"I don't think you are a druid." I pushed at the arm locked around my waist but he growled, holding me in place. "I can talk and fuck you, *annwyl*."

"I think this conversation requires our full attention."

"And I will give it that. I promise." He skimmed his nose up my throat. "My full—" He tugged my earlobe. "—undivided—" His lips brushed my cheekbone. "—attention."

I shivered, grinding myself against him. "I'm serious, Jack."

"I know. I can smell it on you." He tilted my face until my lips brushed his. "And before you ask, I don't know. I'm not quite sure what you are, but I promise I will devote every resource at my disposal to figuring it out. Tomorrow."

He kissed me, but I turned away. "Should I be worried?"

"No." The word came too harsh, savage. That only made me more nervous, but he whispered, "If I was worried you would know it. Nothing about this will harm you. I'd die before I let that happen."

I brushed my hand across his face. "No need to be so dramatic."

"You're *mine*," he growled. He pushed his cock against me, slipping along my wet center, but not inside. "I protect what's mine. Always. So when I say it's fine, and we will discuss it more in the morning . . ." He kissed me again, running his tongue against mine. "You are perfect, *annwyl*. We will figure out the rest together."

"Okay." But the nervous feeling never left, the sudden sense something could be seriously wrong. If I wasn't a druid, what could I possibly be? Maybe this was just a strange step to my final evolution, or some side effect because of the ritual. He transformed me without a Bogoran, something that has never been done before. It was uncharted territory, and while we had always been in that, it was a lot different when it literally altered my being . . .

"First thing in the morning, I want to ask Arthur."

Jack went taut behind me. His arm dug into my waist, cock slipping *deep* inside me. I moaned, breathing fast as he rocked against me, at the vicious words he breathed against my ear. "The only man's name you say undressed is mine." He slammed into me harder, rubbing at that little spot I loved. "Whose name do you say while I fuck you, *annwyl*?"

"Jack."

He fucked me so hard I could no longer think. "Scream it."

"Jack. Oh god . . . Jack . . . Jack. *Jaevidan.*"

He didn't stop until we both broke again. We never went back to sleep.

SOMEONE KNOCKED ON THE foyer door three times. "You two done in there yet?"

A low sound went off in Jack's throat. He was sitting in his desk chair, stark naked, with me straddled on top of him. At the moment, he was very busy writing his name over my nipples with his tongue. I grinned, running my hands through his hair. "Maybe we should come up for air."

His hands found home on my hips, digging in. He nipped at my breast. "No."

"It's been three days!" The voice called, which I now recognized as Lillian's. She sighed. "Addie, can you talk some sense into him?"

It wasn't until two days ago I realized the bond made Jack a bit . . . testy. It was something he hadn't mentioned earlier, but apparently it was fairly common—or as common as it could be, for such a rare bond—for a freshly paralleled couple to, well, go into a frenzy. Which made sense, if the whole thing was about mating and such. I'd already secured all my human and magic means to prevent pregnancy, which I suspected only made things worse. If the bond sensed it wasn't getting a baby, it might not want to let up.

Men in particular were affected, even if they were human, but I didn't need Jack to tell me that. He'd reverted into something closely resembling a caveman. Which meant he'd done very little besides eating, sleeping and fucking, and the first two only enough to maintain his pulse.

I ran my hands through his hair, forcing his head back. Maybe a new tactic would be more effective. I pouted, streaking my thumb across his face. "I want to get out for a little bit."

His eyes narrowed. "Why?"

"Jaaaaccck. If you don't come out, I'm selling all the stock on the hoteeel," Lillian sang.

"We could go dancing. Get something to eat." I kissed his cheek, breathing in his ear, "Is the movie theater always that dark?"

"And on your oil company! J.W. enterprise will go bankrupt!"

"On the fucking fates, *Lillian,*" he snapped. She went silent behind the door. "Do not sell my fucking stock."

I grinned. "I think she's serious."

"I am!"

His eyes roamed down my bare chest, settling a few inches below my navel. "Worth it."

"But I want to see the others. We still haven't gotten to ask about my change." His mouth set down in a frown. "We have to get out sometime."

He shook his head.

"Yes, Jack."

He shook his head again.

"And while we're at it, I think I'm going to give myself a raise! Double the salary, and *fifteen weeks* of paid leave a year."

I walked my fingers down his chest, brushing my nose against his. "I'll do that thing you like tonight."

He stilled beneath me. "Which one?"

I grinned, tugging his lower lip between my teeth. "All of them."

JACK SAT IN A chair all to himself in the red room, foot bouncing against the floor with his hands laced between his knees. Each time someone wanted to talk to him he gave clipped answers or made slightly inhuman noises, so I performed the niceties on his behalf.

The Band of Banished threw me a little *Welcome to Immortality!* dinner—all Lillian's idea—at the Silvertongue. Fae wine (which I could now safely drink) made several rounds, along with a spread cooked by Charlene herself. At my insistence, Lillian shaded her in so I could say thank you, but she only told me to enact corporeal punishment for theft and asked to be taken back to the kitchens.

Violet said I looked slightly less hideous and Harold hissed at me. Sensing how on edge Jack was, Arthur and Will put as much distance between us as possible in the packed room, keeping the conversations brief. Meanwhile, Lillian skipped circles around us all, saying she knew everything would work out perfectly and she was so happy we still had a month until killing Delsaran and my hair just looked so beautiful and *shiny* and she couldn't wait to play with it.

After packing away Charlene's third course and getting another round of wine, we all settled into our respective seats and discussed exactly what the transformation meant.

"I think Jack is right, you really don't smell like a druid," Will said. The latter's sharp eyes fell on him with viciousness. Will shrank down into his seat.

"Druids don't generally change either," Arthur weighed in. "I mean, the differences are subtle, but you have definitely *changed*."

"There's nothing else she could be," Violet said. "So she's a fucked up druid, what did we expect?"

"Ooo! What if she's a siren? Addie, try and sing for us."

I shook my head, swirling my glass of wine around. "Whatever I am, I just want to know if it will be a problem."

Arthur shrugged. "Do you feel okay?"

"I guess . . . I don't know, I don't feel all that different. It keeps feeling like there's something in my hands though, like beneath my skin."

"Power," Lillian said. She frowned. "That's more of a fae trait though."

"She's definitely not fae," Violet said. She took a bored sip of her drink, dribbling some out for Harold to lick off the table. "She smells rotten."

I paused. "What?"

"Not in a bad way," Lillian rushed. "More like . . . wilting flowers. Very, very sweet. With a hint of decay."

My stomach hit the floor. "I smell like *decay*?"

"You're not decaying," Arthur cut in. His eyes roamed me up and down. "It would be much easier if I could do an exam . . ." He turned his slow gaze on Jack, who clutched his armrest until the stitches popped.

I sighed, making my way over to Jack and fell in his lap. His arm came around me immediately. "As long as you think there's nothing to worry about for now." To Jack I whispered, "Do I smell bad?"

He breathed deep, nuzzling his cheek against my hair. "You smell so fucking good."

"As long as *you* feel okay, I'd say there's very little to worry about at the moment. For all we know, this is simply what happens when creating a druid utilizing the, um—" Arthur's stare fell on Jack, who was currently unworking the top button of my blouse. "—method, you did."

I grabbed Jack's hand, gently placing it back in his lap. It came back up to my collar immediately. "In that case, I feel great actually." I removed Jack's hand again, lacing my fingers through his. "It gets a little more intense every day, but in a good way. I have a lot more energy, and I'm stronger, my eyesight has been getting sharper, my hearing."

"All fae qualities," Lillian pointed out.

"Jack is also very strong, you have to remember that," Will said. "It's not like you were paralleled to your run-of-the-mill high fae, and since you're now a Morrigan with Violet, it could be making you into some sort of . . . super druid. Who knows."

I eyed Violet, who had been very quiet the past few minutes. As far as we knew, the Morrigan was automatic with my acceptance of the parallel bond to Jack. I expected to feel something from her since we were now connected, but she had said herself she only sensed Jack in extremes, so maybe it would be the same for me. "Vi, do you feel anything?"

She shrugged. "Superior to you in every way. Other than that, maybe a little stronger. I used to have a tweak in my elbow, that's gone. So your contribution to our power has been fucking riveting."

Okay, so she was feeling like herself. Jack placed his hand on my knee, roaming beneath my skirt and up my thigh. "Does anyone know how long he's supposed to be like this?"

"Er, no," Arthur said. He turned a splotchy maroon. "I think you just have to . . . um, well, get it out of his system. If you catch my drift."

Jack's sharp eyes fell on the druid, who held his hands in a defensive position. I sighed, turning Jack's face back to me. "Be polite."

He growled at me. Honest to god fucking growled. "I'm being very polite."

I narrowed my eyes. On the other side of the room, Violet coughed. "You two are fucking disgusting."

My lips cracked with a smile. Jack's didn't. His hand drifted across my face, snatching a lock of my hair and letting it drift through his fingers. "I told you I would keep you safe."

I laid my hand over his. "I know."

"Whatever you are, I love it very much," he whispered. Warmth unfurled in my chest. I smiled.

"Addie, do you want to visit a flower pixie colony with me this week? I have to pick up tithe from them and they may recognize your scent. Or . . ."

Lillian's words faded to background noise. "I'm worried this is a bad thing. We don't have a lot of time to figure everything out before . . ."

Jack pulled me closer, his lips inches from mine. "I already told you, if I thought it was something bad I would have intervened immediately. You are very powerful. I can feel it." His fingers shifted over my cheek, brushing my hair behind my ear. "And I can always feel you. So the moment something feels wrong, I will let you know. I promise."

I brushed my lips against his. His scent washed over me, rain and oleander. "You are so sweet to me."

"Do you think we dragged them out too early?" Will asked.

Jack's scent grew stronger, taking over all my senses. I brushed my lips against his again, a heady fog rolling through my brain. God, he smelled so good. And he was so warm, and *solid* beneath me. He made a satisfied little grunt and nipped at my lips, tugging the bottom one between his teeth.

"No . . . no, they're fine."

First his scent, then his taste. On the fucking fates, his taste. Wetness gathered in my panties and I shifted, a little noise breathing past my lips. His hands tightened on my waist, his breaths coming faster. I kissed him again, running my tongue over his. I wanted his tongue on my breasts again, between my legs. I suddenly felt so empty, so distant from him. I wrapped my arms around his neck, tugging him closer.

"Jack, Adeline? Anyone home?"

I blinked and we were in the Abstruse. I swiveled around, but Jack shoved me against the wall, lifting my skirt and ripping my undergarments to my ankles. "Should we have said goodbye?"

451

"No." He grabbed my hips and sheathed himself inside me.

FORTY-FOUR

IN THE WEEKS THAT followed, I received quick and dirty training on adjusting to my new body and abilities. While no one could quite figure out what I had become, Arthur promised to solve the case after Delsaran was dealt with. But as long as Jack didn't seem concerned, neither was I.

So far, I had done little more than float at will. I couldn't glamour or use compulsion like the fae, nor use the spells and enchantments Arthur tested with me. I was surprisingly efficient at using the shade, setting Jack's teeth on edge each time I did. But after a week of proving I not only wouldn't get lost, but could utilize it in ways the others had never seen, his anxiety faded and he pushed my power to its limit.

As it turned out, I could not only pull objects through, but *people*. I'd adamantly refused at first, but Jack insisted I test the theory on him. Standing in Arthur's living room and Jack in our apartment three blocks away, I reached through a mirror and brought him to me.

Jack landed on the checkered tiles, bewildered. Arthur had leapt from his chair, hair askew. "On the fucking fates."

I grinned with pride.

Like all magical creatures, I was also faster, stronger, and had more energy than I knew what to do with it. Power coursed over my skin night and day, making it hard to do anything but find outlets to pour it into. I hardly slept, but I didn't need to. It became instantly clear why Jack always rose before me in the mornings, because after three or four hours of rest, I was wide awake and ready to practice again.

Will made it his mission to train me with a sword and daggers. Guns didn't mute my abilities like they did with the others, and neither did iron. While everyone else needed extensive safety measures to keep their iron weapons from poisoning themselves, it turned out to be no trouble for me. But becoming proficient in swordplay would take many years, and that wasn't something we had time for. Samhain was only two weeks away, when Delsaran had promised to unveil his newest threat to humanity. If we were going to kill him, it had to be before then.

So I trained with Will in the early hours of the morning, then Jack and Arthur with the shade. In the afternoon, we joined Lillian and Violet at the Silvertongue, crowding the red room to its limit and formulating our plan for confronting Delsaran. He had been noticeably silent these past few months, even in the human world. Jack pulled strings with the police to see how his liquor business had been running, but even the authorities claimed he vanished, assuming a rival gang may have killed him or he went underground. Lillian had been busy running around Chicago with Violet for protection, extracting memories from any creature they could. And on October 20th, only eleven days before our doomsday, they found him.

"Currently, he's holed up in an ironworks on Lake Michigan," she said. We crowded the velvet booths, pouring over the map of Chicago spread across the table like a shrine. "Which, as I am sure you can imagine, makes things much more difficult for us."

Like me and whatever I was, druids weren't affected by iron, but Arthur repeated the Guild chose to remain neutral on this matter, and druids were few and far between. As far as I knew, no other magic species were resistant, meaning Delsaran kept his current circle small, or he was alone.

"What else in the memories you pulled?" Jack asked.

Lillian shook her head. "Not much. Even his supporters knew very little, but many had their memories scrambled."

Jack frowned. "How?"

"I don't know, it shouldn't be an ability Delsaran has, unless there is another fae doing it for him."

That made no sense either, since affinities ran in family lines and Lillian was the last living member of her kin. She echoed my very thoughts to the room.

"Theoretically, if he possessed one of the other Dianomicans, it's an ability he could create," Arthur pointed out.

"But we have the second. The first, sixth and eighth are in Ildathach, the third, fifth, seventh and ninth have known owners and the tenth has been lost for centuries." She ran her hands through her hair in a very un-Lillian like way. "I don't know what he's doing, it makes no sense."

"That's not important, killing him is," Violet hissed. "Jack and I can handle some iron and Addie is resistant. As long as we know where to find the fucker that's all we need."

I wanted to agree, but without any knowledge of what he planned to do, it was difficult to say if killing him would resolve the issue. It would certainly solve a handful of problems, but if his plans were already set in motion, it wouldn't be enough.

"What if we trap him?" I asked. "There is no need to kill him right away if we could obtain valuable information first."

But Jack shook his head. "That's too much of a risk. If there is an opening, we need to take it."

We all fell into pensive silence. My fingers caressed the diamond hanging from my throat, seeking the comfort. Once, it had been an iron crucifix. Old habits die hard.

"So, it's settled, then," Violet said. "Lillian, Arthur and Will remain in New York while the rest of us go to Chicago. We find Delsaran here—" She pressed a finger to the thin X Lillian drew. "—we kill him, then we do our best to mitigate the aftermath."

I nodded. "When?"

Jack folded the map, taking a long sip of his drink. "Three days. Until then, we prepare."

I DIDN'T SLEEP THAT night, partially from nerves but mostly Jack's insatiable needs. He undressed me the moment we appeared in the study and bent me over the back of a settee. After that, it was against his desk, on the floor beside the bookshelves, then we broke apart long enough to retreat to the bedroom. I had mere moments before he shoved me on the bed and buried his face between my thighs.

I wished there was more to say, but Lillian had already given us everything she could and the rest would be dealt with as it came. Jack and Violet had already selected everything we would take— weapons, mostly, with a few provisions from Arthur that would be useful when facing a druid. Other than that, there was little more to do but hope Lillian could find more information in the meantime. At this point, everything else was unfamiliar ground.

"Have you ever been in battle?" We lay in bed, both pretending to attempt sleep..

"Here or in Ildathach?"

Well, that answered my question. "Ildathach."

"Yes."

I realized it may not have been the best pillow talk, but after a long moment he said. "When I was younger, against a nation neighboring Lillian's."

I turned on my side, fighting the weight of his arm wrapped around my stomach. When we were nose to nose, I asked, "Why?"

"Why does any country go to war?"

"I've heard the reasons vary."

"No, in the end, it all boils down to the same thing." He sighed, running his thumb over my lips. I kissed the calloused pad of it. "People are greedy."

I mulled it over. "What about now?'

"As I said, people are greedy." He shifted, pulling me up until I lay directly on top of him. I folded my arms over his chest, resting my chin on my hands. "The greed in this case is Delsaran and we're on the other side of it."

"The right side?"

He leaned to the side. "Why do you ask?"

My eyes darted everywhere but him, but after a long pause I whispered, "I have never killed another person. And I know it is for the right reasons, that it will save many in the long run, but it still feels . . ." Like my humanity could suffer for it. It was something I'd been warned time and time again to keep an eye on, seeing the results myself with druids like Henry Foster. Jack said we couldn't risk entrapping Delsaran, but a childlike naivete wished it were still an option. That maybe with some time and reasoning, he could be reformed as Lillian had once been. Then we could all hold hands and sing and world peace would prevail.

"It will lay heavy on your consciousness, *annwyl*, and always let it. It is how you keep this." His fingers drifted down my face, settling in the dip of my chin. "It is not our good deeds that make us just, but our hard choices. Everyone is perfect when there are no difficult decisions to make, when they are on the outside looking in. But hardship defines our true nature. And I will be here for you, always."

I kissed him. "I know. Thank you."

"We should really get some sleep."

I settled back on my side of the bed, savoring the arm he tucked around my waist. His quiet breaths skimmed the back of my neck, growing even and slow after a few minutes passed. I reached for the diamond hanging from my neck, running the warmth through my fingers. *You must always listen to Jaevidan.*

Still, as sunlight touched the carpet and Jack found home between my legs, I couldn't help but feel like I had missed something.

FORTY-FIVE

AFTER BREAKFAST, JACK WENT off to discuss something with Violet. I used my new ability to carry Will through the shade and to the study. He swayed on his feet, hand on a knife at his belt. "On the fucking fates, that is strange."

"Very convenient though."

"Perhaps for you." He grinned, tossing a bandolier over the back of a chair. The silver practice weapons glimmered in the firelight. "Jack actually has me running around today, so I'm afraid you won't get to practice stabbing me."

"I'm not very good at it anyway."

"And you won't be for many, many years." He patted my head, swiping an apple off the abandoned breakfast table. "I am heading downtown if you would like to come."

I wanted to practice manipulating the shade more. Arthur had a theory the shade itself was made of matter. Matter that could be bent and utilized similar to how fae work compulsion and glamour. But Jack—along with everyone else—provided endless warnings about experimenting without supervision. The shade was an arcane entity that was deserving of respect. It'd killed enough people they knew to make them all antsy about my sudden draw to it.

"What do you need to do?"

"Human things, actually. I need to send a telegraph off to an associate in Wales and make a bank deposit."

Power swarmed beneath my skin, itching to be used. Because I could easily pull things to me, I had been wanting to attempt sending items to other places, a very difficult skill if your body wasn't traveling with said item through the shade. Jack could do it to some extent, but said he never bothered because of how often objects ended up flying through the wrong mirror. And to send something that far was out of the question. As adept at shading as Jack was, he could only travel himself about ten miles at a time. I managed fifty the other day.

I shoved the notion down, fingering the chain of my necklace. "I think a morning of normalcy may be nice for once."

Crisp, autumn air hit my skin, but I wasn't cold. I wore my favorite autumn jacket and wool hat to blend in, but ever since changing, temperature differences hadn't bothered me much at all. Jack's study used to be sweltering on a good day.

Orange and yellow leaves littered the sidewalk. Wreaths of African daisies and purple corn adorned front doors and pumpkins littered the stoops. Restaurants boasted marigolds and mums in their flower pots and shop windows held advertisements for Halloween costume sewing patterns. Children huffed hot breath into red-tipped fingers and women pulled their coats tighter against the October breeze. Lillian mentioned they held a delightful parade in midtown every year, but for obvious reasons, we would not attend. On the actual holiday, my fae companions never partook in human festivities anyway, not that Samhain would be celebrated this year.

Will made his bank deposit and we found our way to the local telegraph office. A line stretched halfway down the block. He sighed, rolling himself a cigarette on the sidewalk. "It's only crowded the days I come here."

I spun on my heel, smiling at a little girl behind us in her mother's arms. "Bad luck charm?"

"Arthur has checked me for one thrice, but I never trust him with hexes."

The woman behind us stepped back, frowning.

"May I ask you something?"

The line shuffled forward. Will leaned against the frigid stone building, puffing his cigarette. "By all means."

"Have we overlooked something?" I chose my words carefully, not wanting to raise any alarms to the humans around us. "I just can't shake this feeling that something is wrong."

"I'm sure it's just nerves." He flicked ash onto the ground, shrugging. "Or an aftereffect of your . . . previous condition."

Right, my curse. Just another thing no one had knowledge of. Even when Lillian rooted through the memories she took from my head, she couldn't make sense of them.

"Perhaps." I knew in part it was due to all the secrets Jack still withheld, but there was nothing to be done with that for now. The star told me to wait until he gave permission to search his memories.

"There are many things we don't know yet. Mostly about you." He pointed the lit end of his cigarette in my direction. "It would make anyone nervous, we simply need to keep our wits about us for now."

"I know." Sighing, I looked up the line. A man argued with someone in the doorway to the telegraph office, gesturing down the row of people. The tired worker tried to calm him, clearly exasperated with the display.

Several quiet moments passed, people sniffing and shuffling their feet in the cold. A siren whistled in the distance, followed by a police car rolling to a stop on the sidewalk.

Two officers stepped out, scanning the line. When they found Will and I among the throng, they stepped closer.

Will sighed, throwing his cigarette to the ground. "On the fucking fates."

"We have to ask you to leave. This is a whites-only establishment."

Will shook his head. "Since when?"

"Last week. It's posted in the window." The burlier of the officers gestured up the line, to the fogged window too far away to see. "There's an office uptown you can use."

"It's just a telegraph," I said.

"Please stay out of this, miss."

"No, he's with me." I gestured at Will. "Or am I not allowed to use the telegraph office either?"

The officer scowled, distaste clear as his eyes bounced between Will and I. "The new rule was posted in the window last week. You can use the service if you wish, but he has to leave."

Red tinged my vision. The line shuffled forward. The woman holding her baby stepped around us, taking our spot ahead.

"This is bullshit."

"Okay, Addie." Will placed a hand on my shoulder, tugging me back. The officer eyed the touch with clear disgust. "We can go uptown. We're not trying to cause trouble."

Restless power swarmed down my arms, gathering at my wrists. I bit my lip, containing the urge to indulge it. "They can't do this, it's not right."

"They can, and they will." He eyed the officer uneasily. "I know you have the best intentions, but this will only make things worse. Trust me. Let's just leave, please."

I knew he was right, but that energy swelled, burning along my sinew. I stole a deep breath, nodding. Control. Now was most certainly not the time to lose it. I looped my arm through Will's, scowling at the officer as we made our leave.

But he wasn't done yet. Hands on hips, he nodded his head at the cigarette butt on the ground. "What's that?"

Will closed his eyes, breathing a heavy sigh. Our footsteps halted on the cement, the officer's heated voice lifting on the bitter wind.

462

"It's mine. I can clean it up," I said, already circling back for the cigarette butt.

"I didn't see you smoking. I did see *him* smoking," the officer said, gesturing back at Will.

I snatched the butt and threw it in my purse. "Well the issue is resolved. Good day, officer."

"We have fines for that sort of thing."

"I'm sure you do."

"Hey, I'm not done talking to you."

Will snatched my arm. "Just keep walking."

The second officer stepped in front of us, blocking the sidewalk. I shifted around him but he grabbed Will, slamming him against the building. "You don't just walk away when an officer of the law is talking to you."

I grabbed his jacket, trying to pull him away. "What are you doing? Get off of him."

"You want me to take you in too?"

A crowd gathered closer. The first cop came closer, pulling out a pair of handcuffs. "I wasn't going to do this, but we don't accept this kind of behavior."

I grabbed the first officer, but he was already slapping the handcuffs on Will. The latter rolled his eyes, glamour flickering around his face but I was the only one who noticed. "*Stop it.* He didn't do anything. You can't do this."

The first officer shoved me aside. "I can add resisting arrest to his charges too."

"I already told you, asshole. The cigarette butt was mine."

An old woman gasped, eyes raking down my rolled stockings. "If you were my daughter . . ."

Ignoring her, I grabbed Will's arm, but he shook me away. "It's fine, Addie. Just go get Jack." His eyes sharpened on me, flickering down the street.

I shook my head. "No, no way, they can't just—"

"Go. Get. Jack. We've dealt with this before, and we have an image to uphold, in case you forgot." He tried to smile, but it was ruined by the second officer shoving him forward. "Alright, alright, I'm going. Calm yourself, lad."

God, I hope he killed them. "He's a good friend of Jack Warren."

The first officer laughed. "Yeah, and I go out to dinner with Coolidge. Get out of the way." He shoved me onto the sidewalk, where the crowd was thick with curious onlookers. Of course, none of them fucking helped.

"Move," I snapped, shoving people aside. The cops threw Will in the back of their car, then stood smoking on the sidewalk with a third officer who arrived on scene. Fury choked my throat as they left the butts on the ground, all three climbing into the car as the sirens flickered on. Will turned in the back, mouthing, *I'm fine* through the glass.

The third officer turned next to him, staring at me. Something glinted beneath his waistcoat, slipping forward as the engine roared to life. A medallion. White with a red cross in the center.

He grinned.

No.

No.

"*Wait.*" I shoved people aside, stumbling into the street. "Wait, stop!"

I reached the car just as they hit the gas. My fingers slipped from the dusty trunk as it peeled into the street. Every other car shifted out of the way. I ran after it, heels smacking the asphalt and horns going off around me. "Stop, stop, stop, *Will, get out!*"

They floored the gas. I skidded to a stop in the middle of an intersection. "*Fuck.*"

I had to find Jack. *I had to find Jack.* I ducked into an alley, looking for the first reflective surface I could find. It came in the form of a dusty bedroom window, where a little girl brushed her hair in the mirror. She glanced at me, wide-eyed. The last thing I saw was the drop of her jaw before entering liquid darkness.

I thought of the study, but remembered Jack wasn't there. *Of all fucking days.* I didn't know where Violet resided, had never seen her apartment. I did the next best thing and shaded to Arthur's.

Three fizzing vials tumbled smoke onto a table. A mouse ran beneath my feet and scurried for a hole in the wall. In the kitchen, a tea kettle began a slow whistle, but Arthur wasn't in either room, his study or bedroom. I brought my hands to my head, flicking my eyes to the mirror and shaded to Lillian's, but just like everyone else, she wasn't in her apartment.

I felt for the bond, jerking and tugging for something, anything, but Jack must have been not paying attention. Shit, shit, shit. There was nowhere else to go, and Will was running out of time. If the Knights took him in, if my brother, maybe Tommy . . .

I walked across the hall and pounded on the door. When there was no response, I kicked it in, but the apartment on the other side was completely empty. Even the furniture that had been present on our arrival was gone, nothing but dust motes and open air to fill the room.

I tugged the bond one more time. *Jack!*

What if something had happened to him too?

No time. I knew where Will was and I had to get to him first. Jack forbade me, and I mean *strictly* forbade me from attempting to shade into a moving vehicle until he could teach me, but he would be a whole lot angrier at what I was about to do. I ran for the empty bathroom. Fingerprints from another life still marked the mirror. I stared deep into my reflection, breathed—

And landed in the backseat of a car, directly between Will and a Knight of Templar.

The first officer whirled in the passenger seat. "What the—"

I kicked my heel into his eye and grabbed Will by the collar. The car swerved, sending the side mirrors and windows into blurs of color with no discernible reflection. Will screamed and grabbed a handle on the ceiling, but I reached over his lap and threw the door open, praying his faeness and my gods-knew-what-ness would break the fall. The car screeched into a tail spin and I pushed us out, rolling over and under Will as my head repeatedly smacked the asphalt. A horn blew heavily in my ears and tires swerved just beside my head. I landed on top of Will with a grunt, cringing at the sound of bones snapping in the arms still cuffed behind his back.

He inhaled and exhaled, wide eyes falling on me. "*Adeline, what the fuck?*"

I grabbed his waistcoat and pulled him up to sit. Both wrists fell at peculiar angles within the cuffs, blood smeared across his skin and pebbles embedded in his face. Behind his head, the Knight stepped out of the cop car and leveled a gun in our direction.

"*Addie.*"

I focused on the shimmering silver of his cuffs, the gray light bouncing off the silver. We entered the shade, a gunshot popping in my ears as cold liquid swallowed us.

I kept a firm grip on Will, thinking of the mirror in the study, but we remained buried in darkness and an endless chill. Shivers coated my bones, the sound of Will's heavy breaths. I thought of the mirror, physically *reached* for it, but each time I came close, something bounced me back.

A low moan came from Will. Ice crept across my skin, coating my tongue. We couldn't stay in here much longer, something was wrong. I turned my thoughts to the alley across the street from the hotel, the shimmering pipes atop the adjacent building. I landed on cold cement with a grunt, an icy breeze throwing my hair into my face.

Will shuddered beside me. Birds chirped and took off in a flap of wings. Cars honked their horns from a distance, along with low chatter and the steady wail of police sirens. I pulled Will up to sit, dabbing at his face. His wide eyes scanned the rooftop we sat on, the upper windows of the hotel glimmering across the street.

He took a calming breath. "Addie, I am going to give you the benefit of the doubt, but I have to say, I am absolutely, beyond fucking—"

"There was a Knight in the car." I tore the edge of my dress, praying to the stars Lillian didn't suffer a stroke when she saw it. Blood soaked the light fabric as soon as it touched his face. "I looked for help, but I couldn't find anyone and Jack isn't answering the bond. I think something is wrong."

He ignored me, wrenching his face away and pushing to his feet. His broken wrists hung limp and useless behind his back. "Oh, fuck."

I jumped to my feet. A hundred feet below, about twenty police cars surrounded the hotel. The street had been blocked off, angry pedestrians being guided through alleys and cars directed to turn around. Angry guests stood with suitcases on the ground, screaming at officers while men in black suits entered the hotel with guns.

"Are they raiding it?"

Will shook his head. "Doesn't fucking matter, Jack already moved everything." He bounced his wrists. "Could you get these off of me please?"

I touched the handcuffs, focusing on nothing but the silver metal and praying I didn't take pieces of Will away. I blinked and they disappeared into the shade. He rolled his shoulders, shaking out his wrists.

"Are they broken?"

"They'll heal within the hour. Why did you put us on the rooftop?"

"I don't know, I couldn't enter the study all of a sudden. It felt like someone was throwing us back."

"They shattered the mirror." He bounced on his heels, teeth clenched. "You couldn't find *anyone*?"

467

"No one was home. We can check the Silvertongue."

"No, they won't be there either." Will turned in circles, bringing his hands to his head before realizing those didn't work. "Do that thing. Try to summon Jack."

I did. Staring at metal pipes puffing smoke into the sky, I reached for Jack and tried pulling him through the shade, but he either was nowhere near a mirror or was resisting me. "I can't. And I can't feel him through the bond either." I peered over the edge of the building, ducking down when an officer's eyes shot to the roof. "Are they Knights?"

"Likely." He chewed his lip. "This had to be fucking Delsaran."

Violet once postulated he had tipped them off. It made sense, but that didn't tell us where Jack was. "They still think I'm human. I can go—"

Will shook his head. "No, absolutely not. We need to find the others first. There are contingency plans in place for things like this."

"Okay, so what now?"

Will blew out a breath, sinking to the ground. "Just . . . give me a second to think."

Blood pooled beneath his legs, his breaths slowing. I scrambled forward, tearing off his jacket and waistcoat. Nothing in front, but when I circled him, a tiny hole filled with blood beside his lower spine.

"Will, I think you got shot."

He nodded. "I just realized that myself."

I touched the wound, wrenching my fingers back when he hissed in pain. "Why won't it stop bleeding?"

"Iron," he gritted out.

Shit. I dabbed at the blood with his ruined clothes, but no matter how much I tried blood kept pouring onto the cement. "There's too much blood, I can't find the bullet."

"It's too deep, don't bother." He breathed hard through his nose. "We have to take it out the old fashioned way, it won't heal otherwise."

I hadn't the faintest clue how to dig a bullet out of someone. Will grunted, splashing a hand in a pool of his own blood. "I have an old medic kit in my bedroom."

"Okay, okay. I'll go get it." I tore another strip of fabric and bundled it tight. "I'm really sorry."

He screamed as I shoved it in the bullet hole. The fabric was red within seconds, but a steady stream no longer left his body. I grabbed his hand and kissed his cheek. "Five minutes. Can you manage?"

He nodded, dark skin turning an unsettling pallid shade. "Get some whiskey while you're at it."

I left him on the rooftop, landing in a darkened living room.

All the shades had been pulled tight. The white tiles were streaked with dirt, the immaculate couch toppled on its side. Throw pillows were cut open and feathers drifted across the floor. The wallpaper had been sliced and the wood beneath hacked into with an ax. I turned in a circle, breath faltering, when three sets of eyes landed on me.

Shadows clung to the men, making their features indiscernible. Smoke curled from one of their lips, their eyes trained on me and something behind me. I turned, but not before someone grabbed me around the waist and shoved a rag against my mouth. I screamed but the poison took effect immediately, vision crumbling away at the corners. The last thing I saw was a pair of dark brown eyes wide with fear.

FORTY-SIX

A METAL CHAIR PRESSED against my spine and my cheek lay flat on a frigid table. My hands were cuffed and chained to the surface, outstretched before me. I blinked, lifting my head and scanning my surroundings. A cement floor with a rusted drain ran beneath my feet. On three walls, floor-to-ceiling mirrors, with a darkened hall at my back. I tried craning my neck to look behind me, but my restraints kept me still.

I yanked my wrists against the cuffs, foggy mind slow to catch up. The dark metal absorbed the light, coming from a sea of flickering bulbs suspended above my head. Everything was iron.

Reflections stared at me, hundreds of images of my wide eyes bouncing back at one another in the mirrors. I stared dead ahead, trying to discern if there was anything behind me, but the hall was too poorly lit to see more than a few feet past my back into darkness.

Fine. I wasn't weak to iron, so I could shade. I found my eyes in the mirror, waiting for the image to shimmer and go molten. Nothing happened. I tried again, but nothing.

Grunting, I shook my hands again and tried a different mirror, moving between my true reflection and the illusion of a thousand eyes looking back at me. Nothing worked. I was still in this room, the shade just out of reach.

"Don't bother. It won't work."

I froze. The low voice came from behind me, followed by the rich scent of smoke. Tobacco infiltrated all my senses and sweat ran down my spine. Someone shifted, then emerged from the endless black. Silver hair gleamed in the orange lightbulb, reflected in the mirror across from me. Agent Rodney took the chair opposite me, spun it around and sat with knees splayed.

"Hello, again," he said.

I bared my teeth, silent. A light bulb swung ominously above our heads, making our shadows writhe in yellow along the floor.

"Adeline Colton. Born January 21st, 1906 in Bellevue Hospital to Jonathan and Clara Colton. Reborn September of 1926, only several blocks away." Smoke curled through his mustache and swirled back into his nostrils. "And what a shame that was. Arguably one of the biggest failures of the Knights of Templar."

I shook my head. "I haven't the faintest clue what you are talking about."

"Let's skip ahead to the point where you realize I know everything, and neither of us feign ignorance." He sent a plume of smoke in my direction. I wrinkled my nose at the sour smell. "I know what you are. You know what I am. All I want to do is chat."

Except, he didn't know what I was. No one did. I kept that information buried, schooling my face into a hard mask. "Where is Tommy?"

"I asked him not to be present for this."

Dark eyes filled my vision, the last thing I saw before everything faded to black. I swallowed. "I want to see him."

"I may allow it, with your cooperation." He reached for something on the ground. I used the opportunity to scan the mirrors again, but the shade didn't respond.

"As I said, don't bother. You see these mirrors?"

I didn't respond.

"They're very special. About . . . twenty or so years ago, it was discovered that if one side was coated with a film, where there was light, a reflection would be seen. But on the other side, it was nothing but a window. We call it one-way glass." He smiled. "Very useful to police, but even more useful to us. Because as it turns out, occult creatures cannot travel out of it."

My heart sank low in my chest, ice pricking along my vertebrae.

"Even better," he continued, "The occult creatures can still enter. Making this room—" He waved a hand around. "—the perfect trap."

I felt for the bond, the ever-present tug in my chest, but that was silent too. "Does that make me bait?"

He grinned. "Oh, no. We have already completed our hunting for the evening."

Fury bled hot and vicious. "Why am I here?"

"I wanted to chat. I already told you this." He pulled a thick file from a satchel on the floor, the topmost page written in several languages. I recognized none of them.

"Where is Jack?"

"Being handled at a safer location. You are welcome, Miss Colton. It may be too late to save your soul, but there is still time yet to save you from a bleak future. You have been the Knights' priority for many years, you see."

I rattled my hands against the chains. "Fuck you."

"Without hearing what I have to say?" He shook his head with a low tsk. "It is unfortunate your father never told you more of his history, raising his children to be ignorant of the true evil lurking in this world. He once held my deepest respect, you know."

My pulse stalled. "What are you talking about?"

"I thought I was to go fuck myself?"

I pressed my lips into a hard line, remaining silent.

"Anyway . . ." He flipped open the file. The first page was nothing but a yellowed photograph. Even sun-faded and cracked in the corners, I recognized the two people at once. Papa and Mama in their finest clothes, standing outside a cathedral. Their wedding day. "Jonathan Colton. Born November 4th, 1743, and Clara Colton, maiden name Loran, born July 28th, 1877."

I scowled. "I think you skipped a century or two."

Chipped eyes fell on me. "When inducted into the Knights of Templar, one must go through a series of challenges to prove their valor and loyalty. Something that takes many years. Once we determine a candidate is worthy to join the everlasting order, we give them a gift. The means to continue our holy fight until they are slain in the battle against the occult." He produced a second item from his satchel. "I'm sure you recognize this."

I stared at the dark leather book. A sigil coated the front in muted silver, splotched with green and black stains. It was nearly identical to the second Dianomican, but the sigil was slightly different, the old stains not present on our book.

. . . and the tenth has been missing for centuries . . .

"That doesn't belong to you," I said.

"It does not belong to fae either, yet they covet these books all the same." He tapped the surface. "This section has been of great use to us, as it contains a ritual for immortality."

I shook my head. "What does that have to do with me?"

He blinked. "Well, everything." He pointed at the photograph of my parents. "Once, your father was one of my best knights. Thomas has very large shoes to fill."

"That doesn't make any sense."

"Of course it doesn't, because unlike your father, Thomas is not a traitor to his species." His eyes flicked to one of the mirrors—the one-way glass, as he called it. I searched the reflective surface, but couldn't tell if someone stood on the other side.

"Once, Jonathan Colton dedicated his life to our cause. It was never a question whether he would be inducted into the order—he had the potential and drive from the moment we met. Fae took everything from him. His entire family . . ." His eyes scanned over me. "He held a rage the likes of which I'd never seen. Couldn't stay out of trouble. When I found him, he was two days away from being hanged in London for murder. But I gave him something, a chance to reform. He could never return to his former self, but he could channel his anger into something better. And for many years, he did."

The thought of my father murdering anyone . . . "I don't believe you."

"Don't, then. It means very little to me." He dabbed his cigar on the iron table and swiftly lit another. "He could have been something great, had he not met your mother."

My eyes flicked to the faded photograph, my parents' beaming faces.

"All of a sudden, our creed, the occult, nothing else mattered. Clara got into his head. Told him she wanted children, a normal life. And of course, he did not want to live without her. He knew I would never allow her immortality, so he begged me for any means to break the immortal shield around his own soul. I bided my time then, knowing she would one day die and he would come back. When she got pregnant, it turned out to be a good thing. A son. All we had to do was mold him into the order when he came of age, and there would be no more mutiny."

He flipped the page, again and again. Documents passed by—a marriage form, birth certificates, the deed to a home. "But it was the second time that ruined everything." He stopped on a copy of my birth certificate, my name shimmering in bold, black letters. "A girl. Useless to us, therefore you needed to die."

I leaned back in the chair, putting as much distance between us as I could with my handcuffs. "I had an umbilical cord wrapped around my neck."

"I am aware, as it was just about the only convenient thing to happen." He sighed, expelling smoke and inhaling thick tendrils back through his nostrils. "Unfortunately, you didn't die right away. Of course, the first thing Jonathan did was approach us, begging to take this cursed thing and find a way to save you." He tapped the tenth Dianomican. "His precious Clara was already gone. But I have been entrusted with this book for a very long time, Miss Colton. Power breeds sin, so we use it for one purpose only."

"Clearly, more fucking power," I snapped.

"As much as I am repulsed by the vileness now flowing through my veins, we cannot beat an enemy that we can barely live long enough to fight. It is a sacrifice of the greatest means to forgo our eternal place in heaven to protect humans from the occult. A sacrifice you will not insult." He glared. "We hold this book to complete our ritual, and nothing more. Your father's desire to study it was to spit on the face of God himself."

My words came through gritted teeth. "He lost a wife and child."

"Something he knew would happen, should he indulge in sins of the flesh and greed." Agent Rodney scoured me, irises spider-webbed with red fissures. "But he didn't let it happen. He took the natural order of things in vain, the souls God himself kept pure for us, and decided to seek out one of *them*."

Jack, he had to be speaking of Jack, but it was the other way around. My father didn't seek him out. Jack found him.

He confirmed my exact thoughts. "Though, before he even could, one arrived right on his doorstep. An occult creature of poison and darkness, inquiring about my knight's dying infant daughter.

"Jonathan knew why. We all knew why, as we had been following this particular specimen for many years. He would find you because you possess a certain birthmark. Right on the back of your neck."

I lifted my hands, forgetting they were still bound to the table. I never knew of any birthmark, but wasn't sure how I would with the location.

"And what a strange opportunity it afforded us, an occult specimen coming right to one of our own. Had your father done the right thing he would have reported it immediately. Instead, he committed the ultimate betrayal." Agent Rodney lifted the Dianomican. "The creature fed him poisonous lies, saying you were special, born with magic in your blood. He was intrigued by you because of the birthmark, and was willing to bargain with your father. If he could steal this book from us, just for a few hours, the creature could perform the ritual called parallelling. And with that, you would be strong enough to survive."

I shook my head. "The parallel bond is something you are born with."

He raised a brow. "Is that what he told you? Surely, something about soulmates. Put a romantic spin on it, right?"

I shook my head. "I don't know what you want from me."

He ignored me, flipping the Dianomican open. Power leaked from the pages, raising the hair along my arms. When he found what he looked for, he set the book down and spun it to face me. "The Bogoran were crafty creatures, I will give them that. These books are spelled so they may be read in the native language of the reader. So, I believe you should have no trouble deciphering this."

I refused to look at the page. He scowled, shoving it closer. "We can do this the hard way, Adeline."

My eyes flicked down.

At the top of the page in sweeping, bold letters read, *The Parallel Bond*. Beneath it, a short inscription, describing the ritual's use. *For those of great power seeking an everlasting slave.* And below that, *May be utilized with a glamour-touched human or previously transformed druid. To complete a bond, part one must be performed when the veil is thinnest. After twenty years and twenty days, part two may be performed and the bond solidified. Upon the ritual's completion, the slave will be immortal and eternally bound to the caster, providing power and other services to their master for the remainder of their life. Particularly useful in the case of breeding heirs, as the bond promotes procreation . . .*

Blood roared in my ears, the sound of Agent Rodney's voice fading in the distance. It could be a trap. Who knew if the Dianomican he held was even real. For all I knew it was a replica, written with fake incantations to gain trust from others.

All of Violet's strange cautionary words came back, each time she tried to tell me something.

I warned you to stay asleep.

When did you turn twenty?

Is this a price you are willing to pay?

"The Knights use a ritual that stops aging on the day it is performed. Had he used this one, you would have remained an infant forever. Judging by the ritual he chose instead, I would say that was not what he had in mind for you." He raised a brow. "Of course, unlike the other rituals in this book, he couldn't complete this one without a Bogoran, and no one ever thought he would. Not only had it never been done, but the second half of the ritual isn't in this text, but another long-lost Dianomican. It is safe to assume scrambling the pages into ten separate pieces was another way for the Bogorans to smite the fae from their graves. Either way, he'd done enough to keep you alive and healthy, figuring he would bide his time for the next twenty years and twenty days until Jonathan gave his enslaved daughter to the master who bargained for her. But instead of Jonathan doing that, he used all his knowledge from years of servitude to the Knights to hide from him, as well as us. My only regret is that he was killed by his insidious actions before he could be tried and executed in the name of God." Agent Rodney cocked his head to the side. "So, no, Adeline. One is not born with a parallel bond. Jaevidan Valdivia *created* it."

My hands trembled in the cuffs. There had to be a reason, a good reason. Jack always allowed me my freedom. He stated over and over the bond was my choice. If I were a slave, those things would never be an option.

Unless, he only made me think I had those choices.

The diamond containing his memories burned where it rested on my chest. *You must always trust in Jaevidan.* It wasn't as if he had the best record, though. He had done something similar to Lillian in the past, but he'd freed her once she proved her loyalty.

Is that what I was supposed to do . . . fulfill a purpose before being given my freedom?

Particularly useful for breeding heirs. The Woman in White was angry at Jack. She said he *cheated*, right before ensuring I would never have children. I thought she meant I cheated death, but what if she meant something else?

"Now, with all that behind us, I am sure you are wondering . . . why you?"

My hands balled into fists. "I don't want to hear anymore."

"Oh? But this is the most interesting part." He flipped the page to a list of names. Below some were question marks, then notes scribbled in corners. But at the very bottom said, *Adeline R. Colton.*

"Let's talk about your birthmark." He stood, retrieved a hand mirror from his bag and circled around to my back. I jerked as he touched me, lifting the short locks of my hair and angling the mirror just so. "If you look in that mirror, you should be able to see it."

I looked. It was faint, such a pale brown it barely stood on my skin, but the shape was strange, the lines too neat and sharp. And it looked . . . it looked just like two downward crossing swords.

"Very unique, wouldn't you say?" He returned to his seat. "So unique, it made it easy for us to hunt down any women born with one. Unfortunately, it was the same for Jaevidan.

"You see, we have—I'd say, nearly three-hundred and fifty years of data on women born with this birthmark. Always women, in case you were wondering. Often blond." He grinned. "Why don't we take a look at the first?"

He turned the page. "Agatha Remington, born sometime between 1560 and 1563 in Wales. Not much information on this one, and it was only by a stroke of luck we found her. She drowned in a river when she was approximately seven. A local priest thought the marking was strange and requested a Knight examine the body before allowing a Christian burial. The Knight drew this, but it was dismissed as nothing. It wasn't for many years we would know just how important this marking would be." Agent Rodney showed me the parchment, so aged it had to be preserved with lacquer. It was an exact replica of the birthmark on the back of my neck.

Something pawed at the back of my mind. A memory, but it faded before I could see it, slipping away before I had time to grab it.

"I always find this one quite devastating. Elizabeth Carrow, a puritan woman born in 1587. She was married to a prominent colonist governor. Until he realized she had been sneaking off into the woods to cavort with the devil himself. When her husband discovered her treachery, he strangled her to death in their home." Agent Rodney tsked. "Probably for the best, but he was quite devastated when we informed him her soul was long gone by then."

Another memory, something I couldn't catch. I squeezed my eyes shut, thinking. I reached for the power that usually flowed along my wrists, but whatever they gave me had to have silenced it.

"And this one is my absolute favorite. The easiest to hunt down." He turned the book toward me. "Marguerite DuPont, Duchess of Valois from the years 1738 to 1741. She had a very short reign, poisoned by her own servants at a dinner party. She was well known for her exuberant behavior and many, many paramours. The most prominent of which was a Welsh advisor, a man heavily disliked and distrusted within the courts. Would you like to see a portrait of them?"

He didn't wait for a reply, reaching back into his satchel. "We had this recreated several years ago, but I assure you the likeness to the original is unparalleled."

My breath faltered.

My heart stopped.

The duchess sat in an elegant chair, hands folded neatly in her lap. A man stood behind her in a navy military jacket and white britches, a golden hand on her shoulder. Even across centuries, his face was as familiar as my own. Black hair, warm skin and brown eyes, so light they were nearly golden. The face of Jack Warren. The face of my parallel.

There was something so familiar about her, about the story, but it was like waking from a dream one couldn't remember.

"I believe that is sufficient for now," Agent Rodney said, removing the portrait. "All of these women have your birthmark. All of these women—barring early deaths—were found and coveted by Jaevidan Valdivia, or Jack Warren the Fourth, as we've known him by for the past thirty years or so. But do you want to know the most interesting part about all of these *human* women?"

I shook my head. I had truly heard enough.

"Oh, but you do. Because they all died horribly." He snapped the file shut. "Until you. The first among any of them to be born glamour-touched. The first one Jaevidan finally had the opportunity to turn into something else." He reached across the table, streaking his sweat-soaked fingers down my cheek. "Without getting into the nitty-gritty, he tried with others. Many times, but they always died, their human blood unable to withstand an infusion of power. So how lucky for him that Jonathan was willing to barter away his daughter's immortal soul in order to keep her alive, all so Jaevidan could become something new himself."

I swallowed, "Become what?"

"You already know the answer to that. A Morrigan." His hand drifted from my face. "Something about this birthmark holds power. We do not know why, but Jack does, and he has spent the past three and a half centuries hunting down any woman who has one. Pride and greed, Adeline, are two of the worst sins."

I couldn't think, couldn't *breathe*. I replayed every moment from the past few months, searching endlessly for every vague warning, every hinting sign. I'd trusted him. I'd trusted all of them, but they must have known, how could they not? They had followed Jack for hundreds of years. And among all of them, the only one who gave any sort of indication, any sort of sign I was in danger, was Violet.

The star said, *you must always trust in Jaevidan. It is the only way to stay in the light.* But that could have meant anything. Estheria was a goddess herself, all-knowing. *Stay in the light* didn't necessarily mean happiness or goodness, but keeping my life, retaining my freedom of will. It could have been a warning. If I tried to fight him now, I wouldn't win.

A short, heated breath passed my lips. "What do you want from me?"

Agent Rodney leaned his head to the side. Observing, like I held the key to a long-locked door, a mystery he longed to solve. But the Knights of Templar didn't exist to gain knowledge. Their only mission was to destroy.

"Let me speak with Thomas first."

He stood, grabbed his things and left me with nothing but the flickering lights for company.

I already knew what my fate held. Tommy recited it to me himself many years ago.

Theirs but to do and die.

FORTY-SEVEN

I SCREAMED, JERKING MY hands against the restraints. It was useless. Blood poured down my left wrist, a deep laceration from the metal stabbing into my skin. I'd spent the past hour using the other cuff to try and break it. When I realized the iron wouldn't give, I broke my wrist instead.

The smashed bones in my hand screamed in agony, but I still couldn't pull my hand through. The power I felt these past few weeks hummed beneath the surface of my skin, but was still inaccessible. I reached for it over and over, but it wouldn't listen to me, nor would my hand come through the cuff. My body was still something new and the magic locked inside. My bones healed shortly after snapping, too quickly to make any progress. I broke my hand a fourth time before giving up, sinking low in the metal chair with a sob.

This was it. This was truly how I would die. After being hidden away most of my life, my father hunted by the Knights and myself hunted by a fae. After following Tommy to New York and narrowly escaping the cult he was sucked into. After bargaining with Jack, learning to trust him and his cause, battling a phooka and a wyvern and transforming into something new, I would die bound to an iron table, alone in a cement room.

Shamefully, that wasn't what hurt most. Jack. I'd given everything to Jack. My hopes, my fears, my allegiance, my virginity, my *life*. How many of those other women did he whisper lies to? Did he tell them how special they were, how strong they could become, that they were the most beautiful thing he had ever seen too?

The prettiest flowers are always the most poisonous.

My gut. I should have trusted my fucking gut the first time.

A thick tear streamed down my cheek, hot and itchy as it ran down my throat. At least I would see my father again in hell.

"The *dramatics*."

My head snapped up. The Woman in White sat across from me, lounged in the iron seat previously occupied by Agent Rodney. Her pale mouth split into a sharp-toothed grin, wicked claws clicking on the table.

"What—how are you—" I looked around, but there was no one else. The mirrors gleamed back at me, empty except for my own reflection. Undoubtedly, someone watched me through the mirrors, but no one burst through the door. I'd never questioned before why I was the only one who could see her, but if she could hide even her reflection . . .

"This is not how you die." Her sharp smile faded. "Unless you wish to."

I rattled my chains against the iron table. "You cursed me for that already."

"An unfortunate necessity." Pale eyelids closed over her milky irises. "But we both got what we wanted."

I most definitely did not get what I wanted. "Why are you here?"

"I have not decided yet." She resumed her clicking on the table. "Do you wish to know what you have become?"

Trying to remain calm, I said, "You can tell me all about it if you help me escape."

"Well, that may be a problem. Do you know where we are, *annwyl*?"

I shook my head. "I don't know, somewhere with the Knights. Do they have a headquarters, a building they use?"

"Not that specific." She splayed her white hands flat on the table. "Outside of these four walls. Do you know where we truly are?"

My broken hands squeezed into fists. I remained silent.

"We can still find our way back to him."

"Back to who?"

"Jaevidan."

My blood turned to slush. I remembered something, a memory that finally broke from the hazy cloud of them locked away. The Woman in White running her hand down his face. *He still looks exactly the same.*

Violet said her and Jack killed the last Bogoran, shortly after it created this very wraith. "What is Jack to you?"

Pale lips turned up in a scowl. "That is not his name."

I sighed. "Jaevidan. What is Jaevidan to you, how did he play you?"

But she wasn't looking at me. Her fingers stilled their steady clicking, coming to grasp the veil around her face. "I do not have these memories."

Eyeing her white dress, the gorgeous veil and satin slippers, I murmured, "If you are a wraith, you were created from fragments of many souls, yes?"

"No." I frowned, but she only whispered, "You are the thirteenth one."

I tried to think of how many names I saw written in that file, but couldn't recall. I didn't think it was thirteen, but I still had a theory.

The Woman in White didn't think her soul was fragments sewn together, but maybe she was confused, or didn't understand what she was. I tried a different approach. "Have you lived multiple lives?"

"Many."

Nodding, I continued, "In one of your lives, did you have a birthmark?"

"In every one of my lives. They all looked like yours."

485

Goosebumps erupted down my arms. "Okay, I think I understand now. You are the amalgamation of all . . . of every woman Jaevidan found. . ."

"He loves me," she breathed. "He loves us. He did. We were . . ." Her claws dug into the edges of her veil, scoring the perfect lace with deep grooves. "When she made this wraith, she only used a piece. Just one, tiny, little piece of my soul. Fractured, I could not move on. "

My eyebrows furrowed. "She?"

"The Bogoran." The Woman in White scowled. "I heard she is dead."

They were all dead, but I didn't say as much. "What do you mean you were fractured?"

"That is what she did. I am made of fragments of my former selves. Nothing but the memories of my many deaths. All I know is how I died before, because this is all I have, all I am. Even my names are lost to me from so many lives. And where the rest of me is . . ." Her claws finally tore through the veil. The ribboned pieces floated around her face "I cannot move on until I am reunited with what remains of me, but only one of the *beansidhe* can heal a fractured soul. If I can bring one my remaining pieces, it will make me whole again."

I wasn't sure how that could possibly work. If she were truly made of fragments belonging to many different women, she would need to be reunited with *all* of her souls. And that still explained nothing about what she wanted with me. Or what Jack had to do with it all.

For now, none of that mattered. Escape did. "I know how you were made. I can help you. A Bogoran created you, but I think Jaevidan was there for all of your following deaths. That's why you are drawn to him, and maybe why you feel cheated by him. But I can help you. I can help you with whatever it is you want. Reuniting with your souls, or . . . if you want to be rid of him—"

"*No.*" My spine smacked the back of my seat. Her claws gouged into the iron table, her white eyes darkening to black. "We do not harm him."

I shook my head. "Okay, we don't harm him."

I added several more placating apologies, hoping I hadn't ruined any chance of her aiding my escape. She ignored me, eyes returning to their milky white and falling to my chest. "You have memories."

Hushing mid-sentence, I blinked. "Yes, from the eighth fallen star."

Her voice grew quiet, trembling. "*His* memories."

I nodded.

She climbed on the table, face swimming a hair's breadth from mine. She snatched the diamond, holding it in her palm and wrenching my neck forward on the chain. Silence passed with her eyes closed, stuttering breaths passing her shaky lips.

Something clicked behind us, the sound of a key turning in a lock. Her eyes snapped open, her claws going around my throat. "Do not trust Rodney, he is not what he says he is."

"What?" I whispered. "Where are you—"

"I will return. Do not trust him. Do not trust anything you see."

She disappeared.

AGENT RODNEY RETURNED, BUT this time he wasn't alone.

Tommy didn't look at me, didn't so much as breathe the air I exhaled. Agent Rodney fell into the seat across from me, practically glowing. Behind him, Tommy crossed his arms and leaned against a mirror.

"Adeline." Rodney's eyes fell on my broken wrist. Now healed, but at a strange angle. Dried blood coated my skin. "I'm sorry for the delay. There was a lengthy discussion on what to do with you."

I scowled. "I thought I would be tried in the eyes of God."

"You already have been, my dear." He patted my blood-streaked wrist. Tommy looked away. "Before I tell you of this decision, I would like to ask you a few questions."

I attempted to catch Tommy's eyes in the side mirror, but each time I did he looked away. "I'm not answering shit."

"I see there were great lengths taken to raise you into a charming young woman." Agent Rodney leaned back, crossing his arms. "What are you?"

"A charming young woman."

"What species are you?"

I leveled my eyes on him, lungs burning. Tommy's eyes finally flicked to mine, something roiling deep beneath the surface, something I couldn't decipher.

"I don't know."

The Knight's mouth broke into a wry grin. "If you wanted to lie, you could have done better than that."

"I don't know. I don't," I snapped. "No one does. None of them could say for sure what I became. Or if they knew, they didn't tell me."

He nodded. "Interesting. And disappointing." Sighing, he flattened his palms on the table. "I had a very difficult decision to make with this."

A heated breath flared my nostrils. Tommy was back to staring anywhere but me. "What is it?"

"After all the chaos that has ensued as a result of you, I hoped your existence wouldn't be entirely in vain. After all, we don't know what you are yet. If there are more out there like you." He frowned. "But ultimately, you create the most evil of Satan's creatures. This Morrigan you form, it is something we cannot allow. It is too much power for our adversaries. Besides, now that you are transformed . . ."

He gestured for Tommy to come over. He hesitated only a moment before standing beside him. "You will not understand. And your soul may still burn in hell, but know we seek to expunge you of your wickedness. God has made this judgment and I carry out his word, to protect the immortal souls of all his children."

I stared at Tommy. His flat eyes fell on me, seeing, but not looking. Hearing, but not listening. "What are you going to do?"

"We have decided it is time for Thomas's final test of faith before joining the order." He stood, clapping a hand on my brother's back. "For it is most fitting that it is your own flesh and blood who delivers you from evil. He will take on the heavy burden of freeing your soul, and afterwards continue his own journey into knighthood."

I stared at Tommy. He couldn't actually agree to this. Not my brother. Not the little boy who helped Papa feed me bottles. The teenager who taught me to read, who whittled me ponies from fallen branches to play with. The man who tucked me into bed each night and followed me to the river, went off to war and came home for *me*. No matter what they told him, no matter how much they brainwashed him, he couldn't possibly do this. I refused to believe that.

"Tommy," I said, each letter shakier than the last. "Tommy, I am still Adeline. I am still your sister."

He finally spoke. My heart broke with each word. "I want to help you. That is all I ever wanted."

"This isn't helping me, this is *killing* me."

He swallowed. "I am saving you."

Rodney nodded, producing a key. Iron. The exact right shape and size for the chains binding me to the table. "She will tempt you, brother. This is what they do, but you must be strong." He dropped the key onto the table, only inches from my trembling fingers. "Retrieve me when the task is done."

The door slammed shut behind him. We stared at one another, unmoving.

He reached for a knife hanging from his belt.

The iron table had to weigh hundreds of pounds, but I was stronger now. I stood, shoving all my weight forward and not stopping until it pinned Tommy against the glass mirror. He screamed, fingers snapping as they were caught between the iron edge and his hip bone. "*Addie.*"

I reached for the key, but in my mission to incapacitate Tommy it had slid across the table, closer to him. His wide eyes fell on it, then on me. His free arm dove for it as I threw myself onto the surface, kicking his arm away and using my foot to slide the key closer. He grabbed my ankle and yanked me forward. I cried out, sending my heel straight into his chest.

He doubled over, gasping for air as I hooked the key around my shoe. I bent my knee, sliding it closer when his broken hand came free from where it was pinned by the table. Along with the knife.

I screamed, kicking my legs until the key was at waist level. He swung down with the knife, just missing my shin as I pivoted on the surface. I curled into a ball, sliding the key closer and closer to my hands. He swung again but I was too quick, spreading my legs so it tangled in my skirts, pinning the fabric to the iron surface.

Get the key. Get the key. Get the key. Tommy grunted, shoving all his weight into the table until it moved just enough to shimmy away from the wall. My fingers fumbled around the iron, finally finding a steady grip. Tommy shuffled forward, breathing hard, as I shakily got it in the lock.

He pulled a second knife just as the cuffs clinked open.

I rolled, just missing the knife whizzing through the air and hitting the mirror. Hairline cracks formed, snaking out from where my head smacked the glass. Dizziness rattled my brain and blood ran into my eyes. Through the crimson sheen, I watched Tommy dive for me again.

I slid to the ground, crawling beneath the table, but Tommy grabbed my foot and dragged me back. I screamed, clawing at the smooth cement. He flipped me over. I'd never thrown a punch in my life, but I balled my fingers into a fist and swung. I got him square in the jaw, knocking him off of me and sending the knife skidding to the drain. I scrambled for it, pushing the teetering weapon until it dipped between the slats.

Tommy grunted, wrenching me back again. He clambered on top of me. I swung blindly, kicking, *screaming*, when his hands came around my throat. I threw my knees between his legs but he pressed down, pinning me to the floor. His hands clutched my throat with vengeance, all the air choking from my lungs.

His dark eyes swarmed above me.

"Tommy," I gasped. "Tommy, please—"

He leaned in close, hissing, "Would you shut up, you idiot? I'm not actually choking you."

A wheezy breath passed my lips, strained and panicked, but I could still breathe. I kicked my legs beneath him and he pinned me harder to the floor. "For the love of god, would you pretend to fucking die so we can get out of here?"

I stilled.

He wasn't trying to kill me.

Oh my god, he wasn't trying to kill me.

Tears brimmed my eyes, streaming down my cheeks. Tommy nodded. "Yeah, just keep that up. Give it a minute." He rattled my head against the floor a little, pretending to hold me down. I thrashed my legs beneath him before finally going still. I let my head loll to the side.

He inhaled a sharp breath, rolling off of me. He smoothed my hair back, bending over with a pitiful cry and his hands over his face. "I'm not sure who's watching. I'm going to pretend to mourn you for a minute."

Great, wonderful. Just another fucking afternoon for the Coltons. He released a couple of fake sobs. I went limp as he pulled me into his arms, bending over me so both our mouths were hidden. "You have so much fucking explaining to do," I breathed.

He rocked me back and forth. "Shut up, you're breaking my rhythm."

After the longest sixty seconds of my life he stood, the look on his face instructing me to remain on the floor. He took several slow steps to the back of the room and a door opened. A moment later, he circled back. "We're clear, get up."

I pushed to trembling knees. "What the *hell* was that?"

He brought a finger to his lips, furiously shushing me. "Just follow my lead." He paused, shaking out his broken fingers. "And did you have to slam the table so hard?"

"I thought you were going to *kill me*."

"What the fuck is wrong with you? You think I would ever actually hurt you? Jesus Christ." He shook his head and grabbed my hand, peeking out the open door. "Rodney should be in his office. I think most people went home by now, but keep your voice down just in case."

I nodded, breathing hard. He tugged us into the hall.

Bright, synthetic lights shined on chipped and fading tiles. It looked like a warehouse, but it was hard to tell. He turned us around several sharp corners, setting a brutal pace. I had to trot double time to keep up with his long legs. "Where are we going?"

"Armory first, then the first train out of dodge."

"You're leaving the Knights?"

"I was never *in* the Knights." He pulled me to a stop, grabbing my shoulders. "Listen to me. These people are fucking nuts, Addie. *Nuts.* They told me I was going to Chicago to train with this unit and

Rodney showed up all of a sudden, spewing all this shit about God's mission to kill fae and how you were a sign of evil. They gave me no choice. Literally, stuck a gun to my head and said I was in or out. I've been trying to find you and escape ever since, but they watch my every goddamn move."

My breaths came in hard pants, my wild eyes scouring his face. His beautiful, stupid, half-burned face. "But at the boxing match, you told me—"

"Like I said, they've been watching my every move. I can never tell when they're listening." His head shot up, eyes darting around. "They've had plans for months now to kill you, Addie. And I've seen what they can do, even to the devil-folk. They're *strong*. I've been trying to play both sides to keep you safe, but last minute they decided to raid the hotel. . ." He shook his head. "It's all in the letters I sent. They read them before I mailed them off, but I used codes. The ones Will and I made up when we were POWs. I thought if they looked strange you would show them to him and he could decode them for you."

The letters I never read, only Lillian did. *This one is very sweet, I thought it may lift your spirits.* She wouldn't have suspected anything because she didn't know Tommy. And after I joined their side, I hadn't bothered . . .

"I'm sorry. I'm an idiot," I breathed.

He ruffled my hair. "Damn straight. Now can we get out of here, please? I've been playing nice with these lunatics for months."

I matched his steady pace. "But you know the devil-folk are real, right?"

He released a short puff of air. "Yeah, I am *very* aware." He cut a hard left, dragging me along. "I get why Dad never said anything though. If I thought he was nuts before, I can't even imagine."

My heart sank. "All those things he said about Papa were true?"

"I'm fairly sure they are." He yanked me around another dizzying turn, stopping us before a heavy, metal door. "It's warded against non-humans."

He scanned me, a question in his eyes. I knew he could see all the subtle differences. He may have known my face better than anyone. But maybe he still hoped.

"I'll wait here," I said.

He nodded, eyes darkening. "Not even a minute. Don't move."

He didn't lie. Less than sixty seconds later he reappeared with two handguns, two knives . . . and a sword.

He thrust one of the guns in my palm. "I'm assuming you can still shoot a squirrel from eighty yards?"

"You have no idea." I gestured at the sword. "What the hell is that?"

"Yeah, they have us fighting like we're in the fucking crusades. Do you have any idea what sword training is like? After this, I'm never touching one again."

Despite it all, I laughed. "I've gotten a little bit myself."

"Good. Take this." He pressed an iron-coated dagger into my palms. "Now that you're something else can you . . . you know, blink in and out?"

I nodded. "Yeah, but it's not working right now."

"That stuff they put over your face, it's formulated ashwood and wolfsbane. Don't ask me how it works, but it won't wear off for a few days."

Lovely. "Okay, so now what?"

"There's an exit a few levels down that dumps us out into the village. The train doesn't come until tomorrow, but we can walk the tracks until we hit the next station. That should be Cardiff, so—"

I paled. "Did you say Cardiff? As in, Cardiff, *Wales*?"

He nodded.

"How long was I out for?"

494

"Only a day."

"Then how—"

"They're hypocrites, okay? Big fucking hypocrites. They utilize that book all the time. Managed to make a portal or some shit from Chicago to here. This is the main headquarters."

They were using the shade. They had to be, but I'd never heard of an open passage that could be used by anyone before. If they existed, Jack surely had no idea.

Or it was something else he kept from me.

"How about after?"

His eyes roamed over me, evaluating. "Why, what did you have in mind?"

I didn't know. I didn't know anything. "Where are they keeping Jack and the rest of them?"

"New York. They only brought you here, it was easier to move only one of you."

And with me halfway across the world, it would weaken the Morrigan. We were stronger with proximity, so they separated us.

I had two options. Back to New York to rescue Jack, or attempt to run somewhere no one could find me. *You must always trust in Jaevidan.* But if the Knight hadn't lied about Papa, he wasn't lying about Jack either. He showed me the proof himself with the portrait, and the Woman in White all but confirmed it just by existing.

"We can talk on the train tracks. Sounds like we have a long walk, anyway."

He nodded. "Alright, good. Let's get out of here."

We snuck down several more halls, Tommy leading the way. When we hit a stairwell we took them three at a time, flying down the steps until we reached a rusted door at the bottom. Tommy flattened himself against the wall, gesturing for me to get beside him. "Whenever these doors are opened, they trigger an alarm. So the second we step through, follow me and prepare to run like hell."

495

"Okay," I slipped my heels off and let them drop to the floor. Cold leached from the tiles through my thin stockings.

Tommy led a silent countdown, then whispered, "Now."

He rammed into the metal door and I behind him.

Heat hit like a brick wall, drying me out instantly. Bugs chittered and nightbirds swooped, the only light the grace of a full moon. Tommy ran several feet and skidded to a halt, swiveling around. I slammed into his back and stumbled back.

There was no village. No lights or any other buildings to be seen. Tommy's good eye went wide. "What the hell? This isn't right, this isn't—"

"*Sh.*" I scanned our surroundings, the endless heat and warmth. Bramble thickets surrounded us, reaching for the sky. Flowing grass ran beneath my feet, softer than any pillow. Hundreds of white flowers opened for the new moon, glowing as if they were lit from within. An owl hooted in the distance, but it sounded melodic, too human-like to be a bird.

Tommy shook his head. "This has never happened before. I don't . . ."

I ignored him, walking across the grass to the crest of a hill. Over a meadow of swaying green, vibrant flowers and small critters shifting through the underbrush, were two massive oak trees. They towered higher than any trees I had ever seen, stretching up until the tops seemed to brush the stars. The branches reached out for another like two lovers embracing, limbs entwining and forming an archway between the trunks. A gate. And between the trunks was the image of a dark field, much different than the one before us. A large boulder was the only thing noticeable in the darkness. Some dried grass and . . . a rusted metal line, like the side rail of a train track.

"Tommy," I breathed. "Was it a new moon last night?"

He brought his hands to his head, turning in circles. "Yes, why? What does that have to do with anything?"

The veil was thinnest during a new moon.

A new moon in the human world, and a bright full one in Ildathach.

FORTY-EIGHT

THE MOON-KISSED FLOWERS SUDDENLY looked horrifying, the pillowy grass a snapping trap beneath my feet. The small movements in the underbrush ahead, the things running across the field . . .

"Tommy, listen to me. Listen." I grabbed his hands from his head, pulling them into my own. "Look at me. Do you see those two trees over there? The dried meadow in between them, with the rock?"

He nodded, paler than the ivory flowers.

"That's where we need to go. I think it's a gateway to get back home," I said softly. "But to get there, we have to run across that field. And I don't know what's in that field, or why we are here. But once we reach those trees, we are safe and sound in Wales. Do you understand me?"

He nodded again.

"So stay close to me," I whispered.

I grabbed his arm, tentatively making my way down the steep slope. Every moment that passed my senses grew stronger, my eyes adjusting to the darkness and my ears tracking the tiniest sounds. Beautiful, sweet scents curled on a hot breeze. Tommy held his gun in his hand, shaking and turning his hearing aids all the way up. Even with the full moon, I knew he couldn't see like I could, so I was careful to guide him around any fallen branches or bumps on the ground.

Tittering laughter echoed from the trees, growing stronger with every footstep. I prayed only my enhanced hearing could pick it up. Things ran through the underbrush, too fast to see. Even my sharp non-human eyes only caught a flash of color here or there. But we reached the bottom of the hill, and so far, nothing bothered us. The low fae could probably scent I was something else, but surrounded by the perfumed air of Ildathach, Tommy smelled overwhelmingly human. I'd never noticed it before, but could tell immediately what it was. Salty and musky, with a hint of decay underneath.

I pulled him forward, careful to keep my footsteps quiet and unassuming. That strange owl hooted again, its drawn O's turning into a lyrical tune. The stars pulsed and danced in the sky, too bright and too close. The dark trees shifted on a groaning wind, the branches seeming to reach out for us.

"Okay, we're nearly halfway across," I said. The branched gateway grew closer, the image of a plain, winter-dry field between the tree trunks. The closer we drew the better my vision became, able to discern the rusted tracks in the grass that stretched into the distance. A cluster of golden lights shimmered on a dark horizon.

Tommy stopped.

I turned sharply to look at him. His eyes became dinner plates, his hand trembling beneath mine. I followed his line of sight up ahead, where three dark figures stood in the grass.

With the full moon behind them I couldn't make out any discernible features, but it was obvious two were women and one was a man. The silhouette of his fedora nearly blended into the trees, his tall form swallowed by darkness. On either side of him, the two lithe women leaned toward him, their long hair flowing on the breeze.

"Tommy. Adeline," the man called out. I recognized the voice immediately, had just spent hours listening to him talk. "Were you planning on going somewhere?"

499

Tommy tried to step in front of me, but I wouldn't let him. The three figures walked forward, completely in unison. The movements were too fluid, limbs slinking like predators on the prowl. They stopped fifteen or so paces ahead, the full moon illuminating them.

It was, in fact, Agent Rodney in the middle, but he looked wrong. His skin too tight over his face, his sharp smile glimmering too white. The women next to him were nearly identical, their silky black hair falling to their hips like running ink. Their matching white dresses caught the moonlight, pronouncing the sharpness of their blue eyes.

"I thought I said to kill her," Not-Rodney said. He gestured a flippant hand at me, still smiling. "You were a good soldier, Thomas. Always followed orders."

Tommy put his arm in front of me, but I gently pushed it away. "What are you?"

"Me?" Agent Rodney smiled, the edges of his figure shimmering in the light. "Oh, no, Adeline. I want to know what you are."

"You first," I breathed.

His grin only stretched wider, trembling in the corners. "Now, the same thing as you. One of the things you are, at least."

"Tommy, run for the trees," I whispered beneath my breath.

"No, no way." He grabbed my arm, pulling me back. "I want out of this, Rodney. I'm done. If you touch my sister I'll pull a bullet in your fucking head, you hear me?"

I grabbed Tommy's arm, pushing him toward the trees. "Tommy, that's not who you think it is."

"Listen to your little sister, sweet Thomas," one of the women called. He swiveled around, as if he couldn't tell where the voice came from. "This is not the man you have come to know."

"Where the fuck is that coming from?"

"The trees," I snapped.

"No, he will never leave his sibling," the other woman said. She played with a loose strand of her hair, eyeing him curiously. "As I would never leave my sisters. It is a family's biggest weakness."

Tommy stepped back. "Addie, what's happening?"

Agent Rodney snapped.

His male form shimmered away, leaving behind the most beautiful woman I had ever seen. Her dark hair lifted around her face as if she floated beneath waves, her crystal blue eyes like beacons in the dark. Long pointed ears tapered on either side of her head and her gown captured moonlight, flowing across her skin. Her two sisters stepped closer, grinning.

"He made this weak thing into a Morrigan, sisters." The ethereal triplet raised a hand, fingers gliding through the air. "A little human, the dark one, and our dear old friend, the Poison Prince."

"Tommy, *run.*"

But Tommy didn't move, spine straight like he'd been petrified. His eyes darted between the three sisters—the *true* Morrigan—with depthless fear.

"He sullied our name," she continued. She lifted a second hand and twisted it in the air. The edges of her dress lifted like her hair, floating on non-existent liquid. Tommy screamed. His back arched and he dropped to the ground. "Does he not know there can only be one?"

I dropped to my knees, grabbing Tommy. He convulsed on the ground, eyes rolling back in his head. Foam lined the corners of his mouth, the veins popping in his neck. I ran my hands over him, trying something, anything, but my abilities were still locked beneath my skin. "Stop. *Stop.* You're killing him."

"Very well," she dropped her hands and Tommy slumped to the earth. I shook him, running my hands over his face. "Tommy, Tommy, are you okay?"

A few mumbled incomprehensible words, but he didn't open his eyes. I pressed my fingers to his neck. A pulse beat steady and low, but he was alive.

I looked at the sisters. "What do you want?"

"The human speaks to us," one of them said.

"Is she though?" The other asked. A cruel smile lifted her lips. "Can you tell us Badb?"

The middle sister—Badb—cocked her head to the side. "It depends. Do we let her live and seek answers, or do we destroy her now?"

"We don't want to harm you," I said. "We were never competing for power, we only made the Morrigan to kill Delsaran."

They all laughed, the sparkling notes bouncing and playing off one another. "Delsaran, Delsaran, Delsaran," Badb hummed. "As if that insolent little druid could have swayed anything, even in your world."

But Delsaran had—or had he? I saw him in the flesh only a few months ago, but I also saw Agent Rodney in the flesh just a few hours ago. If they could create illusions like that, even ones Jack and the others couldn't detect . . .

"It was you," I breathed. My eyes darted between the three of them. "But why? Jack said you had no interest in human affairs."

"She asks us why."

"She asks the wrong question."

"She asks nothing," Badb said. "She does not know what we seek. She does not know what the poison prince did to her, let alone how. But if we take her, maybe he can tell us himself." Her eyes flicked to Thomas. "But what to do with him?"

Tommy moaned, rolling onto his side. I pushed him back down, scrambling in front of him. "Let him go and I will do whatever you want."

Babd smiled. "You will do that anyway."

Tommy screamed, clawing at his face. Years of nightmares swarmed back, lying in bed and listening to Tommy scream through the walls. Sobbing alone each night as I waited for him to come home, striking a deal with a woman in a white dress beside a river. Images flitted past, of a faded book with a bullet in the center, of soldiers carrying a gurney with a bandage-wrapped man lying on the surface. One dark, brown eye looking at me, then no words between us for months. Cries about Argonne, my father being thrown into a kitchen chair. Then speaking for the first time in months, carried in Tommy's arms with golden eyes watching across the river.

"Stop, please, I'll do anything," I sobbed. Tommy writhed, the blood vessels bursting in his foggy eyes. The veins in his face swelled, his skin turning purple. "Stop, stop, *stop.*"

Adeline.

My cries faded to background noise, the forest going dark.

Adeline Ruth Colton.

I looked up.

The Woman in White stood behind—*above* the three sisters. She was floating, arms spread wide like Jesus on the cross, her white hair a floating crown around her head. Her white eyes fell on me, the dress rippling over her bare feet. *Do you want to know what you became?*

Tommy gurgled beside me, his head smacking into my knees.

Do you want to know what I made of us?

A single word came forth, barely a whisper. "Yes."

Her lips stretched into a razor-sharp smile. *Then scream.*

I looked at the three sisters, laughing at the display before them. Then Tommy, turning violet beside my knees. I ripped his hearing aids off and threw them across the grass. I stood on trembling knees. I balled my hands into fists and took a deep breath.

Between her jeering sisters, Babd's face melted into a frown.

I screamed.

Power flickered across my skin, sharp and raw. My flesh turned red, my hands blackening at the fingertips. Wind blew through the field like a tornado, lifting roots from the ground. White flowers took to the sky and turned the air into a moonlit maelstrom. My eyes glazed over, nothing but darkness and swirling ivory. Sounds screeched passed my ears—a distorted wail, a keen of death.

My jaw ached, snapping at the hinge. My tongue turned heavy and molten in my head, my feet lifting above the ground. I floated higher. Higher. Until the Woman in White drifted before my eyes. She reached out for me, claws digging into my cheeks. *This is it*, she breathed into my mind. *This is what the last fate destined us for.*

I couldn't move. My torn and bloody dress drifted around my legs. The white flowers consumed my vision, the relentless wind bursting my eardrums. The Woman in White laughed, throwing her head back. "This is what you did," she screamed. "You created the next *beansidhe.*"

Her nails dug into my cheeks, her eyes scouring mine. *Are you ready, annwyl?*

I fell.

The wind stopped, the flowers drifting to the grass. I hit the ground with a thump, my legs crumbling and snapping beneath me. My arm bent at an odd angle, my blackened fingertips absorbing the moonlight. Tommy rolled to his side, moaning in pain.

Darkness cornered my vision. No, I had to . . .

"Adeline." Tommy released a hacking cough, reaching for me. "Addie . . ."

The darkness grew stronger, the world fading away. Tommy's frightened eyes swam before me, turning into a starry night. The last thing I saw was my hand, twitching and pale in the grass.

Am I alive? I asked the darkness.

Yes, she whispered. *More alive than we ever were before.*

FORTY-NINE

WHEN I CAME TO, stars littered the sky in every direction. A barren field stretched out like a yellow sea. Tommy prodded at my face, saying he dragged me through the branched gateway. He didn't understand what happened. Where we were. Why walking through that archway landed us outside the village he spoke of in Wales. I could barely move, but even still, I wasn't sure how to explain we'd been somewhere else, and that he took us across a break in the veil.

An hour later I could move better. He helped pop my bones back into place, setting them for when the healing took over. Within minutes they were back to full strength, all the cuts along my face from my fall sealed closed. All that remained were my ruined fingertips, scorched like frostbite from the second knuckles to blackened nails.

Either Tommy still hurt badly, was shocked, or simply didn't want to know, because he was silent as I grabbed his arm and hobbled down the train tracks. Two more hours passed before I found a puddle. I stared at my moonlit reflection and it swirled and melted. I told Tommy to close his eyes. I didn't know a single place to shade to in Cardiff, but I knew it was along the sea. I shaded us to a dark beach, our feet dipped in the frigid, glass-like water. Tommy vomited several times, but remained otherwise silent. We made for the city, got turned away at three inns, and finally found one on the outskirts willing to give us a room. The woman at the front desk eyed us suspiciously, but handed us a key.

I threw Tommy to the bed, finding him some water and forcing him to drink. His eyes were completely red except for the brown irises, the shade of his skin still scarlet, but he insisted he was fine. Within moments he was fast asleep.

I pulled a faded chair to the window and threw it open. The gossamer curtains lifted in the salty wind, reminding me of the Abstruse—of home. Or whatever would remain of it after tonight. I still had no clue what I would do about Jack. If he was even still alive after the Knights took him, the *real* Knights. I felt for the bond, but I knew I was too far away. Somewhere across the sparkling sea outside this window he was either dead . . . or waiting.

Someone shifted in the dark room. I turned in my chair, but the only other living thing was Tommy, snoring softly against faded floral sheets. Turning back to the window, I froze as something flickered in my periphery. I stared at the mirror propped over a broken dresser. The Woman in White stared back from inside the glass.

Frowning, I leaned to the side to catch my reflection. She moved with me, blocking the view of my own face. Her lips matched my frown, her eyebrows scrunched together like mine were. I raised one tentative hand and she did the same, coiling her fingers the same time I did.

"What are you doing?" I whispered. Her mouth mimicked the words before I had time to complete them.

Sharp nails dug into my shoulder. I jumped, turning as the Woman in White leaned against the window. Her bleached gaze found the open water, a strange look flickering across her expression. "I recognize this place."

Shaking my head, I glanced back at the mirror. It was my reflection this time, the Woman in White not visible where she stood at the window. "From one of your lives?'

"I think," she leaned her head against the molding. The breeze drifted in, lifting her hair beneath the veil. The white strands coasted across her cheeks.

"Why are you here?"

She didn't answer. Her fingers drifted down the condensated glass, leaving no tracks. She pulled her hand away, bringing both to her chest. After a long moment she whispered, "I found it."

"What did you find?"

She took her ruined veil between her fingers, stroking the scalloped edge like a harp. "The rest of me."

"Oh." I wasn't sure what was appropriate in a situation like this. Congratulations, maybe? "Does that mean you can move on now?"

"No." She didn't clarify, so I didn't ask. But she continued, "I will rejoin with what I lost. I will no longer be fragments, but whole again."

I nodded. "That's good. Very good. I am happy for you."

For the first time, her white eyes flickered to me. "But not yet."

Chilled air tumbled through the window, caressing my skin. It lifted the veil around her face. The sight brought a strange feeling, of my hands drifting over swaths of lace. Of fabric brushing my cheeks as pins were stuck in my hair.

"Why not? I thought this was what you wanted."

"I wanted to move on." She resumed her stare out the window. "I needed you to die so I could, but he made you immortal. So I settled for the next best thing."

Wrapping my arms around myself, I mumbled, "What is that?"

"Being reunited with what I strayed from. As a banshee, you can make this so."

I stared at her. "Well, when you have the rest of your soul, let me know. I will help in anyway I can."

Her mouth stretched into a humorless grin. "You were always so innocent."

Sure, and speaking of innocence . . . "The curse you put on me when I was eleven—now that you have made me something else, can it be taken back?"

She nodded absently, pressing her forehead to the window. "It is gone. I no longer need you dead. In fact, I need you alive."

To heal her soul, because apparently I was whatever a *beansidhe* or banshee or whatever was now. Hopefully, it would be a long time before she required that of me, if she ever did. I'd had enough of her presence for a lifetime. "Is there anything else I should know? I still don't understand what I am."

"The memories," she breathed. Instinctively, I touched my throat and brushed the diamond. "The memories will tell you everything. They told me. They told me who I used to be."

Jack's memories, a gift from the star. I didn't think anyone else was supposed to see them, but it was too late now. Estheria told me to wait until Jack gave me permission to view them, but if the Woman had already looked, maybe I should too.

"Can I trust him?" I asked.

But she said nothing, closing her pale eyes as a final breeze tumbled into the room. She wrapped the veil around her face, breathing deep. "I want to see him before I go."

She stood straight. The veil disintegrated around her face, her beautiful dress fading on the wind. Her fingertips crumbled away, the dust forming white flowers on the salty wind. They drifted out the window, one at a time, little teardrops floating to the heavens.

I reached for her. "Wait. Before you leave, I need to know if I can trust him."

Her arm crumbled beneath my hand. She smiled. *The memories. The memories will tell you everything.*

She fell away, drifting into nothing but snow-white petals on the wind. The curtains drifted back to the wall, the room turning silent and cold.

I sank back to the chair, listening to the soft sounds of Tommy's sleep. I had my brother back. I had my curse lifted. Once, that was all I ever wanted.

It would be easy to run. It would be easy to follow in the footsteps of my father, using mistrust as a weapon, drawing conclusions before finding answers. He spent so much of his life hiding away, and it killed him. It nearly killed me. But now I could do something, I held the key to everything I wished to know right in the palm of my hands. I was terrified, but even if they held answers I didn't want to see, I knew now ignorance was not bliss. Because no matter what Jack may have been, what his role in this swiftly changing world could be, I wanted him. I wanted him from the depths of my cursed soul to the tips of my scorched fingertips. So I needed to know if he could truly be mine.

The star told me to wait, but if he was good, he would understand.

I caressed the diamond in my hand. With the darkness of a foreign city around me, and the sound of my brother's soft breaths behind, I reached for Jaevidan Valdivia's memories.

EPILOGUE

JACK

PRISON WAS GETTING QUITE boring.

I paced the confinements of my cell for the hundredth time, wondering when Violet would hurry this the fuck along already. The fates were rarely on my side as of late, but they had given me one thing—the Knights were too fucking impatient for their own good. They raided the hotel, undoubtedly assuming their cover with the normal authorities would be an extensive cache of liquor. Violet and I already threw that shit in the shade months ago, so there was nothing.

Therefore, I currently sat in a lonely cell within a very human and very normal penitentiary upstate. All while they desperately searched for any means to book me. They wouldn't find any, because I was too smart for them. The Knights placed me in a cell with iron bars, because they were fucking idiots and thought that would stop me. I was truly trying to do the right thing here and wait for everything to be cleared legally before leaving, but they were testing my patience. And I never had much.

I felt for the bond again, but either Adeline was confined somewhere too or the iron was masking it. I'd only been able to make a brief phone call to Violet yesterday and she said everyone was fine. Some were still in questioning, but she was keeping tabs. So now, I just had to be patient.

510

Fucking patience.

"Would you quit that shit? Some of us are trying to sleep."

"Fuck off," I snapped. Prisoners in the cells beside me piqued up with interest. I already had one beg me for a job, another asked questions about the bootlegging business and a third threatened to kill me for shooting his brother last year. His cellmates silenced him immediately.

Someone knocked on my bars. "Can't sleep?"

I looked up and into the shit-eating grin of Agent Robert Rodney. What a dumb fucking name. "Not at all, I find the accommodations quite lovely, actually."

"Good. You should get used to them." He leaned against the bars, clutching a steaming cup of coffee. I debated glamouring it into piss. "As soon as they find something, Warren, your ass is ours."

I grinned. "May their search be star-blessed, then."

He scowled. They always hated when you brought up fae shit. "I wouldn't be laughing too much if I were you. We have plenty of leads. Not to mention, the girl you're keeping prisoner."

"Oh, are you speaking of Adeline? She's my girlfriend actually, though I see where the confusion may come in."

Agent Rodney shook his head, pressing a hand to his cross medallion. "The evil you must have placed in that young woman's mind."

I placed plenty of things in Adeline, just not in her mind. I tugged at the bond again, already knowing the result but unable to curb the urge. She was probably losing her head right now, with everyone getting swarmed by the Knights. Surely, her brother took the opportunity to try and preach their nonsense to her. I only hoped the fallout wouldn't be too severe when he realized what she became. I couldn't care less about him, but I didn't want her to be unhappy.

Maybe I'd compulse him to apologize or some shit.

"You know I've dated around a bit myself. And I have to say, I've yet to lock up any woman, or worse, make her completely disappear."

"I'm sure that shriveled brain of yours has a hard time keeping track of memories, but if you recall, she told you herself she was staying with a friend at the hotel. I wouldn't call that missing."

"And since then?" He raised an eyebrow. "You know, we have her sibling. I'm sure he's very concerned right now as to where she is. I would hate to tell him at the bottom of the Hudson."

My rushing blood came to a still. "And why would you assume that?"

"Since no one can find her, I'm not sure what else to assume." Beady eyes leveled on me, crawling over my skin. "Tell us where the Colton girl is, Jack."

I didn't think, not as a million alarms swarmed my mind nor when my hand shot through the bars and latched around his throat. The metal burned along my bicep but I ignored it, yanking his face against the metal. "Don't fuck with me."

"Hey!" A sleeping guard jumped to his feet, pulling out his gun. "Release him. Now."

"I'm not," Agent Rodney wheezed. "No one has seen her for days, not even your fucked up band of merry men."

"I will shoot!"

I released Rodney. He fell to the floor with a heaving gasp, clutching his throat. "Just say you got her killed, Jack."

No.

No, this was a lie. This was antagonism. I was smarter than this. I was *fucking patient*. She was fine, waiting at home. She was most certainly sitting on the settee, obsessively reading one of Arthur's books, or making niceties with the feral brownie in the kitchen, or practicing her shading, or—

The shade. What if she got lost in the fucking shade. I kept telling her not to push things, not yet. She may have been a master at it already, but it was dangerous and she always pushed herself too hard.

Or Delsaran had found her.

Violet told me everything was fine, why the fuck would Violet—

I bent down, grabbing Rodney by his waistcoat and jerking him against the bars. "I want a phone call."

He stared at the iron bars, twitching. "We can't, we're not—in your rights—"

Fine, we would do this my way.

I stopped holding in power. It killed me every second to do so, the poison burning beneath my skin. It was moments like these I finally felt relief, a breath of air in calculated violence. Darkness seeped from my skin, coating my fingertips and blackening his waistcoat. His eyes went wide, a scream lurched in his throat as it crawled up his skin. The pool of death formed a circle around me, melting the iron bars. The guard's gun wavered in the air, knees trembling as he stepped back. I threw Rodney to the side before I could kill him and pushed open the melted door.

Tattoos coated my hands, which meant I had lost the glamour. Fuck. The guard stared at me, a wet spot growing in his trousers. "What the hell are you?"

I shoved him aside.

A bullet tinged off the cell beside me. Another one. The prisoners jumped to their feet, screaming and clawing at one another to get a look. Another round fired off and I stumbled, looking down to where it tore through my stomach. Blood seeped across my waistcoat, but stopped mere seconds later. No iron bullets. What fucking idiots.

The guard screamed behind me and ran for the next cell block.

Annwyl was in danger. I could feel it, like a stain on my soul. I needed to find her, needed to make sure my fucking sister hadn't lied through her teeth. I pushed into the next cell block. A group of guards looked up in alarm, smoke curling from their mouths and cards frozen in their hands. In a blink they were on their feet, guns raised. I let the poison seep again, this time in a depthless fog across the ground. Belladonna bloomed in my wake and they screamed, clawing at their skin wherever the fog touched them. I grabbed one idiot by his collar and wrenched his face to mine. "I need a telephone."

He choked on the air he was breathing. "What's wrong with your fucking eyes, lad?"

I threw him down. Idiot. I grabbed the next closest one. "Telephone. Now."

He pointed a shaky finger to an alcove against the wall. An older guard sat at a desk, trembling but otherwise unmoving. I sat on the wood and grinned, pointing to his telephone. "May I borrow this for a moment?"

He nodded.

Violet picked up on the first ring. "What?"

"Where the fuck is Adeline?"

Silence descended on the other side. "Jack, I swear I've been looking for her. I didn't want to say anything because I know—"

"Where. The fuck. Is Adeline?"

Another beat of silence. The guards screamed behind me, calling for help. The prisoners joined the fray, slamming against their bars and demanding to be let out. Violet didn't answer me. Instead, she said, "Delsaran is dead."

I froze. "Violet, that sounded a lot like you just said Delsaran is dead."

"Not only is he dead, but he has been for years."

I closed my eyes, pinching the bridge of my nose. "Come again?"

"They found his bones at the bottom of Lake Michigan. Human dental records and our own resources confirmed it. He's been dead for a long time."

I smiled. That was the only thing to do in moments like this. "We saw him just a few months ago, Violet."

"Well, it wasn't fucking him." She took a steadying breath. "There's only one thing with the ability to transform like that."

And it wasn't a fucking phooka. "Do they have her?"

More silence. The screams grew louder in the background, the sound of a metal door clanging open and shut. "I think you already know the answer to that."

I was going to kill every last one of those dark-haired cunts.

Every.

Last.

One.

"Be at the prison in ten minutes."

"Jack, I know how you feel, but we still have to—"

"*Just fucking do it.*" I slammed the phone down so hard the desk collapsed. The trembling guard cried out and crumbled with the debris. I turned back to face the cell block. A row of six guards faced me with rifles.

"Put your hands in the air."

I shook my head. "You really don't want to do that."

"*I said grab some fucking air.*"

I sucked on my teeth. "Of course."

I lifted my hands above my head.

And snapped.

Clicks fired in rapid succession, every cell along the row losing its lock. When this row was done, the rest echoed throughout the prison, a symphony of dropping metal and swinging doors.

Beautiful, blessed silence. A quiet breath between life and death. Then the prisoners screamed and rushed forward, toppling the guards onto the ground. Bullets fired into the crowd and fog swirled among the gunfire. A stream of black and white uniforms rushed in an endless tide. I slipped into the fray, keeping my head down.

Guards hollered for order. A bullet tinged off cell bars and landed in the head of someone beside me. A prisoner knocked a gas lamp over. Kerosene splattered the walls and fire licked up the cement. I kept walking, hands in pockets, listening to the screams erupt around me.

The prisoners already handled the front guards for me. The doors swung open, fresh air and a starry-night sky. It was a new moon. But wherever Adeline was, I had a feeling she saw a full one.

Prisoners streamed into the packed yard. The fire must have hit something important back in the prison, because an explosion showered us in debris and glass. Heat scorched my back and I kept walking, kept hoping—

A sliver of white—pure white—stood out among the crowd.

She didn't move. The prisoners swarmed around her, oblivious to nothing but the sense they should step away. Her long white hair tumbled down her back, her ruined wedding dress brushing her bare toes. She pulled her veil around her face, white eyes wide on the burning prison behind me.

I quickened my pace.

"It's burning," she whispered.

I cupped her lifeless face in my hands. "I know, I know. It's fine."

"Fire," she said, lips trembling. "He—you—supposed to—"

"It's okay. Don't look at that, look at me." I spun her away from the prison. Behind her head the fire crawled along the roof, screaming prisoners climbing down from windows.

"It's okay," I repeated. "But I need you to tell me, do you know—"

"We are safe." Her white eyes turned on me, empty and haunting. "The Morrigan stole Adeline's body, but she escaped. We became a banshee."

My hands trembled around her face. "What?"

"It was the only way to free these fragments," she said. "And it saved us when the Morrigan came. Our body screamed." She swallowed, tensing as another explosion went off. "We killed Macha, but Babd and Nemain still live. They will want revenge."

My hands fell to her shoulders. "Where is the rest of you?"

"In Cardiff, with a brother." She leaned into my touch, closing her eyes. "I told us to look at the memories. The rest of me was scared of you. The Morrigan told her things. Terrible things, but I remembered. I saw your memories, and I realized I was not fragments of many souls, but only *her*. So I told her to look. Please, do not be angry."

I shook my head. "I'm not angry. I am glad you did." I wrapped my arms around her. "What are you doing here?"

Her face tilted up, milky eyes clouded with tears. "I will join her now. I wish to be whole again, but these fragments became something of their own these last few centuries. I wanted to see you once more before losing myself."

I swallowed. "I am sorry. You have to know, I am so fucking sorry. I never meant to do this to you. Fragmenting you was the only way to keep you tethered here. If your soul moved on you would be lost forever."

"Never apologize for finding me." Her lips pulled into a watery smile, white tears brimming over her lashes. "But these pieces wish to join the rest of our soul now. I do not think we will remember all of our lives inside this new body, but we have your memories. We will learn."

I kissed her forehead. "I will find you. I promise."

"Thank you." She wiped her eyes. "I love you most."

It had been years—*years*—since I heard those words. Three hundred and fifty of them, in fact. I nodded. "I love you too."

She smiled—a brilliant, lovely smile. Then she was gone.

I stood there, hands empty while prisoners ran around me.

She was okay.

She was in Cardiff.

She was safe.

I crossed the yard, footsteps pounding into the dirt. The west wall of the prison crumbled in an eruption of fire and dust. Addie. I had to get to Addie.

Violet leaned against a Rolls Royce, smoking a cigar with no glamour. Prisoners took one look at her eyes and ran from the car. I jogged up to her, running my hands through my hair. "Addie killed Macha."

Her eyes became slits. "How?"

"She became a banshee."

Violet slapped a hand on the hood, pushing herself to stand. "She's a fucking *what*?"

"I just saw the wraith." I turned, half expecting to see her standing in the yard. "That is what she told me."

Violet blew out a breath. "Okay." She reached for a purse and pulled out a second cigar, patting the hood. "I want to talk for a moment."

"No, I have to—"

"*Jaevidan*." Her eyes scoured me, her darkness leaking around her. After a moment she pulled it back, wrapping her arms around herself. I sighed, sitting on the hood beside her.

"So it's done?" She asked.

I clipped the cigar and lit it, puffing smoke into the blazing night. "Yes, it's done."

She shook her head. "And now, she is this. Do you even understand what we did to her?" Her cold gaze fell on me, lips turned in a sneer. "I love you, so I will only ask this once. Don't you think it's about time you allowed her to die . . . and to stay that way?"

I didn't even need to think. "No."

Violet squeezed her eyes shut, voice cold with anger. "She died almost four hundred years ago. And again. And fucking again. Twelve times, Jaevidan. She had to die twelve fucking times. And now, this version of her, Adeline." She waved her hand in the air. "She's cursed. Forever."

"I will handle it. I will take care of her. I always have."

"*You can't cheat everything.*" She shook her head, stealing a deep breath. "She was haunted by chipped-off pieces of her own soul, for fuck's sake."

"And they have rejoined with her," I snapped. "The wraith knows what she is now. Her soul is back in one piece, and she is alive. That is all that matters."

Violet shook her head. "You can't bring someone back thirteen times and expect no fucking consequences."

I knew that. I knew that the first, second, third and twelfth fucking time. But I made a vow all those centuries ago. I vowed to love her, and protect her and most of all, to always find her. And this time, I did—*truly* did—because on her thirteenth and final reincarnation, she was born into a glamour-touched body. I made the parallel bond so she could become immortal. She would never face death again.

"You know, you once told me we do terrible things for power, courageous things for hope, desperate things in fear, but we will do anything, absolutely anything for love."

I ran my tongue over my teeth. "Sounds uncharacteristically poetic for me."

"If you love her, maybe you should let her go." Violet's eyes found mine, deep with everything we didn't say, all our own secrets we buried. They mounted high over the centuries, but she knew what this meant to me. And Violet loved her once too.

"She's in Cardiff," I said. "And I want to be with her now."

When she looked at me, it was with all those things we didn't say. But she threw her cigar to the ground, sighing. "Let's hope she accepts you this time."

She would. I knew it like the sky was blue and the grass was green. Like a full moon shone in Ildathach when an empty sky darkened this world. I flexed my fingers, staring at the black letters written over them. I had thirteen tattoos, but this one—the most recent one, finally gave me hope. Twenty years ago, I woke up with eight words inked across my knuckles. *Yn y bywyd hwn ac o hyn ymlaen.* In this life, and hereafter.

I finally had her back in one piece, and I would never fail her again.

I nodded, slapping the hood of the car. "Let's go get my wife."

Books By Marilyn Marks

Fantasy Romance

The Prince of Prohibition

The Veil of Violence – *coming soon!*

Dark Romance by Mallory Hart

Hit

Marked

Second Son

ACKNOWLEDGEMENTS

I've said this in the past and I will say it again, it takes a village to raise a book. There are several people I want to give endless thanks to for making this novel ready to see the light of day.

First and foremost, Melissa and Erica, who are not only my lovely sisters but amazing beta readers. Thank you for listening to me sob on FaceTime at two in the morning for about three weeks straight. You are both getting very expensive birthday presents.

As usual, my wonderful PA Kayleigh Reid who I would simply cease to function without. One day, I will actually get things to you on time.

Rin Mitchell, a very dear friend and the reason the cover and interior of this book has so much beautiful art. We worked together for months to get everything just right and I couldn't be happier with how it turned out. Truly, you have an amazing talent.

Noah Sky, for painstakingly combing through this book and teaching me the difference between lay and laid in past participle.

My amazing and dedicated ARC team, who have all shown so much enthusiasm about the book. It has made this one of my best and most exciting releases yet.

And finally, to everyone who has taken the time to read and follow Jack and Addie's story. Thank you for being here and I hope to see you back for book two!

About the Author

Marilyn Marks is a fantasy romance author who loves all things swords and sass. With a weakness for bad men and time periods that aren't her own, she loves to pen books featuring otherworldly creatures, epic duels, high stakes and lots of steamy romance. When not writing, she can be found watching anything based in the early 1900's, hanging out with her husband, or fending off her vicious and deceptively spry one-eyed shih tzu.

Ingram Content Group UK Ltd.
Milton Keynes UK
UKHW010621160423
420232UK00005B/334